THE LAWS OF MAGIC

OF

BLAZE OF GLORY

VOID

THE LAWS OF MAGIC SERIES

THE LAWS OF MAGIC

BLAZE OF GLORY

MICHAEL PRYOR

RANDOM HOUSE AUSTRALIA

A Random House book
Published by Random House Australia Pty Ltd
Level 3, 100 Pacific Highway, North Sydney NSW 2060
www.randomhouse.com.au

First published by Random House Australia in 2006
This edition first published in 2010

Addresses for companies within the Random House Group can be
found at www.randomhouse.com.au/offices.

National Library of Australia
Cataloguing-in-Publication Entry

Author: Pryor, Michael
Title: Blaze of glory / Michael Pryor
ISBN: 978 1 86471 862 1 (pbk.)
Series: Pryor, Michael. Laws of magic; 1
Target audience: For secondary school age
Dewey number: A823.3

Cover illustration by Jeremy Reston
Cover design by www.blacksheep-uk.com
Internal design by Mathematics
Typeset in Bembo by Midland Typesetters, Australia

10 9 8 7 6 5 4 3 2

Printed and bound by The SOS Print + Media Group

FSC
Mixed Sources
Product group from well-managed
forests and other controlled sources
Cert no. SGS-COC-3047
www.fsc.org
© 1996 Forest Stewardship Council

The paper this book is printed on is certified by
the ©1996 Forest Stewardship Council A.C.
(FSC). SOS Print + Media Group holds FSC
chain of custody certification
(Cert no. SGS-COC-3047).

FSC promotes environmentally responsible,
socially beneficial and economically viable
management of the world's forests.

For Wendy, Celeste and Ruby.
I'm a lucky man.

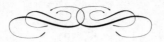

One

AUBREY FITZWILLIAM HATED BEING DEAD. IT MADE things much harder than they needed to be.

'When you're quite ready, Fitzwilliam! We haven't got all day!' bawled the pimply-faced Warrant Officer. Aubrey stood up straighter and glanced at him. The WO was Atkins, a fellow sixth-former, a newcomer to Stonelea School. He had an Adam's apple that made him look as if he'd swallowed a melon and he was taking great pleasure in his small position of authority. 'Two laps of the Hummocks, full pack.' Atkins paused to gloat. 'Lovely weather for it, cadet, if you enjoy heatstroke.'

Aubrey said nothing. He lifted his chin, stiffened his back and stared straight ahead to study the rounded hills of the Hummocks. The pounded earth trail he had to follow wound its way up and down through the sparse growth of the training course. Heat haze made the air ripple over the farthest reaches, obscuring the fence that separated the training course from the school playing fields.

Two miles, more or less. His task was to complete the circuit twice, at the double – in early afternoon heat that had already sent the tennis players from the courts and the birds to drowsiness in the trees around the fence line.

Before his accident, Aubrey knew he would have completed the challenge without difficulty, even though, at the age of seventeen when many others were filling out and taking on their adult strength, he was still slight. He had pale skin, black hair and dark-brown – almost black – eyes, and he looked frail, a poet rather than an athlete. But he'd always managed to surprise people with his determination in running, boxing, or games. Boys much larger than him had learned that provoking skinny Aubrey to fight could be a poor idea. He could drag himself over broken glass if he set his mind to it.

But since the disastrous magical experiment, things were different. Balanced on the edge of true death as he was, physical strain – even emotional strain – could tip him over. He only kept the semblance of a normal existence by a combination of arcane spells and strength of mind. If his magic failed, it would be the end for him.

I'll just have to make sure I don't let that happen, he thought. He adjusted his shoulders.

'Step lively, now!' Atkins said. 'The clock's running! Don't keep us waiting! Remember, no magical assistance!'

Aubrey set off, grinding his teeth. *Steady on*, he told himself. *He was probably bullied by his older brothers. And sisters.*

The heavy woollen uniform itched, but Aubrey had no time to scratch under the khaki. With the weight of a full field pack on his back, it was all he could do to retain his balance as he shuffled along as fast as he could in a shambling gait that resembled a drunken sailor more than a well-trained soldier.

Heat hammered down from the cloudless sky and radiated from the hard dirt path. Aubrey staggered up the first hill that gave the course its name. His breath rasped in a throat that felt as if it was made of sandpaper.

Dimly, he could see Atkins and his cronies standing in the shade of a row of elm trees. They were sniggering and pointing, but Aubrey was pleased to see that they became more circumspect when George Doyle sauntered over. With his massive shoulders and height, George looked more like a wrestler than a student. For years, Aubrey had seen George stop arguments and make fists drop simply by appearing on the scene. It was an ability that Aubrey had used, on occasion, to his own benefit. After all, what were best friends for?

Aubrey's forearms ached as he held the heavy Symons rifle in front of him. The wretched thing was thirty years old, if it was a day, but — thanks to Aubrey's meticulous maintenance — was in perfect working order, even if it hadn't seen live ammunition in decades. Aubrey had even replaced the bolt action, using a spare part he'd found in one of the outbuildings at Maidstone.

Whatever gets me there, Aubrey thought and he gritted his teeth again.

He felt the webbing straps of his pack cutting into his shoulders and decided, not for the first time, that his desire for promotion to Warrant Officer was one of his more stupid ambitions. He'd sailed through the written examination and the interview from two army majors was straightforward. All that remained was the physical test.

Aubrey reached the next hill and stumbled. He heard laughter. 'Come on, Fitzwilliam! You want to fail, like your old man?'

Uneasy laughter greeted this jibe. Aubrey tightened his grip on the rifle and slogged up the slope, cursing the varying height of the hummocks that made it hard to maintain a rhythm. His pack threatened to topple him backwards, but he was prepared. He leaned forward, bent at the knees, and forged up the hill.

When he reached the summit, Aubrey tried to shake sweat from his brow, but just managed to make his helmet slip. It hung there askew, and he tried to nudge it back with his shoulder.

For a perilous moment, he was on the brink of going headfirst down the slope. He caught himself and fought momentum as he descended. His boots threatened to skid out from under him and every step jarred his teeth, but he made it to the bottom.

The next hummock was a short trot away.

Through a combination of doggedness and good decision-making, Aubrey endured for nearly half an hour, but by then he felt as if he was wandering in the bowels of a furnace.

His rifle was a mass of hot iron and wood. He could feel blisters sprouting every time he moved his grip. His helmet seemed to think it was an oven and his head was the Sunday roast. He could feel the sunlight on his back as an actual weight, as if it were heavy rain. His breath was ragged, each sip of the hot air searing his throat.

His head sagged. His gaze was on the yard or so of the path directly in front of him. *If I can manage this step,* he thought, *and the one after that. Then the next . . .*

That was all he had time to contemplate. The ground suddenly fell away from underneath him and he realised, a little too late, that he'd reached the top of another hummock and he should have been easing down the other side.

By then, his balance was completely upset. His right foot insisted it was still climbing, while his left knew perfectly well that it was time to start heading downwards. The weight of the pack, however, had no time for Aubrey's feet to sort out their dispute, so it took over.

Aubrey had time for a startled yelp, then he pitched forward.

There was a fraction of an instant, a moment where all the forces conspiring against him were in balance and he knew that if he could angle his hip left, and flex his right knee while striking the ground just *so* with his heel, he could catch himself and all would be well.

Then his helmet slipped over his eyes and gravity was in charge.

Aubrey flew forwards, somersaulted once, then landed on his chest. He slid the rest of the way down the slope on his chin, his arms stretched out in front of him, still holding his rifle with both hands, according to regulation.

Atkins and his cronies were helpless with laughter. 'Oh, lovely style, Fitzwilliam! Lovely! Do it again!'

Despite the heat, a shiver ran through Aubrey. The perspiration drenching his body turned chill and he closed his eyes. The blackness behind his eyelids rippled and he knew that he was in trouble.

His control was wavering. The heat, the exhaustion, the physical strain had taken their toll. He was on the verge of losing his grip.

Hold on, he thought and he looked within himself for strength.

A voice nearby came to him. 'Aubrey.'

'George,' he said without opening his eyes. 'Wait. I must concentrate.'

'Your shadow,' George said. 'It's fading.'

It's worse than I thought, Aubrey decided. He breathed deeply, carefully, looking to stabilise his condition. He muttered one of the web of spells that was keeping him from the true death. He strove to pronounce each element as crisply as possible, particularly those dealing with duration, trying to re-establish their power. The strain of preventing himself from dying was a constant pressure, and he was still searching for the best combination of spells to counteract the implacable tugging on his soul. If the spells collapsed, his soul would pass through the final portal into the great unknown. Not for the first time, he cursed his own foolishness for putting himself in this perilous position.

Heavy footsteps made him open his eyes.

George was squatting next to him, shading him from the sun. Next to George, Atkins stood, hands on hips, a silhouette against the blue sky. His cronies stood around him, a straggly group of supporters. 'On your feet, Fitzwilliam,' the WO growled. He nudged Aubrey in the side with his boot. 'Your old man isn't here to help you now.'

Aubrey didn't move. *A minute*, Aubrey thought. *That's all I need. Then I'll stand, brush myself off, salute, apologise for my poor form . . .*

George straightened and dusted his hands. 'I don't think you should say things like that,' he said to Atkins, his voice low, his face mild. 'It gets him angry.'

'Hah!' one of Atkins' cronies said. 'So?'

'You should be afraid of getting him angry,' George said. '*I* get afraid when he's angry.'

The guffaws died down as they waded through what George had just suggested. Aubrey could see their laboured brain processes as they squinted and took in George's size, and wondered what on earth could make him afraid . . .

Atkins cleared his throat. His slender grasp of military authority and decision-making was apparent on his face. He was groping for the best course of action that would allow him to keep his dignity, while maintaining that Aubrey was a worthless piece of cadet trash unsuited for officer training.

'I think I should get him to the infirmary,' George suggested.

Atkins nodded. Slowly at first, then more vigorously as the idea took hold. 'Yes. Quite right. See to it.'

He tried to gather his cronies with a glance. They stared at him, then he pushed the nearest in the direction of the gate. He strode off; they trotted in his wake.

Aubrey lifted his head and tried to prop himself on an elbow. After three attempts, he was successful. 'George, can you get this bloody pack off first? Might make things a little easier.'

George slung the pack over one shoulder. Balancing the load, he reached down and helped Aubrey to his feet. For a moment, Aubrey's head swam and his knees threatened to buckle. George slipped an arm under his. 'Ready?'

'Of course. I should be, after that nice lie down.'

Blood dripped from Aubrey's chin and onto his uniform. He took a half-hearted swipe. It smeared.

They limped to the gate, past the glowering Atkins, past the snickering cronies.

'He's failed, you know that!' Atkins called. 'All his father's influence can't change that!'

Aubrey let out a bitter snort of laughter. 'That's the last thing in the world I want, favours from my father.'

George sighed. 'I know, Aubrey. I know.'

Two

THE DISASTROUS MAGICAL EXPERIMENT HAD TAKEN PLACE
three months earlier.

The evening was mild for early spring, although the
wind appeared to have ambitions greater than mere
breeziness. The smell of honeysuckle came through the
open window to the room Aubrey shared with George at
Stonelea. It was the heady, redolent scent of late spring.

The rooms at the school were spare but serviceable,
which was very much the Stonelea way. Aubrey wished
that comfort had been part of the four-hundred-year-old
school charter, but the glowering portraits of the founders
in Clough Hall announced to the world that comfort was
for other people, not for Stonelea boys. Judging by the
portraits, it seemed that rigid posture, enormous bushy
eyebrows and lack of a sense of humour were the qualities the Stonelea founders most approved of.

The beds had thin mattresses, lest anyone be tempted

to sleep too long when there was work to be done; but desks were large, all the better to study. Aubrey had covered most of his with as much alchemical apparatus as was allowed, although he'd often wished he'd brought the larger alembic from home. The chairs were wooden and straight-backed, but George had somehow obtained a battered armchair, which took up its position under the single window. Boxy wardrobes completed the furniture in the room. Aubrey's was topped with suitcases, while George had perched his cornet case on top of his.

Aubrey sat at his desk in a fury of planning. At times like these, the outside world seemed to disappear and he became lost in the intensity of his devising. He was ablaze, as he knew he was on the cusp of moving from preparation to action. He was burning to launch into the experiment that had absorbed him since he'd made his remarkable find.

A week ago, while he'd been doing some idle research into the history of magic, Aubrey had found some ancient scraps of parchment inside a book on classical magical philosophy. The spells were incomplete, but intriguing enough to set Aubrey on a researching spree. Now, he was nearly ready to put his findings into action and undertake a grand experiment.

'So, Aubrey,' George said, 'd'you think the King's decision to marry a tree was a good one or not?'

Aubrey lifted his head from his papers, straightened, and turned to find George nodding at him seriously from the depths of the moth-eaten armchair.

'The King's marrying a tree?'

'Some sort of beech. Lovely bark, apparently.'

Aubrey's mind was still on the details of spell duration, magical forces and the dangers of concatenation. He tried to drag his attention back to the mundane world in order to follow what George was talking about.

The King's behaviour had been slowly becoming stranger and stranger in the five years since the death of Queen Charlotte. The Crown Prince was, in reality, handling all official functions of the monarchy, even at his tender age of eighteen. Most people understood, but it wasn't the sort of thing that was spoken aloud in good company. The public still seemed to like the King, but the affection had been growing strained as his behaviour grew more and more erratic.

Marrying a tree, though, was taking eccentricity to a level that even the most loyal Albionites were uncomfortable with.

'Where's the ceremony to be held?' Aubrey asked cautiously.

George grinned. 'Ah, at last, a reaction! Do you realise that's the fourth question I've asked you in the last half an hour? And the first one you've actually heard?'

'So the King's not marrying a tree.'

'Not that I've heard. But there is a rumour that no-one is allowed to use the word "porridge" in his presence, so I wouldn't be surprised at anything. Thank goodness for the Crown Prince.'

'Mmm,' Aubrey said. His mind was already turning back to his books.

George stood and sighed ostentatiously. 'I can see that you're not going to be any use for a while.'

'Sorry, George. This Nature of Magic stuff has me excited.' Aubrey pushed his hair back from his eyes. 'In class today Mr Ellwood said that unlocking the Nature of Magic will be the greatest advance in magical theory since Baron Verulam's Magical Revolution –'

George held up a hand. 'That's enough, old man. You know that magic talk makes me dizzy.' He reached on top of the wardrobe and seized his cornet case. 'I'm off to practise. I'll leave you to your stuff.'

Aubrey didn't hear the door close behind his friend. He was already immersed in the intricacies of arcane magic theory and feeling the thrill that comes from exploring the frontier of knowledge. He wondered if this was how one of his personal heroes, the great Baron Verulam, had felt.

Baron Verulam's staggering insights three hundred years ago were the birth of modern magic, taking it out of the dark ages of superstition and trickery. Verulam's insistence, despite the scorn of his contemporaries, was that magic should be treated in a scientific manner, through experimentation and observation, to try to establish consistent laws that would lead to reproducible results. This empirical approach to magic was the great leap forward, and light was brought to bear on what had previously been a dark art. Modern magic grew from ancient magic in the same way that the half-mad, half-intuitive fumblings of alchemy gave birth to the rational science of modern chemistry.

Slowly, great minds came to see the worth of Verulam's ways. Spells became more reliable as the underlying laws were established. Fewer disasters resulted from spell casting. Gradually, magic became dependable enough to be used to assist the growth in mechanics and technology in the Industrial Revolution, much to the benefit of the nation of Albion. Its growth as the powerhouse of the modern world could be traced to the savants, thinkers and practitioners who were alive to the possibilities of a rational approach to both magic and technology.

The growth in technology outstripped the rise of magic, however, due to one important aspect: magic could only be performed by those few with the natural aptitude for it. This aptitude also brought an awareness of magical forces, and an ability to see the effects of magic in a way others could not. It could be enhanced by study and diligence, but without the inherent magical capacity, spells could not be cast.

From an early age, it was apparent Aubrey had this ability. It had appeared in his family over the centuries, but only rarely, skipping whole generations and then blooming unexpectedly. It was a gift, much like a gift for higher mathematics or a gift for music. Aubrey was humbled by it and determined to make the most of it.

He seized his copy of Tremaine's *Towards a Theory of Magical Forces*, which he'd had sent down from the university library. He'd used Mr Ellwood's name on the request, but he was sure he'd have it back before his teacher noticed. The Tremaine book was large, leather-bound, and very, very new. When he opened it the heady fragrance of fresh print rose from the pages. He enjoyed the sensation for a moment, then began to read the introduction.

Dr Mordecai Tremaine was the Sorcerer Royal, adviser to the government on all matters magical. From his studies, Aubrey knew that Dr Tremaine was a radical thinker on the Nature of Magic, and since that subject was the current hothouse of argument, debate and occasional fisticuffs between major magical academics, Aubrey wanted to know what the Sorcerer Royal's views were.

Aubrey began to frown as he read. It didn't take long before he closed the book in disappointment. He rubbed his eyes and sat back in his straight-backed chair.

The book was nothing new. It was a compilation of a series of groundbreaking papers published last year in *The Greythorn Journal of Magic*, papers Aubrey had already read in his quest to know more. Dr Tremaine's notion was that magic was a phenomenon with some similarities to electricity, magnetism and light. It obeyed laws and it could be manipulated by magicians, who have the special ability to draw on a vast magical field, channelling it to their ends via the mechanism of properly constructed spells. But where did this magical field come from? In the final paper of the series, Dr Tremaine explored the possibility that it was humanity that brought about such a universal magical field, caused the generation of such a reservoir of enormous magical force. Was it human awareness? Human intelligence? Human souls? In the end, he left this question unanswered – tantalisingly so to Aubrey's way of thinking.

In class, Aubrey had learned of the shock this series of papers created in magical circles. Fusty academics who for years hadn't considered anything more important than whether to have another cup of tea or not were almost rioting in the corridors and cloisters of the universities. Dr Tremaine was praised, condemned, questioned and even, in one overdramatic display, burned in effigy. How could humankind possibly have an effect on such a powerful force? Alternative theories sprang up, where magic was compared to an invisible fluid that filled the cosmos, or a form of power bestowed by creatures unknown.

Such controversy excited Aubrey's curiosity and fired his imagination. He wanted to be part of the great enterprise, to debate, to spar, to cross intellectual swords with others afire with the quest to discover the Nature of

Magic – and more. Magical Theory still had much to do. Many areas were virtually untouched as savants experimented, observed and tried to quantify the effects of magic. Names were made in an instant by researchers stumbling on new laws or new applications of old laws. Great and powerful functions were being discovered almost daily. These were heady, exhilarating times, but Aubrey's great fear was that everything would be discovered before he could finish school and begin serious research. So he'd decided he couldn't wait.

He scanned the pages he'd been working on. All his preparations were in order. It was time. He closed the books on his desk and gathered his papers. He slipped them into a satchel and threw it over his shoulder. He found several sticks of chalk, which he dropped into his pocket.

He left a light on for George, then hurried out of the room.

The corridor was still lit by gas jets, the program for converting the school to electrical lights having stalled at the library and the assembly hall while contractors and the headmaster argued over costs. The gaslight gave Aubrey's shadow a yellow cast, as if it were jaundiced. He reached the end of the corridor and went into the night.

The wind seemed to have leapfrogged 'breeze' and gone directly to 'gale'. Its ambition seemed to be causing as much mischief as possible. Aubrey held a hand in front of his face to avoid the dust and shredded ivy leaves. Assorted bangs and clatters echoed around the quadrangle as unfastened shutters enjoyed their freedom and branches whipped at stone and glass. He squinted and leaned into the wind and, in the manner of a man walking through thigh-deep mud, pushed step by step towards the Magic Laboratories.

The Magic Laboratories were contained in a large stone building a hundred yards to the south of any other structure at Stonelea. After a series of fires and explosions and one memorable earthquake had destroyed fourteen centres for magical experimentation, it had been decided that moving such a facility away and surrounding it with a good deal of open space was a wise step in assuring the ongoing future of the school.

Aubrey had trod this path many times before, so his feet took him automatically through the darkness and the wind. It gave him time to think as he pressed on through the avenue of elms and past the broad sweep of lawn that led to the caretakers' barracks. The wind was coming from his right and he had to lean to one side to counter it. He screwed up his eyes as a blast of sand flew from the mound near where builders were constructing an extension to the music wing. The music wing was dark and silent and Aubrey wondered idly where George was practising his cornet.

His thoughts turned to rehearsing some of the more difficult parts of the spell he was about to cast. Much of it was in language unfamiliar to him, but there lay its potential.

Language was at the heart of magical manipulation. Baron Verulam had established that language was part of the vital talent that enabled magicians to bend magic to their will. The trappings of spells since the dawn of time – incense, hand-waving, ingredients rare and often distasteful – were simply not essential. Sometimes they could be used as props to help focus the magical force, but that was all. Language was the key.

Magical energy was so powerful, so wild, that every spell had to be organised in meticulous detail, with every element in the spell naming and limiting the variables and constants involved. There was no room for inaccuracy, ambivalence or ambiguity. Precision was the paramount quality of each spell, and magicians shared this painstaking approach with watchmakers, accountants and tightrope walkers; only the last had the same awareness of the perils of not achieving perfection.

Aubrey knew that much magical language used today was the descendant of spells that had been used from the earliest days of shamans and hedge wizards, a language quite unlike the language of everyday communication. It had grown into an argot, a jargon special to spells, and it had been augmented by every language imaginable, especially any with pretensions to learning. Latin and Greek elements were common in the language of spells, and experimentation threw up other possibilities as well. Magical language was an unruly beast with a thousand fathers and a thousand mothers, none of whom would recognise their offspring. The result was a language that tended to be inexact.

This had always irked Aubrey. He was dissatisfied with every scheme to reform magical language. None had the clean, systematic structure that he dreamed of. He saw the construction of a universal language for magic as the true culmination of Baron Verulam's Magical Revolution, when spells would be clear and consistent at all times.

The wind shifted slightly and, as if sensing Aubrey's slight imbalance, buffeted him anew. He staggered and turned his head in time to see certain death hurtling towards him.

It was a large plank, six feet long at least. The wind had picked it up from the building site near the music wing and it was tumbling towards him. He had time to straighten and it speared past his nose, whistling as it went.

Aubrey was counting his good fortune when a crash came from the Magic Laboratories ahead. He sprinted as best he could through the wind and arrived to see that the plank had crashed through the large, expensive and famously ugly leadlight window above the front door. It had been donated forty years ago by the large, wealthy and famously tasteless Lord Wallington, who'd made a fortune in soap by selling it by the ton while not using it himself. The plank jutted from the remains of the window like an arrow in the eye of a king.

Aubrey surveyed the damage and decided he was better off well away from the Magic Laboratories tonight. Not that he'd be accused of anything, he assured himself as he slipped into the darkness. It was just that he'd made a number of disparaging remarks about the window and had often mused about the best way to rid the school of it.

He struggled against the wind and made his way to dark and silent Clough Hall, the oldest part of the school. It was a gaunt Gothic monstrosity, a collection of towers, steeples and pointed arches. Its upper reaches were the home of thousands of pigeons in a state of constant warfare with the groundskeepers, one division of which had the sole job of trying to keep the dark slate roof as free of white streaks as possible. It was a futile task.

Clough Hall was used as the assembly hall for the school. Its main hall was filled with wooden seats legendary for their hardness, despite centuries of being smoothed by the rear ends of schoolboys. A gallery looked over the ranks of seats, but it was strictly OUT

OF BOUNDS to students. It was for the use of parents and dignitaries, once or twice a year, to endure prize-giving or the school play.

Aubrey was seriously keen about the stage. Ever since he'd been at Stonelea he'd been part of the school productions, playing everything from a tree stump to a murderous librarian. He'd worked backstage, helping to paint backdrops and haul sets. He'd swept, cleaned, prompted, sewn and applied makeup. He'd fumbled lines, gone blank and tripped on props. He'd made entrances, sung in the chorus and revelled in applause – something he adored.

In this, his final year at Stonelea, he was looking forward to *The Barrister's Lament*, a chance for a grand finale to the acclamation of parents, staff and students.

Aubrey found a door at the rear of the building and slipped into the crowded space behind the stage. It was full of canvas, rope and timber, the remains of productions from years gone past. He conjured up a small glow globe with a spell he'd perfected through repetition. It used an application of the Law of Aspiration, and Aubrey's clipped, careful syllables conjured an orb the size of his hand. It floated at his gesture and cast a soft, golden light on a rolled-up backdrop. He recognised the storm-tossed sea from *Sailors of the King*, which was used again in *The Adventures of Sir Augustus Frog* before making a surprise appearance as a dream backdrop in *A Night of Memories*. Aubrey shuddered when he remembered how his part in that play required him to sing a duet with Mrs De-Winter, the sweet-voiced but vast wife of the Geography Master. George had later remarked that he was afraid that Aubrey was going to be eaten, so wide did Mrs DeWinter open her mouth when straining for the high notes.

Aubrey started to make his way to one of the small rooms off the main hall. He'd used it for some of his experiments before and it was private enough – and solid enough – for his purposes. But he paused. Was that a sound? With a word, he extinguished the glow globe. Carefully, he felt his way past boxes of costume remnants and trunks of wigs, scarves and other accoutrements, making his way to where he'd heard the sound. *Probably some third-formers having a secret feast*, he thought and decided it was his duty as a sixth-former to throw a decent scare into them, as it would be theirs when they were sixth-formers. It was traditions such as this, Aubrey reflected with a grin, that made Albion great.

Judging from the crashes and stifled oaths, the intruder wasn't entirely familiar with the cluttered confines. And it wasn't one of the more magically talented boys, either, or else he wouldn't be blundering around in the dark.

Light flared. Aubrey stood back behind a tattered fishing net as the intruder held a match high and peered around. Aubrey smothered a laugh as the match burned quickly and singed the intruder's fingers, followed by more oaths – less stifled this time. He summoned his glow globe again. 'Stay there, George,' he called. 'You're right next to the throne of the fairy queen from *Aurelia*. Topple that on top of you and you'll regret it.'

Aubrey clambered over to join his friend, who looked as if he'd been on his way to visit the King, discovered he was wearing someone else's trousers and it was now too late to do anything about it. 'Ah, Aubrey. You're here too.'

Aubrey shrugged. 'I was about to try a few things.'

'I take it these would be unauthorised magical experiments?'

'Only if you were being picky.'

'I see. I'd expect as much, finding you skulking around Clough Hall in the dark like this.'

Aubrey raised an eyebrow. 'Skulking? And how would you describe *your* movements?'

George looked around at the tangled, jumbled, cluttered space that surrounded them. 'Boyd says his sister is coming to visit next weekend. I thought I might take her on a tour of the school.'

'Boyd? Fifth form? Tall, dark hair, good painter and –'

'Extremely ugly. Yes, that's him. Nice chap.'

'And you want to show his sister around the school?'

'It's amazing,' George enthused, 'how heredity works. Boyd is grotesque – hideous, really – but his sister is heart-stoppingly attractive. Red hair, freckles, quite lovely.'

'I thought you were more interested in country girls, husky milkmaids, that sort of type.'

George drew himself up. 'I may be from the country, Aubrey, and I may have done my best to uphold the traditions of country friendliness and hospitality among the female folk in our district, but I'll have you know that I'm an admirer of all members of the opposite sex. Bless them all.' He grinned. 'And bless Boyd for bringing his sister next weekend.'

Aubrey grinned in response. George was incorrigible. He enjoyed the company of females with a fervour that was only matched by the enthusiasm they had for him. The life he'd led on the Doyle farm had given him an aura of extraordinary good health and vigour that they found highly attractive.

Aubrey admired him. 'Good luck, George. Don't let me keep you from your scouting expedition.'

George thrust his hands in his pockets. 'I don't think I'll

bring her here, though. Too dusty.' He squinted at Aubrey. 'So you're about to do some experimenting?'

Aubrey patted his satchel. 'I could be onto something.'

'Dangerous?'

'Perhaps.'

'I'd better come and keep an eye on you, then. Besides, I might learn something.'

'George, you're probably the least magical person I know. I think the school dog has a better chance of learning magic than you do.'

'Probably. Let's just say I'm interested. Which way?'

Aubrey's destination had once been a small office, longer than it was wide. It opened from the entrance vestibule at what was now the rear of the main hall. Its walls were solid stone, while its slanted ceiling was a good eighteen feet overhead. One small window, with diamond-shaped panes of glass, opened onto the night sky but Aubrey pulled heavy, blue velvet curtains across it, turned on the electric light, and dismissed his glow globe. The floor was parquetry, but most of it was covered with a worn rug of vaguely Eastern design. The only furniture was a rectangular table made of dark wood, with four mismatched chairs around it.

'Make yourself useful, George. We have to move the table and chairs out of the way. Then the rug.'

George grumbled, but soon the floor was clear. Aubrey studied it with a scowl. 'I really should be tidier,' he muttered.

'That awful scrawling? Looks as if someone gave a baby a packet of chalk.'

'It's the remains of the last focusing figure I drew here. I should have erased it better. I can't leave it as it is – it will interfere with the new one I need to draw.'

Focusing figures were the refinement of the pentacles and mystical symbols from the dark days of magic. They were a diagrammatic representation of some aspects of the spell being cast – mostly the restraining and limiting factors. They tended to be combinations of geometrical shapes, and Aubrey found the clarity and precision of their drawing aided his concentration.

He took out his pocket handkerchief and got down on his hands and knees. With George's cheerful supervision, he scrubbed at the parquetry until every trace of previous figures was gone.

He sat back on his haunches. 'How's that?' he asked George.

George was leaning against the wall, arms folded on his chest. He cocked his head. 'You missed a tiny bit near your right knee. Apart from that, you've done enough to suggest you'll be a wonderful charlady one day. Outstanding, using a silk cleaning cloth like that.'

Aubrey stood and dusted off his knees. 'Admirable though charladies are, my ambitions go a bit further.'

George dropped his arms. 'I say, old man, this isn't about ambition again, is it?'

'George, don't you have dreams, goals? There's so much I want to do that the hardest thing is to decide what to try first.'

'I'll wager that you've been specifically told not to do this,' George said gloomily.

'Sorry to disappoint you, but I haven't.' *Not that I'd let that stop me if it was important enough.* 'Mr Ellwood simply said that this was a forbidden area of magic.'

'Aha!'

'But he didn't say we weren't allowed to explore it.'

George looked unconvinced. 'Explore what?'

Aubrey had hoped to avoid telling George this, but his friend had left him no choice. 'Death magic.'

George's eyes went wide. 'You're joking.'

'It's perfectly safe, George. I just want to do some simple experimenting, and then document my findings. There's been nothing done in this area for ages!'

'With good reason, I'd say.'

Aubrey began to pace the length of the narrow room, his hands behind his back. 'But it's so crucial! Death magic impinges on the whole question of the Nature of Magic. How does humanity create this remarkable magical force? At what point do we stop creating it? It's our very place in the universe that's at stake here!'

'And if you can find something useful, you'll make a name for yourself?'

'I never said I *wasn't* ambitious, George.'

'And you can do this? Safely?'

'It's all under control,' Aubrey said, waving a hand. 'This isn't some primitive hocus-pocus we're talking about. This is a rational, empirical exploration of natural forces. I can do it.'

'Aubrey, you think you can do anything.'

Aubrey didn't even answer this. He stood in the middle of the room, mapping out in his mind the complex diagram he was about to draw. At the same time, he was rehearsing the elements in the spell, making sure he had them all memorised.

The outcome Aubrey wanted for this spell was quite simple. The laws for death magic had never been quantified and clearly expressed. Throughout history, it was an area of magic only attempted by the mad, the desperate or the depraved. The results – when recorded – had been horrible beyond belief. Sacrifice, massacre and insanity stalked the murky history of death magic, with practitioners who survived being shunned. And yet, because it dealt with the threshold between being and unbeing, death magic held the prospect of uncovering much — perhaps the fundamental nature of magic itself.

Aubrey wanted to see if he could establish some parameters for safely dealing with death magic. If he could determine limiting factors, ways to shield an experimenter probing this area, it could be of incalculable worth. He could turn death magic into life magic and open a whole new field for research.

He put his hands together and prepared to cast a spell that would momentarily put him in a state of death.

When he'd first contemplated this, he was quick to discard it as foolishly dangerous. Then, after the notion refused to go away, he decided that people suffered worse every day. Hearts stopped and were restarted, with no ill effects. People were discovered not breathing and revived none the worse for wear. Eventually he decided that, although some risk was part of this procedure, it was reduced by careful preparation. Aubrey was proposing a spell which would stop his life for an instant, much less than a heartbeat, much less than the time between one tick of the clock and the next, and then he would resume his normal state. He would be stepping across from life to death and back again in a perfectly controlled way. A well-thought-out, careful, rational procedure from which he'd eliminated the danger.

His heart began to pound, apparently not convinced.

He got down on his hands and knees again and began drawing the first of the many-sided figures on the floor. It was soothing, familiar work, but — despite his confidence — he felt his nervousness increasing. His throat grew dry, but his palms were sweaty and the chalk became slippery in his fingers.

Somewhere between tracing the second and third interlocking figures, Aubrey's stomach began to knot. It was like the feeling he had before a performance on stage, but it gripped more fiercely. He winced.

'You all right?' George asked from his vantage point in the corner of the room nearest the door.

'Fine, fine,' Aubrey muttered, but vowed to hide any further discomfort from his friend.

When he had finished, Aubrey stood and dusted his hands. He slipped the tiny nubbin of chalk into his pocket. 'Done.'

George frowned. 'Looks like some of those mathematical curvy things . . .'

'Parabolas?'

'They're the ones. You've got a bunch of them trying to dance with some sort of lopsided stars. And you've thrown in a few twisty rings for good measure. Very nice.'

'Thanks, George. I'll see if I can get you a spot as one of the judges for the next school Art Show.' He drew a breath and tried to slow his racing heart. It felt as if it was knocking on his ribcage and trying to get out. 'Now, keep your distance and whatever happens, don't interfere. It's all perfectly safe, but the focusing figure will confine the effects of the spell, regardless.'

'That's reassuring,' George muttered. 'Perfectly safe, you say?'

'Perfectly.'

'As safe as the time you made that set of wings out of cardboard?'

'That was a long time ago. Now, I need some quiet. I must concentrate.'

Most of the language for the spell was derived from ancient Sumerian, but the difficult middle section was a variation of an Akkadian spell he'd found recorded in an ancient text lent to him by a friend of the family. The Akkadian spell was mostly nonsense, but Aubrey had been excited by what he saw as some extremely useful, but throat-straining, elements which he couldn't wait to link with two fragments of Latin spells that dealt with death magic in an oblique way. He'd found these Latin spells misfiled under 'Hearth Magic' in the National Library on one of his frequent research trips to the city.

He rubbed his hands on the legs of his trousers. He closed his eyes. He took a deep breath. He began his spell.

He spoke firmly, striving for perfect enunciation and articulation and no hesitation, leaving no room for uncertainty in constants, variables or the transitions between them. Each element in the spell had to be perfect for his manipulation of the magical force to work as planned. It was like building an arch, where each block depended on the other. If any was to fail, the whole structure would collapse.

The unfamiliar syllables twisted in his mouth, as if they were reluctant to be uttered, but he formed them and spat them out, one after the other. He could feel sweat springing from his brow, but he didn't spare time to wipe it.

He came to the last three elements – one for duration, one for intensity and the last a 'signature', a unique item that made the spell his own. He felt a moment of doubt, but he thrust it aside and pronounced each component crisply.

As soon as the last element left his lips, Aubrey knew something had gone wrong. He was plunged into blackness, utter nothingness, then pain seized him, a shattering, all-consuming agony that tore a howl from his lips. His mind reeled. It was a raw, overwhelming shock, as if he had been flung against something hard, dropped into ice water, smashed between hot irons, slashed by a thousand razors, rolled in acid. He felt as if a great beast was shaking him by the neck, as if he were being squeezed through a hole the size of a pencil, pummelled, flayed, burnt alive. It was beyond a simple physical sensation. He was torn apart and exposed, beyond hope and beyond help.

With a final wrench which seemed to upend the whole universe, the pain suddenly stopped. It was replaced by an insistent tugging sensation. Aubrey was able to see again, but his mind recoiled from what he saw.

He was looking at his own body, collapsed on the floor.

It took him a giddy moment of denial and confusion, but he knew that his soul had been separated from his body.

His vantage point seemed to be somewhere near the ceiling. George had approached the boundary of the focusing figure and was looking distressed. His mouth was working, but his words were muffled, unclear. Aubrey wondered if his hearing had been affected by the spell. Hovering, he noticed that something was wrong with the focusing figure, but he couldn't determine exactly what it was. Something to do with duration, intensity?

In the midst of a sense of dislocation that could be like no other, Aubrey found time to berate himself – for heedless bravado, for reckless posturing and for shoddy preparation. His anger blazed, then he quelled it. He had other charges, but they'd have to wait. Methodically, he began to search for a remedy for his stupidity.

His body looked forlorn, crumpled as it was. His dark hair was obscuring one side of his face and he wanted to reach out and push it back.

With what? he wondered. He turned his attention and discovered what a soul looks like.

He told himself it was a failure of imagination, or perhaps simply a handy representation using available materials, but his soul looked just like the body he'd left crumpled on the floor, down to the tweed jacket and high-waisted trousers. He found he was actually disappointed that, apart from a level of insubstantiality, it wasn't more startling in form.

Interestingly, his soul-self was holding a translucent golden cord tight in its right hand. It was stretched taut and was the source of the tugging sensation, which was a deep, nagging feeling at a most fundamental level, far below conscious thought. He groped for a comparison and the nearest he could come was the need to breathe.

Aubrey was doing his best to cope with the sense of displacement he was experiencing. Terror threatened to envelop him, but he kept it at bay thinking rationally. If he could observe things carefully, he was sure he could work out a solution.

Then he traced where the golden cord led and he felt like a man whose house had been invaded by assailants, who had then been kidnapped, stripped, beaten, and imprisoned, before being told that all his family had died. It was an almost unbearable shock on top of a series of almost unbearable shocks.

A void had replaced one of the longer walls of the room. The other end of the cord disappeared into it. Pearly-grey tinged with silver, like massy clouds caught by sunlight, the void was in motion, boiling and turning, and he was being drawn towards it by the tugging on his golden cord.

In an instant of complete apprehension, Aubrey knew that the true death lay on the other side, the place from where no traveller returns. His current state, this soul-self floating above his erstwhile body, was a halfway stage, a moment to pause *(for reflection?)* before the final departure.

No, he thought. *This is not right.* He tried to let go of the golden cord and found he couldn't. He shook, but his fingers remained wrapped around the mysterious cord. He could shift his grip, he could move along it, but otherwise the cord was as much a part of him as his hand was.

Aubrey twisted, trying to turn away. It felt as if he were trapped in a river, fighting against a strong current. He thrashed, struggling to resist the tidal pull of the way that he'd inadvertently opened, straining to increase the distance between the void and him.

In his flailings, he came to face downwards, towards his vacated body. Another golden cord lay in its hand. The end of this cord was flapping loose, as if it had recently been severed, between Aubrey's soul-self and his body. It drifted in the air, but it was losing its vitality and colour. Even as he watched, Aubrey could see it coiling back on itself, the loose end falling back to drape over his body lying on the floor.

Aubrey didn't think. He lunged for the loose end, but the cord in his right hand pulled back. The pull from the void was growing stronger. Inch by inch, the void was drawing him towards it.

Suddenly, the irresistible pull eased. Aubrey jerked around to see that George had ignored his instructions and had blundered through the focusing diagram, scuffing it with his shoes.

Aubrey gathered himself and dived towards the receding end of the golden cord. He seized it with his left hand, but nearly let go when he was convulsed with a familiar pain; it was the wrenching that had marked the separation of his soul and his body. But having felt it once, this time he was less overwhelmed by it. Despite being racked by spasms, he didn't let go of the cord in his left hand.

Below, Aubrey glimpsed George working frantically on his motionless body. The golden cord leading from it was becoming fainter. The one in his right hand was vibrant and glowing, and still tugging at him. Aubrey's soul was caught between his body and true death, suspended on the ultimate brink.

He knew that he couldn't remain like this, in an unnatural halfway state. The void was urgent, insistent. He found himself wondering about what lay on the other side of the opening. Perhaps it was a chance to find out the answer to the greatest mystery of all.

Later, he said to himself. *It's not the time for that now*. He ran through spells in his mind. He wanted something to spring from all his reading, all his wide research, something that would save him.

It came to him. It was a humble spell, a piece of everyday magic that he'd learned so long ago that he'd forgotten where. It was a spell to splice the ends of a rope together.

Aubrey ran through the spell in his mind and realised it wasn't enough. It needed strengthening. He realised, wryly, that he needed to splice some elements of his death magic spell into a spell that dealt with splicing. Even then, it would only be temporary – but a temporary respite from being taken by the true death would do, for now.

He lined up all the elements. He inserted the variables. He organised the limits and specified the parameters. Aubrey felt as certain about this spell as he had of anything he'd done. All that remained was to see if a soul could utter a spell.

Aubrey brought the two ends of the golden cord together. He pronounced the spell, the short, sharp syllables marching off his soul-tongue. With a burst of wild, fierce relief, he saw the two extremities of the golden cord fuse together, ends interweaving in a way that would make a sailor proud.

The cord leading from his body began to fill out, regaining colour, strengthening and tautening even as he looked at it. He still could not release his grip from it, however, and he was caught holding the entire cord two-handed, with the dreadful pull of the open way on his right.

He refused to be taken. This was premature and he was not going to let a moment's stupidity be the end of him. He would save himself. Gone was any thought of complicated spells. He slipped his left hand along the golden cord, hauling himself towards his inert body. Then he dragged his right hand until it met his left. He kept his head turned away from the awful void, but he could feel its attraction. It pulled at him with the force of destiny.

No, Aubrey vowed. *I will not go.*

It became a test of his will. Aubrey had to force himself, inch by inch, away from the other side. Every infinitesimal gain was achieved against the awful pull from behind. He dared not look up as he edged his hands along the golden cord, gripping and releasing, slipping back and then moving forward, moving away from the void and towards reuniting his body and soul.

An eternity passed, and another. A thousand times Aubrey contemplated giving up and a thousand times he rejected it. Nothing distracted him from his goal and he promised himself he would maintain his laborious progress until the end of time if that was what it took.

Finally, he looked up to see that he was close to the outflung hand of his motionless body. An almighty effort, a lunge, a horrifying moment when he thought he was going to fall short, then –

Agony. He felt as if he was putting on a suit of red-hot armour. Every fibre of his being burned. His nerves hummed at the farthest extremity of pain. He gasped and opened his eyes, then realised he'd been able to do both. He looked up to see George glaring at him.

'George,' he mumbled. He was weak, new-born. The floor felt hard beneath him. The sharp smell of ozone hung in the air. Aubrey found himself looking for thunderstorms. 'Remember: interfere whenever you want to.'

George let out a sigh and Aubrey felt his friend's grip on his shoulders tighten. 'What happened?'

'I died. More or less.'

George looked flummoxed. 'You're better now?'

Good question, Aubrey thought. He felt bloodless, feeble, as if he'd been ill for a very long time. He used his magical senses to examine himself. 'Ah. Well. Not entirely.'

'What do you mean?'

Aubrey glanced at the focusing figure. Yes, something was definitely awry there. 'I think I'm still dead, old man. Technically.'

'Technically dead?'

'My sloppy spell-casting opened the door to my true death, and it hasn't closed. At the moment, I've brought my body and soul back together, but the true death is calling.' He still felt it — a deep-seated inner summoning. 'I've stopped things, for the time being, but I'm afraid it's only temporary.' He shook his head, then bit his lip and looked away as emotion threatened to overwhelm him. 'I'm sorry, George. I've overstepped myself, rather.'

George gripped his shoulder. 'You'll figure out something, I'm sure of it. Besides, you've been in worse spots.'

Aubrey turned and stared at his friend. 'Worse spots? Worse than being dead?'

George scratched his head. 'Well, I'm not, I mean, I didn't exactly mean . . .'

Aubrey watched his friend with gratitude. George's support was enough to bring him around to face his situation. Inaction — never his friend — would in this case probably prove fatal. 'Help me up, George. I need to get to my books. I have to close that door.'

Three

AUBREY AND GEORGE DIDN'T GO TO THE INFIRMARY after the debacle on the training ground. Aubrey refused. Even though George was dubious, they went back to their room.

Boarding at Stonelea School was not Aubrey's idea. Nor his parents', really, even though his father had attended the school himself. It had simply been assumed, from Aubrey's earliest youth, and emphasised by Aubrey's grandmother, his father's mother. Duchess Maria had appointed herself the upholder of the Fitzwilliam family name. Despite the twin handicaps of not being born into the family and coming from overseas, her knowledge of the family tree was formidable. Since her husband, the Duke of Brayshire, had passed away, Duchess Maria oversaw the family traditions. In her eyes, this included boys attending Stonelea — and boarding there even though Maidstone, the family home, was only a short walk away.

Since she was the fiercest old woman he'd ever known, Aubrey had never questioned her decision.

Aubrey eased himself down on his bed and draped an arm across his eyes. 'Put a chair behind the door, would you, George? "Never disturb a wounded soldier", or so said the Scholar Tan.'

No locks on the doors at Stonelea, so a chair under the doorknob was the best security available. Unless one used magic – and using magic for such trivial things was frowned on as a waste.

George dropped Aubrey's pack on the floor. 'I'm sick of your Scholar Tan. He's always droning on about battles and tactics and retreats. It's so depressing.'

'Have some respect. A thousand years ago he was a revered expert on the art of war.' Aubrey's head was throbbing. He heard the sounds of ball sports coming from the courtyard below and was glad when they were muffled by George closing the curtains.

The physical test had been a shambles. Aubrey tried to relax, to rest and regather himself. Since the bungled experiment, he'd managed to find a few spells that eased his situation somewhat, but he still had to take more care of himself than he'd been accustomed to. He found it difficult to put on weight, regardless of how much he ate. His skin remained pale, even after time in the sun. The hold his soul had on his body was tenuous. Physical or emotional strain made it much harder to resist the call of the true death.

So far, he'd been able to hide these things from others. Even from his mother and father.

His motives for not telling his parents were clear to him. At least, he'd thought them through carefully and arranged them neatly, much in the way a barrister would

organise a defence for a client before going to court. His
aim was to avoid divulging his mistake by finding a
solution for his condition before anyone found out.

Being *ashamed* of what he'd done wasn't quite right.
Being *embarrassed* was more accurate. As a dedicated
perfectionist, getting something wrong on this scale was
deeply mortifying.

He was willing to admit there was more to it than that.
A son who had managed to suspend himself between
life and death through experimenting in forbidden magic
would certainly be exploited by his father's political
enemies. They would question Sir Darius's fitness for
public office, with many a shake of their bewhiskered
heads.

Lastly, Aubrey was determined to clean up his own
mess. It was a question of honour.

With that in mind, he managed to slip into a troubled
sleep.

AUBREY RESTED, MARKING TWO HOURS BY THE TOLLING OF
the clock over the library. Refreshed, he opened his eyes
to see George slumped in the armchair asleep.

Aubrey padded to his desk, his bare feet hardly making
a sound. He took some books from the bookshelves over
the desk and soon was lost in the world of arcane magical
research.

Evening was drawing in when Aubrey heard a grunt
from George. He turned. 'Awake, I see. I thought I was
the one who needed the rest.'

George rubbed his eyes and yawned. 'Well, I was the

only one who managed to carry a full kit back here.'

Aubrey shrugged. 'Why should I carry all that gear when someone's willing to do it for me?'

George snorted. He stood, opened the curtains and came to the desk. 'What on earth are you doing?'

Aubrey held up his hand. Between his forefinger and thumb were clamped a piece of glass and a copper penny. 'Experimenting. Mr Ellwood was rambling on about the Law of Contiguity and I had a few ideas I wanted to follow up.'

George snorted again. 'I'm glad I'm not taking Magic this year. Too taxing on the brain. I'll stick with Sport and Music.'

Aubrey glanced at his friend. 'You don't know what contiguity is, do you?'

George nodded and adopted an air of ancient wisdom. 'Of course I do. Contiguity. Closeness. Proximity.'

Aubrey smiled. 'You continually surprise me, George. Yes, that's what contiguity means. With the right spells, a magician can invoke one of the variations of the Law of Contiguity.' Deftly, he separated the two items and held the coin in front of his eye. 'Look.'

'Fascinating. A penny.'

'I can see you, George.'

George raised an eyebrow. 'You're looking *through* the penny?'

'The Law of Contiguity, in action,' Aubrey said. He was pleased with himself. He hadn't been sure if his variations on an approach he'd read about in an obscure tome would work.

'Ah,' George said. 'The coin and the glass were in contact. Close proximity.'

'Contiguous. That's right. Go on.'

'And so, magically, the coin has become a little like glass?'

'Exactly!' Aubrey jumped to his feet and flung the curtains wide. 'It cuts both ways, of course.'

He held up the fragment of glass. Through it, the light was decidedly coppery. George took it from his hand and stared at it. 'So, with some effort we can have transparent metals?'

Aubrey threw his hands in the air. 'George, don't be so straightforward. If the Laws of Contiguity can be properly fathomed and codified, the possibilities are endless.'

'Well, that's all very good.' George looked away.

'Yes? You have something to say?'

'Today's little spectacle on the Hummocks isn't going to impress your grandmother, is it?'

Aubrey made a face. 'I'm not worried about her reaction.' It wasn't a lie. He didn't have to worry about her reaction. He *knew* what it would be.

'You must be the only one in the entire country who isn't.'

'I'm more concerned about my father.'

'He won't say anything, will he?'

'That's the problem,' Aubrey muttered. He glared at the window, not seeing the view of the ivy-covered library.

Aubrey readily admitted – to himself – how difficult it was to be Sir Darius Fitzwilliam's son. His father being one of the most prominent men in the country, a war hero and former Prime Minister, meant that Aubrey had much to live up to. Everywhere he went he was faced with expectations and people who wanted to measure him against the great man.

'You know how it is, George. I want to please him, but

I end up disappointing him. Not that he'd say anything. It'd be the "Gallant try, Aubrey" speech.'

'Awkward, that.'

'Indeed.' Aubrey sprang out of the chair and grinned. 'And tonight you'll see just how awkward it is.'

'Tonight?' George frowned.

'When we have dinner at home at Maidstone. I have special leave from the school and I asked for one for you, too.'

'Me? I can't go. I've got to study. I have cornet practice. I've got something else to do.'

'Good food at our table, George,' Aubrey purred. 'Succulent beef, roast potatoes, green beans. Nothing overcooked, watery or cold.'

George brightened. 'Pudding?'

'Of course. Cook is superb at pudding. It'll probably either be bread and butter custard or jam roly-poly.'

'When do we leave?'

Four

'How's my collar?' George asked Aubrey as they stood on the doorstep.

'Perfect.'

'The tie?'

'Elegantly and firmly knotted.'

'My hair?'

'On top of your head, as it should be. Now, do you want me to produce a full-length mirror?'

The walk from Stonelea School to Maidstone, the Fitzwilliams' city residence, hadn't taken long. On such a pleasant summer's evening, many people were abroad. Courting couples were strolling arm in arm, oblivious of the passing parade. Families were walking with more purpose, mostly led by parents whose faces seemed to suggest that they knew the walk was a sound idea but that they'd rather be at home with a good book.

Maidstone was the house where Aubrey had grown up,

and where generations of Fitzwilliams had grown up. It was one in a long, curving row of elegant three-storey townhouses facing a small park in Fielding Cross. The park was dominated by an ancient willow tree which shaded a tiny pond. Aubrey had spent many hours there, sailing wooden yachts and studying tadpoles.

The entire neighbourhood was clean, quiet and reeked of money.

Wealth was in the discreet, but expensive, brass door-knockers. It was in the uniformed domestic staff who appeared at doors whenever they opened. It was in the curtains, the clothes of the passers-by, the prize-winning dogs being walked by anxious-looking kennel lads. It was in the smoothly gliding prams pushed by pretty young nannies.

When growing up, Aubrey had taken some time to realise that the whole city wasn't like this. Small things, like the shabbiness of the visiting knife grinder and wondering where he came from, had aroused Aubrey's curiosity and sent him out of Fielding Cross and into the sprawling streets of the city.

He'd discovered the vast Newbourne railway yards and the blunt engineers and navvies who worked there. He'd found the Narrows, Newpike and Royland Rise, each with their thriving communities so different from the gentility of Fielding Cross, and visited Little Pickling, Crozier, and even the Mire, despite its reputation.

The city was a grubby, brawling conglomeration, and Aubrey loved it, but Fielding Cross remained home.

The entrance of the Fitzwilliam residence was grand. A sandstone portico that would have done justice to a minor pagan god sheltered the door from the elements. The door itself was painted a glossy, dark blue. A bell pull on the wall didn't draw attention to itself, but was there for those who were brought up well enough to know what to look for.

Aubrey took a deep breath, bracing himself. It was always tense, returning home. Sometimes it was like entering a battleground and he knew he had to have his wits about him.

He reached out and rang the bell.

'Ah! Master Aubrey! Master George!'

The butler who answered the doorbell was tall, silver-haired and ruddy-cheeked. The fact that Aubrey had always thought he looked like a weary basset hound didn't detract from the affection Aubrey felt for him. 'Harris. Good to see you. Is he in?'

'Not yet, young sir. Something has come up in Parliament. The PM's called an early election.'

Aubrey whistled. 'An early election? Something must be afoot. When?'

'He's called it for just after the King's birthday.'

'Very clever. No doubt he hopes the goodwill from the King's Birthday procession will spill over to the election.' He shook his head. 'What about Mother? She's not at the museum, is she?'

'No, sir. She's bathing. She said she stank of formaldehyde and needed a good long soak before dousing herself with Padparadsha.' Harris said this with an impassive face, as if he were reporting on the weather. He did not have a high opinion of Lady Fitzwilliam's choice of perfume.

'Good. Good. George and I will be in the library.'

Harris looked as if he were about to say something, but simply nodded. He shut the door behind them before disappearing into the cloakroom. Aubrey stared at Harris's receding form, wondering what it was that he had been about to say.

When they entered the library, Aubrey found out what the butler's discretion had prevented him from mentioning.

Aubrey's grandmother was in the library.

Duchess Maria was sitting in a huge armchair, facing the door. The room smelled of old leather, cigar smoke and woollen carpet that's absorbed too much port and too many secrets.

Duchess Maria was over eighty years old, but her face was smooth and unlined. She was tiny, almost lost in the leather immensity of the chair. Her silver hair was arranged under a black snood and she wore black lace gloves on her long, thin hands. Her eyes were bright and attentive. Aubrey knew, from past experience, that those eyes didn't miss anything.

She didn't look surprised to see them, something Aubrey attributed to her legendary network of informers and spies. An image of Duchess Maria as a spider at the centre of a web stretching across the country and much of the world came to him and he shuddered.

He bowed and kissed her hand. She smelled of violets. 'Aubrey. You're too thin.'

She turned to George. George had learned enough to kiss the hand held out to him. 'George Doyle. It has been six months since I've seen you. You have grown.'

In someone else it would have been a cliché. In Duchess Maria it was a careful observation. 'Yes ma'am. Five inches in the last year.'

'Well done.' She turned her attention back to Aubrey. 'You didn't complete the training course today.'

'No, I didn't,' Aubrey said. Then he waited.

'I see. And you know that this will make it difficult for you to become an officer in the cadets?'

'Yes.' Aubrey kept his answers brief and, he hoped, not open to misinterpretation.

'You know that every Fitzwilliam male in the last two centuries has been a cadet officer at Stonelea School?'

'Yes.'

'So what do you have to say for yourself?'

Aubrey looked mildly at his grandmother, knowing that anger was not a useful reaction where Duchess Maria was concerned. 'I'm allowed one more attempt. I'll make sure I complete the course.'

Duchess Maria nodded. 'I see.' She turned back to George. Aubrey thought the smoothness of the action was like a swivel-mounted machine gun. 'Are you keeping up your cornet practice, George?'

It was an hour before they escaped.

'I feel as if I've just been over the Hummocks myself,' George said as he closed the library door behind them.

'You see why I don't much mind living at the school?' Aubrey said. 'Let's go to the billiards room.'

Aubrey enjoyed a contest. He always felt that he could make up for any lack of skill with a good grasp of tactics, strategy, and the weaknesses of his opponent. He had been playing against George in all manner of games since they were four years old, and despite George's easy co-ordination and strength, he usually managed to beat him.

Aubrey was ahead by a few frames when Harris found them. 'Dinner, sirs.'

Aubrey racked his cue. 'Lucky for you, George, that this table has just been relaid. I was just starting to get the feel of it.'

George shrugged into his jacket. 'I'm sure. A few more decades and I would have been begging for mercy.'

Aubrey laughed. 'Harris, are my parents seated?'

'They are, Master Aubrey.'

Aubrey sighed and his head drooped for an instant. Then he gathered himself. 'Tally-ho, then!'

Gaslights shed yellow softness on the dark, polished wood that was the dining room. Wood panels, wooden floor, immense wooden sideboards and mirrors with heavy wooden frames filled the room, leaving space for the large oval table in the centre. Aubrey had eaten a thousand meals in this room and had always wondered how many trees had gone into the making of the Fitzwilliam dining room. A small forest or two, he was sure.

Duchess Maria was motionless, while seated at either end of the table were his parents.

He looked at his mother, Lady Fitzwilliam. Masses of dark blonde hair were flung over her shoulders, eyes the colour of summer sky at midday, a face that the greatest portraitists would fight to paint . . . Only her sun-tanned skin prevented her from being universally acclaimed the foremost beauty in the land in an age when white skin was the hallmark of those who didn't have to work in the sun and who – therefore – came from the leisured classes.

Aubrey glanced at George. George's face was red and he wasn't looking at Lady Fitzwilliam. Anywhere else in the room, but not Lady Fitzwilliam. Aubrey knew that George had always been totally devoted to his mother, and that she was the only female who unsettled him. Agog, enraptured, in love, George was all of these things. Aubrey was sure his mother knew it, and she tolerated it with warmth, never embarrassing George or revealing she knew of his infatuation.

A discreet throat-clearing drew Aubrey's attention to the head of the table.

Sir Darius Fitzwilliam was tall and slim. His centre-parted hair was beginning to grey, dramatically standing against the original blackness. Aubrey had often heard his father described as dashing but he'd always thought that if he grew a beard he'd look like a pirate, such was the glint in his eye.

'Father,' he said. He kissed Lady Fitzwilliam on the cheek. 'Mother.'

'Aubrey,' she said. 'Are you well?'

'Of course he is, Rose,' snapped Duchess Maria. 'Can't you see?'

'I'm not sure.' She put her hands on Aubrey's arms and turned him this way and that, allowing the light to fall on his face. 'You look pale.'

'He always looks pale, Rose,' Duchess Maria said. A touch of acid lay on her response like frost on a well-kept lawn.

'George, Aubrey, why don't you sit down?' Sir Darius said, amused. 'They could be at this for hours.'

Aubrey admired his father's voice. He could understand why the man had been able to inspire loyalty in his troops, leading them into – and out of – certain death. He also knew why the government flinched every time Sir Darius stood up in parliament.

'Thank you, sir,' George mumbled, taking his seat.

'Your parents are well, George?' Sir Darius asked.

'Mother's healthy as ever, sir. Dad's leg has been playing up, but he doesn't complain.'

'He wouldn't,' Sir Darius said. 'He never did complain.'

George's father had been Sir Darius's sergeant-major, saving his life in the Battle of Carshee – but losing his leg at the same time. Sir Darius had never forgotten, making sure that William Doyle received the best hospital treatment. After the war, Sir Darius had kept up the friendship and their sons had grown up together, Aubrey spending much time at the Doyles' farm. Aubrey knew that his father had sponsored and paid for George to attend Stonelea School, but only after much arguing with George's father. This was only one small part of Sir Darius's ongoing gratitude, but Aubrey also knew that such things were not spoken of. Loyalty, duty, honour were fundamental values, as important and as unnoticed as breathing. Debts were repaid, friendships maintained.

'You too, Aubrey. Don't let the ladies keep you.'

Aubrey nodded and took a chair. The instant he had, servants brought soup.

Lady Fitzwilliam wouldn't be diverted. 'I hope this has convinced you that the army isn't for you, Aubrey.' Her gaze was direct, not allowing him to escape.

'Of course he hasn't,' flared Duchess Maria. 'Every Fitzwilliam goes into the army.'

'And many's the Fitzwilliam who regretted it,' Sir Darius murmured. 'If they had the chance to. As the Scholar Tan said: "Warriors are often chosen, sometimes made, but seldom remembered."' Every eye at the table was on him. He lifted his head. 'My, this soup is good.'

Aubrey looked down. He realised it was pumpkin and that he'd eaten half the bowl. He hadn't tasted it, which was fortunate as he hated pumpkin soup.

Lady Fitzwilliam picked up her spoon and attacked the bowl much as she took to her specimens at the museum. 'George,' she said, 'you were there, weren't you? Tell us what happened.'

George froze in the middle of buttering a roll. 'Tell you what happened?' he repeated.

'I don't think so,' said Sir Darius. He wiped his lips with a napkin and glanced at Aubrey, then George. 'Hardly fair to expect a brother-in-arms to report on another. Loyalty, you know. Camaraderie, the spirit of the regiment, that sort of thing.'

Neither Lady Fitzwilliam nor Duchess Maria looked happy at that. 'Ridiculous,' Lady Fitzwilliam said and attacked her soup again.

'Splendid soup,' George said into the silence. 'Much better than anything we get at Stonelea. Potato and leek, isn't it?'

'It's pumpkin, George,' murmured Aubrey.

'Ah.'

'School food is meant to be bad,' Sir Darius said, the corners of his mouth twitching upwards. 'It means you'll be grateful for the comforts of home.'

So the rest of the evening went. Nothing more was discussed of Aubrey's failure, nor of his future. Lady Fitzwilliam and Duchess Maria were polite as they asked after school affairs, George's musical studies and his family. Sir Darius regaled them with gossip from parliament. Aubrey noted how George looked shocked at some of this, and he chaffed him. George tried to explain that he wasn't accustomed to knowing so much about the great figures of the day, but they would have none of that.

'Sweet, innocent George,' Lady Fitzwilliam said, smiling and touching him on the arm. 'May we always have plenty of sweet, innocent Georges.'

Much to Aubrey's amusement, George blushed mightily and tried to hide it under his napkin.

It was when an immense coconut, strawberry and cream pudding had been placed in front of them that Duchess Maria directed a fierce gaze at Sir Darius. 'Now. How are you going to win this election, Darius? You've been out of power for too long. Look how the Royalists are ruining the country!'

Sir Darius looked pained. 'Mother, I don't want to discuss this at the moment.'

Aubrey wanted him to. He wanted to know how his father was going to combat the Prime Minister's sublime scheduling of the election. The traditional King's Birthday procession, with the King and the PM in the great golden open carriage, would be winding its way from the Palace, over the Old Bridge and the other six great bridges and through the heart of the city. It was one of the few public roles that the King had insisted on maintaining and that the Crown Prince had been unable to distract him from by adding another exotic beast to the burgeoning royal menagerie. The parade was vastly popular, hundreds of thousands of people lining the route and cheering. What a start to the Royalists' campaign, as long as the King didn't do anything bizarre.

What were the Progressives going to do?

'I wasn't happy when you renounced your title,' Duchess Maria went on. 'But if you're going to keep up this ridiculous pastime of being in the Lower House, then at least you should be at the forefront again.'

Aubrey leaned forward, not wanting to miss a word. Since Sir Darius had lost the position of Prime Minister and been expelled from the Royalist Party, he'd been doing his best to consolidate the Progressive Party, the new party he had founded. The difficulty was that the

Progressives were a disparate lot, with many different needs, desires and motivations. Making sure that they were all pulling in the one direction was a gargantuan task.

'We face a difficult election,' Sir Darius said.

'If the Royalists win,' Duchess Maria said, 'you'll be condemned to the Opposition benches for years. I couldn't imagine anything worse.'

'What about the war we're about to have with Holmland? Surely that would be worse,' Aubrey put in, before he realised it. *Did I actually say that aloud?* he thought and he chased a strawberry around his bowl.

All faces turned to him. Duchess Maria looked shocked, as if a dog had spoken up. A smile hovered on Lady Fitz-william's mouth and she covered it with one hand.

Sir Darius put an elbow on the table and rested his chin on a fist. 'War?'

'It may not be inevitable, but it is more than likely. This is why we should be preparing.' Aubrey stared at the strawberry on his spoon for a moment then looked at his father. 'Isn't that what you said in your letter to *The Argus?*'

'And faced a good deal of heat in the party room for it. Some of us aren't sure what we think about Holmland.'

'Surely they can see what's happening on the continent?'

'Some of them don't even see the trouble that rabble-rousers like the Army of New Albion and the Reformists are stirring up. I'm not saying that they don't have some genuine grievances about the state of the country, but their methods . . .' He made a face and picked up his spoon. 'Good strawberries?'

'I won't know until I taste them,' Aubrey said.

Duchess Maria made a noise of disgust. She dabbed at her mouth and rose from the table. 'If you'll excuse me.'

After she had gone, Sir Darius shook his head. 'That

woman can gently close a door louder than a thousand cannon.'

'She's anxious, Darius,' Lady Fitzwilliam said. 'She's seen so much before.'

'Upper House politics?' Sir Darius snorted. 'Any place where entry is based on your owning a title becomes party games for the rich and idle. The Lower House is where government happens, where decisions are made. The Upper House members just glance at the bills and approve them, those who are awake. I don't know how Father put up with the Upper House.' Sir Darius looked at his son. 'And what do you think, Aubrey? What's the best way to win this election?'

This was a typical Sir Darius challenge. Aubrey knew that he expected a reasoned answer. Wit was acceptable, but it had to have a backbone of rigour. 'Well, sir,' he began, 'it's a short campaign, and I'm not sure the party is totally united.'

'True, true. Much to my chagrin.'

Aubrey chose his words carefully. 'And the situation with Holmland makes things awkward, wouldn't you say?'

Sir Darius sat back. 'Holmland is arming itself and growing stronger every day. I don't trust it, even though its Elektor is our King's cousin. I see ambition overriding any family loyalty. Strength, not words, is what the Holmlanders understand.'

'Darius,' Lady Fitzwilliam said, 'you're making speeches again.'

He grinned and suddenly looked years younger. 'I need the practice.'

Later, as Aubrey and George walked back to school, George said, 'Your father knows how to inspire people. If he led, I'd follow him.'

Aubrey didn't say anything for some time. Eventually, as they neared the school gates, he turned to George. 'His men always said that,' he said softly. 'Even the ones he later led to their deaths.'

Five

THE NEXT DAY WAS SUNDAY. AUBREY FELT THAT GOING to chapel might be good for his soul, or for his conscience, or both. He roused George, who would have preferred to sleep in.

After the service, Aubrey shook hands with the minister on the stairs in front of the chapel. The minister fell into the short, round category of clergymen. Aubrey liked him because he was a practical, down-to-earth sort, whose sermons were short but had lingering effects. Aubrey often found himself thinking about them days after they were given.

'Thanks, Reverend,' he said. 'You put it all very clearly. To the church, magic is neither good nor evil – it's the user who turns it to good or evil ends. So it's a matter of free will again, correct?'

The minister chuckled. 'Free will. That's what it's all about, young Fitzwilliam. The church has come a long way since the dark ages.'

The sun was warm and golden. Aubrey stood with his cap in hand enjoying the moment as the masters and the other boys swarmed down the stairs and out into the day that stretched before them. The scent of the roses and lavender planted around the chapel came strongly to him and mingled with the smell of cut grass on the playing fields. One of the groundsmen was slowly working his way around the oval, marking the boundary with lime. High in the blue sky, an ornithopter flapped its way across the heavens, taking important people from one important place to another.

Aubrey enjoyed Stonelea and its challenges, but the world was out there and, with his usual impatience, he wanted to tackle it. Finish this year – but then which of his ambitions was he to tackle first?

'A beautiful day,' George said.

Aubrey wrestled briefly with his impishness and lost. Making sure George was watching, he glanced at the cloudless blue sky. 'Thank you,' he said and strolled off, leaving George gaping.

Aubrey had difficulty keeping the smile from his face as he ambled along the path towards the boarding house.

George caught up. 'You're not fiddling with weather magic again, are you? Remember what happened last time?'

Aubrey relented. He grinned. 'No-one's called you Gullible George for a while, have they?'

George thrust his hands in his pockets, after a quick glance to see if any masters were watching. 'Dash it, Aubrey. There's no need for that sort of thing. I was simply concerned for you.'

'Sorry, George. I don't know what got into me.' Aubrey paused. 'Going to this morning's lecture?'

George looked longingly at the cricket oval. Half a dozen fourth-formers were doing some catching practice. 'I have to. The headmaster put me on the list for luncheon with our guest.'

'You? With all of sixth form to choose from?'

'Yes.' George put his hands in his pockets. 'Who's our guest lecturer this time?'

'It's Dr Mordecai Tremaine. I'm looking forward to it.'

'The Sorcerer Royal? Of course you are, magic and all that.'

'Naturally. I hope I'll get the chance to ask Dr Tremaine a few questions.'

CLOUGH HALL WAS ALMOST FULL WHEN AUBREY AND George arrived. The Sorcerer Royal's notoriety had attracted a larger attendance than usual.

Ever since Aubrey had begun seriously studying magic, he'd admired Dr Tremaine. His copy of the definitive reference work – *Tremaine on Magic* – was battered and dog-eared through repeated readings.

Dr Tremaine had risen from obscure beginnings to become a public figure after being appointed to the post of Sorcerer Royal by the King. His shadowy past had given rise to many stories. He often featured in the popular newspapers, which were attracted by his feats. What was known was that he'd fought in duels, both magical and physical, over matters of honour. His output of poetry was small, but highly praised. He was a champion fencer and rider. His singing voice was legendary, and he was constantly sought for roles on the stage, all of which he declined. It was rumoured he'd fought in foreign wars, always on the side of the insurgents, and that he swam four miles across the Sardanis Strait to rendezvous with one of his many lovers.

Aubrey had also heard that Dr Tremaine had once been offered the throne of Baltravia but did not accept, much to the disappointment of all Baltravians, saying that the climate disagreed with him.

Clough Hall was one of the showpieces of Stonelea School and was naturally where Dr Tremaine's address was to be held. With a soaring fan-vaulted ceiling, arches, pillars and stained-glass windows, it was undeniably impressive. Its great failing was that its acoustics were dreadful.

In his early days at the school, Aubrey had sat on the hard wooden seats and struggled to hear headmasters and other speakers. For anyone beyond the first row of seats, speakers' voices became woolly, muffled and – further back – lost in muddy echoes.

One of Aubrey's current duties was to adjust the recently installed equipment that was meant to solve this problem. The headmaster had chosen an expensive, newly developed magical amplification system instead of non-magical mechanical devices, as a sign of Stonelea's being at the forefront of all things. Aubrey approved of this, but when the system proved to be temperamental, he was given the task of the necessary periodic adjustment.

Aubrey thought the theory of the system was good. Using spells that applied a reciprocal function of the Law of Attenuation, the company manufactured a number of brass horns that were magically linked. One horn was to be positioned on the lectern to capture the speaker's voice, the other horns were to be arranged around the hall and the speaker's voice would emerge clear and undistorted, to be heard by those assembled.

But applying the Law of Attenuation was notoriously fiddly, and inverting it made things even more of a headache. The positioning of the outlet horns was important, and they tended to lose their connection with the capture horn with changes in temperature, fluctuations in light, numbers of people present, or even phases of the moon. Aubrey was given a manual with a range of maintenance spells and his role was to attend to the system and make sure all was well. Some of the spell elements used derivations of the Inorian language and Aubrey enjoyed the challenge.

He'd been doubly careful before the Sorcerer Royal's lecture. It wouldn't do to have the foremost magician in the land let down by magical apparatus.

Aubrey sat with George and the rest of the sixth form at the rear of the Assembly Hall. He could see the brass horns, situated on brackets high on the walls. Of course, the privilege of the sixth form in their last year at the school – to sit at the back of the hall and doze through the unintelligible announcements – had been ruined by the installation of the system. Aubrey had been offered bribes to make the horns fall out of synchronisation but, despite the temptation, he'd refused.

Dr Tremaine stood at the lectern. He was a large man, with a build more like that of a wrestler than an academic. He wore his wavy hair to his shoulders, and parted in the middle. His eyes were very, very dark and Aubrey thought he looked liked a gypsy; he was sure Tremaine would have ladies swooning whenever he appeared. He wore a long frock coat and he carried a cane with a large baroque pearl as a knob, though Aubrey could see no reason for it, since Dr Tremaine didn't appear to limp at all.

The lecture, which Dr Tremaine gave without using notes, was about his life in magic. Throughout, he used his deep, musical voice to charm the assembly and he paced across the stage with the energy of a tiger. He used anecdotes which were humorous and thrilling and he emphasised the challenge of dedicating oneself to the world of magic.

Aubrey was struck by how Dr Tremaine ended his lecture. He stood, hands grasping the sides of the lectern, leaning slightly forward, sweeping his dark gaze across the boys, teeth bared in a fierce grin. 'We are standing on the brink of a great age,' he said after a long pause. 'Nations are striving against nations to redefine our globe. Our understanding of the fundamental nature of magic is being torn down and built up again. Science and technology are changing the way we live our lives. In front of me I see young men, lucky young men. You are embarking on a voyage that will take you into times that our grandparents could not imagine. Young as you are, you will see more of it than I, and I envy you for it.' He bowed. 'Thank you for your attention.'

LUNCHEON WAS NOT IN THE DINING HALL WITH THE REST of the school. For special meals, the school opened the old Refectory.

The stone walls of the Refectory had small windows, high up, which meant that artificial light had to be used even in the middle of the day. Proudly, the headmaster showed

Dr Tremaine the magical lighting orbs that floated over the long table. 'More than three hundred years,' the headmaster said from his position at the head of the table, 'those orbs have been shedding light uninterrupted.'

'Remarkable,' Dr Tremaine announced after gazing around the chamber. He was seated in a high-backed chair at the headmaster's right, and had propped his pearl-headed cane by his side. Aubrey was on the headmaster's left, directly opposite Dr Tremaine, with George next to him. George sat glumly, running a thumbnail over the tablecloth.

A dozen boys from the sixth form had been invited to the dinner. Most were from the Advanced Magic class, with a few others – like George – for variety. Aubrey's prime position was thanks to his excellence in magical studies.

As the meal went on, the headmaster became increasingly nervous, watching Dr Tremaine dispatch vast amounts of the school's best wine. As far as Aubrey could judge, the Sorcerer Royal was not affected at all, apart from the gleam in his dark eyes becoming brighter.

Dr Tremaine dominated conversation around him, telling story after story. But Aubrey noticed how he made sure to include everyone at the table, calling for responses and opinions from those at the far end of the table as well as nearby, pointing at boys with his cane and refusing to allow them to sit unengaged in the middle of the animated discussion he was conducting. He even managed to engage George by accurately guessing that George would rather be elsewhere and admitting that he enjoyed the outdoors more than being cloistered on such a fine day.

After a particularly fine steamed pudding and custard,

Dr Tremaine pushed his plate aside, put an elbow onto the table and dropped his chin into his hand. Hair fell over one eye as he jabbed at Aubrey with his cane. 'Fitzwilliam, you're Sir Darius's son, aren't you? And don't sigh or roll your eyes.'

'Yes, sir.'

'I thought so. Tell me, Fitzwilliam, you're in sixth form, finishing up here at Stonelea, fine school as it is.' He grinned at the headmaster, who smiled back awkwardly, then he turned his intensity back to Aubrey. 'What's next? What are you planning for your life? I'm interested.'

Aubrey folded his napkin and smoothed it in front of him. 'Army and university. I'm not sure in what order.'

Dr Tremaine pursed his lips. 'And then?'

Aubrey wondered at his interest. Dr Tremaine had questioned others at the table about their plans, but there was something insistent about this attention. 'I'm not sure,' he said, and he spread his hands. 'Travel? Stay in the army? More study? I've plenty of time to decide.'

Aubrey wasn't sure why he didn't reveal his true ambitions. He'd been impressed by Dr Tremaine. His immense energy, his spirit, and his profound knowledge of things magical set him apart from most of those who chose magic as their life. While most magicians were retiring, studious types, Mordecai Tremaine swaggered through the world of magic as if it he was a pirate captain on the deck of his prized flagship.

Is that why I don't want to tell him that magic won't be my entire life? Aubrey thought. *Is it that I don't want to disappoint him?*

He felt Dr Tremaine's compelling gaze as he tried to frame a suitable response.

The headmaster coughed, and Dr Tremaine seemed to

remember he was there. 'Headmaster! You do fine work here!' He swept his arm around the table. 'Your students! I drink to them!'

He raised his wine, drained it and studied the empty glass. 'Fine vintage, headmaster.'

'Yes, well . . .' The headmaster grasped for a conversational straw. 'Tell us, Dr Tremaine, what are you working on at the moment?'

Dr Tremaine sat back in his seat and placed his arms on the rests. 'Many things, headmaster, many things. Foremost is my work heading up a top secret research establishment. Some fascinating magical work going on there. Can't say much, though.'

'Of course,' the headmaster said.

Aubrey couldn't help himself. 'Defence-related, is it?'

Dr Tremaine narrowed his eyes. 'Why do you say that, Fitzwilliam?'

'Well, doing work for the army or the navy would be the quickest way to earn top secret status, especially with the way things are going on the continent, hints of war and such.' He paused, then plunged ahead. 'There are rumours of Holmland aggression in the Goltan states, and even that they've used new magically enhanced weapons.'

Dr Tremaine was silent for a while, then he grinned and slapped the armrest. 'Damn me, Fitzwilliam, I like the way your mind works!' He turned to the head of the table. 'Headmaster, let me know if he wants to study magic at university. I'll put in a good word for him.'

Aubrey smiled, but he didn't fail to notice that Dr Tremaine hadn't answered his question.

Dr Tremaine pounded a fist on the table, pushed back his chair and stood. 'Staggeringly good meal, headmaster!'

The headmaster rose and looked worried. 'You'll stay and talk to some of the boys?'

Dr Tremaine shook his head and picked up his cane. 'I'd love to, but I have a young lady I promised to meet at the theatre. Hopeless actress, but you can't have everything.'

The headmaster looked nonplussed, but Dr Tremaine saw the direction of Aubrey's gaze. 'You like my cane, do you, Fitzwilliam?'

Aubrey had actually been wondering how he'd look with a cane like that. It was a dashing accessory. 'Yes, sir.'

'Well, I'd love to give it to you as a reward for your stimulating company, but,' he held it up in both hands, at chest height, 'this is special. Damned nuisance, but special.'

'It's handsome, sir.'

Dr Tremaine rubbed the pearl head with a thumb and stared at it. 'My sister gave it to me. Just before she died, she made me promise that it would never leave my side. Like a fool, I agreed.'

'Is it magical, sir?'

Dr Tremaine's face was thoughtful and he didn't take his gaze away from the pearl. 'No, not unless you mean the ordinary magic of memory.' He sighed. 'Every time I look at it, I remember her.' He shook himself. 'Enough of that.' He seized the headmaster's hand. 'Goodbye, head-master. Best of luck with the gout!'

After Dr Tremaine left, driving an outrageous open automobile, Aubrey and George strolled back to their rooms. A spindly figure appeared around the corner of the gymnasium and tottered towards them.

'I wonder what Addison wants?' Aubrey said.

Addison was by far the oldest porter at Stonelea School, being young when Aubrey's grandfather was at the school. It was rumoured he'd been in the place longer than many of the buildings.

Bandy-legged and bald as an egg, he hurried towards them. One outstretched hand held an envelope and he had a newspaper tucked under his arm. 'Master Fitz-william!' he called. 'Master Fitzwilliam! Letter for you!'

'On a Sunday?' George said. Aubrey shrugged and held out his hand.

It was obvious that the letter was important. The envelope was a heavy, cream paper and when Aubrey turned it over the blob of red sealing wax stood out. He scratched at it with a thumbnail and its greasy solidity spoke of someone with money, a sense of tradition and extremely good taste. Someone very familiar.

A very formal approach, Father, he thought, then he read the letter. When he had finished, he carefully folded it and placed it back in the envelope. He ran one finger along the length of the envelope, thinking. 'Thank you, Addison,' he said vaguely.

Addison tipped his cap. As he turned to go, he remembered what was under his arm. 'Your newspaper, Master Doyle.' He thrust it at George and hurried off.

Aubrey began walking towards the boarding house, thinking deeply. George fell into step beside him. As they walked past the cricket nets, he burst out, 'Dash it, Aubrey! Who's that letter from?'

Aubrey blinked. 'Sorry. I was miles away.' He stopped and rested against the fence. He looked down at the envelope he still held. 'It's from my father. It's his official stationery and seal. He wants me to do something for him.'

'Something official?'

'Yes.'

'And you're wondering why he didn't ask you last night.'

Aubrey glanced sharply at George. His friend's broad, friendly face frowned back at him. With his height, massive frame and sandy hair, George looked every inch a country bumpkin, but Aubrey knew his friend was no fool. *People don't know how shrewd you are, do they?* he thought.

'Am I that easy to read?' he laughed. He set off again, striding comfortably. He felt strong, eager and alive, ready to challenge the world.

'Well, it's obvious that's what you'd be thinking,' George persisted.

Aubrey stopped and turned. He thrust out his chest, drew in his chin and looked at George over imaginary spectacles. 'Obvious, Doyle?' he barked in his best imitation of the Advanced Magic master. 'Be so good as to share the obvious with us all!'

George laughed. 'One day, Mr Ellwood will catch you doing that, Aubrey, and you'll be suspended from his classes. Then you'll be sorry.'

'You cannot deny an artist his craft,' Aubrey said. 'When the impulse comes on me, the actor comes out.' He chuckled. 'But I'm still interested in why you think I was wondering about my father.'

'It's not difficult. When you look particularly thoughtful and sombre, it's usually your father you're thinking of.'

Aubrey let out a long sigh. 'You've known my family for too long.' He looked away. 'Perhaps he simply couldn't ask me face to face.'

'Of course he could. Whatever it is.'

'You know, this is the first time he's ever asked me to do something official like this. I've been impatient, but now it's come I'm feeling a little —'

'Anxious? Nervous? Petrified?'

Aubrey glanced sharply at George. 'Anxious will do, old man.'

He turned away and gazed over the oval. *How do you live up to a man like Darius Fitzwilliam?* he thought. *It was hard enough for the men he commanded in the army. But for me, his only son?*

He knew many people simply wouldn't try. Casting such a bright light makes all others seem pale and insignificant. Better to turn away, not attempt the impossible. Achieving even some portion of his success would be a fine achievement. To others, though, having the bar set at such a dizzying height meant the challenge was greater.

Aubrey wasn't about to give up. His ambitions were very, very lofty.

'Well?' George said. 'Are you going to tell me what this mysterious task is?'

Aubrey considered for a moment. 'How's your aim?'

'My aim?'

'Shooting, George. A country boy like you should be a crack shot.'

'I do well enough.'

'Grand. You're doing nothing next weekend, I take it?'

'Aubrey, you know very well that I'm stuck at school every weekend during term time, home being so far away. What are you getting at?'

George's home may have been far away, but Aubrey had spent much time at the small farm in the weary old hills near Green River. George was an only child, and Mr and Mrs Doyle were always happy to have Aubrey visit – and it gave Mr Doyle and Sir Darius a chance to reminisce in the guarded, elusive way that old soldiers often have. Aubrey remembered lingering in the warm kitchen, amid the hunger-inducing smells of baking bread and spice cake, hoping to hear stories of the old regimental victories, but the two men tended to talk of comrades and their circumstances, Sir Darius usually providing most of the details.

'Bertie is hosting a shooting weekend at his estate and my father has been invited. Unfortunately, he's been called away, can't be there. He's asked me to deputise for him.'

'Bertie?'

'The Crown Prince, George. The heir to the throne of Albion. The oldest son of the King. My cousin. You know the one.'

'Ah. Prince Albert.'

George had never grown used to Aubrey's closeness to the Royal Family. Prince Albert was only a few years older than Aubrey and they'd spent much time together when younger.

Aubrey felt sorry for Bertie. He would have made an excellent banker or a businessman but instead he was destined to be a king. Fortunately, he had a strong sense of duty. He never complained and, in time, Aubrey had come to the conclusion that Bertie's sense of duty – and his thoughtfulness – would mean he'd work hard to become the best king he could.

And that should be very fine indeed, he thought.

'Think, George,' Aubrey continued, 'a relaxing weekend in the country. Plenty of good food, fine accommodation, interesting company . . .'

George grinned. 'A pity you're perfectly dreadful at shooting.'

Aubrey shrugged. 'I've had all the lessons. I'm adequate.'

'Adequate? I suppose it depends on what you mean. If you mean that you haven't actually shot yourself by

accident, then by all means describe yourself as adequate.'
George laced his fingers together and placed them on his
chest. 'I'll come, then. I might be able to spare you some
embarrassment.'

'I'm honoured.'

Aubrey's father shot, of course. And played golf off
scratch, was an expert bridge player, a champion horse-
man and sailed in international ocean races. Any pursuit
that important men indulged in, Sir Darius Fitzwilliam
was a leading light.

And here Sir Darius was asking Aubrey, for the first
time, to deputise for him.

Aubrey decided that the official request meant that this
was too important for an informal approach. This was the
Leader of the Opposition needing someone to stand in
for him. Aubrey felt a momentary glow at the trust this
implied, but it faded when he realised that it was also a
challenge, as was Sir Darius's wont.

Deputise. A simple word, but it was full of meaning.
Aubrey knew he was able to chat to Bertie well enough,
but 'deputise' meant more than that.

He tapped the letter in his pocket. *Why didn't he give me
a list of duties?* he thought, but he knew the answer. It was
like the dinner table challenge of the night before. The
test was how Aubrey responded to such a broad brief as
'deputise'.

Aubrey ran through some possibilities. Observe. Be
discreet. Keep up the Fitzwilliam name. Be diplomatic.
Report back.

They set off again. In the distance, past the hockey
field, the cadet corps were drilling. Fragments of shouted
commands drifted to Aubrey, sounding like the yipping
of excited dogs.

'It's a special weekend, George,' he said as they mounted the stairs to their room. 'The Crown Prince has asked some Holmland diplomats along.'

George raised his eyebrows. 'So soon after the sinking of the *Osprey*? Won't that be a little . . . well, awkward?'

'That's one of the things the Crown Prince is good at, smoothing over awkwardness. Much better than the King, at the moment, anyway. The Elektor of Holmland has publicly apologised for sinking our cruiser, the Holmland navy has expressed regret and called it a tragic error. Our government is apparently taking them at their word and trying to patch things up.'

Aubrey was sure that the King had had something to do with the invitation. It was probably another of his efforts to show all Albion what splendid fellows the Holmlanders were. As they had to be, ruled by the King's cousin. The Elektor of Holmland was one of his many kin on the continent and the King couldn't bear to see disharmony between the two countries. His efforts were genuine – as were the headaches they caused the Crown Prince and the government.

With the messy situation on the continent, especially the constant strife between the nations on the Goltan Peninsula, Aubrey was not about to disagree with attempts to keep the peace. Although he wondered what the wives and children of the lost sailors from the *Osprey* would say.

'Prince Albert enjoys hunting?' George threw open the door. The help had made the beds and rearranged the mess so it looked almost habitable again.

'Lord no, he can't stand it.' Aubrey stood at his desk, pushing his hair back out of his eyes.

George sat in the comfortable chair and unfolded the

newspaper. 'I must have missed something. Prince Albert hates hunting but he's holding a gala shooting weekend and inviting a horde of Holmlanders to come along?'

'Duty, George. It's all about duty. Host the Holmlanders. Show them what a decent lot we are really. Emphasise the family ties, too, with Bertie playing the expansive host with one and all.'

Aubrey pulled a book from the crowded shelf over the desk.

'This wouldn't have anything to do with the war?'

Aubrey raised an eyebrow. 'What makes you think that?'

'Well, with the way your father has been making noises . . .' George paused, then he nodded. 'Ah.'

Aubrey turned back to his book. 'You see why Sir Darius Fitzwilliam was invited to this shooting weekend? And you see why he has to send someone in his place so it won't seem like he's snubbing the whole affair, thereby insulting not only the heir to the throne but the Holmland delegation, thus adding to the tension between our two countries?'

'I see why you have to go. And what the deuce are you reading?'

'*Tremaine on Magic.*'

'I see. A racy little story?'

'I wanted to check something. I had a thought about a novel method of applying two disparate magical laws in a way that may have a useful effect.'

'Something to make the Snainton Prize even more securely yours? I can't imagine anyone else matching you for Dux of the school.'

'No. This is more to do with our engagement next weekend. I was thinking about a way to improve my aim.'

George snorted. 'Practice being out of the question.'

'No time for that, George.' He pointed at *Tremaine on Magic*. 'The Law of Animation is reasonably well established – how to give lifeless objects some vigour through a variation on the Law of Contiguity.'

'Walking broomsticks fetching water, that sort of thing.'

'Exactly.' Aubrey nodded. 'It's not foolproof, but the variables are fairly well worked out. I was thinking of the shot used in the cartridges. If I could apply the Law of Animation and find some way to guide them, the shot could compensate for my inadequate aiming.'

'Ingenious.'

Aubrey seized *Tremaine on Magic* and flipped through the pages. 'Here it is: "The Law of Propensity – the tendency of objects towards certain actions. For example, most objects have a tendency to fall when dropped from a height."' He snapped the book shut. 'I think I can work this law so that the shot almost has a *desire* to go in the right direction, towards the target.'

George frowned for a moment. 'If you can perfect this, there may be many people who'd be interested in such a process.'

'Of course. Our friends in the army would love ammunition that wouldn't miss.'

'Smart bullets. Clever shells. Intelligent bombs.'

'Hmm.' Aubrey narrowed his eyes. 'If I can do this discreetly, no-one need ever know.'

George picked up the newspaper. 'Very discreetly.' He tapped the front page. 'Some Holmlander archduke or other is making rather colourful suggestions about your father and the policies he stands for.'

'Again?'

'You're not worried?'

Aubrey took another book from the bookshelf and sat at the desk. 'It wouldn't do much good if I were. Father won't stop making speeches, nor would I want him to.'

'You think he's right?'

'In standing up to bullies? Certainly. In bringing us closer to war? I'm not sure, but I'm not sure of the alternative, either.'

'Tricky thing, international relations.' George shook the newspaper. 'Let's bypass them and concentrate on something important.'

'The Personal Advertisements?'

'Precisely.'

'George, I've never understood your fascination with the agony columns.'

'I'm simply curious. Insight into other lives, glimpses of how strangers live, colourful details. Interesting stuff.'

'That's right. "Mr G. Brown will no longer be responsible for any debts incurred by his father as he is now dead." Profound, that.'

'What about "C.J. Send £10 at once. D.W."? Anything could be going on there. Blackmail, embezzlement, secret plans.'

'It's more likely that D.W. needs money and thinks C.J. is a soft touch.'

'Where's your imagination, old man?'

Aubrey chuckled and returned to his reading.

'What are you going to wear, Aubrey?' George said suddenly.

'To the shooting weekend? No idea.' Aubrey didn't look up from *An Inquiry into Enchantments of Motion*. He'd found some interesting approaches to the problem of changing momentum by spells that worked on variables of mass and velocity. 'But I'm sure Grandmother will have sorted that out. She'll probably get a trunk or two of clothes organised.'

'Ah.'

'Don't worry. The Holmlanders are notoriously bad dressers. They spend enormous amounts of money on clothes whenever they're posted over here, but they have abominable taste. They'll either look like walking haystacks or they'll scare away any game for miles.'

'That's not much consolation. "There goes George Doyle. He doesn't dress quite as badly as a Holmlander."'

'George, you have tweeds, perfectly acceptable shooting clothes. You're from the country, we're going out to the country. You'll be at home.'

'I hate tweed,' George mumbled. 'It itches.'

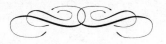

Six

AUBREY LIKED TRAINS. HE FOUND IT HARD TO PASS A station without pausing to take in the steam, smoke and organised business that was railway life. The smells of oil and coal appealed to him, as did the knowledge that every station was the beginning of a thousand destinations, all waiting at the other end of the vast steel network that was the railways.

He saw trains as the result of a hundred and fifty years of accumulated expertise and refinement. He admired the power and precision in the engineering that went into engines: the way that coal and water was turned into enough horsepower to pull a laden goods train was testimony to years of practical thinking, each engineer adding his competence to those who'd gone before him.

Or her, Aubrey added mentally, thinking of Lord Ashton's daughter, Sophie, who had recently invented a particularly clever magically augmented anti-blowback valve for locomotive boilers. Extraordinarily expensive, it was, so it was only found on the showpiece locomotives, such as the one he was gazing at.

He stood on the platform of Ashfields Station, the busiest in the city, admiring the *Teal*, the latest of the Northern Line's engines, the pinnacle of the Hurricane class of engines. The dark green paint glowed on the streamlined cowling as a stoker polished brasswork that already glistened in the morning sun. A thin wisp of steam came from the smokestack, indicating it was some time before the train was to leave.

Aubrey wanted to stop and chat with the driver, but George was looking pained as he waited. 'Come on, George,' Aubrey said, with a lingering glance at the great driving rods and wheels. 'Let's find our compartment.'

Aubrey led the way. He'd been feeling ill at ease all morning and his stroll around the station had done him good, allowing him to think clearly about the looming weekend.

He was willing to admit that he felt ambivalent about the shooting party. The lack of clear direction from his father was awkward. Aubrey was tossing up if it meant that his father had confidence in Aubrey to know what to do, or whether it meant a *lack* of confidence.

Of course, the sinking of the *Osprey* was going to make the weekend tense. Aubrey smiled to himself as he imagined how the Albion politicians and generals would be polite through gritted teeth, saying they understood how these things happened while seething underneath. The Holmlanders would be stiff and diplomatic and manage to offend everyone without realising it, as Holmlanders usually did.

It was bound to be a weekend of walking on eggshells.

He wondered if his father really had another engagement to go to.

Aubrey marched down the platform, studying his ticket and peering at the carriages. The porter with the bags had to hurry to keep up.

'Here, George,' Aubrey gestured. 'Climb aboard. Next stop, Penhurst Estate Station.'

'Why couldn't we take an ornithopter?' George asked. 'It'd be fun. We'd be there in no time.'

As if to emphasise George's suggestion, an ornithopter rose clattering into the air from the ornithopter port nearby. Aubrey shaded his eyes and watched as it swooped, steel wings beating birdlike at the air, righted itself and then rose over the neighbouring Engineers' Guild headquarters. Aubrey approved of the way the pilot rolled the aircraft around the dirigible tethering mast on top of the building and then mounted even higher.

'I wanted to think,' he said. 'Ornithopters are so noisy it's hard to talk, let alone think.' He looked up again and followed the ornithopter as its metal body caught the sun. Someday, he'd like to learn how to fly one of those magically enhanced machines. 'Another time, George.'

AFTER THE PORTER HAD STOWED THE LUGGAGE, HE BACKED out of the compartment.

With blue velvet bench seats, chintz curtains, brightly polished brasswork and turned wood, the compartment was fit for a king, Aubrey decided, and most probably had hosted royalty. He approved of the combination of luxury and cunning artifice, showing that comfort need not be sacrificed in an efficient, modern world.

Aubrey placed his hat on the wire shelf above the other seat in the compartment and hung his coat in the cleverly designed rack, which was no more than a handspan wide. He sat on the velvet and brushed his hand backwards and forwards, studying the changing sheen of the nap.

George frowned at the compartment from the narrow doorway. 'Don't just stand there,' Aubrey said, 'come in.'

George sat. Then he smiled and ran a hand through his sandy hair. 'Plush, isn't it? I feel out of place.'

'Don't worry about it. Relax, enjoy the ride.'

George sat back, realised he was still wearing his jacket, stood, took it off and hung it up. He took a position by the window.

Unlike George, Aubrey had some experience in dealing with royalty and foreign diplomats. A constant stream of the powerful and famous had run through Maidstone over the years of Aubrey's growing up. George was a country lad, not accustomed to the brittle world of precedence, protocol and politics. He was more at home in the fields and woods than in the drawing room.

At least he should enjoy the shooting, Aubrey thought. He remembered the letter his grandmother had given him before he left Stonelea that morning.

'Something amusing?' George enquired.

'Grandmother. She gave me a twelve-page letter, detailing everything she thought I'd forget.'

'Stand up straight, eat all your greens, things like that?'

'Protocol, George. How to address the Crown Prince. How to address a foreign diplomat. Correct forms of praise for good shooting by one's host. That sort of thing.'

'Twelve pages,' George mused. 'You read them all?'

'Hardly.' Aubrey grinned. 'But I'm sure it's nothing

personal. I'm certain she would have written such a tome for Father if he were going instead of me.'

George smiled and then looked serious. 'How are you feeling?' he asked.

Aubrey shrugged. 'I'm all right at the moment. I'm rested, the spells seem to be holding . . . There's not much more I can do.'

'Have your researches given you any hope of a lasting cure?'

'I've found a few small refinements to the spells I'm using, but that's all. I have a few prospects to investigate, but . . .' Aubrey's good mood began to evaporate. Thinking about his condition made him depressed. He'd achieved an equilibrium state where maintaining his integrity was almost automatic. Focusing on it made him aware of how precarious his state actually was, how fragile the grace afforded to him by his spells.

Aubrey brooded, cursing the impetuousness that had led him to the disastrous experiment. He had grown good at this self-chastisement and he took a moment to give himself a good dressing-down. He deserved it.

In addition to castigating himself for bungling the experiment, he spent time dissecting his actions. As well as the failure in the focusing figure, he was sure that, despite his efforts, the problem had arisen from a slight looseness of expression in one element in the spell. It was enough to introduce an error, which had influenced a variable and thus created another error, which led to more. Subtle, infinitesimal, but errors nonetheless. The result was death's opening in front of him. It was still there, waiting.

Aubrey felt cold when he thought of it. He had so much he wanted to do in his life that the idea of leaving it now appalled him. He didn't want an obituary that included phrases such as 'too young', 'cut short' or 'before his time'. He smiled wryly. If nothing else, he was determined to leave more than clichés behind.

The trip took just over an hour and a half. They had had time to visit the dining car, with George tucking into a huge plate of scones. The landscape rushed by, the steam whistle split the air and the deep-throated chuffing of the locomotive underlined everything.

The conductor was a roly-poly man who looked as if he'd break into a sweat if he even thought about climbing stairs. He assured Aubrey and George that Penhurst Estate Station was not a regular stop on the line and it wasn't to be confused with Penhurst Station. Penhurst *Estate* Station was actually part of the Crown Prince's Penhurst Estate and only used for his business and guests. Anyone wanting to go to the town of Penhurst had to get off some two miles further down the track.

As the train began to slow, Aubrey peered through the window. 'No brass bands to welcome us.'

George was struggling into his jacket. 'Just as long as there's someone.'

Aubrey looked again, with a level of careful appraisal. 'There is. It's a girl.'

Standing alone on the platform was a girl. A young woman? Aubrey found it hard to say, with the swirling smoke and steam. She was dressed for the outdoors, with leather gloves, a small cap, a tweed jacket and a heavy skirt. Dark brown hair. The more she tried to wave the smoke and steam away from her face, the more it seemed to cling, attracted to her.

George hurried to the window and joined Aubrey. 'Well,' he said. 'Charming. This weekend is looking more promising all the time.'

'We're here out of duty. Remember that.'

'And it looks as if this duty may be a pleasure. Come now, old man, the train isn't going to wait all day. Tally-ho!' He fairly bounded for the door of the compartment. Aubrey wondered if he should point out that they weren't going fox-hunting, but shrugged instead. It wouldn't make any difference.

Once they'd alighted, Aubrey saw that the young woman was closer to his age than he'd thought. 'Fitz-william, Doyle? I'm Caroline Hepworth. I've been sent to fetch you.'

She held out a leather-gloved hand. George looked nonplussed, but took it and she shook in a businesslike manner. Before she could repeat the process, Aubrey held out his hand first. 'Miss Hepworth,' he said, looking her directly in the eye and smiling. 'Thank you for coming out for us. I hope we haven't kept you waiting.'

She hesitated, then took his hand. 'Not at all. It gave me a chance to get out of the Big House and all the nonsense that's going on up there.'

Aubrey blinked. 'Nonsense?'

'Politicians and diplomats. They love a chance to scheme and plot away from the eyes of the public. They're more excited than a class of schoolboys on a field trip.'

'I see.' Aubrey was a little taken aback, but intrigued all the same. 'I'd guess you're not a politician, Miss Hepworth, so your role here is . . .?'

'My father. My mother made me accompany him to keep him out of trouble, but there's only so much guff I can stand.'

'I'm sure,' Aubrey said.

At that moment the conductor appeared with their luggage. George took his bags and placed them on the trolley that was waiting for them. The conductor hurried back for Aubrey's trunk.

'Good Lord,' Miss Hepworth exclaimed. 'How long are you staying? Six months?'

Aubrey shrugged and spread his hands. 'My grandmother packed for me. I could insist, but she feels I can't do the job properly without her.' He paused. 'Miss Hepworth, your father would be Professor Lionel Hepworth?'

'Quite. And my mother is Ophelia Hepworth.'

The name was familiar. Aubrey hazarded a guess. 'The artist?'

George looked from Aubrey to Miss Hepworth, puzzled.

'Sorry, George. Professor Hepworth is renowned for some extraordinary work at Greythorn University. Uncertainty Theory, if I'm not mistaken, Miss Hepworth? Working with Winslow and Tremaine?'

She nodded, but Aubrey saw wariness in her eyes. 'That's his field.'

'I haven't read anything about his research for some time,' he said. 'I hope I'll get the chance to meet him. It'd be an honour.'

Miss Hepworth glanced at George and added, 'My mother is Ophelia Hepworth. Her works are hung in the National Gallery as well as in major galleries overseas. Her paintings are sought after by private collectors and the Royal Family own several. She's a genius.'

'I'm sure she is.' George smiled.

She turned back to Aubrey, who was trying to keep up with the mercurial Miss Hepworth. 'Your mother is Lady Rose Fitzwilliam, the famous explorer and naturalist?'

Aubrey was surprised. It was his father that most people were immediately interested in. 'Indeed.'

'I'd like to meet her.' With that, she swept towards the station exit, not looking behind to see if they'd follow.

'A modern young woman,' George said, after a moment's silence.

'Certainly,' Aubrey said. 'Let's go and join her, George. I'm sure she has more surprises for us.'

The station was a tribute to the stationmaster's care, with climbing roses growing along the picket fence and up one side of the tiny house. The stationmaster himself came bustling out, tucking his shirt into his trousers. 'Here, young sir,' he said to George. 'Let me take that.'

George happily relinquished the trolley. The station-master took the handles, and it was only a short distance through the gate before they found Miss Hepworth.

She was standing by a carriage, stroking one of the matched pair of black horses that looked as if they'd been prepared for dressage. The driver nodded approvingly at her handling of the animals.

The stationmaster frowned at the lightly sprung carriage and then at the luggage. He pushed back his cap, scratched his head and then shrugged. 'You go ahead. When you get there, tell them they'd better send the wagon down.'

Aubrey offered his hand to Miss Hepworth, but she climbed into the carriage unaided. Aubrey and George sat opposite her. The driver clicked his tongue and they moved off.

George waved a hand. 'You've been to Penhurst before, I take it, Miss Hepworth?'

She had been studying the elms that lined the long avenue leading from the station towards the house. She looked at George and inclined her head a little. 'Father has been working nearby. Prince Albert has made his colleagues and him welcome a number of times. He says that their living circumstances are too spartan.'

'And are they?' Aubrey put in, leaning forward.

'I wouldn't know.' Miss Hepworth returned her gaze to the trees she obviously found more fascinating than Aubrey and George. 'I haven't seen them.'

'Ah,' Aubrey said, his mind racing. His curiosity was pricking at him. A number of things Miss Hepworth had said — or not said — were intriguing, but Aubrey knew better than to force matters. He sat back and let his mind work.

After fifteen minutes travelling through woods and well-kept fields, the avenue brought them to a large set of gates in a tall stone wall that stretched as far as Aubrey could see in either direction. The gates bore the coat of arms of the Royal Family. 'The Big House,' Miss Hepworth said, pointing.

Still some distance away, well inside the walls, was a huge, rambling building, four storeys, brownish stone, many windows looking outwards. A flag flew from the tower, indicating the Prince was in residence.

Aubrey smiled, remembering the happy times he'd spent at the Royal Family's favourite country estate. Its popularity, no doubt, arose from the King's fondness for shooting and Penhurst's possessing some of the finest country in the land. Of course, the King had done a great deal to improve its natural advantages. Much replanting of coverts was undertaken, woods were cleared to suit efficient beating, all with an eye to providing superlative shooting opportunities for the King and his friends. No-one was considered a serious shooter until he or she had scored a bag at Penhurst.

A dapper young man stepped briskly out of the

gatehouse. He was tall, lean and wore his hair and mous-tache clipped short. 'Good morning, Miss Hepworth,' he said, then he peered at Aubrey and George. 'Mr Fitz-william and Mr Doyle?'

'That's right,' Aubrey said.

'We are expected,' George added.

'Of course,' the young man said. He gestured over his shoulder and after a moment another young man left the gatehouse and drew back the gates.

'Very good,' Aubrey murmured as the two young men ushered the carriage through the gates. He leaned out and watched them lock the gates behind.

Military men, both of them, he thought. *No mistaking it. It was all they could do not to salute.*

He straightened to see Miss Hepworth looking quizzi-cally at him. 'Lovely gardens,' he said, gesturing at the trees, the rolling expanse of lawn and the small, but exquisite, lake, the result of a few centuries of dedicated labour. 'Competence Rowe, if I remember correctly?'

'Yes,' Miss Hepworth said. 'It's said to be his best work. See how the stone bridge over that end of the lake takes you to the grove of linden trees? It's a fine place for contemplation. Or so I'm told.'

George seemed to feel he should make some contri-bution. 'So, you like shooting, Miss Hepworth?'

He hadn't slapped her with a dead fish, but her face said he might as well have. 'No,' she said. 'And it's only been made barely tolerable by the banning of blood sports.' She looked at Aubrey. 'That was your father's doing, wasn't it?'

'Yes. He pushed that bill through Parliament while he was Prime Minister.'

'Not an easy task, that. Nor many votes in it, either.'

'He felt it was the right thing to do. He'd always been

sickened by fox-hunting and the like. He couldn't see how a country could call itself civilised and still allow such things.'

'Clever, though, how he managed to promote an alternative. Without it he wouldn't have had a chance of getting a ban on live hunting made into law.'

'The theory for magical hunts had been around for ages,' Aubrey said. 'Father simply brought the right people together and they perfected the spells needed, translating some of the Traskentian elements into more modern language.'

Miss Hepworth held her hands together tightly. Her face was set, Aubrey noticed uneasily. 'And he made quite a deal of money from it, didn't he?'

Ah, I see what's bothering you. You're an idealist. 'Yes,' he said simply. Aubrey glanced at George. 'Scandal has a habit of never going away, George, remember that. Even if a Royal Commission clears your name.'

'I will.' George gave him a look that promised all sorts of retribution if Aubrey didn't explain exactly what was going on.

'Miss Hepworth,' Aubrey said, 'my father stepped down as Prime Minister as soon as the Opposition raised the issue of conflict of interest. Even though he'd *given* the magical hunt company to the university as soon as it was making a profit, he *still* stepped down, confident that the matter would be cleared up and he would be able to return to his position.'

'But he didn't,' she said.

'My father has been involved in politics for years. This means, through no fault of his own, he has made enemies. Some of them were once his allies. It was people in his own party, the Royalists, who conspired to keep him from the leadership after the Royal Commission, saying there was a cloud over his character and such. Then they expelled him. For the good of the party, they said.'

She nodded carefully, thoughtfully. 'I see.'

I believe you do, Aubrey thought. He decided to move the conversation to something less prickly. 'And what are we hunting this weekend? Gryphon? Manticore?'

'Stymphalian birds, I believe,' she said. 'And here's the house.'

They were greeted by a regiment of the Prince's staff. Footmen, stable boys, butlers and other indeterminate – but obviously essential – helpers swarmed over them, whisking them inside. Before he knew it, Aubrey had been separated from George and Miss Hepworth and deposited in a sunny bedroom.

He had barely sat down in the armchair when his luggage arrived. The under-butler who delivered it was young and dapper, and he carried Aubrey's trunk as if it was a feather. 'Where'd you like this one, sunshine?' he asked.

Sunshine? Aubrey gestured at the expensive burl walnut wardrobe, and the trunk was deposited next to it. The under-butler ticked a merry half salute as he left, closing the door behind him.

Aubrey stared at the door. *Another soldier*, he thought. But in plain clothes. He rubbed his hands together. Something interesting was going on at Penhurst.

He stood and walked around the room, examining its expensive but far from gaudy furnishings. The single bed was covered with a heavy, brocaded quilt. A dressing table with a large oval mirror stood next to the window. Aubrey parted the drapes and gazed down at the drive-way and the gardens beyond.

Immediately, he closed the drapes and stepped back from the window. Not that he had anything to hide from, he told himself. It was simply that he'd seen Sir Guy Boothby – the Foreign Secretary – and the Holmland Ambassador talking.

The brief glimpse he'd had was enough to make him wonder, for the two men gave every indication that they did not want to be seen. They were near the bridge over the ornamental lake, by a copse of birch trees which – Aubrey was sure – they felt screened them from the house.

It was only that Aubrey's room was on the corner of the house, and on the third floor.

Aubrey slipped off his boots and stretched out on the bed. He put his hands behind his head.

It looked as if it was going to be a very interesting weekend.

A knock came at the door. 'Yes?'

George walked in, smiling broadly. 'Friendly staff here, Aubrey.'

Aubrey knew that look. 'We'd be talking about the maids, the scullery girls and the like?'

'I think there are a few ladies-in-waiting, too, or whatever they're called.'

'You've changed your mind about the weekend, then?'

'I'm suddenly looking forward to it. Like to go for a walk?'

Aubrey rolled off the bed. 'Capital idea.'

The house itself was grand. Aubrey counted fourteen doors on the floor where his room was, and this floor looked over a vast entry foyer. Paintings and prints covered almost all the available wall space. He saw a Dellarte, a Carpenter, and a rather good Marceau that hadn't been on display last time he was at Penhurst. He didn't care for the rest.

Aubrey noticed small groups of people wherever they went. Quite a few of the fit young men seemed to be loitering, making desultory efforts at polishing furniture or mopping floors. Aubrey was asked several times if they were looking for anyone or anything, always in unfailingly polite tones.

Discreet, well disciplined, watchful, Aubrey thought as he watched another of the young men leap up the stairs, balancing a tray full of crystal glasses, a decanter and a soda siphon. *And no shortage of them. Is someone expecting trouble?*

It was the guests, however, who intrigued him most. They were everywhere. Five serious-looking older men were sitting in the billiard room, ignoring the tables that looked like slabs of green turf. They stared at the two intruders in the doorway, moustaches bristling. Aubrey and George hurried out.

Half a dozen more were discussing matters in the library. Weighty matters, to judge from their frowns and the careful arrangement of standing shoulder to shoulder to exclude anyone joining them. Elsewhere, some stood in porticoes, others talked while they walked along the colonnaded east wing, others sat in the conservatory amid lush tropical plants and spoke in solemn voices that stopped whenever Aubrey and George came close.

'The garden?' Aubrey suggested after they withdrew. The voices in the conservatory resumed as he closed the glass doors, but more softly, as if the guests were speaking behind their hands.

It took a few false turns and a number of locked doors but they managed to emerge into a small garden dominated by a magnificent pin oak. The garden opened out onto the grounds on the western side of the Big House and a serene view presented itself. Aubrey went to the bench beneath the tree and sat. He pursed his lips and hummed tunelessly.

'You're thinking,' George said.

'That I am.' Aubrey glanced at him. 'How'd you know?'

'Your awful humming. You do that when something's on your mind.'

'Nothing gets past you, does it, George?' Aubrey crossed his arms and the humming resumed.

George sighed and sat on the seat next to Aubrey.

George was right. Bits and pieces were gnawing at Aubrey, little fragments he'd heard and noticed since arriving at Penhurst. But they were jumbled, unconnected, and the harder he tried, the more the connections eluded him.

He knew what to do. He had to distract himself.

He found he was staring at the house, and he let his gaze roam over it. He felt odd calling it a house. 'House' seemed too cosy, too domestic. The building before him was as large as one of the best hotels in the city. Aubrey could count twelve chimneys, just on the wing in front of him. Castle wouldn't do, though. No battlements, nor any crenellations. Mansion sounded too ostentatious.

But the King refused to call it a palace, even though that probably was the best name for it.

Aubrey's gaze drifted away from the house. He frowned.

'George,' he said, 'what do you make of that chap over there?'

'The gardener?' Cloth-capped and gumbooted, the man was raking leaves near a privet hedge thirty or forty yards away. His sleeves were rolled up and he was taking great sweeping strokes with the rake, side to side. 'He seems to be enjoying his job.'

'It's interesting,' Aubrey said.

'What is?'

'You noticed his tattoo?'

George squinted. 'Let me guess, Aubrey, before you do. A sailor?'

Aubrey nodded. 'Look how he's raking. Legs wide apart, long strokes side to side. That's more like mopping a deck than raking leaves.'

'What's a sailor doing here?'

'Whatever he's doing, he's not alone. See that fellow on the roof mending the drainpipe?'

'Another sailor?' George said, shading his eyes against the glare of the sky.

'Perhaps. Would you say he had anything in common with the gardener?'

George looked at them both. 'I'm not sure what you mean.'

Aubrey glanced at the roof and then at the hedge. 'I'll wager they can both whistle.'

'I beg your pardon?'

Aubrey didn't say anything. Smiling, he stood and stretched. Then he put his hands in his pockets and strolled around the trunk of the tree, his attention on the ground. He didn't look at the two men and did his best to appear every inch an idle and vacant young man of breeding. Halfway around the tree he found what he wanted. He bent and re-tied the laces on his boot. 'Watch the two men, George,' he muttered without lifting his head. 'Be discreet about it.'

Aubrey stood and flexed the small twig he'd picked up from the ground. He sought in his memory for the spell he needed. He mumbled a string of syllables, making sure he limited the scope of the effect, then the twig split apart.

Immediately, a crack like gunfire came from overhead. A large branch tore from the oak tree and crashed to the earth.

George leaped to his feet. As he did, a chorus of whistles echoed from the walls of the house.

Aubrey watched carefully. He saw the gardener sprinting towards them, having abandoned his rake. The man on the rooftop had his fingers to his lips and was unleashing volley after volley of whistles.

'Watch, George. We'll compare notes later.' Aubrey put his hands back in his pockets.

'Sirs! Are you hurt?' The gardener stared at the enormous branch. He wasn't panting, despite running all the way in gumboots. His arms were spread and his gaze was darting from side to side. He was young, in his early twenties, Aubrey guessed.

'No harm done,' Aubrey said. 'Just frightened, that's all.'

George glanced incredulously at Aubrey.

'You were lucky,' the gardener said. He studied the oak branch, then pushed back his cloth cap and scratched his head. 'Never seen that happen before.'

More staff began to appear and several men appeared from inside, attracted by the commotion. 'Not in spring,' Aubrey said. 'I've only seen it happen in autumn, when the acorns are heaviest on the limbs.'

'Aye,' the gardener agreed, but his expression made it clear that Aubrey was speaking gibberish to him.

The whistling stopped. An older man hurried from the house. He was short, stocky and obviously in charge. He surveyed the scene, studied Aubrey and George for a moment, then caught the gardener's eye. As Aubrey and George left they were conversing in low voices. Others stared at the massive oak branch and the wound in the side of the tree. Nothing seemed to be happening until an ancient gaffer wheeled up a barrow and started pointing towards a shed in the distance.

Aubrey held the door open for George and they found ourselves in a corridor with a bare wooden floor. Their footsteps echoed. 'Well, Aubrey,' George said softly, 'how did you know they could whistle?'

'Wait a little, George. Let's go back to my room.'

AUBREY DROPPED INTO THE ARMCHAIR. 'LINE OF SIGHT, George,' he explained. 'That's what it was all about.'

'Line of sight?'

'Indeed. Our gardener who was a sailor, he was part of it.' He tapped his chin with a forefinger. 'At least, he *had* been a sailor. Until recently, given the suntan on his arms. He didn't know anything about gardening, judging from his reaction to my oaks in autumn story.'

'Naturally. The whistling?'

Aubrey nodded. 'I could see that the man on the roof had a clear line of sight right along the east wall. The gardener could see into the kitchen garden where the rooftop watcher couldn't. They were perfectly placed for observation. And what would observation be without some method of signalling what they saw?'

'The whistling.'

'George, do you remember at the gate, the two young men who greeted us?'

'Of course.'

'Military types. Ex-army, I'd say. Did you notice how the man who greeted us always stood to one side, never getting between us and the gatehouse?'

'Line of sight.'

'Exactly. The second young man in the gatehouse probably had a rifle on us the whole time, until he received a signal that we were all clear.'

George's eyes widened. 'Are you saying that there are guards everywhere here?'

'Special Services, I'd say. They're the only division that recruits from both the army and the navy.' Aubrey stood and began to pace the room. 'Not the Magisterium. I'm not sensing a trace of magic about these fellows. They're just good, honest servicemen, the best of the best, creamed off from the regular army and navy and recruited to do extraordinary duty.'

'And what's extraordinary about a shooting weekend?' George said.

Aubrey grinned wolfishly. 'That's what I'm curious about. I can't wait for dinner.'

Seven

*A*UBREY RAPPED ON GEORGE'S DOOR. WHEN IT OPENED, he put his hands on his hips and scrutinised his friend. George had dressed in his dinner suit, which the house staff had pressed. His shirt collar had been freshly starched and stood high and proud. He tugged at it, but Aubrey batted his hand away. 'Quite presentable, George.' He reached out and adjusted his bow tie. 'There. Perfect.'

'We're not late?'

'Nothing to worry about.'

'Let's go, then. I'm hungry. If it means getting some food, I'm prepared to sit next to a hundred boring Holmland diplomats.'

To Aubrey, the dinner was a vital chance to survey those invited to the weekend. All the guests would be in one place. By watching who sat next to whom and which direction the conversations flowed, he'd be able to determine some of the alliances, some of the tensions and some of the possibilities.

Since the King's eccentricities had become pronounced enough that he'd been effectively eased out of sensitive matters, Penhurst had become known as a place where political agreements were reached before they ever came to Parliament. Diplomatic agreements were also concluded here over a glass of port and a handshake, language differences disappearing in the convivial surroundings.

Aubrey also saw this as a sign of the Crown Prince's increasingly important role in matters of the nation. He grinned. This was the hurly-burly of upper echelon decision-making. He loved it.

Before they reached the stairs, George tugged at his elbow. 'Dash it all, Aubrey. I can't wait any longer. Tell me how you made the branch fall!'

'I knew you'd ask.' Aubrey reached into his pocket and pulled out a broken twig. 'A practical application of the Law of Sympathy.'

George grimaced. 'Like affects like?'

'Very good, George. You learned something before the masters gave up on you.' He held up the twig and pointed to where it had snapped in the middle. 'I picked up a twig from the oak tree and after the right spell to link it to one of the branches of the tree, I broke it. The branch had no choice but to snap. Like to like. In the dark ages, those poor misguided souls would hurt dolls to inflict injuries on their enemies. The principle is the same, but now we understand magic better we can control the spells, carefully delineating variables.'

'We could have been crushed.'

'Hardly. I chose my branch well.' Aubrey reached out

and dropped the twig into a vase that was sitting on a spindly side table. 'Food is calling.'

A footman, his hair brilliantined until his head shone like a beacon, directed them to the main ballroom, which was being used as a banquet hall. It was large, with a lofty ceiling. Aubrey decided that grapes must have been the plasterer's forte, as vines snaked along the cornices and great bunches festooned the tops of the six mock pillars spaced along each wall. A gallery at one end of the room overlooked the throng, empty and somewhat ominous.

Two rows of tables stretched along the length of the room. A smaller table, obviously for the most important guests, was at right angles to them at the opposite end to the gallery. Modest bowls of chrysanthemums were arranged on the white linen tablecloths. Ranks of cutlery shone with the sheen that only comes from sterling silver. Five glasses of various sizes and shapes stood in front of each setting. It was a display of serious wealth that was meant to impress and the organisers had not missed any opportunity.

At the door, they handed their cards to the major domo and waited while he scanned his seating list. The major domo frowned and gestured to a footman. A muttered discussion ensued, and Aubrey took the opportunity to study the guests who had already been seated.

At first glance, the only thing the guests had in common was that most of the men were old. At least in their forties, he guessed, from the grey hair and bald heads. The women were harder to gauge.

Aubrey blinked. Miss Hepworth. He almost didn't recognise her, sitting between a tall man with old-fashioned muttonchop whiskers and a woman who was wearing so many jewels that she looked as if she were carrying a chandelier.

Aubrey did his best to stop himself goggling. Miss Hepworth was wearing a black dress that was shaped in ways that defied his understanding, and her hair was piled up on top of her head in a braided curly arrangement that made her look quite different. However the effect was achieved, it made her look compellingly elegant and unapproachable.

She was speaking with animation, leaning towards the old gent as if she wanted every word to be as fresh as possible. The old gent listened to her with stunned attention. She didn't look in the least nervous to be in such company.

And such company. When Aubrey dragged his gaze away from her, he saw, a few places away, Wammersley, the Chancellor of the Exchequer, speaking to the owner of the largest steelworks in the country. Opposite them was an actress who was the current toast of theatreland; she'd captivated two of the most conservative peers in the land. They looked as though they wouldn't tear themselves away if someone told them they were on fire.

The major domo loomed. 'Young sirs? We have your places for you.'

Aubrey spent the next part of the evening listening to a Holmlander accounts clerk telling him of the glories of the fatherland and how the Holmlander way of life was the finest in the world. The accounts clerk seemed to be able to eat, talk and drink, all without interrupting his stream of praise for his country, its people, its leaders, its forests, its mountains and its cheese. Aubrey was unreasonably pleased to see that George was trapped with a junior under-secretary from the Royalist Party, a notorious bore who had obviously mistaken George for someone important, to judge from the way he was doing his best to impress.

To his disappointment, Aubrey couldn't see Miss Hepworth without turning his head one hundred and eighty degrees, something he thought even his Holmlander dining companion would be bound to notice.

He was, however, able to see the head table. Prince Albert was obvious from the throne-like seat he was installed in. Tallish and slim, dark-haired and with refined, thoughtful features, the Prince was the focus of attention of every unmarried woman in the room – and their mothers, who would give anything to match him with their daughters. He was quite unlike the ruddy-faced and extravagantly bearded King, having taken after his mother, who was from Torremain.

Aubrey recognised the dapper, languid Home Secretary, Phillips-Dodd, and several older military men. These bearded gents were doing their best not to be offended by the assortment of Holmland diplomats and generals who dominated the table. Sir Guy Boothby, the Foreign Secretary, was seated between the military and the Holmlanders, no doubt a deliberate arrangement by Sir William Brasingham.

Sir William was Prince Albert's equerry and the man responsible for the detailed planning and execution of the Prince's daily program. He was dressed in the uniform of the regiment from which he was seconded, the Midland Guards. His gaze was never still, but instead of roaming over the guests, as Aubrey's did, Sir William's attention was on the footmen, the servers, the major domo and anyone else involved in the running of the evening.

Aubrey could see, even from this distance, that Prince

Albert was nodding his head and wearing the careful smile that was his standard expression on these occasions. It reinforced Aubrey's belief that the Crown Prince had one of the worst jobs in the country. It seemed to consist of innumerable dinners with guests not of his choosing, hundreds of openings of buildings he'd never seen and was likely never to see again, and making presentations to people he didn't know for doing things he'd been told about five minutes before the actual handing over of the diploma, medal, award or whatever it was that day.

Of course, all these duties had to be done with good grace, without the slightest hint of bad temper or boredom.

Aubrey shuddered. Even though Prince Albert had been brought up for this sort of thing, Aubrey didn't know how he managed it.

Between the first dessert course and the second, the major domo rang a small bell. It precipitated a mass turning of heads by those who knew what the signal meant and a delayed, consequent movement by those who followed their lead. The final effect was like a breeze blowing over a field of wheat.

It was time for the Prince to make a speech. Aubrey sent mental thanks heavenwards, for it meant that his Holmland dinner companion had to interrupt his litany of Holmland achievements, just as he was beginning to delve into pre-history.

'Lord Ambassador of Holmland,' the Prince began, nodding to the man on his right, 'lords, ladies, friends. I should like to welcome you here to Penhurst. I hope you are all comfortable in your rooms and that your stay here will be a pleasant one.

'I especially wish to welcome our friends from

Holmland – the ambassador and the delegation who have just arrived from the court of our cousin the Elektor. It is good to have you here and I hope that I may be able to visit your country again one day soon.'

The reaction this seemingly bland statement caused was minute, but unmistakable. A slightly raised eyebrow here, a faint stiffening of posture there. *Interesting*, Aubrey thought as he tried to catalogue who reacted in what way. His father would want to know.

The Prince went on. 'I also wish to welcome our researchers from Banford Park, whom we've grown fond of in this last year. I'd especially like to welcome Professor Hepworth, who has stepped into the breach as the leader of this vital establishment since the death of Dr Mordecai Tremaine in a tragic ornithopter accident, something we are only now making public.'

This announcement created more consternation in the gathering, some mutters, a scene bordering on bad manners. Aubrey felt as if he'd been struck. Dr Tremaine dead? Stunned, he realised that this Banford Park must be the research facility Dr Tremaine had hinted at when at Stonelea School.

Aubrey rubbed his forehead. Magical studies would be put back decades by the loss of Dr Tremaine. It was a staggering blow.

He straightened in his seat and peered at the tall, lanky man the Prince indicated. The professor's dinner suit looked a little frayed around the edges. He had a large, round face, and he looked very, very serious. The Prince smiled at him. 'Professor Hepworth, I am assured that your researchers will not use their magic to assist them in any way in tomorrow's hunt.'

Professor Hepworth looked bemused for a moment,

then frowned and dabbed at his lips with a napkin, oblivious to the polite laughter that this mild quip brought forth.

Prince Albert waited until the chuckles had died down. 'I must extend apologies to you on behalf of the Minister for Magic. Sir Philip is, naturally, bound up with sorting out the consequences of Dr Tremaine's passing.'

The professor waved a hand, almost knocking over a candlestick.

'And now,' the Prince continued, addressing the entire assembly, 'I wish you all the best of luck for the shoot and I thank you for coming.'

After the dinner had ended, the diners broke into smaller groups and took themselves off to private corners, nooks, corridors and rooms to discuss and dissect the evening and its announcements. Cigars were produced and servants rushed in all directions carrying decanters of port on silver trays, on occasion barely avoiding nasty collisions with each other. Intrigue, conspiracies and schemes were so prevalent it seemed as if they were necessary to sustain life.

Aubrey managed to disengage himself from his Holmland companion. George was still politely listening to the junior under-secretary, nodding as the under-secretary dropped name after name that Aubrey knew would mean nothing to him. The under-secretary seemed to be taking George's lack of reaction as a sign that he was unimpressed and was desperately trying to find the names of richer, more aristocratic or more powerful people he was friendly with.

Aubrey tapped George on the shoulder. ''Ere, young'un. Time you were a-bed. Stables'll need good mucking out in the morning.'

George blinked, but quickly saw the opening Aubrey had provided. 'Aye,' he said broadly. 'Muck waits for no man.' He thanked the under-secretary for his company.

Aubrey was pleased that they left the junior under-secretary displaying a mixture of bafflement, disdain and pique. The expression on his face nearly made Aubrey laugh out loud, but he whisked George away while managing to keep a straight face.

Eight

THE MORNING ANNOUNCED ITSELF WITH A KNOCK AT Aubrey's door. He sat up in the dark, rubbing his eyes and groping for the electrical light cord, just in time for George to burst in.

He was wearing a grey tweed outfit and stout boots. Leather gloves hung from the pocket of his Norfolk jacket. The whole ensemble looked as if it was well broken in, with genuine-looking stains and frayings that couldn't have been bought in any shop.

Aubrey stared at George through bleary eyes. Despite how much he enjoyed the experience, the journey to Penhurst and the stimulating surroundings had been an unexpected strain. This meant he was less able to resist the call of the true death. Alone in his room, he had felt the pain which signalled his soul was on the verge of separating from his body, succumbing to the ceaseless pull of the unknown. He had not slept very well, as his condition continued to deteriorate, no matter how much he tried to resist. Eventually, he was forced to use one of the spells he'd found, a counter-intuitive application of a minor aspect of the Law of Adherence. He was extremely careful to pronounce the elements with his best Chaldean intonation. For some time he was unsure whether it had taken effect, as the tugging on his soul continued, but gradually, as the night wore on, the sensation eased. His body and his soul settled. He slept. The last thing he wanted was for his control to fail while he was asleep.

'I thought I'd locked that door,' Aubrey mumbled.

'No.' George beamed. Aubrey thought he looked disgustingly healthy and rested. 'Hurry up. The shooting party's about to leave.'

'What about breakfast?'

'No thanks, I've already had it. Get dressed. I'll meet you downstairs.'

George slammed the door behind him. Aubrey winced.

It took him some time to get out of bed. His muscles complained and every movement was an effort. Getting dressed was another trial. He opened the wardrobe where the footman had neatly stowed his clothes. He glared at the racks of tweed his grandmother had packed. He felt sorry for the dozens of sheep who had gone cold to make the jackets, trousers, hats and unnameable oddments in front of him.

By the time he was dressed, Aubrey was beginning to feel better. He trotted down the stairs, whisking a slice of toast and marmalade from the tray of a startled maid. George leaped from a red leather chesterfield and bounded to the door. Aubrey followed, trying not to glower.

In the grey light of early morning they assembled at the rear of the Big House, near a large greenhouse that was misted so heavily that all Aubrey could see was a few palm fronds pressed close to the glass. He counted forty-three in the shooting group, both men and women. There were three times that many attendants, carrying guns, food hampers, spare boots and all manner of other things to make the time comfortable. The morning was crisp and Aubrey was grateful for his gloves, but the sky was clear and promised a sunny day ahead.

At that moment, Aubrey realised he hadn't rehearsed his aiming spell. His hand went to the inner pocket of his jacket, searching for the scrap of paper where he'd written down the spell, but came back empty.

How good was his memory? The awkward syllables came to mind, and he felt confident that he had all the elements in the correct order. A lingering doubt, however, hovered. The language of magic was like trying to make a pet of a wild animal – it was never fully tamed and always liable to turn on its master. Even familiar, well-worn spells sometimes twisted on the tongue and went awry. With this spell, he had to make sure that its parameters were clearly limited to the lead shot he'd be using. He didn't want other objects suddenly flying in unexpected directions.

Aubrey repeated the spell in his mind again, then once more, until he felt assured.

George nudged him. 'Fine bunch, wouldn't you say?'

Aubrey looked around. The kennel master was a thin, wiry chap. He wore a short-sleeved shirt, a leather vest and a dull bowler hat. He had three boys helping him. They were marshalling a dozen or so retrievers, all of which were glossy-coated, bright-eyed and eager to be off, straining at their leads and testing the resolve of the dog boys'. The dogs whined, but didn't yelp. Aubrey approved of their good training.

Prince Albert emerged from the house, accompanied by Sir William. The equerry puffed steam through his grey whiskers as he surveyed the scene. He nodded to the Prince, the kennel master, and the stocky man Aubrey had noticed the day before at the site of his experiment with the falling branch. He decided that this was the man in charge of the Special Services squad.

Prince Albert tugged on a pair of fine leather gloves. He was dressed in brown tweed, but his hat had a jaunty red feather in it.

'The Prince doesn't look keen,' George said to Aubrey.

It was the sort of thing Aubrey had grown used to George noticing. A thousand people would have looked at the Prince and commented on how interested he looked. George had glanced at him and known differently.

'Why do you say that?' Aubrey asked him.

George shrugged. 'Little things. I don't know. Clasping his hands behind his back?'

'He could be cold.'

'So you think he's eager for some sport?'

'No. I'm sure he'd rather be in the library.'

George snorted. 'I thought so.' He pointed. 'Look. There's Miss Hepworth.'

She was with her father. Aubrey hazarded a guess that she was wearing a skirt and jacket combination suit sort of thing, in a pale grey. Her hat was small, with a high peak. Aubrey thought she looked fresh and alive, unlike some of the more jaded people around him, but her face was as solemn as the Prince's.

Her father was dressed in a baggy suit that looked as if he'd slept in it. He leaned on a walking stick and gazed at the throng, his forehead furrowed. He, too, looked like a man who wished he were somewhere else.

'I wonder if she'd like company,' Aubrey said. 'She looks a little lonely.'

'That Holmlander fellow seems to have the same idea. Nice moustache.'

Aubrey grimaced. 'Hugo von Stralick. The fellow next to me at dinner pointed him out. Couldn't stop talking about him. He's the junior attaché for cultural affairs at the Holmland Embassy.'

'Impressive title.'

'He's a spy, George.'

'What?' George stared until Aubrey nudged him.

'Junior diplomatic staff are always spies. It's well known. They meet people, look around and send lots of reports back to their own country.'

'But shouldn't the police do something about him? Or the Special Services?'

Aubrey shrugged. 'They're generally harmless and we know all about them. The dangerous spies are the ones we *don't* know about.'

'He should be deported.'

'Why? He's considered to be good company. He tells reasonable jokes, he plays excellent billiards and he enjoys watching cricket. Besides, he'll be back in Holmland in a year or two, having sampled the delights we have to offer here. We'll have a friend over there for life.'

A beefy man with a spectacularly red face strode around the corner. He caught the eye of one of the Prince's assistants and soon he was talking with the Prince himself, with Sir William in close attendance. From the mud on his boots and the direction he was pointing, Aubrey guessed he was the head gamekeeper.

The beefy man beamed, clapped his hands together and clumped off. The kennel master followed, with his dog boys and retrievers, and gradually the whole party fell in behind them. Aubrey looked for the Special Services commander and saw him at the rear of the party, with a dozen of the fit young men, while others of this type scattered themselves throughout the group. Aubrey nodded at this, noting the careful way they took up position near both the Prince and the Holmland Ambassador. Their eyes were constantly moving, watching members of the party as they milled around, and also peering into the distance, at hedgerows and the trees that surrounded the fields they soon found themselves in.

Aubrey looked at the sky. It was growing lighter as morning unfolded itself and he felt it was time for decisive action. He left George to his own devices, then, by carefully adjusting his pace and moving sideways through the crowd, he managed to bring himself close to Professor Hepworth and his daughter. It was a skilful manoeuvre, and he was quite proud of how accidental he made it look.

'Professor Hepworth!' he said as he came alongside. 'I didn't get a chance to speak to you last night.' Aubrey tipped his hat to the professor's daughter. 'Miss Hepworth.' She nodded, but her expression did not change. Aubrey had hoped for a more promising reaction, but he knew he was now committed.

'Eh?' said Professor Hepworth. He turned, almost tripping on his walking stick. 'Ah, it's Fitzwilliam's son, isn't it?'

'That's right, sir. My father sends his best wishes.' While this may not have been strictly true, Aubrey felt he would be forgiven for the white lie. Sir Darius was an admirer of Professor Hepworth's work in highly esoteric magical theory. Aubrey had heard him insist that people like Professor Hepworth should be supported, for the good of the country.

Aubrey was familiar with Professor Hepworth's name through his Advanced Magic class at Stonelea. It was often mentioned in conjunction with significant break-throughs in magical theory, either alone or with other great thinkers. Unlike most of the brilliant men of his kind, Professor Hepworth roamed across disciplines. Aubrey had come across his name in areas as diverse as the Mental Domination Conjecture, Colour Transference and Transient Bodily Shaping. No-one else had made such a range of discoveries or advanced understanding in so many different areas.

The professor's frown relaxed for a moment. 'Ah, Sir Darius. He was a rare one, Caroline. A politician who listened to experts, but didn't let them get away with balderdash. Asked damned good questions, he did. Brooked no nonsense.' He shook himself and blinked. 'You've met my daughter, have you, Fitzwilliam? Caroline?'

'She met us at the train. Lovely morning, isn't it, Miss Hepworth?'

'It's too fine to waste on foolishness like magical hunts.'

Aubrey almost smiled. A young woman of forceful opinions was Miss Hepworth. Aubrey was pleased that the forceful opinion agreed with his own. And yet, as his father's representative, he couldn't agree outright with her, not in public . . . Shooting was much too popular for that.

A hubbub went up. 'Reached a fence,' Professor Hepworth said, craning his neck. 'This should be chaotic.'

The head gamekeeper and squads of footmen were directing the party to a stile some fifty yards away. As they ambled towards it, Aubrey went on. 'Professor Hepworth, have you made any progress with your work on Uncertainty Theory?'

Professor Hepworth glanced sidelong at Aubrey. 'No.'

'Fascinating area of endeavour, I would have thought,' Aubrey continued. 'The possibilities – inducing effects at a distance, reversing cause and effect. It could have a great impact.'

'I'm not working on Uncertainty Theory any more,' Professor Hepworth jabbed at the ground with his walking stick. 'It was a dead end.'

Before Aubrey could tease out this intriguing hint, it was their turn to mount the stile.

Although it was only four steps high, footmen were struggling to help portly figures – both men and women – up and over. The simple fence crossing was fast becoming the equivalent of the journey over the mighty Tanskadi Ranges, complete with near disaster at every turn.

Professor Hepworth ignored the offers of help and mounted the stile as if it were a staircase. Aubrey stood back and held out a hand. 'Miss Hepworth?'

She looked at him, then at his hand, then at the stile. 'Thank you,' she said, then lifted her skirt a little and climbed the stile easily.

Aubrey was left there holding out his unused hand. He felt the flush rise to his cheeks, but he was impressed despite it. *Remarkable young woman*, he thought.

On the other side of the fence, the countryside was altogether more wild. As Aubrey gazed out over the rolling expanse of grass, bushes and scrubby growth, he could see they'd left behind the sculpted world of the gardens. This was a large expanse of heath, dotted with hummocks and bushes, small stands of thorn trees, with some marshy areas away to the north.

With a practised eye, Aubrey looked for traces of magic and was pleased to see only a few. Whoever had been hired for the job were professionals. Sir William would only hire the best for the Prince, and the best were almost always the most discreet. The quarry had been summoned, let loose and limited to the bounds of the estate, all ready for the guests.

They reached the shooting ground, a windswept area with tall forest on three sides, a mixture of oak and beech, old trees, survivors of an ancient, vaster forest. Tents had been set up, some distance away from the butts, for those who weren't actively partaking in the shooting. A steady stream of wagons was arriving at the tents, disgorging hampers, trestle tables, crockery, crates of wine and other necessities for an outing in the country.

Nothing like getting away from the creature comforts, Aubrey thought.

A smaller tent was near the bustle of activity, and it was altogether more businesslike. People – mostly men – were making their way towards it. Aubrey excused himself from Professor Hepworth and his daughter.

He hadn't gone far before George appeared at his elbow. 'I say, Aubrey, where have you been? I couldn't find you anywhere.'

Aubrey waved a hand. 'Oh, talking to people.' He didn't feel it necessary to tell George who he'd been talking to. Not at the moment.

'Time to get our guns, is it?' George nodded at the tent.

'It wouldn't be much of a shoot without them.'

The Holmlanders were gathering eagerly at the tent. Their clothes were dark, navy blues mostly, of a slightly old-fashioned but expensive cut. Their boots were rather heavier than fashion dictated, however, and looked as if they were of military issue. There were half a dozen older Holmlanders, distinguished by their heavy whiskers and quite startling moustaches. The younger Holmlanders were mostly clean-shaven and generally of a brooding aspect, apart from a few like Hugo von Stralick, who were cheerful and jovial, enjoying the carnival atmosphere.

All of the Holmlanders had upright postures, as if a steel rod had been sewn in the back of their jackets.

As well as being flanked by two of the fit young men, the Prince was accompanied by a gaggle of other men and women. Aubrey recognised most of them as the younger sons and daughters of peers, the sort of carefree, unoccupied crowd that could be relied on to present themselves at any social occasion, as long as it had sufficient wealth and prestige attached. Most of them did little more than float from gala opening to coming out ball to Empire celebrations, exquisitely dressed and immaculately polished. Aubrey tried to imagine them actually *doing* something, but found it difficult. He thought they probably spent their time between social engagements simply propped up in a corner in their vast, ancestral homes, like waxwork dummies, waiting for the next party.

Aubrey recognised others from the previous night's dinner. They were the researchers, colleagues of Professor Hepworth. They looked a little puzzled in these surroundings, peering at the sky and the open field as if they'd been shut away for days and had emerged, like moles, blinking in the light. Most of them were dressed even more eccentrically than Professor Hepworth – patched woollen overcoats, hats that looked as if they'd been worn on expeditions to the tropics, tennis shoes with tartan socks. The bright young things with the Prince were careful to keep their distance from the researchers, as if they feared they were contagious.

The rest of the crowd out that morning were the assistants and beaters recruited from the village.

Aubrey pointed. 'A shooting weekend like this must be a good source of income for them.'

'A shooting party couldn't happen without them,' George said.

There were boys and girls who couldn't have been more than ten years old and a few grey-haired gaffers who would have been too old to fight in the last war. They wore an assortment of old but clean clothes.

Aubrey narrowed his eyes. All of the assistants were wearing identical headgear – a hard rounded hat with a metal flap at the back that projected down to cover the neck. He looked around. The gamekeepers had all donned similar apparatus.

'Interesting hats,' he pointed out to George.

George raised an eyebrow. 'I don't think they'll become fashionable in the city.'

The head gamekeeper was speaking to this raggedy army. They were obviously well accustomed to the rituals of the hunt, for they spread out quickly and headed towards the forest at the far end of the shooting ground, getting ready to drive the game towards the shooters. The older hands ran close to the ground, bent almost double. Two youths, one with a red flag and one with a blue, were dispatched to either end of the line to mark the extent of the beating.

George steered Aubrey towards the entrance of the gun tent, but they had to stand aside to allow a pair of Holmlanders to exit. The Holmlanders were comparing the gleaming shotguns the Prince's staff had lent them, which they carried broken on their forearms. George nodded in approval. 'Roberts and Malone. Top manufacturers.'

Aubrey stared at him. 'I never knew you were so knowledgeable about shotguns.'

George shrugged. 'I managed to make some money as a gun boy on the estates around our farm. The more you know, the better off you are.'

Indeed, Aubrey thought.

'Those guns, the ones the Holmlanders had, were both hammerless breechloaders. Single trigger. Very nice. I don't think anyone will be able to blame the guns today, if they have any trouble.'

'I prefer an over-and-under,' Aubrey said airily, grasping at something he'd recently skimmed in preparation for the weekend. 'Helps me feel as if I'm looking right along where I'm aiming.'

George snorted, perfectly aware of Aubrey's tenuous understanding of shotguns.

They entered the tent. Some quick negotiations with two armoury keepers and George handed Aubrey a gun.

Immediately, Aubrey knew he was handling a piece of fine machinery, the culmination of a hundred years of skill and refinement. The wood was dense, highly polished and so smooth it felt like glass. The metal was dulled to avoid reflection, but had a satin lustre that made it almost soft to touch.

As they left the tent, Aubrey made sure he was carrying the gun correctly – broken over the forearm. 'The only time a gun should be shut is when it's loaded and ready to fire,' he remembered his father saying.

One of the fit young men came up to them. 'Sirs, Collins is my name. I'm your loader and assistant for today's shoot.' He was tall, broad-shouldered, and wore a waistcoat over a white shirt with the sleeves rolled up. He had an open, sunny face and he carried two guns over his muscular forearms.

'Excellent,' Aubrey said. 'Glad to have you aboard, Collins.'

George led the way to the butts, which were stretched over about fifty yards of broken land. The stone semi-circles looked as if they had been freshly scrubbed and Aubrey thought that Sir William might actually have organised such a thing for the Prince.

'Collins,' Aubrey said as they found themselves an empty butt, about two-thirds of the way along the line, 'any idea what these Stymphalian birds are? They sound familiar, but I just can't recall . . .'

'Not exactly, sir.' Collins grinned. 'Something out of the ordinary, that's all I've heard.'

Around them, people began to spread out. A more serious mood came over the party as the non-shooters retired to the tents for refreshments. Aubrey saw much studying of guns, discussions with loaders and looking to the sky to judge wind conditions. The Holmlanders marched to their positions, issuing orders to their loaders in clipped, no-nonsense accents. Prince Albert was ushered to a butt in the middle of the line, no doubt chosen by Sir William to ensure the best shooting.

The dim light of dawn had given way to the soft gold of early morning. The air was still and cool, with the heavy smell of damp earth and vegetation. Aubrey looked along the line of shooters. Some were slouching, guns still broken; others were leaning against the stone walls of their butts. The Holmlanders were alert, guns at the ready, eyes scanning the forest ahead.

Aubrey's gun was still broken and he wondered if it was time to load. The back of his neck began to itch and he rubbed it.

'Nearly seven o'clock,' George said and tucked his watch away. 'We should hear something soon.'

Aubrey nodded, and the prickling sensation at the back of his neck returned. 'Odd,' he muttered.

'I beg your pardon?' George said. He handed his gun to Collins for loading.

'There's some strange magic afoot, George. I can feel it.'

George frowned, but before he could reply a hulla-baloo erupted from the tall trees at the end of the shooting ground.

Between the shouting, whistles and sound of pots and pans being struck, it sounded to Aubrey as if all the fiends of hell were tuning the instruments of an infernal orchestra.

'Ready, sirs,' Collins said from behind them. He took Aubrey's gun and, as Aubrey turned, thrust another on him. 'The beaters are doing a fine job of driving the game towards us.'

A new sound rose over the din in the forest, a shimmering noise like metal sliding on metal. Aubrey held his gun loosely and tried to see what was happening in the trees.

Something brass-coloured shot out of the woods and climbed, whirring, into the sky. From Aubrey's left, someone stifled an oath and the bird arrowed overhead, sun reflecting from its wings. It had gone before anyone had time to loose off a shot.

Aubrey looked at Collins. The young man grinned and pushed back his cap. 'No expense spared here.'

'Stymphalian birds,' Aubrey said and he suddenly remembered stories he'd heard years ago.

George grimaced. 'Tell me quickly, Aubrey.' Another metallic shape whirred from the trees and darted overhead. This time, the shooters were more prepared. Three or four shots rang out, but only expressions of disgust and disappointment followed the salvo. 'What are they?'

'One of the twelve labours of Herakles was to rid Lake Stymphalus of a flock of brass birds.'

'Brass? That'll make the shooting tricky.'

More shots came from the other shooters. George brought the gun to his shoulder.

Three birds flew out of the woods and soared upwards until they were yards overhead. They hovered, clattering, and began to swoop.

'Of course Herakles found these birds to be more than a little aggressive,' Aubrey added.

George had time for a startled glance at Aubrey and then the birds were on them.

Aubrey was sure it hadn't been Sir William who'd decided to make the shooting party more interesting than the usual affair. Adding a touch of danger to an occasion where the Crown Prince was present was not Sir William's way of thinking. Perhaps it had been Bertie's idea. Aubrey knew he had a wicked sense of humour that, unfortunately, had few avenues for expression. He may simply have dropped in a few suggestions, then let Sir William make the arrangements.

A scream like a sheet of metal being torn in two came

from the birds as they swooped. Two beaters who had emerged from the woods threw themselves flat on the ground and the birds shot past them, shrieking in disappointment. 'I think I see why the villagers have those hard hats,' Aubrey said.

The Stymphalian birds drove upwards. As they did, three or four of the guests fired. Their guns coughed with the sound of expensive firearms, but the birds flew higher and circled, unaffected.

George shot, then looked at Aubrey. 'You're not shooting.'

'In a moment. Just readying myself.'

A few more volleys thundered out. One bird, instead of retreating, screamed and dived towards the shooters.

One of the guests was braver, or more foolhardy, than the others. While they scattered, she stood there, slim and dressed in grey, calmly holding out her hand for the gun the nervous loader was thrusting at her.

Caroline, Aubrey thought, and he held his breath. Without consciously willing it, he began measuring angles, widths, going over spells in his mind, gauging the wind, a hundred things at once.

He had actually taken a few steps towards her when she snapped her gun shut, raised it and shot at the bird, which had obviously decided who its chief tormentor was.

A loud 'Spang!' came from the creature, followed by an indignant squawk. Caroline took a neat step to the side as the bird tumbled past. She swivelled, tracking its progress, but she didn't use the other barrel as the bird flapped and mounted into the air again. She watched it, gun pointed carefully to the ground. As the bird laboured into the air, a feather detached itself and fell to the ground with a clank.

Aubrey, by then, was hurrying towards her. More birds were driven out of the woods and the shooters were suddenly busy not just idly shooting, but defending themselves.

When he reached Caroline, she glanced at him while keeping most of her attention on the swooping birds. 'Careful,' she said.

'You shoot well. Very well.'

'It's a stupid waste of time, but my father insisted I learn. One of his friends is Lord Sumner. He taught me.'

Aubrey blinked. Lord Sumner had won the King's Prize for the last six years in a row. He was considered unbeatable at any form of shooting.

She bent and picked up the brass feather. 'Stymphalian bird.'

Aubrey took it. He turned it over in his hands. It was about ten inches long and, apart from the fact that it was made of brass, looked identical to an ordinary bird's feather.

'Fine work,' Aubrey murmured.

'It should be. Your father's company was responsible.'

With an effort, Aubrey didn't roll his eyes. 'It's no longer my father's company.'

'It's appalling, all of this,' she said, ignoring his protest. 'Using magic to create monsters and legendary beasts, then shooting them. Your father has a lot to answer for.'

'Well,' Aubrey said, searching for a reasonable tone to overlay his desire to defend his father, 'surely it's better than shooting real animals. No blood and all that. Shoot a gryphon and it just vanishes.' He waved a hand at the line of shooters blazing away. 'They seem to be having fun.'

Caroline rounded on him. 'That's not the point. Hunting is a trivial thing to waste powerful magic on.

Hundreds of hours of skill and effort are wasted on rubbish like this!' She swung one hand wide, while cradling her gun in the other.

'Ah, I see.' Aubrey felt her blistering glare as he sought for a suitable response. 'Umm . . . Well, it keeps the shotgun makers in business.'

Caroline stared at him. Then she handed her gun to the loader, who had been doing his best to appear invisible. She turned and marched off towards the tents.

George strolled up. 'Nice chat?'

'What?' Aubrey closed his eyes for a moment and then opened them. 'Fascinating.' Aubrey couldn't remember the last time he'd made such an inane response. He didn't blame her for walking off.

'Bagged myself a bird,' George said. He held up a handful of feathers. 'When you manage to drop one, they vanish and leave these behind. Nice souvenir.'

Aubrey made admiring noises. He turned to go after Caroline and explain that his gaucherie wasn't usual, that he was usually much more lucid than that, almost always putting two or three words together in the correct order, but George caught his arm. 'Not now. Not a good time, I'd say.'

Aubrey nodded. He took a deep breath and let it out, then looked around.

To judge by the infrequency of shots, the flights of Stymphalian birds had lessened. Aubrey shaded his eyes, but couldn't see anything.

The head gamekeeper stepped out of the woods, slapping at his jacket. After he'd dislodged a cloud of dust, he waved his bowler hat over his head.

Sir William appeared to have been waiting for this. He waved back. After a moment, he managed to get the attention of all the shooters. 'The birds have gone to ground. Time to do some walk-up shooting.'

Aubrey took a gun from Collins. 'Bertie will like this much better,' he said to George. 'At least there's some exercise this way.'

George exchanged his gun for a loaded one. 'Always seemed like better sport to me, anyway. Just waiting for game to be driven one's way feels a bit lazy.'

'Stay alert. We might hear some interesting discussions in Holmlander.'

'I don't speak Holmlander.'

'It may be time to learn.'

The ground ahead of them was a mixture of open country, heath, scrubby bushes, and a scattering of forlorn, wind-blown trees. Aubrey and George formed part of a long line of shooters, walking slowly towards the woods. Soon, Stymphalian birds were everywhere – being flushed, diving on people, climbing high into the sky. The reactions of the shooters were a source of amusement for Aubrey. Some people seemed to forget all about their guns and ran, stooping, trying to protect their heads. Others were firing away, grinning as they were handed reloaded guns.

Aubrey saw one young man pick himself up from the ground. He had a sour face as he tried to brush mud from what had been expensive and neatly pressed clothes. His friends were laughing at him and consoling him all at once, and they didn't seem to notice the contradiction in this.

Some people were simply spectators, watching and commenting on how the others were coping. A few of them were drinking from hip flasks. Aubrey made a mental note to keep away from those particular indivi-duals if they started shooting again.

They were skirting a low thicket of thornbush when Aubrey stopped. 'Collins,' he said, 'George and I will be fine from here. Why don't you go back and get something to eat?'

Collins frowned. 'Beg your pardon, sir? Is it something I've done?'

'No, nothing. George and I have lost interest in shooting. We'll just ramble along after the others. Keep up appearances, that sort of thing.'

Collins frowned. 'I'll be taking the spare guns, then?'

'That's it. We'll keep one each, though. Thank you, Collins.'

When the loader had trotted off, George raised an eyebrow. 'We've lost interest in shooting?'

Aubrey ignored him. He dropped into a crouch and examined the ground. 'George, what do you make of this?'

'Sorry. Can't see a thing.'

'Good. That means it's definitely magical.'

'Magical?'

'Spoor, traces. I've been following it for a while. Something magical has been moving through this area.'

'Stymphalian birds?'

'No. Something altogether different.'

Aubrey straightened. The magical traces were fuzzy blotches, a deep almost-indigo colour that he was only seeing because his senses were magically attuned and trained. He wiped his hands together. The trail unsettled him. There was something about it that made his skin shiver unpleasantly. As he watched, the colour of the blotches changed, skating across purple, black and brown, as if it couldn't hold on to any single hue. It was powerful magic that had thrown off these spatters, but it meant the spell's parameters needed tightening.

The sounds of the shooting party receded. Shotgun reports, dogs barking, cries of delight and exasperation became background as Aubrey tried to make sense of what he was seeing. He rubbed his chin. All this pointed to something dangerous being in the vicinity. For an instant he wondered about calling attention to the magical traces, but his curiosity won. *I can always call them later*, he thought and he began to follow the magical spatters.

Gradually, the trail grew clearer, leading off towards the edge of the shooting ground. 'This way,' he said. He set off towards higher, tree-shrouded ground.

'What is it?' George asked.

'I'm not sure, but it seems fresher up this way.'

No-one hallooed or called them back. Aubrey walked with his head down, shotgun broken over his arm, following the indistinct trail, only occasionally looking up to see where they were heading. He found that if he held one hand out in front of him, palm down, he could feel the magic of the spatters, almost as if he were holding his hand over a hot stove.

They forged through a line of bushes, then were in the undergrowth proper. A matter of a few yards further on and they were among old trees – oaks, beeches and alders.

For ten or fifteen minutes they scrambled over huge roots and trudged through slippery leaves. Aubrey followed the trail to a gully with a tiny stream at the bottom, and they had to jump across. On the other side, the trail led them up a gradual slope.

They came to a gnarled oak tree with a waist-high buttress root. Aubrey propped his gun up against the root and peered ahead.

He saw a stony outcrop, a tumbled collection of boulders. Moss had turned them into a mottled grey-green, somewhat scabrous-looking. The trees around it were thinner than those they'd trudged through, competing in the shade thrown by the ancient, established trees.

A fine position for observing the shooting ground, Aubrey thought and, as he leaned against the rough wood, a wave of fatigue swept over him. For a moment, his stomach felt as if it had disappeared and he found he was trembling. The physical exertion on top of the lack of sleep was making things difficult.

'Are you all right, old man?' George said.

Aubrey closed his eyes. 'It will pass.' *I hope.* He put a hand to his head and massaged his temple.

'Is there anyone up there? On the rocks?'

Aubrey opened his eyes and sighed. 'Let's find out, shall we?'

'Grand.' George vaulted the buttress root and helped Aubrey clamber over.

They scuttled up the slope towards the rocky rise and Aubrey found time to be grateful that he didn't have a full pack on his back this time. The shotgun was awkward enough and he bit his lip when he slipped forward, jamming his fingers between it and the rocky ground.

The closer they came, the more clearly Aubrey saw that this position had an almost unimpeded view of the entire shooting ground. Some time ago, a swathe had been cut and trees had been felled, leaving only stumps extending down the slope to where he could see the tweedy folk going about their business.

The ghostly glowing trail led to the outcrop, but Aubrey couldn't see any movement. He motioned to George that they should approach from the rear.

Every slip they made, every footfall, made his heart
lurch. He tried to divide his attention between the
uneven ground ahead and the boulders that were their
target. The carpet of fallen leaves made the going difficult, and soon the legs of his trousers were covered with
leaf mould and mud.

When they had skirted the boulders, Aubrey saw that
the rocks opened up in a rough horseshoe arrangement,
bending back up the slope at either end. He estimated that
they stood some twelve or fifteen feet at the highest point.

'What do you think?' Aubrey whispered as they paused
near the first of the rocks.

'A good observation post. Fine view.'

Aubrey nodded. He'd thought the same. It was a
perfect position for someone to watch the shooting party,
keeping an eye on proceedings. The perfect place, indeed,
for one of the men who were taking such good care of
the Prince. But . . .

'Then where's the observer? And why is the trail
leading this way?' Aubrey chewed his lip. Something was
not quite right here. 'You have some cartridges?'

George raised an eyebrow, but dug in his pocket and
held out a handful. Quietly, Aubrey and George loaded
their guns.

Aubrey nodded, then he darted off, running bent-
kneed, staying low, following the magical trail, George
close behind.

Aubrey reached the rocks, then wound his way upwards as if they were stairs. He felt the prickling of magic
and the trail grew stronger. The awful purple beat at the
back of his eyes, setting his teeth on edge.

He squeezed between two tall rocks and stopped. All
the breath ran out of him in one, long sigh.

The sight of death affected him even more since his accident. It reminded him too clearly of the precarious nature of his own existence, of how close he was to that final, irrevocable journey. He put out a hand and steadied himself against the rock, shaken.

'What is it?' George said. 'Oh.'

Aubrey watched the flies buzzing around the pool of blood. The young man's corpse was stretched out on a flat part of the foremost rock, the ideal observer's position. He looked like a toy that had been flung aside by an irritable child. Aubrey was grateful he couldn't see his face. The remains of an untouched meal was strewn around him – paper-wrapped sandwiches, a bottle of ginger beer, an apple. The ordinariness of the food, the humble, everyday items that were now not needed made Aubrey sag.

He stared at the body and the reality of his own mortality struck him, unbidden and unlooked for, like a fist in the dark. *It's the thought of not being*, he thought, *of life going on without me, that hurts.*

George cleared his throat. 'This is not good,' he said and his hands made small, fumbling motions. Aubrey could see that his friend had blanched. 'Not good at all.'

'True. But we can help best if we can learn something.' Aubrey gathered himself and approached the body. 'Field glasses,' he said, picking up the binoculars. The lens on the right was shattered. He stood his gun against a nearby rock, squatted and studied the corpse.

He was wearing a black uniform, streaked with orange mud. Army boots, no mistaking them, but apart from that, no identification, no regimental badge.

Aubrey was certain the unfortunate soul was another of the Special Services men who were swarming all over the estate.

His dark hair was matted with blood and Aubrey studied the wound for a time before looking up. 'What do you think happened here, George?'

George looked around. 'It could be that he slipped on the mud and struck his head badly. Bled to death.' He glanced at Aubrey. 'You don't think this likely?'

'No. Not likely at all. You see, there are two wounds. One on the front of his head, and one on the back. He wouldn't have fallen forward, killed himself, then fallen backwards again. Besides, where did the mud come from? His boots are clean.' He rubbed his forehead. It was aching. 'I wonder what happened.'

'I've never known you to leave well enough alone, but can't you this time? Let's go and get help.'

Aubrey sighed. 'George, do you remember the Law of Resonance?'

'You're not going to do more magic, are you? You're not in a good way.'

Aubrey ignored him. He straightened, then dusted his hands. 'The Law of Resonance states that actions and objects can, in certain circumstances, leave an imprint on their surroundings. They can resonate through time.'

'I know. And I know that working with that law is difficult, uncertain and taxing.'

'Ah,' said Aubrey lightly, 'but what isn't?'

Aubrey took a piece of chalk from his pocket, glad that he'd come prepared to do magic. He surveyed the area, his gaze skimming over the body of the unfortunate young man. Humming tunelessly, he walked around the observation post, an area about five or six yards across.

As he walked, Aubrey was estimating the area of effect he'd need and how best to limit it. A geometrical focusing figure would work best, he decided, hexagonal to fit the surface area of the rock. For good measure, he thought he'd reinforce it with some boundary curves which would interweave with the straight edges. Just to be on the safe side.

He bent, drawing around the corpse and the site of the disturbance. While he completed the figure, he was sorting through elements and creating the spell he'd need. It would require more than just applying the Law of Resonance, he concluded. He'd need to integrate aspects of the Law of Relevance and the Law of Permanence, to make sure he captured the right moment. And of course he had to be precise with the extent of the spell. He didn't want it going back too far. Perhaps an isolating element as a terminator to the spell? The Endorian language had some useful terminators and he went through them in his mind before selecting one.

He stood and stepped outside the ring. For a moment, while he ran over the spell in his head, he studied the focusing figure. At this stage, it wouldn't do to leave any part of it incomplete.

He took a deep breath. He'd gained his second wind, but he knew he was exerting himself – perhaps unwisely.

Aubrey broke the chalk into small pieces, his fingers working rapidly. He placed them in the palm of one hand and closed the other over it. Grimacing, he ground the pieces of chalk together.

When the chalk was ground finely enough, Aubrey brought his hands up to his lips, spoke the spell in an unforced sequence of liquid syllables and blew through a small hole he'd allowed between his thumbs. Two long strides, then he flung the chalk dust high into the air over the circle, where it burst in a flare of light.

Dizziness hit him like a sock full of sand to the back

of the head. He staggered backwards into the arms of George, who had hurried to him. 'Are you all right, Aubrey?' his friend asked.

'It's working,' Aubrey whispered.

Inside the circle, a scene was unfolding. It was faded, as if all the colour had been washed out of it, but figures moved slowly, clearly.

'Ghosts?' George asked.

Aubrey shook his head and immediately regretted it. Pain rolled around inside his skull and he felt as if he were about to vomit.

Inside the circle, the corpse of the young man could no longer be seen. Replacing it was a night-time scene, with the young man healthy and unconcerned. He stood in the dark, with the field glasses up to his eyes. His untouched meal was near his feet.

Coming up over the edge of the rock, behind the young man, was another figure. Even though the scene was faint, there was no doubt of the malignity of the stealthy intruder. It hunched, then slowly raised itself until it was standing, still undetected.

This second figure made Aubrey shudder. Naked, it seemed out of proportion, with arms that were too long, hanging almost to its knees. Its head was bulbous, hairless, the size of a football.

It moved with terrifying speed. The young man only had time to turn, drop his glasses and his attacker was on him. A blur of motion as the creature swung and the young man was caught a stunning blow on the forehead. He fell backwards like a sawn-off tree, his head hitting the rock with such force that it made George turn away.

The vision faded, and once again Aubrey was looking at the lifeless form of the unfortunate young man.

'A golem,' he said. He knew that only an extremely powerful sorcerer could work such magic. But to what ends? 'Someone has made a creature out of clay to do his bidding.'

George raised his gun and held it in his arms. 'Where is it?'

'Still around here somewhere.'

'And so is the Prince.'

'Really, George, you do have a penchant for pointing out the obvious.' Aubrey was recovering a little, feeling surer on his feet. He walked over to the body and squatted beside it. After some silent contemplation, he reached out and dug some of the thick, orange mud from the young man's uniform. He rolled it between his fingers, making a marble-sized ball, and tucked it into his pocket.

He picked up his shotgun and stood. 'Now, if the golem isn't close by, then where would it be?'

George looked around. 'Aubrey, there's no time for this. We have to get back to the party and warn the Prince.'

'Of course. Just a moment or two.' Aubrey stood there, trying to think like a golem. Or, at least, its master. 'This position is compromised, George. Once it found our unfortunate guard here, it couldn't use this location for whatever it was planning. It's probably looking for somewhere else.'

'Aubrey, stop this!'

He looked around. Trees blocked his view on all sides, apart from the cleared swathe down to the shooting ground. 'As far as I can see from here, there's nothing with quite so sweeping an aspect as this place. So where would it go?'

'Aubrey!'

He had it. 'Come, George, I think I know where our missing golem will be.'

Aubrey led off, limping slightly.

'Aubrey, this is no time to be trying to be a hero.'

He paused on the edge of the climb down. 'Heroes, George, are generally people who don't know what they're doing until afterwards. I, however, always know what I'm getting into.' *I hope*, he added to himself.

Aubrey hurried through the gap in the woods towards the shooting ground. He trotted through the fallen leaves, down the gentle slope, doing his best to look in all directions at once.

It couldn't be accidental, a murderous golem just happening to stumble on the perfect position to observe a royal shooting party. Aubrey had no doubt that this one would still be seeking to fulfil its mission. Somewhere.

Ten minutes later, after scrambling through brush, thicket and straggling undergrowth, Aubrey lunged for the cover next to the fallen trunk of a giant beech tree. George rolled in next to him. 'Have you seen anything yet?'

Aubrey shook his head. He peered over the top of the log, surveying the dense stand of saplings ahead. 'At least tell me what you're looking for,' George whispered.

'Vantage points. I think we're looking for a sniper.'

'A sniper!'

'It's perfect. The sound of a rifle wouldn't be heard today with all the shooting out there.'

'Can a golem be taught to shoot?'

'Oh, yes. They're nerveless, never get tired while waiting, never have second thoughts. If they weren't so difficult to construct, I'm sure there'd be armies of them defending countries around the world.'

George took Aubrey's arm. 'Aubrey, I insist we go and tell the others. It's our duty.'

Aubrey gnawed at his lip while he scanned the trees. What would happen if Bertie was hurt? Aubrey had known the Crown Prince for as long as he could re-member. His playmate had grown up into the sort of intelligent, thoughtful young man that augured well for when he assumed the throne. Many people wanted that sooner rather than later, to put an end to some of the erratic behaviour of his father the King.

Aubrey sighed. 'Duty, George. It's your turn to play that card, is it?'

'Well, I've heard it often enough from you, old man. Seems to work.' George slapped him on the back. 'Shall we go?'

Together, they struggled down the slope, slipping over rocks hidden beneath fallen leaves, weaving between the young trees, heading back to the shooting ground where the guns were still making themselves heard.

At the bottom of the slope stood a vast, spreading oak. It was in a small clearing, a natural dell that opened out onto the shooting ground. As the slope levelled out, Aubrey walked towards the oak in silence, gun cradled in his arms.

When they reached the massive tree, Aubrey put a hand to the back of his neck. The skin there was prick-ling, the ominous sensation that signalled magic was in the area.

He cast around and a trail of purple blotches led to the trunk of the oak tree. He held up a hand, catching George's attention. George raised an eyebrow and Aubrey pointed up, towards the dense canopy of the oak tree.

Aubrey thought quickly. While not as good a vantage

point as the rocky outcrop, the oak tree overlooked the whole shooting ground. Aubrey could see the guests spread out in clumps. It seemed as if some had retired towards the Big House, while more than a few were sitting on blankets near the tents, enjoying the refreshments.

Aubrey searched for Bertie, hoping he'd gone back to the house, but knowing that he was another who would always do his duty and would be out until the last of the shooters had grown sick of blasting brass birds.

George pointed. The Prince was with a small party of perhaps half a dozen people. He seemed to have moved on from the Holmlanders to some of Professor Hepworth's colleagues.

He was only thirty or forty yards away.

George started towards the shooting field, but Aubrey seized his arm. He put his mouth close to George's ear. 'You move or call out and the golem will shoot.'

The Prince appeared to be listening to one of the researchers, who was holding up a stalk of a plant. It looked more like a nature ramble than a hunt.

George bent and whispered into Aubrey's ear. 'You have a plan?'

'I'll shoot the golem out of the tree.'

Aubrey was rather pleased at the surprise on George's face.

He dug into his pocket and held up the marble of clay he'd taken from the dead guard's uniform. 'Golem mud,' he whispered. 'Remember my plan to improve my aim? To make the shot desire to go in a desired direction? This will do the trick. Now, I need some shot.'

George took a shell from his pocket and used his penknife to slice it open. After a moment's work, Aubrey held out his hand and George poured the shot into it.

Then he spoke the spell aloud, applying it to the lead pellets, combining applications of the Law of Animation and the Law of Sympathy. Done, he worked half a dozen into the clay ball. He stowed the rest in his pocket.

George took Aubrey's gun and examined it, cleaning some dirt off the stock, then took another shell and loaded it as quietly as he could.

Aubrey moved rapidly, glancing upwards as he worked. He took the clay ball containing the lead pellets and repeated the spell over it. In seconds, he was done.

Aubrey grimaced. The clay ball was no longer inert material. It was cold and clammy, more like flesh than mud.

'Ready,' he whispered. 'Throw this clay ball as high as you can. I've placed a spell on it. Because the clay came from the golem, it will now be attracted to the same golem – like to like. Then, when I fire the gun, the shot will be attracted to the shot in this clay ball – like to like again, helped by animating the shot to speed it towards the shot inside the clay ball.'

'Which has, by then, found the golem.'

'And so the shotgun blast will follow.'

He dropped the ball into George's hand.

Aubrey took his gun. He raised it and squinted over the sights, peering into the thick leaves overhead. He moved to the left so he wasn't aiming directly at a huge branch. 'Now, George,' he whispered. 'Fling it high.'

George nodded grimly and threw the clay ball upwards. It broke through the leaves and disappeared. When it did, Aubrey raised the gun and fired straight up.

The deep, coughing report startled birds, sending them squawking and flying from the tree. It was followed by a different noise – a flat, deadly crack, altogether different from the hollow roar of the shotgun. Shredded leaves rained down, with a few twigs and dust. A thump came from overhead, followed by a crash and another thump.

Aubrey swept out a hand. 'Step back.'

A figure plummeted onto the large branch just over their heads. It caught for a moment, then slid onto the ground. It landed with a heavy, almost wet, thud. Seconds later a rifle bounced off the branch and joined it.

George loaded his gun. 'Let's see what we have here.'

There was no mistaking the motionless figure, even if half its head was missing. It was the murderous golem they'd seen in the vision Aubrey had conjured at the observation post.

'Good shot,' George said.

I'm glad that worked, Aubrey was about to say when three men armed with service revolvers burst through the bushes.

'Put the guns down, gentlemen,' one of them ordered. 'And do it quickly.' Another turned and whistled. Soon, a squad of Special Services agents surrounded Aubrey and George. Aubrey thought he recognised some of them as loaders, gardeners and even footmen from the meal the night before. One swore when he saw the remains of the golem.

I don't suppose they've come to give me a medal, Aubrey thought. Carefully, he laid his gun at his feet and stepped back from it.

Their commander, the stocky, officious man, appeared from the direction of the shooting ground. The young men straightened when they saw him and one or two caught themselves in the middle of saluting.

Aubrey straightened at the prospect of meeting the Special Services commander at last.

The commander walked up to the golem and screwed up his face. He glanced at Aubrey. 'Well, what do we have here?'

He wasn't tall, a little less than Aubrey in height. His shoulders were broad, however, and his long black coat strained at the seams. He wore a bowler hat and he had a short beard. He stood easily, hands clasped behind his back. His eyes moved quickly over the golem, the rifle, the shredded branches overhead and then fixed on Aubrey. 'Young Fitzwilliam, isn't it?' He didn't smile.

'Yes. And your name?'

The man ignored him and turned to the nearest agent. 'Anyone see what happened here?'

The young men tried to stand even straighter. 'No, sir. Just heard a commotion, came to investigate.'

At that moment, Prince Albert and his party hurried up. 'Aubrey! What's going on here?'

Aubrey spread his hands slowly. 'Your friends here seem to think we're dangerous.'

'Is that right, Captain Tallis?' the Prince said. He didn't raise his voice, but it had the unmistakable tone of someone who'd been taught to give orders.

Captain Tallis stood straighter. 'We're not sure, your highness. There seems to have been an incident here.' He gestured at the body of the golem.

'Well,' the Prince said. 'Extraordinary.'

'Sir!' one of the young men blurted.

The golem was slumping like a jelly in hot weather, rapidly losing all its shape. Extremities melted first, fingers and toes disappearing. Soon it was simply a pool of muddy clay. 'Good Lord,' the Prince said.

Captain Tallis grimaced. He growled at the nearest young man. 'Get back to the Big House. We need someone from the Magisterium at once. Tell 'em there's magic here.'

'Why not ask one of the researchers to come over?' Aubrey suggested as the guard ran off. 'They might have some idea what's going on.'

Captain Tallis glanced at him. Aubrey could see that the man was filing him away for future reference. In all probability he had been marked 'Awkward'.

'That sounds like a good idea, captain,' the Prince said. 'Send one of your Special Services people.'

'Yes, your highness.' He nodded at another of the young men, who headed for the shooting field.

Captain Tallis turned back to Aubrey but, before he could resume his questioning, Aubrey chipped in. 'Captain, I think you need to know that one of your men has been killed.'

Captain Tallis stiffened. 'One of my men has been killed?'

'By the golem. At the observation post.'

'You've seen this?'

'Yes. I'm sorry.' George nodded in support.

Captain Tallis looked around at the young men. A number of them looked visibly shaken by Aubrey's news. 'Who's armed?' he asked.

A young man with curly black hair put up his hand, as if he were in school. 'Baker, Charlesworth and me, captain.'

'All three of you go to the observation post. Report back as soon as you can.'

Prince Albert sighed. 'Aubrey, what have you fallen into this time?'

Aubrey smiled apologetically. 'I'm not sure, Bertie, but I aim to find out.' He gestured at Captain Tallis and the young men. 'Exactly who are they?'

The Prince half-smiled. It was an expression Aubrey had seen many times. It said duty, obligation, protocol and etiquette were about to be involved. 'They're a handpicked squad from the Special Services. Acting as bodyguards is one of their duties.' He looked sidelong at Aubrey. 'Your father advised the Palace that extra precautions might be a good idea this weekend.'

'Ah,' Aubrey said and did his best to appear wise. 'I can't say too much.'

'Understood, old chap. Now, I see Sir William hurrying this way. I don't want to give the old fellow a stroke, so I'll go to him rather than have him come all this way. See you at the Big House?'

Aubrey nodded, and soon he was left alone under the oak tree with George. 'George?'

'Yes.'

'I think I'm about to collapse.'

George put his arm around Aubrey's shoulders. 'Go ahead. I'll get you back.'

'Don't know what I'd do without you, George,' Aubrey mumbled, his head drooping.

'Replace me with two or three patient, tolerant, strong types, I'd think. Hold on, we've a long way to go.'

Nine

A FEW HOURS LATER, AUBREY WAS WOKEN BY THE rumbling of motorcars. He lay on the bed for a moment, aware that — judging by the emptiness in his stomach — he'd missed lunch.

He sat up and swung his legs over the edge of the bed. He was glad to see that they'd stopped trembling. The rest had gone some way to restoring his energy. His body and soul were settled, united; the pull of the true death was still there, but he was strong enough to stand firm against it.

It had been a near thing, out at the shooting ground. Grappling with so much magic in such a short time had stretched him more than he'd been willing to admit. As his physical self weakened, the grip he had on his soul became more precarious. The remorseless summoning of the true death became stronger, harder to resist. All he could do was hold on. Back at the Big House, left in his bed, he spent some hours simply refusing to let go. Finally, the pull slackened and he slept.

He went to the window. The afternoon was well advanced. Four black motorcars were coming up the driveway, identical Eaton touring cars of the latest model. Aubrey could make out shadowy forms in both front and back seats. When they drew up in front of the house, the chorus of doors slamming was like the footfalls of giants.

Aubrey took the knock at the door as a good sign. If he had been in serious trouble over the incident at the shooting ground, he had no doubt that such niceties would have been dispensed with.

The door opened and a footman poked his head through. 'Sir,' he said, and Aubrey relaxed even more, 'if you'd care to get dressed, Captain Tallis would like a word with you.' He looked embarrassed. 'I'll wait outside.'

The footman led Aubrey to a wing of the house he hadn't often been in before. They passed a number of the Special Services men. With no need to disguise their roles, they stood at attention as Aubrey and the footman passed.

At the end of a long, dimly lit corridor, George was waiting on a wooden bench. 'What took you so long, old man? I've been here for ages.'

'Sorry, George. I hope you used the time wisely.'

'I could have been sleeping,' George said mournfully.

The footman opened the door and ushered Aubrey and George inside.

The room had no windows. Dark wallpaper extended from ceiling to floor, which was covered with a thin, grey carpet. The room was lit by a number of hissing gas lantern sconces in the wall, electrical wiring obviously not having reached this part of the house yet.

Captain Tallis sat behind a long table. He looked as if

he'd been sucking on a lemon and was trying to pretend it was the most enjoyable thing he'd ever tasted.

Prince Albert was next to him, along with Sir William. The fourth man sitting at the table was tall, gaunt and wore a severe black uniform with black buttons. Aubrey didn't recognise it, which immediately aroused his curiosity. He thought he knew the uniforms of all the regiments in Albion.

The man's face was striking. His lips were thin, his cheeks hollow. His nose was like a knife blade. His eyes were cold and grey, and glittered with iron intelligence.

'Sit down,' Captain Tallis said. Then, after a pause, 'Please.'

Everything's going to be all right, Aubrey thought, hearing the courtesy. He tried to catch Bertie's eye, but the Prince was looking at Captain Tallis, who cleared his throat.

'His Royal Highness has pointed out that neither you, Fitzwilliam, nor you, Doyle, has his parents here. Therefore it would not be proper to question you about the events of today. Furthermore, he has vouched for your characters and indicated that it is impossible that either of you would be involved in an attempt on his life.'

'Quite so,' Aubrey said. 'But all possibilities must be explored, isn't that correct, Captain Tallis?'

'Indeed, but this shall be done as soon as we can organise it with your parents.'

'By the Magisterium,' Aubrey said.

Captain Tallis glanced at the silent, black-uniformed man and went red in the face. 'What?'

'I saw them. Four motorcars full.' Aubrey nodded at Captain Tallis. 'It's always the way, isn't it? When there's a sniff of magic wrongdoing in the air, the Magisterium rides roughshod over the regulars and gets all the glory.'

From the corner of his eye, Aubrey was watching the black-uniformed man. He didn't change his expression and was watching this byplay as if it were only mildly interesting.

'Enough, Aubrey,' the Prince said. A smile hovered on his lips. 'Captain Tallis has done an excellent job, and our representative of the Magisterium,' he inclined his head to the black-uniformed man, 'has appreciated his thoroughness.'

Captain Tallis pursed his lips even more at this and Aubrey wondered if his face was going to disappear.

'Of course, of course,' Aubrey said. He stood. 'When the time comes, I'll answer every question they have, Captain Tallis, and I'll make sure you get a copy of the report.'

'Very good. You can go, then. But don't discuss this with anyone.'

Together, Aubrey and George left the room. Outside, Aubrey looked at George. 'You didn't say much.'

'Play to your strengths, old man, that's what I always say. One of your strengths is talking. One of mine is staying out of trouble by letting you do the talking.' He paused and looked at the ceiling. 'That last part hasn't always worked, though.'

In silence, they made their way back towards the busier part of the house.

Aubrey walked with his hands behind his back, turning over the events of the day in his mind. He sensed wheels within wheels. The whole weekend had been planned for a number of reasons, and Aubrey wasn't sure he had them all sorted out. Obviously, trying to patch up the differences between Albion and Holmland was high on the list, but politicians would never let such a meeting of

the high and mighty go by without taking the opportunity to advance a few plans, to form a few alliances and
to conclude ongoing business.

Then there was the presence of Professor Hepworth
and his researchers. What on earth were they doing
there?

Aubrey sighed and rubbed his temples. A golem
assassin. No petty crime, this, and a petty criminal
wouldn't be behind it. But who would benefit from the
death of the Prince? Unless it wasn't the Prince who was
the target of the assassin. There were plenty of other
targets. The Holmland Ambassador, for example. Having
him killed in Albion would heighten the tension
between the two countries, perhaps even precipitate the
war everyone feared. So who would benefit from that?
Arms manufacturers? Speculators? What about the
Goltans? If Holmland was at war with Albion, its attention would be drawn away from that troubled peninsula.

Aubrey rubbed his temples again. He was making
himself giddy.

They emerged from a gallery and Aubrey brightened
when they ran into Caroline.

'You two!' she said, glaring, and Aubrey's smile disappeared. 'Where have you been?'

'Seeing what we could do to help,' Aubrey said.

'Help?' Caroline echoed. 'What *did* go on out there?'

'Shooting accident,' Aubrey said.

'One of the guards was killed,' George added and he
frowned. Aubrey could see that his friend was still
troubled by the incident. *You're not alone, George*, he
thought, remembering the desolation of the young man
lying in the pool of blood.

'Oh,' Caroline said. 'You saw this?'

'We found him,' Aubrey said.

'Who was responsible?'

'It's not clear,' Aubrey said. 'That's what we're trying to help with.'

She nodded, but her expression was thoughtful. 'I suppose the Magisterium is here to use magic to help investigate the circumstances?'

'The Magisterium is here?' Aubrey said. It wasn't a lie. Aubrey knew a question rarely was.

'Yes.'

'Interesting.'

She skewered him with a look. 'It's magic, isn't it? Something's gone wrong with your father's hunt magic and the Magisterium has been called in.'

Aubrey opened his mouth to answer, but they were rescued by the arrival of Professor Hepworth. 'Ah, Caroline! I've been looking for you!'

She studied both Aubrey and George for a long, cool moment. 'Father. I've been talking with these two gentlemen.'

'Ah! Fitzwilliam and Foyle! Dashed awful what happened, eh?'

'Doyle,' Caroline murmured.

'Sorry?'

'Never mind, Father.' She nodded at them both. 'We must be off.'

'Miss Hepworth,' Aubrey said. 'We must get together some time to discuss magical matters in more depth.'

Professor Hepworth looked at his daughter with surprise. 'Magical matters? Caroline? Well, well, well!'

Aubrey watched the Professor and Caroline as they left. 'Interesting young woman.'

'I suppose,' George said.

'You don't like her?'

'Her face is too symmetrical.'

Aubrey stared. 'George, you astound me.'

THE WEEKEND WAS CURTAILED, MUCH AS AUBREY HAD anticipated. That evening, another fleet of black motor-cars arrived, this time to take the guests away. All of them were driven by members of Captain Tallis's Special Services squad.

Aubrey and George waited in one of the drawing rooms overlooking the immaculate gardens and driveway. Aubrey amused himself by trying to work out how long it would take to clip such perfect topiary platonic solids. The tetrahedron would be straightforward, but the dodecahedron . . .

His musings were interrupted when a long, silver Oakleigh-Nash Constellation glided around the fleet of anonymous black motorcars and pulled up right in front of the Big House.

Aubrey groaned when he saw it. George looked up from his newspaper. An under-butler appeared at the door. Small, balding, harried-looking, he was definitely not one of Tallis's people. 'Master Fitzwilliam, it's your parents.'

'Excellent!' George said, folding the newspaper and looking out the window. 'They've brought the Oakleigh-Nash. Very nice!' He rushed out of the room.

Aubrey was less pleased. He sagged into his chair, put one elbow on the armrest and rested his chin on his fist.

He'd failed. He'd been representing his father and had

a chance to do something worthy, but with the weekend degenerating into such a fiasco, he accepted he hadn't managed to bring it off. After all, he knew a weekend of such diplomatic importance should be a quiet affair, and an attempted assassination of the Crown Prince would propel this occasion to the top of the list of fashionable gossip topics. Now, his father was coming to the rescue of a son who wasn't quite up to the mark.

The anxious under-butler appeared at the door again. 'Master Fitzwilliam? They're waiting.'

Sir Darius was standing by the motorcar talking with George and Stubbs, the driver. He looked alert, calm, and perfectly pressed, as if he'd just stepped out of the pages of a magazine. 'Aubrey,' he said when he noticed his son approaching, 'what's been going on here?'

Aubrey stiffened, then gave a faint smile. 'Father, a full report may take some time.'

The window of the motorcar slid down. Aubrey's mother smiled at him with an air of amused tolerance. 'Aubrey. Sorry to arrive like this. I realise how embarrassing it must be to be rescued by your parents. I wanted to wait for you to get home by yourself, but Darius wouldn't hear of it.'

Sir Darius brushed his moustache with his forefinger. 'I thought I might be able to be of assistance.' He signed to the driver. 'Stubbs, wait here.'

Stubbs was an older man, grey-haired but with the impeccable posture that was a legacy of his time in the army. He'd had been a corporal serving under Sir Darius and had followed him once he left the military.

Sir Darius strolled off. Aubrey and George fell in alongside him. 'A friend let us know what had happened,' Sir Darius said.

'A friend?' Aubrey said. 'Let me see, which one of your old political allies would that be?'

Sir Darius let that remark go by. 'Bertie isn't harmed, is he? My reports were a little vague on that score.'

'Not a scratch,' George volunteered. 'Thanks to Aubrey.'

'Ah,' Sir Darius said. He looked at Aubrey. 'I see.'

Aubrey looked for any sign of approval on his father's face, but saw only careful consideration. He stifled a sigh of disappointment. *After all,* he thought, *we have a major diplomatic incident on our hands. Even if I did save Bertie, it's the sort of mess Sir Darius Fitzwilliam would never have allowed to happen.*

Lady Fitzwilliam joined them. She took Aubrey's arm and then George's. 'Come, you fine gentlemen. I think there's a long story needing to be told. Do you think you can find a parlour in this great barn of a place? One that's a little private but near enough to food and drink?'

'I'm sure we can,' George said, enjoying both having Lady Fitzwilliam on his arm and the prospect of food. Aubrey nodded, but didn't say a word. He allowed his mother to whisk them off.

The day room they found was near the library. The chairs were upholstered in green velvet, and green velvet wallpaper covered the walls. A pair of framed lithographs hung over the mantelpiece of a fireplace that Aubrey thought was entirely too large for the tiny room.

Aubrey reported. He did his best to keep it concise, in military fashion. While he spoke, he watched his parents closely.

Sir Darius's face was grave when Aubrey had finished. 'I see,' he said. He sat back in his chair and steepled his fingers. His brow was furrowed.

'You're both well?' Lady Fitzwilliam asked.

'Just a sore shoulder,' Aubrey said.

Sir Darius snorted. 'You need to seat the gun more firmly, nestled right into your shoulder. Didn't you tell him that, George?'

'I did. He must have forgotten it in the heat of the moment.'

'Yes.' Sir Darius studied his son. 'Quite a moment it was, too.'

They were interrupted by Sir William looming in the doorway. 'Lady Fitzwilliam. Sir Darius. His Royal Highness would like to speak with you.'

'And the boys?' Lady Fitzwilliam asked.

Sir William frowned. Aubrey guessed Sir William would rather see him in a cage. 'I believe they may accompany us.'

They were taken to a day room on the first floor. It had a glorious view out over the gardens, but Prince Albert wasn't looking out of the window. He was standing near the piano, speaking with the tall, gaunt Magisterium representative Aubrey had seen earlier when questioned by Captain Tallis.

Sir Darius bowed and Lady Fitzwilliam curtsied – a mere bob, but she had observed the courtesy with a knowing smile. 'Your Royal Highness,' they said, almost in unison.

The Crown Prince smiled. 'Rose. Darius. It is good to see you. Sit, sit, we have much to discuss.' He gestured at Aubrey and George. 'And you two. Don't stand around. This concerns you as much as anybody.'

'Your highness,' George mumbled. Aubrey simply nodded and took a seat.

The Prince gestured towards the gaunt man. 'You know Craddock, don't you, Darius? Rose?'

Aubrey blinked. *This is the legendary Craddock? Here?*

Sir Darius nodded at him. It was a tiny nod, a mere inclination of his head. 'I was Prime Minister when Craddock was appointed head of the Magisterium.'

Craddock gave a wintry smile. 'An appointment you opposed.'

'Yes.' Sir Darius met Craddock's gaze with hard eyes. Aubrey had heard much in the tumultuous days following his father's resigning of the prime ministership. Something he'd never forgotten was that his father had suspicions about Craddock's part in his downfall. Apparently time had not lessened his concerns. 'Although how you know of the deliberations inside Cabinet baffles me.'

Craddock made a slight, flipping motion with one hand. 'It was a long time ago.'

Aubrey studied Craddock. He'd heard a hundred stories about the man. The mysterious head of the Magisterium, the man who had never had his photograph taken, who had no friends, no family, nothing to get in the way of his utter loyalty to the Crown. His ruthlessness was notorious, too. While the Magisterium was nominally an arm of the police, it acted as an independent body investigating magical misuse in the kingdom. Craddock, therefore, was an officer of the law, but rumours of the ways the Magisterium was willing to bend the law in pursuit of their aims were multitudinous.

Mention of Craddock's name was often enough to make hardened criminals confess, something that the police had been known to use to good effect. The threat to take miscreants to the Magisterium headquarters in sprawling Darnleigh House often worked wonders.

Prince Albert glanced at the man in black. 'Craddock

isn't happy with what he's found here. The particular magic involved in the creation of the golem is something quite new.'

Craddock took this as his cue. He lifted a long, thin hand. 'His Royal Highness is quite correct.' His voice sounded as if the edges had been smoothed away from it, leaving nothing distinctive at all. It was a voice of everyman and no man, utterly unmemorable. 'This was no ordinary golem. This creature did not register at all on the magical detection devices we'd planted in the woods surrounding the shooting ground.' For an instant, Aubrey thought he saw Craddock's eyes flick towards him. 'Perhaps they need adjusting.'

'A stealthy creature,' Sir Darius said.

'Indeed. The Magisterium is very interested in finding out more about it. And its maker.'

'Of course,' Sir Darius said. He sat back in his chair, his expression neutral as he smoothed his moustache with his forefinger.

'Go on, Craddock,' the Prince said.

'There's little more to tell, your highness. The level of skill required to imbue a golem with marksmanship is extremely high. The planned self-destruction was also neat work.'

'Darius,' the Prince said, 'this contretemps is frightfully inconvenient.'

'Most contretemps are.'

'The Holmland delegation were most indignant at the turn of events,' Prince Albert added.

'Too indignant?'

'Darius,' Lady Fitzwilliam said, 'are you implying that the Holmlanders are responsible for the attempt on Bertie's life?'

'We're living in tangled times,' Sir Darius said. 'There are shifts and feints hiding behind blinds wrapped in mysteries. Are the Holmlanders responsible? I wouldn't discount the possibility.'

'Just as long as you're not jumping to conclusions about Holmlanders,' Lady Fitzwilliam said. 'Fine people, excellent scientists.'

The Prince looked amused. 'Rose, with our family connections, we surely can't be accused of bias against Holmland. Quite the contrary if you read some of the newspapers.'

'Or listen to some of the gossip,' Sir Darius added.

The Prince raised an eyebrow. 'Anything new around the traps, Darius?'

Sir Darius raised an eyebrow. 'Apparently you're going to marry the Elektor's cousin, rule our two countries and declare war on the Tartars. Or else you're going to abdicate and run off with Lily Hartington, if she can get away from her commitments in the world of aviation.'

The Prince seemed to consider this for a moment. 'The Elektor's cousin is how old?'

'Forty-eight,' Lady Fitzwilliam said. 'She's an authority on freshwater molluscs. I correspond with her regularly.'

'And this is what they're saying? Remarkable.'

Aubrey was struck by how reserved Bertie was. Everything was considered, careful, conscious of his position. The times the Prince and he had spent playing games in the succession of palaces – hours of hide and seek, horses and tin soldiers, books and country rambles – seemed centuries ago. Bertie wasn't a playmate any more. He was the king in waiting.

'Rumours,' Craddock said. 'Rumours, your highness. Vapour and fog.'

Sir Darius sighed. 'You'll be able to mollify the Holmlanders, Bertie?'

A smile quirked the Prince's lips. 'Well, this batch, anyway. Speaking their language goes a long way.'

Prince Albert stood and everyone got to their feet. 'We wanted to speak to you, Darius and Rose, to let you know that Aubrey was heroic today.'

'Of course,' Lady Fitzwilliam said. She smiled at her son. Sir Darius seemed to consider the matter.

'And that we appreciate his actions. Of course, we can't let the public know about this. Otherwise, some sort of medal would be in order.'

Craddock shook his head. 'Can't let news of this get out. The Crown Prince being shot at? Unthinkable.'

'Once, perhaps,' Sir Darius said. 'Times have changed.'

With that, they exchanged pleasantries and made to leave. Before they could go, the Prince coughed. 'Doyle. A moment.'

Aubrey raised an eyebrow, but was chivvied outside by his mother.

'What's that about?' he asked as the door closed.

'None of your business,' his mother said. 'You can ask George later. If he's willing to tell you, you'll learn about it then.'

Five minutes later, the door opened. George, looking dazed, was led out by Sir William.

Sir William frowned. 'Best to get back to the city, I'd say.' He shook his head. 'What a fiasco.'

The Oakleigh-Nash was waiting for them, all chrome and silver. Stubbs was polishing the sparkling headlights with a rag that disappeared when he saw them.

Aubrey was bursting with impatience, but he waited until they'd all settled in the motorcar and it had pulled away from the house before asking. 'Well, George? What did Bertie say?'

George blinked. 'Bertie? The Prince?'

'Of course! What did he want with you?'

George reached into the pocket of his jacket and took out an envelope. It bore the Prince's personal seal. George held it as if it were made of solid gold. 'He said I'd done a good job this afternoon, helping you. He said he appreciated it and would send a letter to my parents saying as much. This is a copy.'

Aubrey sat back on the long leather seat. 'Good for you.'

Lady Fitzwilliam leaned over and patted George on the arm. 'Well done, George.' She looked at her son. 'And well done to you, too, Aubrey. Saving the Crown Prince? Quite a feat.' She turned and nodded at her husband. 'Wouldn't you say, Darius?'

Sir Darius considered this. 'Well done, Aubrey,' he finally said. 'In difficult circumstances.'

'Thank you, sir. I did what I could.'

'My letter made it plain that you were representing me,' Sir Darius said. 'You did what you had to do.'

'The letter. Yes.' Aubrey felt his actions had earned him enough to ask something that had been niggling at him. 'If you don't mind, Father, why didn't you ask me in person rather than writing?'

Sir Darius started. 'Why, the matter came up after you'd left Maidstone. Otherwise I would have, naturally.'

Aubrey felt foolish. Where his father was concerned, he often found slights where none were intended. He wondered if he were overly sensitive about these matters and decided that in all likelihood he was – but only because it was important to him.

Aubrey had always thought that George had an exquisite, if erratic, gift for timing. On this occasion, he rose to the challenge beautifully. 'Is anyone reading this?' his friend asked, picking up a newspaper from the seat and unfolding it. 'Look, Aubrey, Dr Tremaine's passing is on the front page.'

Aubrey glanced at the large headlines. 'Well, he was the Sorcerer Royal.'

'Tributes, too, from all sorts of people. Even the PM.'

Sir Darius made a noise at that. It was meant to be ignored, and Aubrey did so. 'He was a great man.'

George folded the paper back. From the way he settled with an expression of great satisfaction, Aubrey knew he'd found his agony columns.

After some time, the drone of rubber tyres on macadam was hypnotic. Aubrey found it hard not to fall asleep in the fading light. His mother had already succumbed and his father was staring out of the window.

George grunted, and Aubrey glanced at him. 'Find something amusing, George?'

His friend held up the newspaper and pointed at an advertisement in a page full of tiny type. 'I feel sorry for the compositor who'll get roasted for this. It's just gibberish.'

'Some day you'll realise that there are more important things in the world than the agony columns.' Aubrey looked more closely. 'Well.'

'Someone must have fallen asleep while they were laying out the type. And while they were editing, too. Quite a cock-up.'

'George, do you know what we have here?'

'Rubbish, I would have said. But look at that one next to it. "Lost: one wooden leg." How'd you think that happened?'

'George, your gibberish advertisement is a cipher.'

'A cipher? Really?'

'You told me that people in these advertisements often used shorthand or subterfuge to hide their true intentions.'

'As in this one: "Meet me at St Giles' at noon. Bring your hat." St Giles' could mean St Alban's or St Catherine's.'

'Or it mightn't even be a church. It could stand for a bridge or a theatre.'

George tapped the paper. 'Noon could mean two o'clock.'

'The correspondents would simply have agreed that whatever time appeared in the advertisement would be two hours behind the real meeting time. Or three hours, or ten.'

'A hat could mean an agreed sum of money.'

'Or anyone of a thousand other things. "Bring your dog"?' Aubrey hummed a little. 'As long as the writer and the reader have agreed beforehand, the correspondence is completely opaque to the outside world.'

'And this gibberish?'

'It's the difference between a code and a cipher,' Aubrey said. 'A code is a secret communication where a word or phrase is replaced with a word, or a symbol or a number. A cipher is much more elegant and more flexible. A cipher replaces *letters* rather than words.'

'Hmm. Someone must have an important secret they want kept private.'

'Or simply something embarrassing. It seems like a commonsense approach to me.'

George stared at the string of letters. 'Very clever.'

'Mildly clever,' Aubrey disagreed. He sat back and

crossed his arms on his chest. 'All ciphers can be broken, with enough time and effort.'

'You could solve this?'

Aubrey closed his eyes. 'I've done some work with ciphers in the past. It's diverting.'

'I see. This looks like a tricky one, doesn't it?' George tore out the cryptic advertisement and dangled it in front of Aubrey.

Aubrey opened one eye. 'Are you trying to challenge me, George?'

'What do you think?'

He took it. 'Let me consider it. It will be a pleasant change from thinking about the events of today.'

And the mysterious master of the golem, Aubrey thought as George went back to the paper. He gazed out of the window at the countryside speeding by. While evening was falling, and all good things were beginning to drowse, somewhere out there was a powerful, elusive adversary.

He turned away from the window and began to consider George's cipher.

Ten

THE FOLLOWING WEEK AT STONELEA SCHOOL WAS THE last before the mid-year break. As was their usual arrangement, George was going to stay with the Fitz-williams for the first part of the mid-year holidays, but Aubrey saw little of him in that hectic final week of term. George was busy with cornet practice for the mid-year concert, and study, for once, had also kept his head down.

Aubrey was again in the thick of everything, trying to devote his energies to a thousand different commitments. He found himself rehearsing lines for his part as the defence barrister in the school play while trying to memorise formulae for his Advanced Magic exam at the same time as he was practising his googly in the nets with the First XI. On top of this, his batting had dropped off and he had to spend some hours refining his late cut.

Aubrey had always been at the top of his class. It wasn't simply because of native intelligence, but because he approached his studies in a rigorously organised way, almost as if study was a military campaign. He mapped out his work, broke subjects down into sections and segments, organised his attack on each one, took notes that were concise but included everything important.

Cricket was different. While he had natural wiry strength and quickness, he knew he wasn't the world's most gifted athlete. So he watched and studied sports, choosing things that would yield to his intellectual approach. In cricket, that was leg spin. The art appealed to him as a combination of guile and misdirection. The complex variety of deliveries was perfect for the way he approached the world in general.

Acting was something he found relaxing. With his good memory, he had no trouble remembering lines and he wasn't at all afraid of the limelight. In fact, walking out on stage allowed him to be someone else for a time – someone who wasn't Sir Darius Fitzwilliam's son.

The teachers and the boys at the school saw Aubrey involved in all these things and wondered how he managed to keep up such a high standard. What they didn't see was the extra burden of struggling to stay alive.

During that last week of term, Aubrey felt the strain. He forced himself to rest, to spend time attending to the needs of his body. Where once he would simply have driven himself to achieve, going without sleep if required, he now imposed a regime of relaxation periods to ensure his physical integrity. With care, he spent evenings researching arcane texts for possible approaches to a permanent solution to his plight.

With all this going on, Aubrey didn't have much time to discuss the events of the shooting weekend with George. They swapped a few thoughts and theories in passing, but too many school commitments got in the way for any detailed analysis.

It wasn't until the Friday afternoon, after the last examination – mathematics – that they were able to turn their minds to matters other than school.

They were sitting on a bench near the cricket nets. No-one was practising, most having already left for the holidays. A broken stump lay against the fence. The grass needed cutting and swallows were swooping low over it, snapping up insects.

Sitting there, basking in the sun, knowing that George was happy reading his newspaper, Aubrey was able to address matters he'd put to one side.

During his preparation for the examinations, he'd stumbled on some decades-old research in an obscure branch of magic concerned with bonding and unification. Apparently the researchers had been convinced that their work was proving barren, but Aubrey wasn't so sure. He felt that this could be a useful avenue to explore for stabilising his condition.

Time, he thought, and rubbed his temples. *That's all I need. About three lives' worth.*

He'd need to spend some of it at one of the big university libraries, perhaps talk to some academics . . .

That made him think of Professor Hepworth and *this* made him think of Caroline.

She was one of the thousand things on his mind since leaving Penhurst after the shooting weekend. He hadn't had a chance to say goodbye to her. Or to arrange to meet again. And that was something he desired. Very much.

Hanging over the memories of that weekend was the great, unresolved question. Who was behind the golem assassin? No-one had questioned Aubrey or George since they'd left Penhurst, but it hadn't prevented Aubrey's mind from circling around this question like a wasp around fallen fruit. He had to admit, though, that he had had no insights.

Intelligence, he thought. *I need more intelligence.*

'George,' he said suddenly, 'fancy a visit to Penhurst?'

George lowered the newspaper. 'Penhurst?'

'Bertie isn't there – he's in the city – but I thought it might be a nice place for a few days' camping in the woods.'

The clock over the library sounded four o'clock and Aubrey absently thought that there was nothing as empty as an empty school. The bell echoed around the buildings and quadrangles as if looking for company.

'Penhurst,' George said. 'Would we take the train?'

'Cycling, George. Haven't you ever been on a cycling holiday?'

'Not really.'

'Jolly fun. Healthy exercise, life in the outdoors, a chance to see the countryside.'

'Nothing to do with a chance to investigate the scene of the crime?'

Aubrey grinned. 'Intelligence, George. That's what we need.'

George snorted. 'Steady on, old man. You're heading for the Snainton Prize as dux of the school. If you get any more intelligence your head will explode.'

'Intelligence in the military sense, George. Information. News. The stuff one needs to make decisions.'

George considered this. 'What about your parents?'

'Mother is away. She's gone up north to gather some specimens. Father is always pleased when I get more exercise. He'll be convinced once he sees you're going along. He thinks well of you.'

'Does he?'

'Of course. You seem to make a good impression on people. The Crown Prince. My father. Who knows where it will end?' He rubbed his hands together. 'Now, what do you say?'

George stood. 'I don't have a bicycle.'

'The least of our problems. Plenty of spare bicycles at Maidstone.'

THEY SET OFF THE NEXT MORNING.

Aubrey had some difficulty extricating himself from the clutches of the staff. Cook insisted on thrusting bottles of ginger beer on him. Stubbs wouldn't let them leave without taking one last look at the chains and gears of both bicycles. Eventually, Aubrey was able to point out that they couldn't carry any more without the bicycles collapsing. Reluctantly, the staff withdrew and waved them off.

They cycled out of the front gates of Maidstone, down the Talavera Road, ready to leave Fielding Cross. George swooped close to Aubrey. 'Sir Darius didn't see us off?'

'He was called to Parliament last night, after dinner.'

George nodded. 'Party business?'

'Party business.'

With the election only a month and a half away, Sir Darius was neck deep in campaigning. Aubrey had grown up with this and knew that politics wasn't just standing up in Parliament and arguing. It was meetings – endless meetings – negotiations, compromises, handshaking, alliances, promises, paybacks, favours, disappointments and finding out more about your fellow humans than you really wanted to know. The hugger-mugger of politics was where people were naked with their wants, desires, needs and fears on display, if one only knew where to look.

Aubrey revelled in it. He loved it because it was subtle and delicate at one moment, and blindingly explicit the next. He loved it because he loved all games; he loved the competition, the cut and thrust, the thrill that came from risk and success, from besting one's opponent, from planning, strategies and tactics.

The difference was that politics was the only real game. It was the game that could change things, could alter the very way people lived. With the right outlook, with determination and clear sight, the game of politics could change the world for the better.

Which was what Aubrey wanted to do.

As soon as he could, he turned off the main road and into less busy side streets.

'You know the way?' George said as they cruised past rows of elegant townhouses. A police officer on his rounds gave them a nod as they went by.

'I have a map,' Aubrey said. 'I studied it last night. If we leave the city on the Harnsby road, that should be best.'

They swept around a corner, skirting a pocket-sized park. At this hour it was free of the nannies and children who'd be gathering later in the day. The morning was sunny, with few clouds in the sky. Aubrey was grateful for the lack of wind. He knew wind was the enemy of the cyclist, never seeming to be at one's back but always in one's face.

After an hour they were out of the city and into the hedgerows and fields of the countryside. They made steady progress and Aubrey called a stop mid-morning.

'Ginger beer?' he offered as they sat with their backs to the stump of an old poplar tree, the last in a once proud avenue. Behind them, a solitary sheep stood in the middle of a field, complaining. Aubrey thought it sounded peevish, as if it had suddenly remembered that it hadn't been invited to the party all the other sheep had gone to.

George shuddered. 'No, thank you. Ghastly stuff.' A crow sat on a hedge nearby and eyed them. George broke a corner off the shortbread biscuit he was eating and flung it to him. The crow lurched into the air and flapped off, cawing.

'George,' Aubrey said, 'there's something distinctly odd about the affair last weekend.'

'A golem trying to assassinate the heir to the throne? What's so odd about that?'

'I was thinking more of the people involved. A rather strange bunch, wouldn't you say?'

'Well, I've never been to such a thing. You'd be more of an expert than I would.'

Aubrey nodded. 'I've been at Penhurst a number of times when weekend gatherings have been held. Some of them were shoots.'

'You didn't go on the shoots?'

'Too young, the same as Bertie. I seemed to be there to give him a companion. Chess, draughts, things like that. And exploring the house, too. Fascinating stuff stored there.'

'And this weekend was different?'

'Indeed. The researchers? The Holmlanders? Members of the government?'

'People like the Chancellor of the Exchequer and the Home Secretary?'

'The Chancellor was at Penhurst to discipline some

backbenchers who had let their private lives become scandalous, shall we say. Not good just before an election. The Chancellor's job was to get them to step aside without a fuss, in favour of some new blood. He took the Home Secretary for support.'

'How do you know this?'

'It's not too difficult to work out. When the Chancellor of the Exchequer takes three long-time MPs aside, it's not because he wants to wish them well. After getting back last weekend, I made some enquiries about what's been happening in Parliament. It was a matter of putting two and two together.'

'And what about Boothby, the Foreign Secretary?' George asked. 'What was he doing there?'

'Interesting, that. I happened to see him talking earnestly with the Holmland Ambassador.'

'You didn't overhear?'

'No.' Aubrey scratched his chin. 'I wonder how talking with the Holmland Ambassador furthers Sir Guy's aim to become next Prime Minister.'

George started. 'Do you think that Sir Guy wants to be Prime Minister?'

'I'm not alone. He's an ambitious one, that Sir Guy.'

'Rather like you?'

Aubrey grinned. 'But unlike Sir Guy, I have the advantage of being on the side of righteousness and honour.'

'And modesty,' George pointed out.

Aubrey stood and started pacing. 'Come, George, tell me what you thought of the researchers.'

'Those scruffy chaps? They didn't seem to fit in with the others.'

'You've hit the nail on the head, George. They weren't part of the usual crowd at all. That's what intrigues me.'

'The Prince feels sorry for them. That's what he said.'

'Yes, that's all well enough. He's a kind-hearted chap and he most certainly does feel sorry for them. But remember that Dr Tremaine told us he was in charge of a top secret research facility and *then* we found out that he was heading this Banford Park. He couldn't be supremo of two research facilities.'

'You thought that he was in charge of something to do with the military.'

'Exactly. Banford Park is highly secret and highly important to the military. Important enough that they tolerate such eccentrics as we saw. You don't hobble genius with rules like a dress code or grooming requirements.'

'Is Professor Hepworth a genius?'

'Undoubtedly.' Aubrey rubbed his hands together. 'Let's get to Penhurst. I want to see what we can find.'

George strapped his bags back on to his bicycle. 'I didn't think you proposed this trip solely as a nature ramble.'

'I could never pull the wool over your eyes, could I, George?'

THEY REACHED PENHURST ESTATE LATE IN THE AFTERNOON.

A grey-haired groundskeeper greeted them, recognised Aubrey, and opened the gates. He waved them through and assured them he'd inform the Big House of their presence.

Aubrey led the way through the gardens. The place looked strangely deserted after the omnipresent watchers of the shooting weekend. He saw a gardener in the distance, raking weeds from a pond, but he didn't look anything like the Special Services agents who had swarmed over the estate last weekend.

A gate, and then they were into less tamed regions, an expanse of fenced-in grass bordered by woodlands. A wagon track ran alongside the fence. It was rough, but usable enough for the bicycles, even if they did have to dismount and walk over some of the more broken patches leading to the shooting ground.

Aubrey found the situation idyllic. The air was full of the smell of green and growing things; the countryside had the composite richness that reminded him that the world was an intricate and mysterious thing.

Aubrey called a halt. George pulled up beside him.

Aubrey could see the Big House in the distance. Smoke rose from its chimneys. From this distance, it looked like a battleship, an enormous bulk on the landscape, reassuring and permanent, much like the Empire itself.

They struck across the fields, pushing their bicycles, heading for the woods and the shooting ground beyond. Aubrey stopped when a horse and rider appeared at a gate to their left. 'Hullo, it's Hoskins.'

Hoskins waved and urged his horse towards them. He was dressed in sensible woollen trousers and jacket. He wore a hat that looked as if a badly made flowerpot had been squashed on his head. A pipe grew from the side of his mouth.

'Fitzwilliam,' he said, without removing the pipe from his mouth. He gestured with his head. 'Who's your friend?'

Aubrey grinned. 'George Doyle. George, meet Hoskins, the farm manager.'

George raised his cap. 'Hoskins.'

'Doyle.' He ran his eye over George, much as if he was a horse. 'You don't look like a cyclist.'

'No, sir. I'd rather a fine horse like you're riding.'

Hoskins smiled at that. 'Bess is a good 'un, right enough.' He ruffled her mane and she snorted. 'Now, young Fitzwilliam, what're you up to in these parts?'

'Camping, Hoskins. George and I have just finished exams and are looking for some peace in the country-side.'

'Nothing to do with the ruction at the shoot last weekend?' Hoskins said. He took out his pipe and studied it. 'Or the Black Beast?'

Aubrey grinned. 'Has the Black Beast of Penhurst been seen again?'

The Black Beast of Penhurst had been a local legend for as long as Aubrey had been visiting the estate. He'd heard many a tale of its nightmarish appearances, of how it had haunted the owners for centuries, the bringer of death and doom. He remembered how both Bertie and he had been deliciously terrified when first told about the apparition.

Hoskins replaced his pipe in the corner of his mouth. He cleared his throat and looked into the distance. From somewhere not too far away came the sound of a wood-cutter and his axe. 'The Beast's been around for a few months, off and on,' he said in his gravelly voice.

'Since before the golem?' George said.

'Aye. Well before the golem.' He was silent for a time after that, seeming to consider this. 'You know what it means.'

'They say that once the Black Beast of Penhurst appears, it doesn't leave until it's taken three lives,' Aubrey explained to George.

'Dr Tremaine from Banford Park, he was the first,' Hoskins said. 'And then that Professor Hepworth. He died too, he did.'

'Professor Hepworth? Dead?' Aubrey gripped the handlebars of his bicycle. 'When did this happen?'

'A few days after the shoot. The Black Beast was howling all night, it was. Next morning, they found the professor, dead, in the woods up that way.' He pointed with his pipe.

'What was he doing up there?' George asked.

'That's the direction of Banford Park. The professor and his chums were always traipsing backwards and forwards between there and the Big House, this last year or so.' Hoskins sucked on his pipe for a moment. 'They've closed the place down, now. All those researchers have been sent back to where they came from.'

Poor Caroline, Aubrey thought. He rubbed his temple. Professor Hepworth gone. Coming on top of the death of Dr Tremaine, this was going to set back magical theory for decades.

Another mystery to add to the puzzle of the golem assassin. Aubrey wasn't inclined to believe that it was the Black Beast of Penhurst who had killed the professor. He'd heard that story too often when he was young to place much credence in it. But what did happen to the professor? And what had he been up to at the secretive Banford Park?

'What sort of creature is this Black Beast?' George asked.

'That'd be hard to say,' Hoskins replied. 'It's hard to get a good look at the creature. Mostly it's the eyes you see. Red, burning eyes.'

George glanced at Aubrey. 'And we plan to camp in the woods.'

Aubrey's curiosity was well and truly roused. He couldn't turn away now. 'We'll be safe.'

Hoskins leaned forward. 'Maybe you would be, at that.' He sighed. 'But I don't think I can allow you to stay out, in all good conscience. If anything happened to you I don't know how I'd answer to Lady Fitzwilliam.'

Aubrey nodded. Hoskins was what the locals called 'a straight 'un'. Utterly trustworthy, reliable and honest, the burden of his responsibilities lay heavily on him. He was stubborn in carrying out what he thought were his duties and this made it difficult to get around him. Unless he was approached tactically. 'You don't want us to stay outside tonight, is that right, Hoskins?'

Hoskins adjusted his seat, then his tie. 'I'm sorry.'

'So you want to take us back to the Big House and have us stay there tonight?'

'Aye.' Hoskins looked increasingly uncomfortable. He had the attitude of a man who is tied to a railway track, hearing a train whistle in the distance.

'And you think you could stop me from slipping out? If I really wanted to, I mean.'

'Well . . .'

'The Special Services have left, now the Prince is no longer in residence, correct?'

Hoskins didn't answer.

'So you're here with the cooks, the gardeners and some household staff,' Aubrey said. 'Hard to cover all exits with them. Especially old Corrigan, with his rheumatism.'

'Ah.'

'So, all in all, I think it better that you allow us to proceed with our plans. At least you'll know exactly where we are, and you can check on us in the morning.'

Hoskins's look was partly hostility, partly admiration, partly recognition that he'd been beaten. 'Hrmph.' He sat up straight. 'You always managed to get your own way, Fitzwilliam.' He managed a chuckle. 'Be it on your own head, then.'

'Don't worry, Hoskins. We'll be safe. We'll stay by the trout stream, near the old bridge.'

Hoskins looked in that direction. 'That should be as safe as anywhere.' He sighed. 'What shall I tell your mother, though?'

He didn't wait for an answer. Bess ambled off.

'The Black Beast of Penhurst?' George said to Aubrey. 'You didn't tell me about that.'

'I didn't want to worry you. Come on. We can land a few trout before the light's gone.'

Once the tent was pitched, darkness closed in. Aubrey cooked some sausages in place of the trout they hadn't caught, and the potatoes he'd popped into the coals were hot and tasty. Sparks flew skywards and the sound of water running over the stony bed of the stream burbled beneath all the other sounds of the woods moving from their daylight mode to their night-time mode.

Aubrey scraped his enamel plate and took a swig of ginger beer. 'In the morning we'll have a closer look at the place where the golem melted. I've brought some materials which may help me reconstruct a thing or two about the creature.'

'I see,' said George. He was stretched out on a blanket, his head propped on a log. 'And this Black Beast?'

'A puzzle.' Aubrey crossed his arms. 'And I'm not sure where it fits in.'

Before George could respond, an unearthly howl split the night air. Aubrey was on his feet in an instant, staring into the darkened woods, his heart pounding, his throat suddenly dry. The back of his neck was prickling.

George scrambled up, wide-eyed. 'Good Lord!'

Aubrey realised he was breathing rapidly and, with an effort, he slowed until he was breathing deeply and slowly. *Fear*, he thought. *It's so thick in the air I can taste it.* 'Are you all right, George?'

'I . . .' George shook his head and stumbled to form words. 'It's . . .'

'George, look at me.' George stared wildly. 'It's magic. It's making you afraid.'

George nodded.

'Deep breaths, George. Calm yourself.'

George blew out his cheeks, then rubbed his face with both hands. 'I say, took me quite by surprise, that.'

'It's some distance away.'

'I'm glad of that.' George brushed down his clothes. 'It's not so bad, now.'

'Once you know what it is, the fear isn't as disabling.'

'No.'

'Did you bring a lantern, George?'

'I thought you had.'

So much for planning. 'Well, we'll do our best without.' He pulled a burning branch from the fire.

George stared at him. 'You want us to go after the Black Beast?'

The chilling howl rose again, closer this time. Aubrey swallowed. The fear was there, but it was now a small thing, easily managed. 'Yes, I think I have to.' *Or my curiosity would never forgive me.*

Aubrey thrust the burning branch in George's hand and hurried to the tent. A moment later he was back with a small bag on a string. He hooked it around his neck. 'Quickly, now.'

Before they had gone more than twenty yards, the comforting light of the campfire was left behind and they were in a world of darkness. The only light came from George's blazing torch.

Aubrey peered into the dark. He knew that night in the countryside was rarely totally black. In his escapades over the years, he'd learned that given time to adjust, the eye can make do with surprisingly little light, picking out objects from among shadows, making sense of blackness. But this night was different. With the erratic, sobbing howls of the Black Beast of Penhurst floating through the night, suddenly shadows were thick and confusing. He found it hard to judge distances between trees and the terrain underfoot was treacherous. Brambles caught his feet and trouser legs, stones conspired to appear underfoot, stumps hid themselves until too late.

'Wait, George.' Aubrey fumbled in the bag around his neck and found a pair of shell-like shapes. He placed one over his right eye and it attached itself there.

Immediately, through his right eye, darkness vanished. He could see no colour; all was in shades of silver and grey, but he could see the trees, bushes, a fence in the distance, the ground beneath his feet. The scene in front of him was ghostly, without colour, but no more than a photograph. Every detail of the night was sharp and clear.

He fitted the other object over his left eye, then found two more in his bag. He handed them to George. 'Here. Cat's eyes.'

'What?'

'Not real cat's eyes. They're something I prepared for our expedition.'

George held up the shells. 'I put them over my eyes, do I?'

'They don't hurt.'

Without much enthusiasm, George placed one of the cat's eyes over his. Instantly, he grinned. 'Very clever, Aubrey.' He fitted the other shell to his eye and looked around.

'Thank you.'

George wrinkled his brow. He sniffed. 'I smell fish.'

Aubrey shrugged. 'The cook at home has a cat. I made a coat for it with pockets for this specially prepared glass. It wore the coat and the glass for a week, not very happily.'

'The cook feeds the cat fish?'

'Salmon. It's a very spoiled cat.'

'I see.'

'I wanted these shells to take on the characteristics of the cat's eyes, so I used the Law of Sympathy. I was pleased with the results for a first effort, but it's not perfect. It's taken on some of the fishy smell, so I expect I'll have to work on setting some of those parameter variables rather more stringently.'

George looked at the blazing torch in his hand and then turned away. 'We won't be needing this?'

'No.'

George threw the branch on the ground and kicked earth over it until the flames were smothered. 'Done.'

The howl of the Black Beast of Penhurst split the night again, sounding like a thousand demons being tortured at once. Aubrey turned, trying to determine where it came from. 'This way,' he said and set off through the undergrowth.

Aubrey moved crouching low, turning his head from side to side. They were barely in the woods, with fields and moorland a stone's throw away.

The howling continued. It rose and fell, at times lapsing into an almost human shrieking. Aubrey could feel it as well as hear it. It made his skin crawl and set his heart pounding, affecting him at a deep, primal level, telling him to run, to flee, to hide in a hole, shiver and hope that the owner of that cry would pass him by.

Aubrey closed his eyes for a moment to steady himself. He motioned to George for silence.

A short crawl through some undergrowth brought them to a fence. On the other side was a field. At first, Aubrey thought it was empty, then he heard cattle. They were bunched in one corner of the field, lowing and trying to get away from the sound that was continuing to rend the night. He could see them tossing their heads and the whites of their eyes stood out in the darkness.

The howling began to move away. Aubrey pointed to George and they hurried on.

The undergrowth began to thin and the woods took on a more cared for aspect. Aubrey slowed. Ahead, he could see outbuildings and the Big House away to his left. It was well lit, and the light flared in his cat's eyes. He put up a hand to shield them.

The blood-chilling noise erupted again. 'It's doubled back,' George hissed.

They plunged back into the woods. Aubrey scanned the ground ahead, hands outstretched, feeling for the presence of magic. Grass, fallen leaves, rocks breaking the skin of the earth . . . Suddenly, his palms tingled.

He stopped and dropped to his knees. George almost ran into him.

'What is it?' George whispered.

Aubrey concentrated and swept his hands backwards and forwards. *There!* 'Magic,' he breathed.

Now that he had locked his magical senses on to it, he could see it: a magical trail stretching away through the woods, glowing a sickly green. 'Magical traces,' he said.

'What sort?'

'Something large.'

George picked up a few fist-size stones and stowed them in his pockets. He saw Aubrey staring at him. 'Better than nothing,' he said.

Aubrey nodded and set off, following the trail and the echoing howls. They were being led away from the Big House and deeper into the woods. Aubrey narrowed his eyes. He attempted to remember what was bordering the estate on this side. Where did the river run? He went as fast as he could, bent nearly double to feel the magical spoor as well as see it.

George swore and Aubrey jumped as the roar of a shotgun sounded up ahead. Then night was suddenly lit by a flare of light, a vivid orange that reflected off the trees and made them look as if they were alight.

'Hurry, George, something's gone awry.'

They charged through the trees, abandoning all pretence at stealth. Aubrey's coat flapped like the wings of a bat as he flew over the rough ground, vaulting fallen branches and small bushes.

A shotgun barked again, twice, and an angry cry rose from nearby.

Aubrey leaped over a log and immediately regretted it. The ground on the other side fell away sharply. He plummeted, sliding and tumbling down the slope, picking up leaves and twigs as he went.

'Aubrey!' George cried, then he, too, was over the log and plunging down into the shallow dell.

Aubrey rolled to his feet and was immediately knocked over by a black-clad assailant. He scrambled to his feet, but the mysterious foe was on him again, grappling with wiry strength. Aubrey had time to notice, with astonishment, that his foe was wearing a loose-fitting black outfit and a balaclava, then he was struggling to avoid being thrown again. He shifted his weight and dropped to one knee, but his foe was too quick, matching his move and countering it by turning side on. An elbow caught him in the jaw and then he was slammed into the ground, all his breath driven from him.

'Aubrey!' George called again. He charged and slammed into Aubrey's attacker.

'Well done, George!' Aubrey panted, his hands on his knees. The black-clad figure had fetched up against a tree stump and was sprawled, motionless, next to a shotgun.

'Hit his head against the stump,' George said. 'Unconscious.'

Aubrey stripped the balaclava from the assailant and stared, open-mouthed.

'What is it?' George said. He came close. 'Oh. I mean, *her* head.'

They were looking at the unconscious face of Caroline Hepworth.

Eleven

'**I** WAS INVESTIGATING MY FATHER'S DEATH,' CAROLINE explained, glaring. Aubrey rubbed his jaw and made a resolution never to make her hit him again.

Aubrey and George were leaning against the wall in the kitchen of the Big House. Aubrey had made sure they'd removed their cat's eyes before they went inside, to avoid comment.

Caroline had been put on a chair in front of the largest stove. Mrs Butterly, the cook, had draped a blanket around her shoulders. Mrs Butterly was glaring, too, and continually rearranged the woolly covering.

'Of course,' Aubrey said. 'I was sorry to hear of it.'

'Yes,' George said. 'Terribly sorry.'

'Mrs Butterly,' Aubrey said, 'you'll organise a place for the young lady to stay tonight?'

The cook nodded, not willing to interrupt her fussing.

'George and I will need rooms as well. If that's convenient.'

The cook crossed her arms across her enormous bosom. 'I'm sure we'd insist on it,' she said in an unexpectedly high-pitched voice. 'At least we'd have some hope of keeping an eye on you, Aubrey Fitzwilliam.'

She rang for a maid. Aubrey wanted to say something more to Caroline, but she was pointedly ignoring them. He shook his head. He supposed he couldn't expect gratitude after they had rendered her unconscious, then dragged her back to the house, while the Black Beast of Penhurst lurked nearby in the night.

When two maids arrived, Mrs Butterly made the arrangements. Aubrey and George left her trying to get Caroline to take some barley water to get over the shock. Aubrey hadn't seen much sign of shock. He'd seen indignation and a desire to rush back out into the night with her magically enhanced shotgun, but shock? He had a feeling that Caroline Hepworth was made of tougher stuff than that.

Aubrey waited while his bed was made up for him and towels fetched. When the maid left, Aubrey went next door to George's room and knocked.

'Well, George,' he said, collapsing onto the chair, 'did you ever have the feeling that you were caught in a very tangled spider's web?'

'Constantly. Ever since I've known you.'

Aubrey clasped his hands together and leaned forward. He grinned. 'Quite right. Exciting, isn't it?'

He rubbed his forehead then, and his enthusiasm subsided somewhat.

George noticed. 'How are you?'

'I'm keeping myself together well enough. I daren't let myself get knocked around too much, I think.'

'You were lucky Miss Hepworth didn't hurt you too much.'

'Quite. I thought she was an assassin dressed in that costume.'

'It wasn't very . . .' George searched for the right word. 'Demure.'

Aubrey smiled. 'No, definitely not demure. A person of surprises is Miss Hepworth.'

'Showing up here in the middle of the night? Rather.'

'It's more than that. She had some sort of magic with her. Remember the orange flash? I managed to look over her shotgun while we carried her back here. It had some interesting magical modifications.'

'Where would she get such a thing?'

'I don't think she'll tell us. Not tonight.' Aubrey hummed under his breath. 'I'm off to bed. Early start tomorrow, George.'

WHILE THEY WERE EATING A GARGANTUAN BREAKFAST UNDER the stern eye of Mrs Butterly, Aubrey looked out for Caroline, but she did not appear. Several times he went to ask the cook about her, but Mrs Butterly's gaze was stony and he left well enough alone.

Feeling as if he'd eaten enough for a fortnight, Aubrey went out into the morning and marched back to where he had encountered Caroline the night before. George accompanied him, totally at ease with the world now daylight had come.

A heavy dew had fallen and their boots were soon sodden. Aubrey scowled but quickly forgot about them. The morning was too delightful, with blue skies stretching overhead and only the gentlest of breezes. Without realising it, he began humming as they climbed the stile and skirted the hedgerows, retracing the path they had taken with the unconscious Caroline the previous night.

When they found the dell, Aubrey stood and surveyed it for a moment.

'Seemed larger last night,' George said.

Aubrey nodded. He found the pouch around his neck and took out a specially treated magnifying glass. He'd magically attuned it by using a combination of spells bound up with sensitivity and appearance. He was pleased with the result, which allowed him to see the most minute traces of magical residue.

With George looking on bemused, Aubrey crept on all fours around the dell, peering through his magical magnifying glass. Eventually, his friend wandered off and Aubrey was left alone with the sounds of the working farm – a lonely dog, cows, an engine of some sort in the distance – filtering through the woods surrounding the dell.

Half an hour later, George ambled back to find Aubrey just completing his inspection. 'It's strange, George,' he said. He stood, wiping his hands on his trousers, which were equally muddy as his hands. He hardly noticed.

'What's strange?'

'If I knew what it was, I wouldn't call it strange.'

'I beg your pardon?'

'Never mind.' Aubrey frowned. 'This Black Beast appears to have left some residue here, but I'm damned if I can determine what it is. I've never seen its like before.'

'Are you sure you're not just seeing stuff left behind by the magical shotgun?'

'No. It was strange stuff, too, but I accounted for all of it. This is something else.'

'Hmm. What do we do next?'

'I want to see where we discovered the golem. Then we go home.'

'If we can stow our bicycles in the guards' van, we could take the train,' George suggested.

'Good idea, George, even if it makes your laziness more obvious. Now, to the shooting grounds.'

THE SITE UNDER THE OAK TREE LOOKED AS IF AN ARMY HAD been through. Aubrey stood back and imagined dozens of Special Services agents trampling the grass and undergrowth as they searched for clues. Even so, the outline of the golem was still clear, because the grass had blackened and died where the creature had melted. Aubrey wondered how long the earth would stay barren.

He scraped some earth samples into small bottles, frowning as he did so. The magnifying glass revealed more of the puzzling residue. Did this mean that the golem and the Black Beast were made by the same hand?

They made their way back to the campsite and packed up their belongings. The tent was a devil to fold and stow, still being wet from the dew. Aubrey attacked it with vigour rather than science, glad to be grappling with something as solid as canvas.

The tent, however, refused to be intimidated. After George managed to stop laughing, he instructed Aubrey on how to hold corners, fold carefully, press seams and roll out air. Aubrey took this as an important lesson in humility, and a timely one at that.

They pushed the bicycles back towards the Big House, stopping at Hoskins's cottage on the way. Aubrey assured him that they were well and that they wouldn't impose on him like that again. Hoskins looked both relieved and dubious.

The stationmaster greeted them as they trundled the bicycles up to the station. He informed them that they'd have a half-hour wait. 'Perhaps you'd like to sit with the young lady,' he suggested.

Aubrey swung around to see Caroline at the station gate. 'I've been waiting for you,' she said. 'What's kept you so long? The Black Beast?'

The stationmaster stared at her, then at Aubrey.

'It's all right,' Aubrey said smoothly to him. 'Miss Hepworth, it's good to see you again.'

The stationmaster went inside, muttering into his beard.

There was no sign of the black outfit Caroline had been wearing the previous evening, and Aubrey was disappointed. On this bright morning she'd donned a smart tweed skirt and jacket. In the breeze, her hat was tied under her chin with a green and white ribbon.

'I need to talk to both of you,' she said. 'And I hope I can do it without your attacking me again.'

'Of course,' Aubrey said hastily. 'About your father, no doubt, and his work?'

'Yes,' Caroline said, her eyes distant. 'His work.' She snapped her gaze onto Aubrey. 'I need to talk to you about that, too.'

'Oh?'

'The waiting room would be more private,' George pointed out. 'We could talk there.'

'Quite right, George. Miss Hepworth?' Aubrey bowed and gestured for her to lead the way.

The waiting room had a settee, a small table, two

armchairs with loose, flowery chintz covers, and a fire-place. This left very little free floor space in the small room. They shuffled around, with Caroline taking the settee. Aubrey and George took a chair each.

'Quite a waiting room,' George said.

'Fit for a Prince,' Aubrey pointed out.

Caroline studied them both dispassionately, which Aubrey thought a great pity. She reminded him of a heroine in a romantic painting, a warrior maid with steel in her spirit and fire in her eye, but he had a feeling that she would scoff at such a notion.

She appeared to come to a decision. 'I don't know if I should be telling you this.'

'Ah,' Aubrey said. 'That's always a good start.'

She frowned, a crease dividing her eyebrows. 'Are you always flippant?'

'No,' George put in. 'Sometimes he's overbearing, sometimes he's rash, sometimes he's maddening, or arrogant. But he's rarely dull.'

'Thank you, George.' Aubrey clasped his hands together and glanced at Caroline. 'He knows me too well,' he said wildly.

She looked at him. He could see her weighing up whether they were worth talking to at all. Something about them must have reassured her, because she went on. 'My father was not happy,' she said. 'For some time before his death, he was trying to escape from his duty.'

'I'm sorry,' Aubrey said. 'His duty? What do you mean?'

'I'll have to go back some time,' Caroline said. She touched the ribbon at her neck, fingering the knot under her chin.

'By all means. We're in no hurry, are we, George?'

'Not at all.'

She put her hands in her lap and composed herself. 'Father was happiest at the university at Greythorn, away from the city. It was where he could talk with like-minded researchers in laboratories just down the hall from his, or over a pint in one of his favourite taverns in the town. The library facilities, the laboratory equipment, all were first class, but it was the people that Father loved. He said it was like being a coal in a furnace, where individual coals make the whole hotter and hotter, each feeding the other.'

'But he left,' Aubrey said.

'He didn't leave,' Caroline said, eyes flashing. 'His commission was activated.'

'He was in the army?' George said.

'He was an officer, a major.'

Aubrey was intrigued. He couldn't imagine Professor Hepworth in battle, leading men and issuing orders.

'It was before I was born,' she went on, 'and it was only for a short time, but apparently he never resigned. He was simply on reserve.'

'Ah,' said Aubrey. 'The military has ways of keeping a hold on valuable people.'

'What do you mean?' She frowned again. Aubrey found himself hoping that he would, one day, see her smiling more frequently than frowning.

He sat back in the armchair. He tilted his head, looked at the ceiling and steepled his fingers in front of his chin. Professor Hepworth in the army. Perhaps not the regular army . . .

'Imagine if certain people within the military had the task of taking a long view of things, charged with the safety of the country, but particularly with preparing for threats that may take years to appear.'

'Doesn't the military ordinarily do that?' George asked.

Caroline rolled her eyes. 'Mostly, the military chiefs are doing well if they can plan what they're going to have for lunch.'

Aubrey continued. 'These long-term planners, shall we call them, may decide to ensure that the brightest brains in the country are in the forces – have taken the King's commission.'

'Oh,' Caroline said.

'Imagine,' Aubrey went on, 'a talented young magical researcher, perhaps just married, certainly struggling for money, being approached by a senior military man. Most likely a war hero, but that may be just a nicety.'

'You're making this up,' Caroline accused.

'Yes,' George said. 'This is what he does. He thinks about things and then spins stories to fit.'

'To go on,' Aubrey said, 'this military man would tell our young researcher that he could undertake a special short stint in the army – or navy, but I can't really see Professor Hepworth at sea.'

Caroline shook her head. 'No. Chronic seasickness. He suffers terribly. Suffered terribly.' Her chin quivered, but she caught herself.

Aubrey resumed. 'The military man would persuade our young researcher by leaning on his patriotism, his duty to the country, and suggesting that a military record would not go astray in applying for academic positions. It would be an irresistible case. A short time in the service, some useful pay, and then our young researcher forgets all about his time in uniform because he finds an academic post and his studies take over.'

'Just in time,' George said. 'Here's the train.'

With the stationmaster's help, they were able to negotiate with the guard and the bicycles were safely stowed in the van.

After they had settled in their compartment, Aubrey weighed up matters then took the chance to resume the conversation. 'And what exactly were you doing out there last night, Miss Hepworth?'

She looked out of the window before answering, through the steam and smoke as the train eased out of the station. 'I was waiting for the Black Beast. It killed my father. I wanted to destroy it.'

George raised an eyebrow. 'With a shotgun?'

'A remarkable shotgun,' Aubrey said. 'Isn't that right, Miss Hepworth?'

She nodded. 'I'm not as credulous as to believe the thing that killed my father was really the Black Beast of legend, but I knew it had to be something extremely powerful, magically. In my father's workshop . . .' Her voice caught a little in her throat. 'I found some magically prepared shotgun shells and a gun. I thought it might work against the creature.'

At the mention of Professor Hepworth's workshop, Aubrey leaned forward. The workshop could hold some useful information about what the professor was working on, and his business with Banford Park. If Caroline had access to the workshop, it could bear investigating.

'You know what the creature is?' George asked. The train whistle screeched as they rounded the bend and steamed up the hill away from Penhurst.

'No. Not really. Not entirely.'

'Tell me, Miss Hepworth,' Aubrey said, 'where did your father work?'

She looked a little puzzled at the abrupt change of direction in the conversation. 'At the research facility. Banford Park.'

'Yes, but where exactly *is* the research facility?'

'Bordering Penhurst Estate, I think.' She pursed her lips. 'I'm sure of it. Father was vague about directions, but that was unsurprising. He was terrible at reading maps and things like that, but he did say that he could walk from the research facility to the Big House in an hour or so, and had done so many times. After the Prince visited their facility, he insisted that the researchers come to Penhurst often. I think he was appalled at the living quarters.'

'The Prince visited the research facility?' Aubrey asked sharply.

'So Father said. I suppose he shouldn't really have talked about all these things, but I'm sure the security people were at their wits' end with the researchers. Researchers simply couldn't understand what secrecy was for. They were used to sharing their work, not hiding it.'

'And did your father happen to mention what *sort* of work they were doing?'

'No. Even he must have realised that he shouldn't discuss some things. All I can say is that, whenever I managed to see him, he was either exhilarated or decidedly unhappy. The exhilaration meant that his work was stimulating, full of challenges and unexpected findings. The unhappiness was the sort of unhappiness I'd only seen once before, when the university forced him to work on a project he didn't agree with, something to do with magical experimentation on animals.'

'Jolly good of him,' George said.

Aubrey glanced at him. George had never approved of such things as cruelty to animals, even in the name of magical enquiry, a legacy of his heritage on the land. Over the years Aubrey had seen the way his friend had made pets of orphan lambs whenever he was on the farm.

'How did that project at the university go?' Aubrey asked. 'The one he was forced to work on?'

Caroline smiled faintly. 'Terribly. With Father's heart not in it, it dragged on and on. I don't think he consciously sabotaged it, but the project went around in circles, mistakes were made, results lost . . . It was eventually abandoned, and I remember Father sheepishly telling us about the dean's displeasure, but he couldn't stop smiling at the thought of moving on to something he really wanted to do.'

Aubrey sat back in his seat and looked out of the window for a time. He jiggled a leg, and began humming.

Caroline stared curiously at this display. 'It's all right,' George said to her. 'He's often like this.'

'George,' Aubrey said, 'do you have your notebook?'

George plucked it from his jacket and produced a pencil.

'Very good. Let us note what we have here.'

Aubrey cleared his throat and held up a finger. 'Firstly, with respect, we have the death of two famous magical researchers, Dr Tremaine and Professor Hepworth, one by sorcerous means.'

Caroline's mouth firmed, but she nodded.

'Secondly, we have an attempt on the life of the Crown Prince. Again, by sorcerous means. Thirdly, we have a highly secret magical research facility near the site of all three of these incidents.'

Aubrey looked at the three fingers he was holding up. 'Have I forgotten anything?'

'A reasonable explanation,' George said, staring at his notes.

'George, simply because we can't see something doesn't mean it's not there. I thought you'd know that by now. Don't you agree, Miss Hepworth?'

She frowned. 'So you're saying, if I follow you correctly, that the research facility may be involved in both sorcerous attacks? The one on my father and the one on Prince Albert?'

'Exactly.' Aubrey sat back and crossed his arms on his chest, feeling reasonably smug.

'But why?'

Aubrey blinked, opened his mouth, then closed it again. He held up a finger and started again. 'I will answer a question with some further questions.' *That should give me some time to come up with something*, he thought. 'Why would someone want both Professor Hepworth and the Crown Prince dead? What do they have in common? Who could benefit from their deaths?'

'Not Banford Park. Father was the leading researcher. He was vital for their work.'

Aubrey thought aloud. 'War work. Banford Park was involved in work for the military.'

'How do you know that?' Caroline asked.

George snorted. 'He guessed when we met Dr Tremaine. It fits, you know. Professor Hepworth's being redrafted. Things are happening with Holmland. It makes sense that we'd have top brains working on magical means for defence.'

Caroline looked at both of them. 'The war.' She looked grim, then distressed. 'That would be it.'

'The research facility could be there to find new sorcerous means to defend the country,' Aubrey said. 'Or it may be for magical offensive weapons, more work of this long-range planning group of the military, no doubt.'

'The Black Beast?' George offered. 'Has someone been using the guise of an old legend to hide these new sorcerous weapons?'

'Perhaps. Imagine such a creature on the battlefield. Panic, terror, troops throwing down weapons and running away. It could be devastating.'

Aubrey stared out of the window at the green and pleasant countryside. He hated to think of such a place as the scene of battle.

He knew that Albion was in an exceedingly delicate situation. It might be an island kingdom, but the continent was only a few miles away. Following the manoeuvrings between the countries and empires there was like trying to keep track of clouds in a storm-driven sky. The Goltan states were a powder keg of shifting alliances, with powerful nations surrounding them and watching closely. It was made even more complicated by the King insisting that his many relations, on the many thrones on the continent, were all to be trusted and supported.

Aubrey paid attention to his father's business inside and outside Parliament and had come to the conclusion that Holmland was the centre of much of the disquiet. It was becoming increasingly warlike; recently, it had been annexing small principalities under the flimsiest pretexts. Now it was looking hungrily at the Goltan states. And though the King had recently repeated his view that Holmland was a harmless friend, a jolly empire which made fine accordions, good beer and better sausages, there were many who thought differently.

Aubrey's father was one. He was a strong proponent of firm resistance, of facing up to bluffs and shows of force from the increasingly strong Holmland. He was not one for appeasement.

'Your father, Miss Hepworth,' Aubrey asked, 'what was his view about the war?'

She was gazing through the window, her chin resting

on a long and elegant hand. She looked at Aubrey and his heart turned an odd corner. 'He didn't have one. He dismissed the continental situation as a lot of silly posturing.'

'There's quite a bit of that, but it does go deeper.'

'I'm sure,' she murmured and returned her attention to the passing countryside.

Aubrey gazed at her for some time. 'What are your plans, Miss Hepworth?' he eventually asked.

George raised an eyebrow, but said nothing.

'Please call me Caroline. Both of you. "Miss Hepworth" sounds unbearably old-fashioned.' She looked at Aubrey evenly. 'I still aim to find out who killed my father. Even if it is tangled up with warmongering.'

'Sounds rather dangerous,' George said.

'It's bound to be,' Aubrey said. 'You're going back to Penhurst?' he asked Caroline.

She shook her head. 'I have to help my mother with the funeral.' She paused and Aubrey was impressed again by her calm. 'I thought I might go to look in Father's workshop.' She sighed. 'There may be something, some indication –'

'Your father's workshop?' Aubrey interrupted. 'At the research facility? How will you get entry?'

She waved this away. 'His private workshop, nothing to do with the research facility. At Greythorn. The university paid the rent on it, hoping his secondment wouldn't last long. He may have left something in his notebook about what he was working on before he went.'

'Excellent!' Aubrey said. 'All we'd need would be a clue, a hint . . .'

'We?' both Caroline and George echoed.

'You are making an assumption here,' Caroline said to Aubrey.

He shrugged. 'I tend to. Forgive me. I feel this may be important.' He grinned. 'I can be ready in a day. When would suit you? The sooner the better, of course.'

Caroline stiffened.

'Aubrey,' George said, 'the funeral . . .'

'Ah.' Aubrey felt like kicking himself. He'd allowed his enthusiasm to run away, again. 'Yes. I'm sorry.'

Caroline didn't look at him, or answer. She simply turned to the window again.

The train whistle wailed and they hurtled towards the city.

Twelve

'*J*'M NOT SURE THIS IS A GOOD IDEA,' GEORGE SAID. 'It's the right thing to do, whether it's a good idea or not,' Aubrey replied. 'Straighten up. Don't slouch.'

'I feel uncomfortable.'

'Sometimes you do things not because of how it makes you feel, but because of how it makes other people feel.'

George scowled. 'I hate funerals.'

'Some people like them,' Aubrey mused. 'In a family like mine, I've had third cousins and great-stepuncles passing on quite regularly. I've been dragged to dozens of funerals, ever since I was born. I'm sure there are people who feel that a funeral is a fine day out, a good social occasion, time to catch up and gossip.'

'Hush,' George said as they reached the stairs of the church. 'Let's find a space in the back pews.'

Aubrey and George had arrived in Greythorn after an early morning train trip from the city. The church was a modest, blocky affair. It wasn't in the university proper, but in a part of the town near a motorbus depot. Aubrey wondered why the professor – or his wife – had chosen this place and not one of the grand chapels at one of the colleges.

He looked at the large congregation who'd assembled to mark the professor's passing. To judge from the crowd, he decided Professor Hepworth had been no academic recluse. Relatives were easy to spot from familial resemblance, and his colleagues were wearing formal academic robes. But there were many others. Quite a few took advantage of the motorbus station to arrive by public transport, but while waiting outside Aubrey had seen a butcher's cart pull up and disgorge half a dozen men, and many bicycles were leaning against the fence.

He also saw famous faces. Phillips-Dodd, the Home Secretary, was perfectly dressed as usual, his black morning suit no doubt worth hundreds of pounds. Sir Guy Boothby, the Foreign Secretary, was also present. Aubrey looked for, but didn't see, Sir Philip Saxby, the Minister for Magic.

The service was difficult. Professor Hepworth was obviously loved and respected, and the distress expressed by many of the congregation was contagious. Aubrey felt tears come to his own eyes as he reflected on mortality and its frailties.

The eulogy was delivered by Sir Isambard Hammersmith, the ancient and revered President of the Royal Society for Magic. He spoke at length, detailing Professor Hepworth's formidable intellect and energy and expressing great sorrow at the loss to magic research. He touched on the dual loss to the field, with the too-recent passing of the Sorcerer Royal, Dr Tremaine. The old man looked crushed.

Immediately after Sir Isambard had finished, the minister signed to another man that it was his turn to speak. '

He was small and nervous, with sharp features, about fifty years old – although Aubrey found it hard to guess. He held a cloth cap in his hands and he continually twisted it as if he were wringing washing.

He announced that his name was Charles Ob and then told of how Professor Hepworth had been his drinking companion for years.

Aubrey's eyes went wide. Professor Hepworth's *drinking companion?*

This claim caused a mass shifting of position in the congregation. Only the fact that it was a funeral service prevented a buzz of puzzled conversation.

Mr Ob went on to tell how Professor Hepworth had helped all six of his children through school. One of them, he said proudly, had gone on to the university. As an afterthought, Mr Ob added that Professor Hepworth had done the same for many families he knew.

AUBREY AND GEORGE SHUFFLED OUT WITH THE REST OF THE congregation, following the pallbearers to the small churchyard burial ground, when Lady Fitzwilliam emerged from the crowd. 'Aubrey! George! I thought it was you.'

Sir Darius appeared, looking unsurprised to see Aubrey there, despite the fact that Aubrey hadn't told his parents of his plans. 'Aubrey. George. A great loss.'

'It's good to see you paying your respects, Aubrey,' Lady

Fitzwilliam said as they walked with the congregation to the graveside.

Aubrey had grown used to the fact that it was hard to surprise his parents. To the best of his knowledge, they hadn't known George and he had left Maidstone early in order to get to Greythorn in time for the funeral. 'It's the least we could do. He was a great man.'

'I wasn't aware you knew him,' Sir Darius said, voice low, as they reached the grave.

'We met on the shooting weekend,' Aubrey said. 'But I'd known *of* him for years. I've read his work.'

'Of course.'

The ceremony at the graveside was brief. Afterwards, they joined the long line to pay their respects to Professor Hepworth's widow.

Mrs Hepworth was tall and extremely beautiful, even in her grief. Her long black hair was wound in an elaborate knot at the back of her neck and she sat rigidly in a chair as the mourners filed past. Caroline was at her side.

'Mrs Hepworth,' Aubrey murmured. 'So sorry. Miss Hepworth.'

Caroline raised an eyebrow when she caught sight of him. She nodded, but said nothing.

Sir Darius and Lady Fitzwilliam were speaking with three older men Aubrey recognised as having visited Maidstone in the past. The tall, lanky one was Admiral Quist, head of the navy. The pot-bellied chap was Thomas Dunleavy, editor in chief of *The Argus*. The one who looked like he wanted to argue but thought it might be a good idea if he didn't was the Dean of St Stephen's College.

Aubrey didn't hesitate. He left George and went straight over. He stood there and refused to be ignored.

Sir Darius smiled wryly. 'Gentlemen, you know my son Aubrey?'

The three elders stared at Aubrey as if he were a performing seal. He inclined his head. 'Admiral. Mr Dunleavy. Dean.'

They huffed and harrumphed, acknowledging and condescending to him in what they thought was the best manly fashion, giving Sir Darius Fitzwilliam's son his due.

Aubrey kept smiling, even though his teeth were gritted. *I'll make you notice me for myself*, he thought, *one day.*

Aubrey's reward for his persistence was ten minutes of extremely boring conversation, as each of the three tried to either impress Sir Darius or enlist his assistance in a home for invalid sailors, a committee on journalistic ethics, and a building fund for St Stephen's College. These proposals were met with interest, incredulity and surrender, respectively.

Aubrey took the opportunity to file away details of the three men, for future reference. He took note of any mention of their backgrounds or family, especially. His father was said to have a card index memory, and his knack for remembering trivial details of people he'd only met once was legendary. Aubrey aimed to be as good, if not better, at this subtle art.

As he listened to the dean suggest that Sir Darius might like to contribute to the college's building fund, he saw a deacon working through the crowd. When the deacon spied George, he hurried to him and thrust a piece of paper into his hand.

Aubrey excused himself and made his way to his friend's side. 'You're looking more than usually befuddled, George. What's going on?'

George didn't say anything. He simply handed Aubrey the piece of paper.

Fitzwilliam, Doyle, can you come to my house tomorrow morning? Yours etc, Caroline Hepworth.

Aubrey was silent for a moment after reading it. He looked at George. 'We can't disappoint the lady, can we, George?'

'We will if we can't find her house. She didn't give her address.'

'A trifle,' Aubrey said and he slipped into the crowd that had gathered outside the church gates.

It wasn't long before Aubrey found the minister and was able to extract the address of the Hepworth residence after disclosing that he wanted to take some flowers to the grieving family.

At that moment, Sir Darius and Lady Fitzwilliam walked over, her arm in his. 'Aubrey, your mother and I are staying here in Greythorn for a few nights. I have to see some people. We can drop you at the railway station if you like.'

'Where are you staying?'

'The Triumph Hotel,' Lady Fitzwilliam said.

'You wouldn't have a suite booked, would you? More than one bedroom?'

Sir Darius stroked his moustache. 'Are you looking to stay here, too?'

'George and I thought we might like to look around the university tomorrow. You've told me so much about it.'

'Ah,' Sir Darius said. He looked at his wife. When she didn't demur, he nodded. 'Very well. Let us go.'

The Triumph Hotel was a recent construction, a monolith in the centre of the town. Eight floors, it looked squat and solid and reputable. It reminded Aubrey of a bank manager with a respectable firm who had a sizeable pension awaiting his retirement.

Sir Darius didn't stay in the suite for long. The telephone rang and, after answering, he excused himself, saying some people had come to meet him already. Aubrey noticed that he looked tense. Lady Fitzwilliam had thrown off her hat and shoes and arranged herself on the blue velvet of the chaise longue. She tapped the back of the chaise longue with one finger as he left. 'I worry about that man,' she muttered.

George having gone to buy a newspaper, Aubrey was left alone with his mother for the first time since the shooting weekend. 'What do you mean?' he asked.

She scowled at the door. 'I do wish these people could come to an occasion like this and not indulge in politics.' She sighed and waved a hand. 'I may as well tell fish not to swim.'

'It does seem to be in their nature.'

'And is it in yours?' his mother said. 'I wonder.'

Aubrey waved a hand, precisely imitating his mother's gesture. She laughed. 'Now, Aubrey, tell me what you're up to.'

Aubrey stretched and laced his fingers behind his head, even though relaxing was the last thing he felt like doing. His mother was among the most perceptive people he knew. She had an unerring gift for detecting falsehood. Her innocent invitation to talk made him feel like he was about to try to pick his way through a minefield.

'I'm well,' he ventured.

'Come now, Aubrey, I think I'm entitled to a little more than that.'

'My studies are going smoothly enough. I'm reasonably confident about the exams.'

'What about the Snainton Prize? I'd heard you were in the running for it this year.'

You'd heard? Aubrey thought. *So Duchess Maria isn't the only one with a network of informants.* 'I'm in the running,' he confirmed. 'But with the school play, the cricket team, the cadets . . .' He spread his hands.

'And what about that incident with Bertie? Has anything come of that?'

Aubrey wondered how much his mother already knew. He decided a partial telling of the truth would be best. 'George and I went up to Penhurst again last weekend, to poke around. We didn't find anything useful.' *Not bad,* he congratulated himself. Nothing he could be hanged for there.

'You were a hero, saving Bertie like that. I was proud.'

Aubrey grinned. 'Thank you, Mother.'

'But be careful. The attention, the thrill of meeting danger and besting it, can be addictive. One can grow to like being a hero. The adulation, the praise . . .' She paused, reflecting. 'Your father learned this. He understood that you should make sure you do these things for others, not for yourself.' She smiled. 'But it was well done, just the same.'

His mother had a habit of doing this. She could go straight to the heart of the matter and touch it lightly. Sometimes it was dazzling, this ability, sometimes frustrating. Aubrey knew that the only way she survived in an atmosphere of constant politics and diplomacy was through her work.

'You don't have to worry about me.'

She smiled, a little sadly this time. 'Aubrey, you can't tell a mother not to worry about her children. I'm afraid it's part of the role.'

'Well, children grow up.'

'Ask your grandmother. See what she says.'

'She worries about Father?'

'Constantly.' She drummed her fingers on the back of the chaise longue and frowned. 'I'm frustrated at being tied up here. I was doing some fascinating work at the museum, classifying some new specimens from the east. Extraordinary birds, they were.'

Aubrey admired his mother. She was a renowned field naturalist, but she was equally at home in the back rooms of museums arguing over taxonomy and out on expedition in jungles. It had been on one of these expeditions that she'd met the Marquis of Rimford – Aubrey's father when he still had his title. His squad had become separated from the regiment in a skirmish in the Mataboro jungle. Rose Hannaford, as she was then, had led them back to civilisation, making them carry specimens she picked up along the way. It was after they married that her husband renounced his title, becoming simply Darius Fitzwilliam, intent on entering the Lower House and gaining the prime ministership, as – according to law – the Prime Minister had to have a seat in the Lower House of Parliament, not be a peer in the Upper House.

She rose from the chaise longue. 'Aubrey, I may rest a little before supper. Will you be happy here on your own?'

'George will be back soon. I'll be fine.'

Aubrey was dozing lightly when George came back. 'I say, old man,' his friend said as he burst into the room, 'I think you're right about this code business. Look at this corker!'

George spread the newspaper on one of the side tables, then dragged it to where Aubrey was sitting. Aubrey blinked away sleep and found George was pointing at some lines in his beloved agony columns. 'Well, ' he said, 'it definitely looks like a cipher to me.'

In the bottom corner of the page, surrounded by curt and plaintive messages, were four solid lines of garbled letters.

George beamed. 'Yes. I've been trying to solve the dashed thing. Devilishly tricky.'

Aubrey ran his fingers through his hair and yawned. 'That? Oh, I solved that last week.'

George stared at him. 'You solved it?'

'If it's the same cipher as you showed me on the way home from Penhurst, I'm sure I have.'

'Aubrey,' George said, exasperated, 'when do you find the *time* to do all these things?'

He looked up. 'Hmm? Time?' He looked back to the newspaper. 'I invented the seventy-minute hour, George. I get more done that way.'

'I see.'

'This cipher took me a while, though,' he said, tapping the newspaper. 'It was devilishly tricky, as you say.'

'I tried everything I could think of.'

'Well, yes. It wouldn't yield to straightforward frequency analysis, I found that out quite smartly.'

'Frequency analysis,' George repeated. 'I see.'

Aubrey snorted. 'I can always tell when you don't know what you're talking about. "I see" is a giveaway.'

George was not a good actor. He tried to look wide-eyed and innocent, but instead looked as if he had heartburn. 'Tell me about frequency analysis.'

'The most commonly used letter in the language is?'

'*E.*'

'Correct. So we look for the most commonly used letter in the coded message and assume that's *e*. The same works at the other end of the scale.'

'So uncommonly used letters like *q*, *x* and *z* would appear least frequently?'

'Indeed.' Aubrey rubbed his chin. 'But this method didn't work. The gibberish remained gibberish. I had to think of something else.'

'Some other pattern?'

'Almost. I put it aside for some time and then, while I was rehearsing for the school play, it struck me. If the frequency of single letters wasn't revealing anything, perhaps I should be looking at the digraphs.'

'Digraphs? Pairs of letters?'

'Exactly. In order of frequency, the way we use the language, the most common digraph is *th*, then *he*, *an*, *in* and so on. The message you showed me last time was a long one, with plenty to work with. By concentrating on the digraphs I was able to uncover enough to read the message.'

'Astounding, Aubrey, simply astounding. What did the message say?'

'Nothing of any real account. Something like "Tomorrow night no good. Wait until Friday. Give the present to my friend at the station. He will have news for you." And so on. Quite banal.'

'Oh,' George said, crestfallen. 'I'd been hoping for something more dramatic. Well, what about this one?'

Aubrey studied it for a moment, then pulled up a chair. 'Pencil, please?'

It took fifteen minutes of effort, with much scribbling and crossing out, but finally Aubrey sat back with a look of satisfaction on his face. 'There.'

'You're done?'

'Now, you can never be totally sure, but I think it reads like this: "Meet at fitness society this Friday. Plans are on course. We are not suspected. The way forward clear. Proceed." Of course, I inserted the punctuation.'

'Hmm. Rather prosaic. It could be a young couple, planning elopement. See where it says "our plans are on course".'

'That could mean anything. And why would a couple who are running away to get married meet at a fitness society?'

'No idea. Another mystery, it looks like.'

At that moment, Lady Fitzwilliam appeared at the door to her bedroom. 'What will remain a mystery, gentlemen?'

Aubrey gestured at the newspaper. 'The agony columns, Mother.'

'Ah, spying on others' lives, are we?' She laughed. 'Your father hasn't returned, Aubrey?'

'No.'

'Well, I shall have two handsome young gentlemen take me to dinner. Aubrey, would you ring the hotel dining room and reserve a table for three?'

WHEN THE LIFT OPENED ON THE GROUND FLOOR, AUBREY was surprised to see Sir Darius waiting to enter. His face was distracted and serious, but it lightened when he saw his wife. 'Rose! I was coming to fetch you to dinner.'

'I couldn't wait,' she said. 'Luckily these two were able to escort me. But we've only reserved a table for three.'

'I'm sure they'll be able to accommodate us.'

As Sir Darius shepherded them towards the dining room, Aubrey's eye was caught by a tall, angular figure leaving the hotel through the revolving door. Once outside, he turned back briefly, much as one would when trying to fix a location in one's mind. In the instant he turned around, Aubrey recognised him.

It was Craddock, the head of the Magisterium.

Thirteen

THE NEXT MORNING, AUBREY SAT IN THE HOTEL DINING room watching George work his way through a breakfast the size of a small country. Poached eggs, sausages, bacon, fried bread and tomatoes, mushrooms, toast and orange marmalade disappeared as George ate with gusto.

Aubrey picked at his food. A sausage sat on his plate next to an untouched fried egg. He'd taken a single bite from a piece of buttered toast.

It had been an awkward night. He'd lain awake, convinced that his soul was about to be pulled from his body, but nothing happened. Then, in the small hours of the night, he'd lain awake simply worrying about the state he'd put himself in. It was pointless, worrying like that, but it overwhelmed him as he dwelt on what could have been and what he should do next. Sleep took him, eventually, but it was fitful, with troubled dreams.

George finished. 'Excellent! Sets one up for the day, a breakfast like that.'

'I'm glad you enjoyed it.'

George studied him. 'You're having trouble.'

'Not a good night. A few aches and pains.'

'Perhaps you should stay here. I'll go and see Caroline.'

'I can manage,' Aubrey said sharply, then he held up a hand. 'Sorry, George.'

George grinned. 'You're interested in her, aren't you?'

'She is interesting. Intriguing. Fascinating.'

'Attractive?'

'That's another way of putting it, I suppose.' He frowned. 'Is there a motive behind this inquisition?'

'No, nothing really. I'm just pleased to see the effect she's having on you. Makes you seem human, old man.'

'Effect?' Aubrey considered the best way to deny this for a moment, before the second part of what George had said caught up with him. 'What do you mean, "makes me seem human"?'

George nodded. 'That took you longer than usual. She *is* having an effect on you.'

Aubrey stood. 'Are you coming or staying here?'

CAROLINE'S MODERN, TWO-STOREY HOME WAS IN A ROW OF houses in a quiet part of town opposite a small, well-kept cemetery which looked to be a favourite place for dog-walkers. Aubrey was disappointed when Mrs Hepworth opened the door. She was pale and drawn. Her hair was unbound, hanging well below her shoulders, and she wore a mauve robe that left her arms bare.

'Good morning, Mrs Hepworth. Miss Hepworth asked us to visit her this morning.'

'Yes,' Mrs Hepworth said. She studied Aubrey for a moment. 'You're Fitzwilliam, aren't you? Darius Fitzwilliam's boy?'

This was a question Aubrey had faced all his life. 'Yes, ma'am.'

'You have his eyes.' She stood back and waved them into the house, oblivious of Aubrey's curiosity.

I have his eyes? he thought. *How do you know his eyes so well?*

Caroline was waiting for them in the hall and Aubrey's train of thought veered in a completely new direction. She looked pale, but determined. 'Do you still want to see my father's workshop?' she said, without any preliminaries.

'Of course,' Aubrey said. George nodded.

'Very well. We'll go now.'

'Caroline?' Mrs Hepworth said. She put a hand to her throat. 'What is this about?'

'I want to show Father's workshop to these two. They may be able to help.'

Mrs Hepworth looked pained for a moment. She took a deep breath and nodded. 'I see.' She turned to Aubrey and George. 'Caroline was always like this. She knows what she wants and I'm afraid that I've encouraged that independence. It's something I must live with, I suppose.' She looked at her daughter with such tenderness that Aubrey thought she was going to cry. Instead, she added in a very soft voice, 'Be careful.' She held her daughter at arm's length. 'You're wearing the diamond brooch he gave you.'

'Yes,' Caroline took her mother's hands. 'I shan't be long.'

Aubrey felt awkward. He looked at George, but he was studying an umbrella stand as if he'd always been fascinated by them.

Caroline tapped her foot as she put on a small hat. 'Come now. We may as well be off.'

They followed her as she strode down the footpath. Aubrey looked up and saw Mrs Hepworth watching from an upstairs window. With her pale face, her unbound hair and her robe, she looked like a figure from an ancient tragedy, a despairing mother watching her offspring leaving for war.

'Shouldn't we catch a cab?' George said.

'I need the walk,' Caroline said, without looking at him. 'It may help clear my head.'

'Ah, indeed,' Aubrey said. 'We're heading to the university?'

'No.'

That was all they had from her for the next hour.

She marched relentlessly through the streets. When they had to stop to cross roads, her face was set and resentful. If pedestrians were slow, blocking the way, she went to the other side of the street. Aubrey decided she was trying to vent her grief, anger and frustration through physical effort. She was making a good job of it.

After the poor sleep of the night before, Aubrey began to feel the strain of keeping up. He swung along easily enough, but since he didn't know how long they were going to be walking, he couldn't pace himself. His knees and the soles of his feet ached.

He really needed to spend a few days recuperating, restoring his strength, doing some more research into his condition, but events were conspiring against him.

Eventually, they found themselves walking through

streets of small factories – metalworkers, cabinetmakers, glassworks. A world away from the cosy, domestic neighbourhood of the Hepworth residence, they were mostly squat, inelegant buildings, many with grubby windows and fenced-off yards. Aubrey saw a famished-looking watchdog studying him intently as they passed and he was confident that Geo. Walsh and Sons, Wheelwrights, was likely to be undisturbed by intruders.

At the end of one such street, beyond a maker of industrial knives, Caroline stopped and they faced a single-storey brick building, perhaps forty years old.

'You have the key?' Aubrey asked. His throat was dry and painful when he swallowed.

'What do you mean?' Caroline asked.

Aubrey pointed upwards. 'This is the only building in the street with an electrical supply. The doors are large enough for a lorry to drive through. No windows in the building, only skylights. It's at the end of a cul de sac with an abandoned building either side. Perfectly private.' He grinned. 'So I'm assuming it's your father's workshop.'

Caroline didn't answer. She simply opened her bag and took out a key.

The doors were stubborn. 'Let me,' George said. He put his shoulder to one and it screeched open. Caroline insisted that he shut it behind them.

'Disappointing, really,' George said after their eyes had grown accustomed to the dim light. 'I'd expect a master magician's workshop to be a bit more dramatic. Where are the stuffed crocodiles hanging from the rafters? The strange mirrors on the walls?'

The workshop looked like a chemistry laboratory. Aubrey supposed at one time the building might have housed a small engineering works or machine shop.

Dusty lathes and turning equipment were clustered at the far end of the room in the shadows, blocking a rear door. Coils of rope hung from hooks on the walls.

The rest of the workshop was filled with three rows of benches. The benches themselves supported forests of elaborate glassware, interspersed with machinery that looked like half-gutted radio receivers and transmitters. Large carboys of reagents caught the light and glowed like a stained-glass window in a cathedral. Pairs of discarded leather gloves, pieces of chalk, crayons and scraps of paper showed that it was a working space. From the disorder it looked as if the owner had simply stepped out for a moment.

Aubrey cleared his throat. 'We should be careful. I'm sure the professor would have some security spells in place.'

Caroline walked to the nearest bench. She reached for a dangling chain and electric light flooded the space. 'I've been here a hundred times. It's perfectly safe.'

Of course, Aubrey thought. *No doubt he would have made sure you were safe if you came without him.*

He stood still, barely a yard from the doorway, right next to an empty hatstand. He felt the prickling on the back of his neck that signalled the presence of magic, but decided that it would be strange if he *didn't* have that sensation in such a place. Still, he felt uneasy, and he scanned the workshop, looking for danger.

George stood next to him. 'I'd usually offer to scout around, old man, but I thought I'd wait until you'd given the all clear.'

'Even though Caroline is moving around?'

'Father's notebook will be here somewhere,' she said, standing with her hands on her hips. 'He never took it out of here.'

George took a few steps towards the benches. At that moment, Aubrey happened to look up.

His eyes narrowed. There, in the shadows, near one of the rafters . . .

'Don't move!' he hissed.

George stopped as if rooted to the spot. He knew that tone of voice. 'What is it?'

Aubrey ignored him. 'Caroline,' he called softly, 'would you please stand still?'

'I beg your pardon?' She gave Aubrey a look of exasperation.

'Something deadly is watching us very closely.'

She froze. Only her eyes moved, her gaze darting around the shelves and cabinets.

'Where is it?' George muttered to Aubrey.

'Look up. Carefully. It's in the corner, on one of the rafters, where it can see the whole room.'

'I can't spot anything up there. It's too gloomy.'

'Wait until it moves.'

'What is it?' Caroline said in a low, calm voice.

'A shade,' Aubrey said. 'I've read about them, but never seen one before. A magician detaches a shadow from something and binds it using the Law of Sympathy, so it retains some of the qualities of whatever it once belonged to. They're not very intelligent, but they can be quite lethal. Thin as shadows, they're like flying razors.' He paused. 'Of course, the original owner of the shadow dies.'

'Why isn't it attacking us?' George asked.

'Good question. Caroline, did your father ever make anything like this?'

'He'd never do something that involved cruelty like that.'

'Then it's been put here by someone else.' Aubrey frowned. 'It's probably been ordered to wait until some-one finds the professor's notebook, then kill them and report the location of the prize.'

George glanced upwards. 'Oh.'

'If it's not harming us, we should leave,' Caroline said. 'We can come back with help.'

'That's probably best,' Aubrey said. *But it's the last thing I'd do,* he thought. 'George,' he said, 'what do you have in your pockets?'

George rolled his eyes. Slowly, he felt in his pockets. 'Some coins, a wallet with very little in it, my notebook, a pencil, a pocket handkerchief.'

'Well, that makes two pocket handkerchiefs,' Aubrey said. He'd left all his magical paraphernalia behind. *Improvise, improvise,* he told himself. He began humming as he looked around the room.

His eyes widened as he saw a shallow rectangular container, about two feet long and a foot wide, on one of the benches. It was filled nearly to the brim with a silver liquid. 'Caroline,' he called softly. 'Can you please look at the bench to your right. Is that a quicksilver bath?'

She glanced at the bench. 'Yes. Father used a lot of mercury in his work.'

'Good, good.' Aubrey glanced up. 'Now, George, I think you should take out any important pages from your notebook. Anything you want to keep, that is.'

'Why?' George removed a few pages and stuffed them in his pocket. 'What are you doing?'

'Plotting, George. Notebook, please.' Caroline stared and Aubrey realised he was grinning. He clamped down on his smile. Everything was clear and sharp-edged as his senses grew almost overwhelmingly alert. He could smell the nitre and the hensbane somewhere towards the back of the room. He could hear crystals forming in one of the beakers to his right. His blood was singing as he thought ahead to what needed to be done.

George shuffled close and handed over the notebook.

'Now, you're not overly fond of that hat, are you?' Aubrey asked.

George took it off mournfully. 'Here.'

'Jacket.'

George slipped out of it, knowing better than to complain.

Aubrey arranged the hat and jacket on the hatstand. 'We must move swiftly,' he said, 'once it attacks this decoy.' He stuffed the notebook into one of the jacket pockets, but made sure it protruded.

'How are you going to make it attack?' Caroline asked.

'An adaptation of the Law of Sympathy – like to like. George's notebook is quite similar in *nature* to your father's notebook. Notebooks being notebooks, they share physical qualities, but they also have commonality of *purpose*. This spell will draw on those similarities and change the appearance of George's notebook until it takes on the appearance of your father's notebook, which, I hope, is somewhere in this room. Otherwise it will be out of range and the spell won't work.'

'I see. Thinking it's seen the notebook it's been waiting for, this shade creature will attack an empty jacket and hat,' George said.

'And we can deal with it,' Aubrey said. He buttoned the jacket. 'Of course, a not-so-empty jacket and hat will be much more tempting.'

This was the easy part. Using a spell he'd perfected through many repetitions, he began to chant softly and ran his hands over the jacket sleeves. Slowly, and to his great relief, the jacket began to swell like a balloon being inflated.

Aubrey heard both Caroline and George inhale sharply when two ghostly hands appeared at the end of the sleeves. They quickly became firm and fleshy, hanging limply.

Aubrey turned his attention to the hat. He put both hands on its crown, then stroked downwards, continuing the spell. He was particularly careful when he intoned the elements setting the solidity of the effect, as this would be important.

'Good Lord,' George said, as a face appeared.

It was his.

Aubrey took a deep breath as a wave of fatigue rolled over him. Caroline began to speak, but he held up a hand. 'The Law of Contiguity. A special variation. The jacket and hat had been touching George, absorbing his Georgeness, if you will. I've drawn on that, added a few elements for appearance and here we are.' *Not bad for such a jury-rigged job.* 'It's not a real body, simply an illusion, no substance at all. A real body would require much more work than this.' He glanced at George. 'But it will do.'

Aubrey began to tremble and shooting pain ran up and down his legs. He leaned against George.

'Is this a good idea?' George muttered.

'Let's find out, shall we?'

Aubrey limped over to join Caroline. George followed, nervously looking upwards as he went. 'It's still there?'

'Yes,' Aubrey said, without looking up. He studied his reflection in the shiny quicksilver. *Perfect*, he thought.

He moved aside all the clutter on the bench – papers, beakers, crucibles, a mug half-full of cold tea, a feather duster – putting them on the other benches until only the quicksilver bath was left. With a grunt, he moved this to one end. The quicksilver rolled backwards and forwards.

'Chalk,' Aubrey said, looking around.

'Here.' Caroline put a piece in his hand.

Aubrey smiled his thanks and drew a large rectangle on the surface of the bench. He dropped the chalk into his pocket, then wet his finger in his mouth. With painstaking care, he traced the outline, his finger moving through the air an inch *above* the chalk line.

Then Aubrey seized the quicksilver bath and upended it onto the bench.

George stifled an oath and stepped back, but the mercury flowed to the edge of the chalk outline and stopped, meeting an invisible barrier. Soon, the shiny, liquid metal lay there, bounded only by a chalk border, making a slab of quicksilver about two feet by two feet, and an inch thick.

'Excellent,' Aubrey said. 'Now for the Law of Opposites. Caroline, would you please hand me those safety matches?'

She had been regarding Aubrey with more than a little scepticism. 'Are you sure you know what you're doing?' she asked as she handed him the box.

'Oh yes. Quite elementary, this part. A minor application of the Law of Opposites. Observe.'

With a flourish, Aubrey struck a match, waggled an eyebrow, muttered a few words, then stuck the lit end in his mouth.

Caroline's eyes went wide, but George gave an exclamation of disgust. 'It's an old trick,' he said to Caroline. 'He mastered it when he was eight.'

Aubrey's cheeks bulged. He pulled the dead match from his tightly closed lips, then leaned over the quicksilver.

With a mighty breath, he exhaled a snowstorm.

Fog rolled across the bench as the heat of the match had been magically transformed into its opposite. Aubrey had not merely conjured a slight chill, either. This was arctic.

Aubrey reached out with a knuckle and rapped on the mercury. 'Good.' He looked at his knuckle and the piece of skin he'd left on the surface of the mercury. 'Ah.'

George held up two pairs of leather gloves. 'You'd better use these.' Fog puffed around his words.

'You too, George. We'll both need them. Now, Caroline, can I borrow your diamond brooch?'

He admired her for the way she simply unclipped it and handed it over. He knew the memento from her father was precious.

He reached out and used the brooch to score a straight line across the middle of the hardened mercury. His breath steamed over the metal as he took one edge. He grunted at its weight, but managed to lift it.

The mercury snapped cleanly in two. 'We now have two mirrors.'

'And what for?' Caroline asked.

Aubrey handed back her brooch. 'A mirror trap, to catch our shade.'

Caroline looked at the two mirrors. 'Perhaps you could have found something in this workshop. After all, Father was not without skill in matters magical.'

Aubrey grimaced. 'I know. I had the highest respect for your father. But blundering around in this workshop would be like trying to use a candle to find a length of fuse in a room full of high explosive.'

She considered this. 'You could be right.'

Aubrey wasn't prepared for how this nod of approval made him feel, as if his heart had given a small, definite hiccup.

He straightened, brought himself back to the task at hand, and looked at George. 'Ready? Time to apply the Law of Sympathy to the notebook. The phantom George will appear as if it has the professor's book, and I'm sure it's been set on guard for just that eventuality.' *And such interest makes me very, very curious about the contents of that notebook, too.* 'When the shade attacks, we have to manoeuvre so that we catch it between our mirrors. Gloves on, George.'

Even through the thick leather, Aubrey could feel the cold bite of the mirror's edge. He looked up at the shade, then he muttered the remainder of the spell that would precipitate the Law of Sympathy.

Slowly, the phantom George reached for a notebook that was suddenly larger and more dog-eared. The cover had a purple stain and the binding was frayed.

'Father's book,' Caroline breathed.

A blur of movement cut through the air and the top third of the hatstand toppled to the ground. The phantom George stood there, unfazed, lifting the false notebook to its face.

'Now, George!' Aubrey shouted.

The shade was buzzing in a tight circle around the hatstand, a vicious whirlwind, trying to slice the phantom George to pieces. An angry hissing came from the creature as it met little resistance.

Aubrey strained and lifted his sheet of mercury, gritting his teeth at the weight of it. He shuffled until he was about six feet away from the shade. The mirror was heavy and cold, and he had trouble keeping it upright. 'George! Trap it between my mirror and yours!'

He peered around the edge of the mirror and saw that George was in position. He began chanting.

The syllables were long, convoluted and scraped on his already raw throat. The pain in his legs grew worse and his arms started to tremble with the weight of the mercury.

'Good Lord!' George exclaimed. An angry hissing went up. 'It's trying to get out, Aubrey!'

Aubrey couldn't see, but his mirror was suddenly buffeted, as if something had been flung against it. 'What's happening, Caroline?'

'The shade is flying from side to side,' she said calmly. 'Like a rat caught in a drain. Hold fast, George.'

'I am.'

Aubrey crouched behind his mirror and felt another blow. The cold was eating its way through his gloves.

'It's flying faster,' Caroline described. Her voice was dispassionate and clinical, as if she were describing a tennis match. 'I'd say it's frantic. It tried escaping the bounds of the trap but it behaves as if it's been caged. The phantom George has collapsed and the hatstand has been reduced to splinters.'

The hissing and the buffeting began to lessen.

'Aubrey?' George called. 'Are we done?'

'It's gone,' Caroline reported.

'George,' Aubrey called. He longed to rub his temples to soothe the pounding inside his head. 'Bring your mirror over here. Don't look into it.'

Caroline guided George with a firm, clear voice. 'A little to the right, George. Two paces forward. A small one. Good.'

'George.' said Aubrey. 'When we fit the two mirror faces together, can you take both and hold them together? It will be heavy.'

'I'll manage.'

Aubrey held up his mirror, guided by Caroline. For an awkward moment, he and George fumbled, but the two mirrors finally came together with a heavy *click*.

'Good,' Aubrey said. 'Place them on the bench.'

George shuffled over and eased the mirrors onto the bench. He stood back, removed the gloves and blew onto his hands.

'They've fused,' Caroline said.

There was no crack separating the two sheets of mercury. They had merged into a single, shining slab.

'And that's the mirror trap,' Aubrey said. He leant heavily on the bench. Despite the cold radiating from the mirror, he was sweating. 'But there is one last thing I must do.'

With a sigh, he turned to look around the workshop. 'Perfect,' he said and took a hammer out of a box of woodworking tools. He fumbled a piece of chalk out of his pocket and inscribed a symbol on the face of the hammer.

When he struck, the merged mirrors shattered like glass.

'Now, all the pieces go back into the quicksilver bath. When it melts it will be simple mercury again.'

George put the gloves back on and hurried to gather the fragments. 'The shade?'

'Is gone.'

Fourteen

AUBREY'S TIRED GAZE FELL ON A STOOL NEAR A RACK of cogs. He hobbled over to it and sat down. 'Caroline,' he said, and he was pleased to hear that his voice wasn't trembling. 'Your father didn't say where he kept his notebook? It has to be somewhere near, otherwise my spell wouldn't have been able to make George's notebook look like your father's.'

'No.'

He scanned the cluttered workshop, still trying to get some of the cold out of his bones. *Where would the professor have kept a notebook?*

He got up and lurched around between the benches, his hands behind his back. 'Now,' he said, 'a notebook is a working tool, something that should be close at hand for reference or for addition, correct?'

George was looking in a wooden cabinet. He grunted.

Aubrey went on. 'And — forgive me, Caroline — the

professor didn't know he was going to die so suddenly, did he?'

'No,' she said, her face set.

'Then I'd say that the notebook would be accessible for the next time the professor needed it, no?'

Caroline smiled crookedly. 'While this may be obvious, I'll grant your point.'

'Thank you.' Aubrey came to the main workbench in the middle of the space. 'We do know what our missing notebook looks like, from our work with the Law of Sympathy and the phantom George.'

'Large, foolscap size at a guess,' George said. He held up a tobacco tin and examined it. 'Brown cover with a purple stain.'

'So we'll recognise it once we see it.'

'Naturally,' Caroline said, with a touch of asperity.

'So we're looking for something that isn't in sight and something which, on the other hand, should be readily accessible.'

'A paradox,' George agreed. He'd discarded the tobacco tin and had found a receipt book, which he was leafing through with some interest.

'Not entirely,' Aubrey said. 'George, come and stand here, at the main workbench.'

The main workbench was bare. The wood was dark, heavily scarred in some places where it looked as if heavy equipment had been dragged. Other scratches, score marks and stains showed that this bench had been the scene of much activity.

Aubrey stood back. 'Stand in the middle, George. A little to your left. Just so.' Aubrey motioned to Caroline. 'Come here, if you please, Caroline. Would you say George is of approximately the same stature as your father?'

Caroline studied George, tilting her head to one side. 'Father was perhaps taller, but only slightly.'

'Your father was left-handed, correct?'

She narrowed her eyes. 'And how did you know that?'

'No mystery there. At the shooting weekend, I saw him with the gun up to his left shoulder.'

She nodded.

'Excellent. Now, George. Can you stretch out your left hand, towards the end of the bench.'

'Of course.' As he reached out, he jerked his hand back, his eyes wide. 'Good Lord! Something's there!' He squinted. 'But I can't see anything.'

'I think we've found it,' Aubrey said. His head was pounding, but he smiled nonetheless.

'It's not a book, Aubrey,' George protested. 'The shape I felt was hard, like metal.'

'Of course. What good would an invisible book be? It's probably in an invisible box or cabinet.'

'Ah.' George fumbled around. 'Here.'

George's hands went through the motions of tipping back an invisible lid. Suddenly, the interior of the box was revealed. There, sitting snugly, was the notebook.

Aubrey opened the book at random. 'Let's hope this can answer some of our questions.'

The pages were filled with the professor's spiky hand-writing, much crossed out and added to, with many different colours of ink. Aubrey stared when he realised that the page he was looking at dealt with death magic and the forbidden Ritual of the Way, but it soon launched from this into a bold new theory on existence itself, before breaking off into an arcane but brilliant set of jottings about the nature of magic.

I can use this, he thought, gripping the book. *It could*

help me step back, return me to the true land of the living.

Suddenly, his neck began to prickle. He felt deep unease in his stomach and his eyes grew wide. He was horrified at what he was doing.

Aubrey dropped the notebook. He put his hands to his face and moaned – then stifled the sound, afraid that it would bring the attention of this place on to him. He knew, with awful certainty, that he was being watched. He'd had the temerity to take the book and creatures of vileness and unspeakable depravity had woken. Once they fixed on him, he was doomed.

Dimly, Aubrey heard whimpering. He cursed it silently, wishing it would stop before it drew *their* attention.

His only hope was that they might not see him. Small and insignificant as he was, perhaps their terrible regard would miss him. He might be able to hide in the mud and slime. He closed his eyes.

A small, frightened sound came from nearby. For a moment Aubrey wanted to open his eyes, take his fingers away from his face and see what it was, but he didn't dare. The cold, malignant gaze of the guardians had been aroused.

He huddled on the floor, bringing his arms over his head, making himself as inconspicuous as possible. His mouth was dry. His jaw ached as he clamped down on the scream that was trying to escape. His heart hammered so fast it threatened to burst from his chest. His hands were clenched in hard, painful fists.

No, he thought, with an effort. *It's a trick. Remember the Black Beast of Penhurst?*

Aubrey opened his eyes. With the strength of will he'd learned since he found himself standing on the edge of the true death, he turned away from the terror. Slowly, it began to recede. His heart started to slow, his fists unclenched. He still felt the terror, distantly, but he no longer wanted to shriek with fear.

It was magic working on him. Gritting his teeth, he noted that the terror had the same flavour as the terror that went with the Black Beast, but here it was closer and a hundred times stronger.

He stood. Panic beat down on him as if he were in a tropical downpour. He shook his head, refusing to give in to it.

A short distance away, Caroline and George were lying on the ground, their knees drawn up as they tried to hide themselves from the horror. Their eyes were screwed tight.

He walked over to them with legs that were heavy and unresponsive. 'George.'

His friend ignored him.

'George. It's all right. Come with me.'

Aubrey touched him on the shoulder. He screamed.

Aubrey stepped back, but George screamed again and lashed out blindly. Aubrey grabbed at him, but his friend shrieked and flailed, rolling along the floor, eyes still shut tight. He gibbered, moaning with fear.

Aubrey tried to subdue him, but George was lost in the grip of terror. He swung his arms and kicked, and it was only because his eyes were closed that he didn't connect.

George rolled over and tried to flatten himself against the concrete floor of the workshop. Aubrey leapt on his back to trap his arms by his side. George thrashed and tried to dislodge him, but Aubrey hung on.

Sobbing, George flung himself sideways. Aubrey threw out a hand to balance himself and he grinned when it touched rope.

Aubrey wrenched at the rope, dragging out a length. He threw it over George's head, slipping it down as his friend clawed at it. Aubrey used the opportunity to pass more loops of rope around his arms and shoulders. George tried to bite, heaving and throwing himself from side to side, but Aubrey eventually had him solidly bound.

Aubrey slumped against the wall, panting. *The things I do for you, George.*

His whole body was a source of pain, with his nose a particularly bright spot. Before he seized up entirely, he dragged George towards the door, passing the still whimpering Caroline lying on the floor.

Outside, the cool air was like a balm. Aubrey threw his head back. The stars looked down on him with astonishment. *It's night?* Aubrey thought, dazed. *We've been in there longer than I thought.*

He looked down. 'George, we're outside the workshop. I have to go back in and get Caroline.'

George opened his eyes. His gaze darted from side to side, but the panic was fading. He tried to shrug, but the ropes prevented him. He smiled, then grimaced. 'I think I'm about to be sick.'

Aubrey managed to untie his friend so that he could crawl to the gutter, then he looked away to give him some privacy.

'You'll be all right?' Aubrey asked when George had finished. He nodded and wiped his mouth.

Aubrey staggered back to the workshop and plunged into the miasma of terror.

This time, Aubrey had rope ready before he tackled Caroline. But when he touched her she slammed an elbow into his cheekbone, just below his eye. It made lights jump around inside his head. He reeled back and she was on him, hands outstretched like claws.

She wasn't as strong as George, but she was quicker and her blows were more calculated, even in her terror. He backed away, tripped, and she threw herself at him.

Aubrey rolled to one side and she hissed, missing him. She came to her feet, eyes wild, but she slipped and her head struck the corner of a bench. She slid to the floor insensible.

Chest heaving, Aubrey lifted her and stumbled towards the door, not too exhausted to marvel at the muscularity, the firmness of her body.

Then he remembered the notebook. He put her down and crawled to where he'd dropped it. He tucked it into his jacket and picked her up again, groaning as his head threatened to explode. Then he saw Caroline's hat, which had become dislodged during their struggle. It had fetched up under a bench. For an instant he was tempted to leave it there, but he thought better of it. Balancing his precious load, he felt around under the bench with his foot, eventually snagging the reluctant headgear. Then, with the hat on the tip of his shoe, he shuffled and staggered out of the benighted workshop.

Outside, he sagged at the knees, but managed to ease Caroline to the pavement.

He sat on the ground for a moment, head bowed, Caroline's hat in his hands. He looked up to see George staring at her. 'She hit her head,' he explained. 'She tried for my eyes, but I was just quick enough.'

'That's twice, you know, that she's been knocked unconscious grappling with you.'

Aubrey sighed. He hoped Caroline wouldn't resent it, but he had his doubts.

'What was it, Aubrey?' George said. 'What happened in there?'

Aubrey looked back at the workshop. 'Terror, George, a purer, more concentrated version of what we felt at Penhurst with the Black Beast. It's powerful magic.'

George was silent for a moment. 'Things were about to attack me. I thought I was going to die.'

'I'm sure Caroline felt the same. We were meant to be reduced to mindless, terrified wrecks.'

'I was. There was nothing I could do about it.'

'It works with primal fears, I'd say,' Aubrey mused. Caroline muttered a few nonsense words and lifted a limp hand. 'Things that haunt us all at some deep part of ourselves. Fear of ancient evil, of powerful things waiting to see us, to devour us.'

George shuddered. 'Enough, Aubrey.'

Aubrey nodded. 'I think she's regaining her senses.' He sighed. 'It probably used some of the professor's recent work. A concentration of emotion, a field triggered by our unauthorised opening of the notebook, designed to incapacitate us. I can see that the military would be interested in such magic.'

'And why weren't you affected by the terror?' George asked. 'Weren't you scared?'

Aubrey looked up at the night sky. 'I was. But once you've gazed on the face of death, ordinary fears don't seem to matter as much any more.'

Fifteen

AUBREY FELT BATTERED, WRUNG OUT AND BRUISED. HE ached all over. George and Caroline weren't much better. As soon as Caroline regained her senses and had the situation explained, all three of them shambled off, looking for treatment, rest and nourishment.

Caroline was irritated rather than grateful. She seemed, somehow, to think that the entire ordeal was Aubrey's doing and that it had been unnecessarily complicated. On top of this, she took the notebook into her keeping. Aubrey wanted it desperately, but he decided not to argue. He needed every ounce of his strength.

Aubrey struggled to stop wincing with every step. His muscles were stiff and all his joints felt as if they were filled with acid. He needed, more than ever, some time to rest. *Thirty or forty years' worth should be enough*, he thought.

They left the warehouses and factories behind and began to move through more populated streets. Houses were lit behind drawn curtains and the smell of cooking was in the air. It made Aubrey's mouth water, but his head pounded whenever he moved it.

Seeking distraction, his gaze swept across the building they were passing. It was a two-storey, red-brick establishment, large and square, stretching back from the street a good way. A small brass plaque near the front door – as would normally signify a doctor's surgery – announced that this was The Greythorn Society for Non-magical Fitness.

He stopped and stared. 'George, what did that advertisement in your agony column say?'

George and Caroline had walked on, not realising Aubrey had stopped, but George turned. 'What is it, Aubrey?'

'The agony column advertisement. The one I deciphered. It mentioned a fitness society.'

'Good Lord,' George said. He stared at the brass plaque. 'So it did.'

'Non-magical fitness?' Caroline said. 'Whatever can it mean?'

George shrugged. 'I suppose one could use magic to get fit. Aubrey?'

'One can use spells to increase muscle tone and endurance. It's illegal in sports, but there are enough private users to keep practitioners in business. Highly expensive business.'

'Non-magical fitness sounds much more wholesome.' George flexed his arms. 'Exercise, weights, things like that. You could join, Aubrey. It might help you with that cadet officer physical test.'

Aubrey ignored him. He was wondering why anyone would use a cipher in a newspaper to meet at a fitness society.

'What are you talking about?' Caroline asked.

George explained about Aubrey's failed cadet test, not sparing the embarrassing details. 'So,' he concluded, 'perhaps Aubrey should make some enquiries here.'

Thank you, George, Aubrey thought sourly. He braced himself. When faced with potential embarrassment, he had one strategy: march straight ahead and let the embarrassment fall where it would. He squared his shoulders, hiding the pain this caused him. 'Very well, George, excellent suggestion. The light's on, let's go inside.'

George gaped. 'You're serious.'

Aubrey opened the gate. 'Of course. Come on now, don't dally.'

'It's hardly the time,' Caroline said.

'Perhaps not.' Aubrey grinned, seized by the moment. 'But opportunity has presented itself.'

Once inside, they found themselves in a waiting room. Tall wooden chairs lined the walls. Their backs were militarily straight, the seats bare of such luxuries as padding. A clerk sat at a reception desk at one end of the room, while stairs led upward to what signs indicated were Meeting Rooms and Gymnasium.

'Gymnasium,' George pointed out to Aubrey. 'This is the right place. I hope they have a branch in the city.'

The clerk stared at them, pencil hovering in the air. He was short, lean, with greying hair. He was dressed in a white shirt and black waistcoat and his whole demeanour said that their appearance was not what he'd expected. He was surrounded by books and pamphlets. Shelves behind him displayed a collection of trophies and shields, mostly tarnished, none remarkable. 'Can I help you?' he said eventually.

Aubrey's burst of energy had deserted him. He lowered himself onto one of the chairs.

George glanced at Aubrey, then approached the reception desk. 'Your society, how does it work?'

The clerk didn't have a chance to reply. A door behind the desk opened and a dark figure emerged. Cadaverous, with a commanding profile, his face was unmistakable. He eyed Aubrey, George and Caroline coldly. 'Get them out of here.'

Caroline didn't move. 'Who are you? Why are you being so rude?'

Aubrey climbed to his feet. 'He's Craddock, head of the Magisterium.'

Caroline didn't look daunted. 'That's as may be. It doesn't mean he should be impolite.'

Craddock ignored them. He turned to the clerk. 'Green, get them out of here. Our targets should be here at any minute.'

'It's too late, sir,' Green, the clerk, said, pointing towards the window. 'The Holmlanders are coming up the path now. Our trap is working.'

'Tallis!' Craddock snapped. 'Remove these people!'

Aubrey was agog when Captain Tallis hurried down the stairs. What were the Special Services doing working with the Magisterium? What were *Holmlanders* doing here?

When Tallis saw them, he looked equally startled. He stared at Craddock.

'Hurry!' Craddock snapped.

Tallis gathered himself. 'This way. Up the stairs.'

'I don't see why . . .' Caroline began, but Craddock cut her off.

'Now. Deaths may result if you don't.'

Caroline stared at Craddock. Not with fear, Aubrey noticed. She seemed to be trying to remember every detail of his face, every line and every feature, saving it up for the future. She did this with a cool determination that made Aubrey promise not to cross her, if he could ever help it.

Caroline followed Tallis. George helped Aubrey up the stairs that led to a windowless corridor. Gaslights were spaced along the wooden panelled walls, but none were alight. The nearest door was marked 'Meeting Room 1'. Aubrey could make out three other doors before the gloom swallowed the rest of the corridor.

'Not the Meeting Room,' Tallis barked. He looked around, jerking his head from side to side. 'The gymnasium. Next door along.'

Tallis stood by the door and turned on the electric lights, exposing a vast space of well-sprung wooden floor. Tumbling mats were stacked at one end of the room and climbing frames covered three walls. Racks of weights and Indian clubs took up the other. Ropes dangled from the ceiling, while a solitary vaulting horse stood in the middle of the floor. On the other side of the hall, across the empty floor, was an exit door.

It looked every inch a gymnasium, but something about it made Aubrey uneasy.

He leaned against one of the climbing frames, clinging with one hand. He felt weak, as if he'd been ill for a month with a fever. The worse he felt, the more he felt the tugging on his soul. The more he felt this, the more his body deteriorated. Until he could rest, he was trapped in a cycle that was undoing him.

Struggling, he tried to decide what was wrong with the place. He turned his head slowly, trying to think through the pounding.

Then he had it.

'George,' he croaked, 'tell me what you smell.'

'Are you all right, old man?'

'Please.'

George looked askance, but took a deep sniff. 'Rope. Floor wax. That's all.'

'It's not a proper gymnasium,' Aubrey said. 'It hasn't been used.'

'How do you know?'

'It doesn't smell of sweat.'

Every gymnasium Aubrey had been in at school or elsewhere, no matter how old or how new it was, had had the indelible, ingrained smell of sweat underlying everything, sour and sharp. It was absent from this place – it was for show.

Voices came from below, raised and angry. Captain Tallis was immediately alert. 'Stay here,' he ordered. He left, shutting the door behind him.

'This way,' George said immediately. He took Aubrey's arm while Caroline darted ahead.

'Thanks,' he said as they tottered across the floor to the other exit. 'I know I'm being such a bore.'

'Never mind, old man. You'd do the same for me.'

Caroline was waiting for them on a landing outside the door. 'Here,' she said, pointing down the dark stairwell. 'Servants' stairs, most probably. I'm sure we'll come out near the back door.'

Just then, the sound of a pistol shot came from the front of the building.

'Hurry!' George exclaimed.

'Wait,' Caroline said. She stepped back into the gym. When she emerged again, she handed Aubrey and George an Indian club each.

Aubrey stared at it. 'It's the nearest thing to a weapon at hand,' she said and she brandished her own. She glanced at him. 'You don't look well.'

'I'll be fine,' he said, even though he'd slumped against the railing. His chest creaked as he breathed and it felt as if hot needles were being stuck between his ribs.

'I see,' Caroline replied, but her face said she didn't believe a word.

'We'll make it,' George said. 'But we shouldn't linger here.'

Another shot rang out, then another, then a fusillade of gunfire. Aubrey could hear at least three different firearms, then breaking glass and heavy footsteps, more gunshots, shouts and wordless threats.

Has the war started? Aubrey wondered, then George dragged him away from the door.

Caroline was already halfway down the darkened stairs. She went quickly, but stopped frequently to look ahead and listen for anyone in the vicinity. She'd lifted the hem of her skirt to allow easy movement, but hair kept escaping from the tight chignon on the back of her head. She batted it away, and Aubrey could see from the gesture that unruly hair was a long-time problem.

She led them to the ground floor which was, mercifully, in darkness. At that moment Aubrey heard footsteps overhead, a dozen or more heavily booted people running along the corridor. Loud crashes seemed to indicate bodies falling or being thrown against walls.

They set out along a corridor, past five doorways, two on one side of the corridor, three on the other. Aubrey paused at the third, which was open and full of wooden crates. 'A minute.' He stood straight and took a deep breath.

Caroline hissed with irritation as Aubrey lurched into the small room. 'What are you doing?'

Aubrey came back with a pamphlet. 'I couldn't leave without seeing what this society has to offer.'

Caroline stared at him. 'You're insane.'

Aubrey considered this. 'No, I don't think so.'

George snorted. Caroline turned and hurried towards the door at the end of the corridor. Aubrey grimly struggled after her, tossing his Indian club aside and stuffing the pamphlet into his jacket pocket. He was in pain, but determined not to lag behind.

The corridor led to a kitchen, lit only by a dim street lamp in the lane behind the house.

'Not used,' Aubrey observed before Caroline found the door to the outside. 'The kitchen,' he added.

He put a hand to the back of his neck. It was itching. He closed his eyes and felt a magical upwelling in the vicinity. He stiffened. 'Close your eyes!' he cried.

He saw Caroline turn, irritated, about to argue. George dropped his Indian club, leaped, clapped his hand over her face and dragged her to the ground.

A flash of brilliant light lit the night. Aubrey could see it through the hands he'd clamped over his eyes. It left red spots dancing in his vision.

'Is it safe, Aubrey?' George said after a moment.

'Yes, I think so.'

He looked up to see Caroline glaring at George. 'What was that?' she demanded.

Aubrey chose to interpret her question carefully. 'Magic. Someone upstairs has unleashed a spell.'

She narrowed her eyes.

'Aubrey knows what he's talking about,' George said.

'Doesn't he always?' she said.

'I beg your pardon?' Aubrey said, but she deflected this with an impatient hand and eased open the outside door.

The back garden was overgrown. In the darkness, trees and bushes loomed over shadowy shapes. Grass had swallowed up garden beds and was knee-high elsewhere.

George peered through the darkness. 'There's a gate in the back fence.'

'It will do,' Caroline decided.

A window broke overhead. They ran along the path through the jungle-like growth. Aubrey was startled to see that the shapes poking through the wilderness were rusty farm machinery: harrows, scarifiers, headers, ploughs. They looked as if they had been there for years.

They'd nearly reached the gate when Caroline glanced back. 'Hide!'

Together, all three tumbled behind the remains of an ancient seed drill. Lying on his stomach and peering through the rusty metal flanges and wheels, Aubrey looked towards the house in time to see figures pouring through the rear door. At that moment, a man leaped from a window on the first floor and landed on the back of another below. A third man ran around the side of the house and tackled two others. It rapidly became a melee.

The overgrown garden became a battleground. Men were brawling, standing toe to toe, trading blows, wrestling on the ground. Some had ripped palings off a fence and were belabouring each other. It was hard to say how many there were, but Aubrey guessed twenty, perhaps more.

A gun fired from a window on the first floor. In return, light suddenly erupted from a figure on the ground. It struck the window, sending glass into the air. In that glaring moment, Aubrey stared. The figure standing at the window was von Stralick, the Holmland spy. He cursed, blood pouring from the side of his head.

Von Stralick awkwardly lifted his pistol but before he could shoot again, a flock of tiny bats appeared from nowhere and descended on him, shrieking and clawing. He lurched backwards, still cursing, and disappeared.

'It's von Stralick,' Aubrey whispered to George.

'You're sure?'

'No doubt.' In the distance, Aubrey could hear police whistles. 'Best to get away from here.'

George looked at him. 'Can you run?'

'If I have to.' He took a deep breath. 'You first, Caroline. Can you get to the gate and hold it open?'

'Yes.'

She moved like a cat, slipping through the shadows, flitting between the skeletons of the farm machinery. She reached the gate and crouched by it.

'Ready?' Aubrey said to George, who nodded.

They went as silently as they could, crouching behind bushes, rushing across the gaps.

The gate opened onto a lane which, after fifty yards or so, took them back to the street. As they emerged from the lane, a dozen police officers were running towards the scene of the uproar, and a police van raced past. They turned and walked in the other direction, trying not to look as if they had just been involved in a desperate escape.

A few streets on, Aubrey took out his stolen pamphlet. He held it in the light of a street lamp.

'You've become a convert to physical excellence?' George asked him.

'No.'

He held it out. George took it and read aloud the large title: 'Darius Fitzwilliam: Friend of Holmland. Traitor to Albion.'

Sixteen

AUBREY WAS SEMI-CONSCIOUS, HALF-SUPPORTED BY George, as they staggered through the front doorway of the Hepworth house.

Caroline's mother stood just inside. She was still wearing the long, trailing robe and her hair was down. 'Where have you been?' she asked, but then she saw Aubrey. 'Bring him in here, into the parlour.'

The parlour was brightly lit by gas jets. Aubrey winced and shaded his eyes as he was helped onto the leather settee.

He felt as if he were falling apart. His joints were hot nuggets of pain and his head pounded. His soul gave small wrenches, heaving against its confinement. Each wrench was a wave of sickening agony.

Mrs Hepworth floated into his vision, which was blurry, with colour fading in and out. 'Here,' she said and held a glass to his lips.

He swallowed, coughed and pushed the glass away. 'Brandy?' he gasped.

'Yes.'

'Oh.' Aubrey closed his eyes for a moment, then he felt his face being bathed. He opened his eyes to see Mrs Hepworth holding a flannel. Behind her, George and Caroline were looking at him with expressions of concern.

'Better?' Mrs Hepworth asked.

'A little.' He didn't know if it was the washing, the brandy, or simply being able to lie down, but the thumping in his head had diminished. The light did not hurt his eyes as much.

While Mrs Hepworth turned away to talk to Caroline and George, Aubrey sought to gather himself. He made an effort to slow his breathing, and he felt his racing heart begin to steady. If he could steady his physical condition, he would be able to hold body and soul together, he was sure. But the spells he was relying on were losing their battle against the pull of the true death. He had to find a better solution.

He sat up. Mrs Hepworth looked at him. 'Now, what happened? Were you assaulted?'

Aubrey was impressed by her calm. She didn't seem unduly fazed by her daughter appearing out of the darkness with two dishevelled youths in tow, one of whom looked as if he were seriously ill, or beaten, or both.

'Not exactly,' he said. 'We managed to avoid that.'

Mrs Hepworth looked at George, who shrugged. Then she turned to her daughter. 'Caroline?'

Caroline was standing by the upright piano and had been working at her hair, removing her hat. She flung the hat at a table in the corner. It nearly knocked over a vase full of irises. 'Mother, we found Father's notebook.'

'I see.' She frowned. 'That explains a good deal. Come here, Caroline.'

Caroline sighed, but complied. 'Let me see your face,' her mother said. After a quick study, she frowned. 'You'll have a bruise on your cheek.'

Mrs Hepworth looked at George. 'You seem not to have suffered.'

'I'm well enough.'

'It was foolish going there,' Mrs Hepworth said. 'Lionel's protective spells always were efficient.'

Aubrey thought back to the terror that had swamped them; how small and helpless he'd felt. 'Efficient, yes.'

'But we still managed to get the notebook,' Caroline said.

'I thought it lost forever after your father died.' Mrs Hepworth turned away for a moment, but when she looked back her face was composed. 'You managed to penetrate the defences?'

'Not easily,' Caroline said. She sat in one of the armchairs. 'It was at some cost.'

She glanced at Aubrey and her mother followed the look.

'I see. Young Fitzwilliam, you have some of the magical arts about you?'

Aubrey nodded. 'I manage.'

'Don't be so modest,' George said. He addressed Mrs Hepworth. 'He's quite good in the magic area. Top notch. Has a few tricks up his sleeve.'

'George,' Caroline said. 'You're repeating yourself.'

'Sorry,' he said. He sat in another of the armchairs. 'It's been rather a dramatic day.'

'Indeed,' Mrs Hepworth said. 'And I think you'd best be staying here tonight. Have you eaten?'

'I beg your pardon?' George said, suddenly alert.

'Food, George,' Caroline said. 'I don't know about you, but I'm famished.'

At the mention of food, Aubrey's mouth suddenly filled with saliva. Visions danced in front of his eyes – plates laden with roast meat and vegetables, followed by rich puddings, jam tarts and orange ice. He dabbed at his chin, certain he was drooling.

'I'll use the telephone to inform your parents of your whereabouts. They're probably fretting at this very moment. They're staying here in Greythorn?'

'The Triumph Hotel,' Aubrey said.

'Of course.' She swept from the room.

Caroline sat on the edge of her chair and watched her mother leave. Then she turned to Aubrey and George. 'I'm glad you've been able to see my mother like this.'

'I beg your pardon?' Aubrey said.

'This is her usual self. You'd only seen her grieving, which isn't fair.' She pushed back her hair with an impatient grimace. 'This is the woman who has an independent existence, a famous painter, a free thinker. This is the woman my father married.'

For a moment, her grief rose to the surface. Tears came to her eyes and she wiped them away without sobbing. 'I miss him,' she whispered.

Aubrey fumbled for words, an unaccustomed experience for him. Everything that came to mind sounded inadequate and he had the sudden understanding that nothing would be sufficient. 'I'm sorry,' he said and that would be the best he could do.

WHEN AUBREY WOKE THE NEXT MORNING, IT TOOK HIM some time to remember where he was. The walls were painted a soft blue and an intricate geometric stencil ran around the room above the picture rail. The colours, the decorations were quite unlike Maidstone. For a moment, he lay and enjoyed the sun spilling in through around the artfully pleated drapes, grateful that he was seeing another day.

The door to the bedroom opened and George stood there. He studied Aubrey for some time. 'You look horrible,' he finally said.

'Ah. An accurate reflection of how I feel, then.'

'You're holding yourself together?'

Aubrey sighed, stretched and put his arms behind his head. 'I woke in the middle of the night and felt myself slipping. For an awful moment I felt as if I'd lost hold.' He paused, remembering. 'I was desperate enough to try something I hadn't tested.'

'I thought you were going to be more careful with magic after –'

'The accident. You're right. I said I would be more cautious. But I was on the edge of despair, George. I was fraying.' He rubbed his chin and the simple physical sensation was reassuring. 'I'd read about some work in bonding and unification magic. I cast a spell and it brought my body and soul together with more stability than I've felt since I dropped myself into this mess.' It was a relief, but Aubrey was not entirely confident. Even when he was speaking the spell, he felt the language was not precise enough. Elements of intensity and duration were *loose*, probably due to the poetic nature of the Ilmyrian language from which they were derived. He desperately wanted to work on a more modern language for such magic to eliminate such uncertainties. It was already on his list of things to do, and – mentally – he underlined it twice.

George shuddered. 'You succeeded, it seems.'

'Barely.' He yawned. 'Not the most restful night I've had.'

'That's what you need, I'd say. Rest.'

'Yes, I know. But there's too much to do to spend time resting.'

'I can see your headstone, old man: "But there are still things to do!"' George clapped his hands together and rubbed them. 'Stay here for a while, at least. I'll fetch you some breakfast. No servants here, you know. Mrs Hepworth doesn't believe in them.'

When George came back he was carrying a tray with porridge, toast, marmalade and a mug of milky cocoa. He also wore a bemused expression.

Aubrey sat up in the bed. 'What is it, George?'

'Breakfast. I said I'd get it for you, remember?'

He handed the tray to Aubrey, who sighed and tried again. 'Why are you looking so baffled, George?'

'Mrs Hepworth. She asked me to call her Ophelia.'

'It's probably her name, George. No need to be upset at that.'

'She's an unusual lady.' George sat in the only chair in the room. 'She asked about you. And your father.'

Aubrey chewed on some toast. 'I see. Anything in particular?'

'Just about what Sir Darius has been up to in the last few years. The way she spoke about him, I had the impression that she knew him well. Or had known him well. She seemed surprised when I told her about the way he'd lost the prime ministership. I don't think she follows politics very closely.' He stared at the ceiling.

The porridge was hot. Aubrey decided to let it cool. 'I see. So you're not the only one, then?'

George ignored the jibe. 'She was crying, Aubrey, when I was talking to her. Not outrageously, nothing like that. Tears simply kept coming to her eyes and rolling down her face. She hardly noticed.'

'She's still grieving. She's lost her husband.'

George was silent for a time. 'We all grieve in different ways, I suppose.' He stood. 'I'll see you downstairs. Bring your tray when you're finished.'

Aubrey sipped his cocoa. *George*, he thought, *you still manage to surprise me.*

Some time later, he dressed and took the tray down to the kitchen only to find Caroline dipping toast into a boiled egg.

'Sit down, Aubrey,' she ordered. 'I need to talk to you.'

'Ah,' he said. He looked for George, but his friend was nowhere to be seen. He busied himself with unloading the tray and placing the dishes in the sink. He took as long as he could, hoping someone would join them and forestall what promised to be an inquisition.

Caroline finished her egg and waited. Aubrey finally gave up and sat across the table from her. 'All done?' she said.

'I think so. Your mother was kind to let us stay.'

Aubrey found that he was admiring the way she'd arranged her hair. It hung in soft curls around her ears.

'It was all we could do, after your efforts.' She leaned forward. 'And how are you?'

'Oh, well enough. A little tired, but that's to be expected after running into such powerful magic. Difficult stuff, that. Still, I think we managed quite well.'

'Mmm.' She looked at Aubrey. 'You're babbling.'

'Babbling?'

'I'd say you're trying to cover up something.'

True, Aubrey thought, *but I usually do a better job than this.* 'I'm not sure what you mean.'

She pursed her lips. 'I see it a great deal. It tends to come from men, usually when they feel as if they're being questioned on matters they really don't want to discuss. It's when they don't want to be rude to the questioner, but they wish they'd go away.'

'Ah. I was doing all that?'

'Yes. I don't think it comes naturally to you, though. You probably picked it up from the masters at your school.'

Aubrey grinned. 'Mr Grimsby, mathematics teacher. He's a very good babbler. He goes all red in the face, then if anyone laughs, out comes the cane.'

'Violence is the last resort of the inarticulate,' Caroline said, frowning. 'But all this isn't really telling me what I want to know.'

'About me?'

'No. Not exactly.'

'Oh, you want to know about my father, the great and famous Sir Darius Fitzwilliam? Do you know how many times people have accosted me about him? It gets tiresome.'

'No, I don't want to know about your father. I want to know about your mother.'

'My mother?'

Caroline's eyes were bright. 'She's a wonder. Her work with the birds of paradise is a landmark. She has shaped modern taxonomy more than any single person alive. Her expeditions have broken new ground in natural history.'

'Well, yes, there is that . . .' Aubrey groped for a witty or earnest contribution, but failed. 'She's very busy,' he finished lamely.

'Busy? Lady Fitzwilliam has had to work twice as hard – *three* times as hard – as others in her field. Other *men*. She's been passed over for grants from the Royal Society and the Explorers Association. All her fieldwork has had to be paid for out of her own pocket.'

Aubrey sat back in his chair. 'You're a Suffragette.'

'Of course. What intelligent, reasonable person wouldn't be? Why shouldn't women have the vote?'

Aubrey had never really considered anything else. With his mother as an example, he was confident that if women could contribute to government, Albion would be a better place.

He did, however, have trouble with the more outrageous actions by the Women's Social and Political Union. Marches, hunger strikes, interrupting political meetings, generally agitating, seemed a messy way to get one's point across. Inefficient, somehow.

Of course, looking at Caroline, he quickly decided that if one belonged to a part of society that had been systematically excluded from power, the only courses of action may be inefficient ones.

'Aubrey?'

'Sorry,' he said. 'I was just thinking. Women voting? Of course. They should have had the vote a long time ago.'

'Well.' Caroline looked mollified, but she still regarded him with narrowed eyes. 'What have you done about it?'

'What have I done about getting women the vote?' He blinked. 'Me, personally?'

'And there lies the problem. I'm sure there are many well-meaning, reasonable males out there like you, Aubrey, who have never considered what they could do to right an age-old wrong.'

'I'm sure.' This conversation had taken a turn in a direction Aubrey hadn't anticipated. It was disconcerting to be cast adrift like this. He tried to strike out in a new direction. 'What have you done with the notebook?'

'I have it safe in my room. Father gave magical strong-boxes to both mother and me, for our valuables. It's well protected.'

'I don't doubt it.'

Caroline studied him for a moment. 'Your parents should be here any moment. Mother rang them last night, and again this morning.'

'I doubt they'll come,' Aubrey said. 'They're most likely to send a driver to fetch us.'

'Surely not.'

'They're both busy people.' He paused. 'Is that the door?'

Aubrey's pessimistic prediction was correct. Mrs Hepworth stood at the front door talking with Stubbs, the driver, and George.

'Thank you, Mrs Hepworth,' Aubrey said when she turned at the sound of their footsteps.

'Ophelia, please. I've managed to get George to use my name, and insist that you do too.'

Aubrey could see that her eyes were red. She noticed his regard. 'It will pass,' she said. 'The sorrow, the grieving. The loss, though, that's another thing.'

She turned away. Caroline put an arm around her shoulders.

Aubrey and George left.

In the motorcar, Stubbs informed them that Sir Darius had been summoned to a hastily arranged meeting at the nearby Grover Hotel. Lady Fitzwilliam had taken the opportunity to visit someone at the university. 'Something to do with birds,' was Stubbs's summation of the purpose of this visit.

The outcome was that, once back at the hotel, Aubrey and George had the rooms to themselves.

Aubrey threw himself on the chaise longue and draped an arm over his face. 'I want to sleep for a century or two.' He lay there for a moment. 'It was a near thing last night.'

'We'd still be trapped in that workshop if not for you.'

'Not just that. I barely hung on, just before dawn.' Aubrey put both hands on his face. His voice became muffled. 'I could feel myself going. It was as if I were turning to smoke and being blown away.'

'Perhaps it's time to seek help, old man.'

'No,' he said sharply. 'This is my struggle. I'll manage it.'

'No-one will think the less of you.'

'No? Not even when I explain what caused this sorry state? How my own stupidity and bravado caused this? Imagine the glee with which Father's enemies would leap on such a thing.' He dropped his hands and looked at George. 'I'm afraid I'm on my own.'

'I'll stand by you.'

'I know. I appreciate it.'

Embarrassed, George turned away. 'Rest. You need it.'

Seventeen

*T*HE NEXT DAY, THEY WENT BACK TO THE CITY. AUBREY felt tired, but his condition seemed steady. George sat with his omnipresent newspaper, alternating between chuckling and tsk-tsking. Aubrey's parents were quiet as the motorcar rolled smoothly down the highway, which suited Aubrey. However, he couldn't help wondering at their silence. His father spent most of the journey staring out of the window and frowning. His mother seemed impatient, her hands never remaining still, tapping on the door or on her bag. With every halt, she clicked her tongue and looked through the window for the source of the delay.

Aubrey rubbed his face with both hands and yawned. Tired, but not dangerously so. His brief contact with Professor Hepworth's notebook had prompted thoughts in new directions, and he had a burning desire to look more deeply into amalgamation as a possible solution, or even some sort of spiritual barrier to prevent the true death from taking him.

Then there was the mystery of the death of Professor Hepworth and the attempt on the life of Prince Albert. Aubrey was convinced there was a link between them, and the presence of the deadly guardian in the professor's workshop added another element to the mix. Who put it there? Was it the same person who had sent the golem after Prince Albert? Or another player in this complex game?

On top of this was the extraordinary confrontation between the Holmlanders and the unheard of collaboration between the Magisterium and the Special Services.

Shadowy figures were at work, indistinct and ominous. Aubrey wished for a bright light to throw on them, to make them all stand out where he could see them.

With so many things to think through, so many challenges in front of him, time was a precious commodity.

So he fell asleep.

They arrived at Maidstone after midnight. Aubrey woke as they glided through the gates, stayed awake until he entered his bedroom, then fell into a dreamless slumber.

THE NEXT MORNING, AUBREY OPENED HIS EYES AND GROPED for his pocket watch on the cluttered bedside table. It was just after eleven o'clock.

He bathed. Then, as he brushed his hair, he looked in the mirror. *Not too bad*, he thought as he studied his reflection.

His skin was pale, but no paler than usual. His eyes weren't dull, for which he was grateful. They did have dark circles under them, but that was the only evidence of strain that he could see.

On the way out of his room, he saw his jacket, thrown across an armchair. He took the pamphlet he'd snatched from the Society for Non-magical Fitness out of the pocket, smoothed it out and stared at the crude lettering that accused his father of being a traitor.

He wondered how it fitted in. He felt as if he were adding another thread to a tapestry where the overall design was hidden from him.

Aubrey hurried down the stairs just in time to run into his father. Sir Darius stood inside the front door, handing his hat and cane to Harris, the butler.

Sir Darius studied Aubrey for a moment, concern struggling with his customary reserve. 'You've slept late.'

'Sorry, sir,' Aubrey said stiffly. He tugged at the bottom of his jacket and straightened his tie.

'You're missing half the day, this way,' Sir Darius said. He turned to the butler. 'Harris, I need a light lunch as soon as possible. Once you've told cook, please make sure the library is arranged for a meeting. Five people.'

'Yes, Sir Darius.' Harris hurried off.

'Sir?' Aubrey said.

'Yes?'

'I have something you should know about.'

He gave the battered pamphlet to his father.

Sir Darius held it at arm's length between his thumb and forefinger, as if it were infectious. '"Darius Fitz-william, Traitor to Albion." Where did you get this?'

Aubrey hesitated, then responded with caution. He avoided recounting the sortie to Professor Hepworth's workshop and concentrated on the battle at the Society for Non-magical Fitness. Throughout, Sir Darius remained silent.

When Aubrey finished, he pointed at the pamphlet. 'You've seen it before, haven't you?'

Sir Darius's mouth was set in a grim line. He folded the pamphlet in half. 'I've seen others like it. My reputation is under attack.'

Red, green and blue light was pouring through the stained glass panels around the front door. Sir Darius was outlined against it. Aubrey could see strength in his face and the way he stood. But could such strength stand against attacks like these?

'That's happened before,' Aubrey said.

'Yes. It should get easier to bear, but it never does. When these times come, I always find that some I thought were friends disappear.' He smoothed his moustache.

'They're not true friends, then.'

Sir Darius nodded and smiled crookedly. 'They're political friends. Remember the Scholar Tan? "Political friends are enemies in waiting."'

'But who do you think wrote this pamphlet? And why?'

'Come now, Aubrey. I'm sure you can think of possible suspects.'

Aubrey had thought, ever since he picked up the pamphlet. 'The obvious answer is the Royalists. If they can sully your reputation, the Progressives' chance of winning the election will take a battering.'

'Good, but who else?'

'The Holmlanders. You're well known as being anti-Holmland. If they can disgrace you, it weakens Albion and makes us vulnerable to Holmland plans.'

'It would be ironic if it were the Holmlanders, if their way of disgracing me is to say I'm their ally. No, I think this plan is too subtle for the Holmlanders. They'd try to libel me some other way.'

'Who else?'

'Who indeed? I have many enemies. I'm afraid I'll just have to keep my wits about me.'

'Who's coming to the meeting?' Aubrey asked suddenly.

Sir Darius seemed to weigh up his response. 'The Prime Minister rang, saying he wanted to see me. He's bringing Craddock, our esteemed head of the Magisterium, and some others.'

'What could they want?'

Sir Darius held out the pamphlet. 'I asked myself the same question. After seeing your pamphlet and hearing of your escapade last night, I think I know.'

AUBREY TOOK LUNCH WITH HIS FATHER, THEN FOUND George reading his newspaper in the conservatory and together they went up to his room.

It was no coincidence that Aubrey's room overlooked the front of the house. He'd chosen it for its direct view of the entrance and the great curved driveway. From any of the three arched windows, he could see who was coming and who was going.

Maidstone was mostly fifty years old, extensively rebuilt at the peak of the boom times. All the rooms were enormous and Aubrey's bedroom was no exception. His bed was neatly tucked into one corner, which left room for an assortment of furniture that he'd chosen. It was, naturally, an eccentric collection. Four overstuffed armchairs, a trio of potted palms that nearly reached the ceiling, a long low table with a glass top, several shelves that looked as if they'd once been shop counters, a gun cabinet that he used for antique wands (curios from the dark ages of magic), a folding table that he'd never got around to unfolding, a red velvet settee, three or four scattered ottomans, vases with dried arrangements of leaves and feathers, a large set of brass scales for weighing horses, and several paintings on the walls, some ugly, some not, but all of Aubrey's ancestors. 'The Starers', Aubrey had called them ever since he was a small boy, when he'd been half-fascinated, half-afraid of their imperturbable expressions.

Aubrey was seated at a large table in the middle of the room. The table was on an oval rug the colour of the sea. On the table was an untidy arrangement of books, pencils, inkpots and newspapers. For a whim, he was wearing an elaborately brocaded smoking jacket, a riot of purple peacocks and Far Eastern bridges. It had belonged to his grandfather.

'Sit down, George. You're making me dizzy, with your pacing like that.'

George went to the window. 'I wonder what the Prime Minister wants,' he murmured. A greengrocer's cart rumbled past the front gate, but apart from that the street was quiet.

'To discuss the events of last night?' Aubrey said without lifting his gaze from the newspaper he was reading. 'And the pamphlet, no doubt.'

'Hmm. Can you remember exactly what was in it?'

'Better than that. I copied it out before I gave it to Father.' He sifted through the paper on the table. 'Here.'

George crossed the room. 'Appalling handwriting, Aubrey. You need to do something about that.' He wandered back to the window and divided his attention between the pamphlet and peering through the gauze drapes.

'Rubbish,' he snorted. 'Rabble-rousers, the lot of them.'

'Yes, George?'

'Listen to this: "Sir Dandy Darius has betrayed us all! His speeches are nothing but a false front! His companies are working with the Holmland military might to crush the workers of Albion! He betrays us all! He grows fat on the blood and sweat of the ordinary working man!" What complete nonsense.'

'It's actually like a hundred pamphlets out there on the street. Did you notice the way every sentence ends in an exclamation mark?'

'But aren't you outraged?'

Aubrey frowned. 'You haven't seen many of these pamphlets before, have you, George?'

'I've seen plenty in the gutters with the other rubbish. Never read any.'

'They're all this passionate, this strident.' He tapped his pencil on the table. 'Sometimes I think they're a sign of the times. It's astonishing, really, the way technology has advanced. We now possess the means for everyone to write, print and publish their thoughts, their creeds, their cries for justice, their rants.'

'And just about every crackpot does.'

'True. But genuine social reformers use this method, too. It's a way of getting their voices heard. Sometimes, it can start a small ripple that becomes a great wave.'

'But this is poppycock! Your father hasn't colluded with Holmlanders at all!'

'Of course not. But whoever wrote this pamphlet has perfectly caught the flavour of pamphlet writers, the anger, the fire. It sounds genuine. People will listen.'

George frowned. 'You don't think it's real?'

'No. It's part of a plot to disgrace my father.'

'By whom?'

'That's what I want to know. And to help me sort out the possible perpetrators, I'm doing some research.' He poked at the piles on the table. 'I'm not simply reading these journals and newspapers for entertainment. I want to see what forces are at work. Care to help?'

George grimaced, but at that moment the grinding of gears and the crunch of tyres on gravel announced that a motorcar had arrived.

Aubrey came to the window in time to see a short, squat man with a dull bowler hat emerge from the motorcar. 'The Prime Minister looks happy,' he observed.

Sir Rollo Armitage was joking with the driver, who held open the motorcar door. His smile split his greying, muttonchop whiskers and made the pince-nez bounce on his nose.

Aubrey knew that his father had little respect for Sir Rollo. After all, Sir Rollo had been Deputy Prime Minister but had not supported Sir Darius during his leadership crisis. When Sir Darius had lost the prime ministership and was expelled from the Royalist Party, it was Sir Rollo who had assumed the position of leader – and had thus become Prime Minister without facing an election.

When Sir Darius founded the Progressive Party and rallied the huge range of disorganised groups together, it was Sir Rollo Armitage who became his greatest political foe.

The second man who emerged from the motorcar was

not smiling, even when Sir Rollo – apparently – repeated the joke.

It was Craddock.

He stood there next to the Prime Minister wearing his customary black suit and wide-brimmed black hat. Tall, spare, he stood with his hands behind his back, his gaze on the ash trees in the front garden. He stood remarkably still, as if he were balanced so perfectly that he could not be moved by earthly forces.

Aubrey wondered how a man could become feared. Was it by committing fearful deeds? Or was it by ordering others to do fearful deeds? Reputation may be enough, he decided, and he knew he didn't want to put this theory to the test.

Two more men alighted from the motorcar, the driver saluting them both. One was beautifully dressed in a grey suit and gloves, his homburg a grey of such an understated nature that it caressed the eye. He carried a brass-topped cane and his shoes shone in the sunlight.

'Phillips-Dodd,' Aubrey said, when he saw George frowning. 'The Home Secretary. In charge of the police, among other things. Loves his racehorses and the theatre and keeps his tailor very, very wealthy.'

'And who's the old fellow?' George pointed at the final member of the visiting party, an old man with a pointed beard. He looked about impatiently as the driver shut the door of the motorcar.

'Come now. Use your powers of observation.'

'Upright stance. Wearing boots. His hand is on his belt, feeling for something that isn't there. A sword?' George looked at Aubrey. 'He was a soldier?'

'Very good, George. He was General Arthur Codlington. Now he's the Minister for Defence.'

'I'd love to be a fly on the wall in that meeting,' George murmured.

Aubrey grinned. 'George, you know I hate to disappoint you.'

'I beg your pardon?'

'This way.'

Aubrey went to the long, glass-topped table. He dragged over a three-legged stool and motioned for George to do the same. 'I'll let you in on a secret,' he said and he wiped the tabletop with his sleeve. 'I've been in a few scrapes over the years.'

'That's no secret.'

Aubrey ignored this. 'Mother and Father always used the library to discuss what to do with me. Naturally, I didn't like to be left out of such talks.'

He placed the palm of his hand against the glass and muttered a few words. The tabletop clouded and suddenly it was like looking through a window onto a foggy day. Aubrey leaned over; the tabletop cleared and the fog was replaced by a bird's-eye view of a table, with five men gathered around it.

'My eye into the library,' Aubrey said. 'A novel variation on the Law of Transference, paying particular attention to the area of effect of the spell. It's very tightly contained so as not to draw any attention.' He tapped his chin. Some of the elements he'd used to shield the fly from magical detection were of his own devising; he'd never seen them used elsewhere. He wondered if the shielding aspect could be used to assist his condition.

'I say, old man, isn't this spying?' George looked troubled. 'It's the Prime Minister, Aubrey. It's not finding out what your Christmas presents are.'

'George, there's something going on here. I'm

involved. My father is involved. I won't sit around and be a spectator. If I wish to do anything, I must know what's going on.' He shrugged. 'It's a fine line between spying and intelligence-gathering.'

He tapped the tabletop with a finger. Voices swam up through the glass and Aubrey studied the scene.

One man at the table was still wearing his wide-brimmed black hat. Craddock. The Home Secretary and the Minister for Defence were sitting opposite each other. The Prime Minister's bald head and cigar were unmistakable. Aubrey's father was sitting upright, opposite the PM. His hands were clasped on the table in front of him.

'You have our every confidence,' the Prime Minister said in his fruity voice. It was the voice he used in public meetings and in Parliament. Aubrey had never warmed to it. It sounded too much like an actor from one of the less successful repertory companies.

The Prime Minister, before he entered Parliament, had been a very prosperous scrap metal merchant. His business background had made him perfect for the Royalist Party, with its belief that healthy businesses meant a healthy country and that anything that helped business was good.

He was widely admired as a self-made man. He was friends with the rich and powerful throughout the length and breadth of the land, but he was notorious as a hard customer, one who never forgot a slight and never failed to exact his revenge for it. His roly-poly exterior had led many people to underestimate him. All of them regretted it.

'Every confidence, Fitzwilliam,' the Prime Minister repeated. He waved his cigar at Sir Darius. 'Of course we don't believe the nonsense in those pamphlets. You? A Holmland sympathiser? Someone's obviously setting out to traduce you and to blame the Holmlanders at the same time. One of those agitator groups like the People's League or the Army of New Albion, most likely. They produce enough pamphlets to wallpaper the Palace!'

Sir Darius did not sound reassured. 'It would suit the Royalist Party if I were discredited.'

'Of course, dear boy, of course. But not like this! Shabby stuff, all round. Bad form.'

'So you'd be willing to denounce the pamphlet and its writers?'

The Prime Minister tilted his head and studied the cigar in his hand. He rolled it between his fingers and Aubrey could see that it was unlit. He lifted his head. 'If that's what you want, Fitzwilliam, I'd be happy to do it. Talk to the press, set the record straight, that sort of thing. Let everyone know that you're not a traitor.'

'I can hear it already,' Sir Darius said. He didn't sound as if he relished the prospect. 'I'll consider your offer.'

The Home Secretary spoke up. 'The police are at work, trying to get to the bottom of the situation but, I must admit, they're having trouble. They've been thwarted in their investigations as to who leased the property. They've stumbled into a maze of false names, empty companies and post office boxes, but it seems as if the place was a base for Holmlander espionage.'

'Special Services?' Sir Darius asked. 'Have they had any success?'

The Home Secretary waved a hand. 'A little. Tallis and his men are pursuing shipping records, consular movements and suchlike.'

The Minister for Defence growled a short, hard laugh.

'Bad lot, these Holmlanders. Below the belt, this. Underhand. I've never trusted them.'

Sir Darius turned to the black-hatted man. 'Your people? The Magisterium?'

Craddock cleared his throat. 'We've been working with Special Services. They handled the mundane matters, my people the magical. Naturally. Once Tallis's men had stumbled on to the organisation that the Holmlanders were using as a front, this Society for Non-magical Fitness in Greythorn, I swung in my magical investigators. They confirmed that powerful magic has been present in the building. Magic of a hitherto unknown sort. Unfortunately, all of the staff had disappeared and our ambush failed to capture any of the people who arrived later.' He paused. 'Your son happened to be there. I'd like to talk to him about it.'

'I know,' Sir Darius said. 'He told me of the events. It was the only way I found out about last night's debacle.'

Phillips-Dodd, the Home Secretary, smiled. 'We were going to let you know. Things became rather busy rather quickly, I'm afraid. The Holmlanders and whatnot.'

The Prime Minister jabbed his cigar at Sir Darius. 'I told you those Holmlanders had something under their hats. Put this with their machinations in the Goltan states and there's a bad smell all around. They're up to something, mark my words.'

'As I've been saying for some time,' Sir Darius replied. He crossed his arms on his chest. 'You'll speak against them while you're campaigning, then? We can have a united front against their aggression. It will force them to back down on the Continent, knowing we're united.'

The Minister for Defence pounded the table. 'Capital idea! Show them we won't put up with any of their nonsense! That's what we should have done after they sank the *Osprey*!'

The Prime Minister looked as if he'd bitten into an apple and found a worm. 'Fitzwilliam, dear boy, you know I can't do that. With the King so pro-Holmland, the leader of the Royalist Party can't come out suddenly and announce the party is anti-Holmland. Impossible, I'm afraid.'

The Home Secretary shook his head. 'Besides, this could simply be the work of some rogue elements in Holmland. I hear they have difficult groups of their own.'

The Minister for Defence snorted and glowered through his beard, but didn't speak against his colleagues.

Craddock held up a finger. 'One more item. We've reason to believe that some of the Holmlanders at this affair were also present at the royal shooting party, the attempted assassination.'

'Who were the Holmlanders at that disaster?' the Minister for Defence barked.

The Home Secretary had no notes but did not hesitate. 'We have our eye on von Stralick, one of their spies. He's disappeared.'

'Find him, will you?' the Prime Minister said. 'We need to speak to the fellow.'

'We're doing our best, Prime Minister.'

'Naturally, news of this won't become public,' the Home Secretary said, his voice as smooth as butter. 'Tallis and his Special Services men have seen to that. One of the newspapers had wind of what went on in that confrontation, but we've managed to bring some pressure to bear there. The managing editor's brother has some business dealings that the managing editor would rather not come to light. Needless to say, we've burned all those dreadful pamphlets.'

'I see,' said Sir Darius. 'To spare my reputation, you're going to cover this up.'

The Prime Minister sat back in his chair and tucked his thumbs in his braces. 'Don't mention it, dear boy, don't mention it. I know you'd do the same for me.'

'Some things the people don't need to know,' the Home Secretary said.

The Prime Minister jammed the cigar into his mouth, clasped his hands, put them on the table in front of him, and leaned forward. 'We don't want this sort of thing out there, do we? After all, with the election only a few weeks away, your party would be ruined by a resignation and the taint of scandal.'

'And you don't want that.'

'Of course not,' the Prime Minister chuckled. 'We aim to beat you fair and square, not through your party collapsing. It wouldn't feel right.'

'I see.' Sir Darius nodded. He stood. 'I'm glad you came, Prime Minister.'

'Don't mention it, Fitzwilliam. Only too pleased to help.'

The meeting broke up quickly after that and, after bidding the vistors farewell, Sir Darius sat down again at the table. He folded his arms on his chest, put his head down, and did not move. Then he tilted his head back and stared at the ceiling.

'He's going through the meeting again in his head,' Aubrey said to George. 'He's trying to work out what went on.'

George looked at Aubrey. 'What *did* go on?'

Aubrey wiped his sleeve across the tabletop. Clouds rolled across, then vanished and they were looking, once again, at a glass tabletop. 'I think the Prime Minister was enjoying his position immensely.'

'He did sound rather pleased with himself.'

'Why wouldn't he be? He has his greatest political enemy at a great disadvantage. He didn't come here to pledge support; he came here to crow.'

'And your father knows this? That's why he wasn't happy at the PM's offer?'

'Of course. The Prime Minister is master of the politics of deceit. Say one thing, mean another.'

'And this is the man who runs our country?'

Aubrey was silent for a moment. 'There are good people in politics, George, many of them, trying to do the best for everyone. Then there are those like Sir Rollo.' He sighed. 'Politics is dangerous, I think. Only the strong can resist being corrupted by the power.'

'I can't imagine why anyone would look for a career as a politician, that's certain.' George stopped. 'Oh. Sorry, old man.'

Aubrey shrugged. 'It's in the blood, George. It's either academia, politics or the military, and the military seems to be doubtful for me at the moment, with my condition.'

Of course, Sir Darius Fitzwilliam had managed to combine both careers, a voice nagged at the back of Aubrey's mind, but he put it aside.

'And what was Craddock doing there?' George asked.

'That's a puzzle,' Aubrey admitted. 'He's not the Prime Minister's man. At least, I don't think so. His motives aren't easy to guess.'

'Unlike yours at this minute.'

'I'm sorry, George?'

'You want to go out and find this Holmlander, this von Stralick.'

Aubrey grinned. 'You know me too well. Of course

I aim to find von Stralick. And, thanks to you, we have a means of doing so.'

'How so?'

'The Society for Non-magical Fitness. Craddock implied it was a Holmland sham. No doubt the Magisterium and the Special Services were trying to ambush the Holmlander spies.' He grinned. 'They said they'd stumbled onto the society, but we happen to know how they arrange their meetings.'

'The agony column code,' George said slowly.

'Precisely. All we need to do is wait until another meeting is planned via the agony columns and there we have them.'

'I suppose it would be too much to hope that you want to tell someone about this?'

'Whom can we trust, George? The Prime Minister? Craddock?'

'What about your father?'

'I can't tell him, George. Not right now. Involving him in this may compromise his position.'

'And having his son caught up with Holmland spies won't?'

Aubrey grimaced. 'You're right.' He got to his feet. 'I'll go and tell him now.'

'Would you like some support?'

Aubrey smiled. 'George, you're a marvel.'

When they entered the library, they found Sir Darius still seated at the table. He looked up as they entered. 'Well?'

'Sir?' Aubrey said.

'What did you think of the Prime Minister's performance? Perhaps you noticed something I didn't.'

Aubrey's stomach sank. 'I was up in my room, Father.'

'I know,' Sir Darius said. 'I also recognise your work when I see it.'

He pointed at the ceiling. There, directly above the table, was a fly. 'You were watching the entire meeting, weren't you?'

Aubrey searched for a plausible story, found none, stood straighter. 'Yes, sir.'

Sir Darius sighed. 'Sit. Both of you. Where I can see you.' He closed his eyes and pinched the bridge of his nose while they drew up chairs.

'I could have you both imprisoned for spying.'

Aubrey nodded. 'Yes, sir.'

'But I don't suppose that would stop you at all, Aubrey. In a few weeks you'd have organised the inmates into an amateur dramatic society which would put on an operetta climaxing in a mass escape.' He shook his head. 'And you, George, would be by his side, making sure no prison thugs damaged him, while reading the newspaper in between cornet solos.'

George opened his mouth and then closed it again.

'You let us watch the entire meeting,' Aubrey said.

Sir Darius lifted an eyebrow. 'I didn't see your blasted contrivance until after the meeting had ended. And I want it removed immediately.'

'Yes, sir,' Aubrey said, then added, 'I have something that may be useful to you.'

Sir Darius drummed his fingers on the table. 'It can wait. I need to consider an appropriate punishment for you. Leave. And take that damned fly with you.'

Aubrey stood and pointed a finger at the fly. It immediately detached itself from the ceiling and flew to his outstretched hand.

With the door to the library closed behind them,

George dared look at Aubrey. 'Well? What now?'

'I'd say we're left with no choice. We have to find von Stralick ourselves.'

THEY SPENT THE NEXT FEW HOURS EXAMINING NEWSPAPERS. After some time Aubrey thought that George must be mad. Reading the agony columns was, frankly, agony.

Having to read them all carefully and then test the coded messages one by one was brain-numbingly tedious. They found many codes, most so simple that a child could decipher them. Backwards writing, simple alphabet–numeral substitutions, shifted alphabet ciphers, and many more.

In the end, it was fruitless. They uncovered five liaisons, two assignations and something that sounded suspiciously like an elopement, but nothing that looked even remotely like a meeting of spies.

Aubrey sat back in the late afternoon light. The drapes were moving slightly with the breeze. Outside, blackbirds squabbled in the ash trees as a steam motorcar chuffed past.

'You know . . .' he said. He was sitting in a wicker chair with his feet on a small sailor's trunk. 'They might have abandoned the agony columns method of communication. They may feel as if it's been compromised.'

George flung the newspaper he was reading onto the table. 'Well, that would leave us in a state.' He stood and roamed around the room, hands in his pockets. The sound of hooves on the driveway drew him to the window. 'It's your mother, Aubrey. She's home.'

They found her in the drawing room. When she saw Aubrey she turned, put her hands on her hips, and glared. 'Aubrey, what have you done to this poor girl?'

There, behind Lady Fitzwilliam, stood Caroline Hepworth, looking partly embarrassed, partly cross and, Aubrey thought, wholly, undeniably attractive.

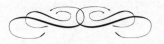

Eighteen

THE EVENING MEAL WAS A TENSE AFFAIR.

Both Sir Darius and Lady Fitzwilliam were not happy, and their attention was on Aubrey more often than not. He did his best to concentrate on his food, keeping what was for him an unusual silence. He wondered exactly how much trouble he was in.

He knew why his father was angry with him, but his mother's displeasure had come as a surprise. *No doubt the Scholar Tan would have an appropriate warning about being aware of the danger of an attack from the rear*, he thought gloomily as he sipped his soup.

His parents had obviously spoken before the meal, with the result that Aubrey was facing a united front. His time-honoured tactic of getting them to work against each other didn't look as if it would succeed.

He spent some time trying to imagine the length, severity and nature of the punishment that was no doubt coming his way.

Lady Fitzwilliam's mood hadn't affected her appetite. She attacked her meal, wielding her cutlery like a fencer with such precision that metal never once scraped china.

Sir Darius picked at his food and sipped from a glass of red wine.

Aubrey's grandmother was there, of course. Duchess Maria spent most of her time examining Caroline, directing thinly veiled questions at her regarding her family. She seemed aware of the tension in the room, turning her head from one side to the other like a bird. She soon realised that Aubrey was the centre of the unease. He knew that it wouldn't be long before she'd be trying to find out what he'd done wrong this time.

George ate with his usual appetite, but kept an eye on Aubrey, looking for cues.

Caroline, alone of everyone at the table, was poised, calm and equable. She sat between Lady Fitzwilliam and Sir Darius, as far away from Aubrey and George as it was possible to get. She seemed to enjoy the meal, but she ate slowly, so that they had to wait for her to finish her lobster bisque before the roast was brought out.

Talk was polite, but clipped, moving around Aubrey as if he were an island in the middle of a river. His mother and father directed most of their conversation to Caroline. After being introduced, Sir Darius had turned his most charming aspect to her, drawing her out of her reserve and engaging her with stories of mild parliamentary scandals.

Aubrey was impressed, all over again, at his father's charisma and the way he was able to win over Caroline. All his life, he'd seen his father do this sort of thing and wondered how he managed it.

When the meal had finished, Lady Fitzwilliam

wouldn't let Aubrey and George leave. She turned to the duchess. 'Maria, you may go. We have things to discuss.'

Duchess Maria picked up her glass of water and sipped, but when she put the glass back down on the table Aubrey couldn't see any difference in the level. She took her napkin and touched her lips. 'I'm quite happy here.'

Lady Fitzwilliam looked at her husband, then back at her mother-in-law. 'While you're always welcome, it may be awkward.'

'Pish! I've been involved in discussions that changed the course of history, ever since I was a little girl.'

Lady Fitzwilliam's eyes hardened. Her knuckles went white as she gripped her napkin. 'Very well.'

Aubrey watched this exchange closely, much as an observer on the heights would study the opening skirmishes of a battle. He cleared his throat. 'Perhaps Miss Hepworth should leave as well. I'm sure we can spare her this.'

'I don't think so, Aubrey,' said his mother. 'After all, we are talking about matters concerning her.'

Aubrey looked at his father. 'Sir?' he squeaked.

'Listen to your mother, Aubrey. And stop trying to think of ways to turn this to your best advantage.'

Aubrey nodded without saying anything. Sir Darius speared George with a glance. 'And George, we want you here so you can tell us what went on from your point of view. I'm asking you to be honest, young man. I know you're loyal to Aubrey, but at this time his best interests lie in your being straightforward.'

Aubrey tried to marshal himself. 'By all means, George, tell them what you know.'

George looked at the faces around the table. Aubrey wondered if his friend was considering making a sudden dash for the door. 'Err. About what?'

Lady Fitzwilliam rolled her eyes. 'About Aubrey's imposing himself on this young lady, of course.'

Aubrey felt as if he'd been hit on the head with a cricket bat. 'Imposing myself?'

'Lady Rose, what are you saying?' George blurted.

Aubrey looked at his father. 'Sir?'

Sir Darius held up a hand. 'We knew that Mrs Hepworth had kindly tended to you after that scrap at Greythorn, but it appears as if it wasn't the first time you'd bothered the young lady here. You've been visiting her while she was still in mourning, intruding on her solitary nature retreat at Penhurst and goodness knows what else.'

'Ah.'

Lady Fitzwilliam let out an exclamation of combined frustration and irritation. She crossed her arms and scowled.

Duchess Maria watched all this like a hawk. After a moment or two of further denials, questions and fragmented explanations, all accompanied by finger-pointing, hand-waving and table-thumping, she tapped her water glass with one of her rings.

The noise cut everyone short. 'Now,' she said. 'One at a time. Young lady, you first.'

Caroline glanced at Lady Fitzwilliam. 'I'm sorry, I didn't mean to imply that Aubrey imposed himself on me at all.'

'I've known him for a long time. I simply filled in the gaps in what you told me.'

Caroline flushed. 'He may have been a little forward . . .'

'And rude, and single-minded, and insensitive,' Sir Darius added.

'Well, yes, all of that. Some of that.'

Aubrey winced, but he didn't argue.

'But he was an enormous help. Both of them were.'

Lady Fitzwilliam sighed. 'When you appeared at the museum and began talking about my son, I thought you were complaining about him.'

'Why? Have many young women complained about Aubrey?'

Aubrey felt his face growing hot. He considered fainting, as a distraction, but decided the nightmare would continue regardless, over his prostrate body.

Sir Darius seemed to be deriving some dry satisfaction from his son's plight. 'Go on, Miss Hepworth. Why, then, did you go to the museum?'

Caroline seemed to find something extraordinarily interesting in her lap. 'I wanted to see Lady Fitzwilliam,' she said in a small voice.

'Me?' Lady Fitzwilliam said. 'Whatever for?'

Aubrey was dazed. He'd had a vague notion that, soon, he would introduce Caroline to his mother, seeing how much she wanted to meet her. Of course, Caroline would be grateful for this and their future would look much more promising than their bumpy beginning might have suggested.

Future? What am I thinking?

'Your work.' Caroline's voice was firmer and she lifted her head. 'You've done so much, you mean so much, I wanted to tell you . . .' Her voice trailed off.

Sir Darius began to say something, but Duchess Maria cut him off with a glance. 'Let the young lady speak, Darius.'

He subsided, still wearing the grim half-smile.

Caroline looked around and saw that she still had the floor. 'I wanted to talk to you. I wanted to know how you did it. Become famous, that is, and discover things, and do what you really want to do in life.'

Lady Fitzwilliam nodded. 'My dear, I think you and I have much to talk about.' She glared around the table. 'By ourselves would be best, I feel.'

'A moment,' Sir Darius said. 'What about Aubrey?'

Caroline smiled. 'George and he were rather kind, really. They helped me recover my father's notebook.'

Sir Darius straightened in his chair. 'Good Lord, you have Lionel's notebook?'

'Yes.'

Sir Darius stared at Caroline. 'Astonishing.' He turned to Aubrey with the clear gaze of a long-distance sniper. 'Professor Hepworth would have guarded any notebook of his. You overcame this protection?'

'Not easily.'

'I hope it's safe somewhere,' Sir Darius said to Caroline. 'Craddock was asking after that notebook, immediately after your father's funeral. Somehow he knew that Lionel and I were acquainted.'

Craddock! Aubrey thought. *That's what he was doing meeting Father at the Triumph Hotel!*

This news of Craddock's interest in the notebook was valuable information. The man who moved in the highest circles and the lowest, the man who spoke to princes, priests and pawnbrokers, the man who was privy to a thousand secrets. What part was he playing in these murky goings-on?

Aubrey felt chilled. Was it possible that Craddock had put the shade in the professor's workshop? He'd certainly have the skill for it.

'The notebook is safe enough,' Caroline said. 'I brought it with me.'

'Where is it?'

'In my bag. I gave it to your butler when I came in.'

Sir Darius rang the serving bell. Harris appeared. 'Harris, you took the young lady's bag when she came in. Go and fetch it.'

Harris's long face lost its impassivity for a moment. He blinked. 'I beg your pardon, sir?'

'The young lady's bag. Bring it here.'

'I'm sorry, sir, but I'm not sure what you mean.'

Sir Darius controlled his exasperation and spoke slowly. 'Miss Hepworth said you took her bag when she came in this evening.'

Lady Fitzwilliam said, 'You took my hat and wrap at the same time, Harris.'

Harris looked distressed. 'Sir, ma'am, miss, I was out in the back garden all afternoon, talking to the gardener about the cabbages. I asked Tilly to attend to anyone who came to the front door.'

'It wasn't Tilly,' Lady Fitzwilliam said flatly. 'You met and greeted us both. Are you all right, Harris?'

He nodded, looking more like a basset hound than ever.

'George,' Sir Darius said, 'be so good as to go to the cloakroom. Fetch Miss Hepworth's bag, please.'

George slipped out. Lady Fitzwilliam looked at Harris with concern. 'Harris, surely you remember. You asked if Miss Hepworth would be staying for dinner.'

Harris, a picture of misery, shook his head.

A shout went up from the front of the house. Sir Darius was on his feet and out of the door in an instant, with Aubrey close behind.

They charged to the cloakroom near the stairs to find George crouching next to a young, red-haired maid. She was lying insensible on the floor of the tiny room.

'Who is it?' asked Caroline, who'd joined them.

'It's Tilly,' Aubrey said.

Sir Darius and George picked her up and carried her to the parlour. She mumbled a little and cried out, but did not open her eyes. They placed her on the leather settee. 'Harris, fetch some water and ring for a doctor,' Sir Darius ordered.

Lady Fitzwilliam placed her hand on Tilly's forehead and then felt for a pulse at her neck. 'It's strong,' she said.

Duchess Maria sat quietly in a corner, her face fearful. Tilly had always been her favourite.

Aubrey gestured to Caroline. She frowned, but joined him outside the room. 'Let's see if your bag is still there,' he suggested.

The cloakroom fairly stank of magic. Aubrey's neck itched as if he had hives. He stopped Caroline from entering until he'd declared it safe.

It didn't take long to check for the bag. 'No,' Caroline said, her face bleak, 'it's gone.'

Aubrey was aware that they were standing very close together in the small room. He could smell Caroline's perfume. Lily of the Valley, he decided.

'You're sure?' he asked.

'Of course,' she hissed between her teeth. 'Now I have to get it back.'

She strode out of the room and back to the parlour.

Remarkable, Aubrey thought, and he followed her.

Sir Darius looked quizzically at them when they re-entered.

'Caroline's bag is missing,' Aubrey announced, 'and there's the taint of magic all over.'

TILLY RECOVERED TEN MINUTES OR SO LATER, JUST AS DR Snow arrived. She reported a thumping headache but no other after-effects; Dr Snow could find nothing wrong with her. Tilly could shed no light on how she came to be lying on the floor of the cloakroom. Harris summoned Maud, one of the other maids, and she took Tilly away to the servants' quarters, with Duchess Maria in attendance, declaring she'd make sure Tilly was well cared for.

Dr Snow was ushered out by Sir Darius and Aubrey. After he'd gone, Sir Darius tested the bolt and lock on the front door. 'I'll check all windows and doors tonight,' he said. 'It's been a long time since I've had to think about security like this.'

'Should you call the police?'

Sir Darius ran his hand along the leadlights on either side of the door. 'I don't think that would do much good. Anyone who can find his way into my house, take the appearance of my butler, and waltz off with property belonging to my guest would leave the police in a state of bafflement, don't you think?'

Aubrey had to agree.

'I'd send for the Magisterium, but . . .'

'You don't trust Craddock?'

Sir Darius nodded once, sharply. 'I have no reason to believe he's dishonest. Quite the opposite. Everything he does shows that he is absolutely incorruptible. And yet I can't forget that it was he who gave Rollo Armitage expert advice which resulted in my having to resign as Prime Minister. Naturally, this meant Armitage became PM in my place.'

'Thanks to Craddock.'

Sir Darius completed his inspection. He straightened

and smoothed his moustache. 'I think we're living in turbulent times, Aubrey.'

'Yes, sir.'

Sir Darius sighed. 'I wish your mother was due to go off on one of her expeditions. For once, I'd actually feel better if she were away.'

'I'll take care of her.'

'Of course you will.'

Lady Fitzwilliam and Caroline were sitting together on the settee when Aubrey and Sir Darius entered the room. George was in a low chair opposite. Lady Fitzwilliam looked up. 'Well, Aubrey,' she said, 'Caroline has done her best to restore the reputation of both George and you.'

He bowed to Caroline. 'Many thanks.'

Lady Fitzwilliam relented and gave a half-smile. 'I'm glad to see you can remember your manners. Now, I'm going to get Stubbs to drive you home, young lady.'

'What about my bag, my notebook?' Caroline said.

Sir Darius stood, hands behind his back. 'If you agree, Miss Hepworth, I think the only way to proceed with this is for a bold stroke which may flush out our enemies, whoever they are.'

'Darius?' Lady Fitzwilliam frowned.

'I'm going to go to Darnleigh House to see Craddock in his own headquarters. Tomorrow.'

'Darius, no!' Lady Fitzwilliam was on her feet and at her husband's side in an instant.

'I've been there before, Rose,' he said gently. 'I'll be all right. There are a few matters I need to put before the Magisterium, I think.'

'Telephone, send a letter, summon them here.'

Sir Darius's smile was wintry. 'No, I don't think so.'

He looked at Aubrey. 'What did the Scholar Tan say about fighting a battle against an enemy in fog?'

Aubrey knew this one well. 'When fighting a battle against an enemy in fog, either move the enemy, move the fog, or move the battle.'

'And I,' said Sir Darius, 'am about to move the battle.'

Nineteen

AUBREY SLEPT WELL, DESPITE THE EVENTS OF THE previous evening, and it was a relief. He realised it was Sunday, but decided not to go to church. He wandered downstairs to the conservatory and out into the garden. The sky was a cheerful blue, entirely untainted by clouds. The leaves on the enormous rhododendron beside the door were still, not a breath of breeze disturbing them. Sunlight was soft on the irises, the daisies, the fuchsias. The air was alive with growth, carrying a thousand floral and vegetative scents. It was a morning where nature itself seemed to be holding its breath in wonder at the perfection it had wrought.

Aubrey stood there a moment soaking it in. *This is another reason I don't want to die the true death,* he thought.

He stepped back inside and closed the door, leaving the lingering golden morning to itself.

Breakfast was in the conservatory, to make the most of

the glorious day. Tilly was setting out chafing dishes.

'How are you, Tilly?' he asked.

She jumped a little, not having seen him approach. She was a tiny thing. 'Well enough, sir, thank you for asking.'

'No headache any more?'

'No, sir. Thank you, sir.'

She hurried off, nearly bumping into Maud, who was coming the other way from the kitchen, armed with a large canteen of cutlery.

A few moments later, Aubrey was the solitary figure at the table, enjoying a plate of scrambled eggs and bacon. He had just concluded that the eggs were excellent, if in need of a touch more pepper, when George dashed through the door, waving a newspaper over his head.

'Aubrey! The code! It's here!'

He thrust the newspaper under Aubrey's nose and jabbed a finger at it. There, halfway down the right-hand column, was an advertisement consisting solely of familiar gibberish. Aubrey saw the patterns in an instant. He dropped his fork on the plate with a clatter, stood, threw his napkin on the table and grabbed the toast rack. While George stared, Aubrey slipped a butter knife into the pocket of his shirt and jammed a pot of black–berry jam in his trouser pocket. He handed George the butter dish. 'We may need nourishment while we work. To my room.'

AFTER AN HOUR AND A HALF, AUBREY THREW HIS PENCIL on the desk and crossed his arms. His head ached. 'There.' He held out the deciphered message.

George had been cutting articles out of past issues of the newspaper, concentrating on anything to do with Holmland. He put down the scissors. *'The burnt church the Mire midnight,'* he read.

'Clear enough, I'd say. They must be confident that their cipher hasn't been broken.'

George frowned. 'The Mire at midnight. I'm not happy about that.'

Every city of large enough size has a place like the Mire, a quarter where the police patrol in pairs, if they go there at all. The Mire was a squalid district, squashed between the vast Newbourne railway yards and the river, full of crooked streets, foul miasmas and short lives.

Aubrey had a different opinion of the Mire from most. He'd been fascinated by its dark energy and over the last few years had taken to spending time there, suitably disguising his background and identity. Using his experience in the theatre, he had created a street persona as Tommy Sparks, a petty thief and procurer of stolen goods. Once he put this on, he was able to move freely around the Mire and found it a useful source of information. At first, he was surprised at who visited the place, but soon realised that the high and mighty used it for their own ends. His experiences had confirmed that there were many wrongs to be righted in Albion, much that was hidden from the law-makers. It made him more determined to enter the world of politics when he was able.

'The burnt church?' George grumbled. 'I didn't know there was a church at all in the Mire.'

Aubrey grinned. 'Now, George, you're being rather prim. It has churches — and the churches have worshippers, too, in case you were wondering. They're ordinary people in the Mire, despite what you've heard, just like you and me.'

George shrugged. 'But what is this burnt church the message mentions?'

'Most of the Mire is low-lying, near the river, hence the name. There is one hill in the Mire. More of a rise than a hill, really. A few centuries ago, when the Mire was different from how it is now, there was a cathedral. St Agnes' Cathedral.'

'A cathedral in the Mire? I don't believe it.'

'You wouldn't know it now. The church burnt down last century, completely destroyed, just ruins and scattered stones.'

'No-one's taken the stones? You'd think good stone would disappear and end up as part of someone's new house.'

Aubrey spread his hands. 'It was tried, soon after the fire. Stones were carted away, hauled to make fireplaces, paths, new homes. But ill luck befell anyone who took the stones, and it usually involved fire. Houses burned down, people fell into the coals, things like that. The stones had a habit of finding their way back to the ruins.'

'Are you saying there's a curse on St Agnes'?'

'So the story goes. Whether it's true isn't important. People believe it, which is enough to ensure that the stones are still on the site where they fell. The burnt church.'

Aubrey felt uncomfortable because he knew he wasn't telling George everything about the burnt church. If he had, he was sure George would refuse to go there because the burnt church was the dumping ground for failed magical experiments of the worst kind.

Aubrey had stumbled on it in his ramblings. In his dealings with the folk of the Mire, few spoke of the burnt church, even though it was a prominent landmark in the area. Those who did speak of it did so in hushed tones. Naturally, Aubrey's curiosity was aroused by this. He was compelled to investigate.

What he found there, late one night, appalled him. In the caves and grottoes far underneath the site were the cast-off failures from forbidden magical experiments. Twisted abominations, these monstrous creations were the worst results of insane tinkerings with spells that twisted bodies and minds. They had once been human, but were now horrors.

Such experiments were, of course, forbidden by the Sorcerer Royal and the Ministry of Magic, but there were always those who went outside the boundaries in the search for power. As Aubrey had with his exploration of death magic. He could understand the urge to explore the arcane regions of magic, the need to try to make sense of the unexplained and the challenging, but he despised those who abused others to achieve their ends. Aubrey had gone into forbidden territory, but he had risked only himself.

And I'm paying the price, he thought grimly.

'The Holmlanders are going to meet there tonight?' George said. 'Let's tell Sir Darius!'

Aubrey was torn, then nodded. After the incident in the library, he felt being open might be the best policy.

They hurried downstairs, only to run into Lady Fitzwilliam. 'Where's Father?' Aubrey asked.

Her mouth was tight. 'He spoke on the telephone for some time. Then he left to see the Magisterium at Darnleigh House.'

LUNCH WAS SUBDUED AND AFTER IT AUBREY AND GEORGE waited for news. George read and Aubrey tried to busy himself with researching his condition, but found it hard to focus. Every time the bell at the front door sounded, he leapt to his feet. Whenever the telephone rang, he opened his door and tried to overhear the conversation.

Lady Fitzwilliam, George and Aubrey ate a light meal as evening drew in. Afterwards, Aubrey sat there, peeling an orange with a silver fruit knife. He looked up at his mother, who was sipping a glass of dessert wine. 'Why don't you ring Darnleigh House?' he suggested. 'It's been long enough.'

She looked at him. Then she put down her glass, nodded once, rose and left the room.

It was only a moment later when she returned. Her face was pale, but her voice was firm. She stood at the head of the table. 'They said that no-one at Darnleigh House has seen Sir Darius Fitzwilliam all day.' She paused to compose herself. 'We'll meet in the library in one hour to decide what to do.'

Aubrey sprang to his feet. 'Why the delay? We need to act now. They have Father!'

Lady Fitzwilliam reached out and put a hand on Aubrey's arm. He subsided, still grumbling. 'I want Miss Hepworth here,' she said.

'Why?' George asked. 'What can she add to our plans?'

'We shouldn't bring others into this,' Aubrey added. 'It's not safe for them, or for us. We can trust ourselves, but others?'

Lady Fitzwilliam's expression was one of intense determination and, in that instant, Aubrey could easily imagine her leading a line of bearers through a swamp, or dealing with rogue traders in an outpost far from the rule of law.

'You don't know Caroline Hepworth very well, do you?' she said.

Automatically, Aubrey began to deny this, offering details about her family, her schooling, her background, but his mother shook her head.

'That's not what I mean. I've only known her for a day, and I've found out what a resourceful, capable, surprising young woman she is. For instance, she's certainly a better shot than you, Aubrey. And she is an expert in unarmed combat.'

George couldn't help himself. 'A girl?'

Aubrey was silent. He remembered grappling with Caroline at Penhurst. She was strong, quick, and her movements were practised. He had no difficulty in believing his mother.

'Her father had many friends and colleagues. Some even came from overseas to work with the professor. Master Wu was one of them, bringing his techniques of Eastern magic to our country and collaborating with the professor on groundbreaking advances. He also taught Caroline Eastern ways of disarming armed opponents and disabling attackers. When she visited me at the museum, she demonstrated on a museum guard. Perkins was quite impressed, when he regained consciousness.'

'Ah, well, I see.' George subsided.

'She has a part in this,' Lady Fitzwilliam went on. 'Her father's notebook is still missing. I believe she wants to see this through.'

'I'm sure she would,' Aubrey said.

Lady Fitzwilliam dispatched Harris to organise Stubbs, the driver. Barely half an hour passed before Caroline was on the doorstep, accompanied by her mother.

Despite this unexpected turn of events, Lady

Fitzwilliam was gracious, leading them to the large drawing room near the front door. Aubrey and George followed.

The drawing room was Lady Fitzwilliam's favourite room in the house. It was crowded with fine furniture, while a large landscape took up most of one wall. An ancient spinet stood in one corner. Aubrey had never heard it played. These items were familiar, comforting to most guests. What made the room unusual was the hundreds of items Lady Fitzwilliam had brought back from her overseas expeditions. The walls were hung with tribal masks and primitive weaponry. Shelves were crammed with statues of earthenware, stone, jade and semi-precious gems. Botanical specimens under domed glass stood on bookshelves. Flamboyant feathers burst from vases. Urns and vases of disturbing shapes were arranged next to carvings that had once protected whole villages from drought. The room was a riot, a carnival, a celebration of the exotic and the outlandish, full of vibrant colours and articles of mysterious origin. Visitors usually stared wide-eyed at the jumble. Aubrey knew his mother enjoyed the unsettling effect it had, and he was impressed when Mrs Hepworth and Caroline took it all in without comment.

'Mrs Hepworth,' his mother said, once everyone was seated, 'I'm pleased you came. Forgive me, I should have asked you in the first place.'

Mrs Hepworth was wearing many layers of brightly coloured silk. A pearl-green scarf was loosely bound around her hair. She inclined her head. 'Indeed,' she said. 'I'm normally not one to stand on outmoded ideas of societal norms, but when my daughter is summoned to the home of Sir Darius Fitzwilliam in the dead of night, I suppose I am entitled to feel curious.'

A *tsk* of exasperation escaped Caroline's lips. 'It's not the dead of night, Mother. Don't be so dramatic.'

Mrs Hepworth smiled a little at that. 'I'm sorry, my darling.'

'Mrs Hepworth —'

'Ophelia, please,' Mrs Hepworth drawled. 'Everyone calls me Ophelia.'

'Ophelia. I'll have someone bring you tea in the parlour, if you wish. The four of us have matters to discuss.'

Mrs Hepworth looked at the door. Then she looked at Aubrey, Lady Fitzwilliam and George. 'Something is seriously wrong, isn't it?'

Lady Fitzwilliam sighed. 'Sir Darius. He's missing.'

Caroline put a hand to her mouth. Lady Fitzwilliam reached for a bell pull. When Maud appeared, she said, 'Tea, for five, in my drawing room.' Maud left and Lady Fitzwilliam turned to Mrs Hepworth. 'It seems you're now part of our war council.'

AUBREY PERFORMED HIS RECITATION OF THE EVENTS OF THE last few days, this time for Mrs Hepworth, with an addendum for Caroline concerning the disappearance of Sir Darius. He left nothing out, but he did it with a sinking heart, certain that the unvarnished account would mean Mrs Hepworth's forbidding him from seeing Caroline again.

When he had finished, Aubrey busied himself with serving the tea, leaving George to answer the inevitable questions. Aubrey chimed in when it suited him, but he concentrated on offering lemon biscuits to the ladies.

Finally, when all clarifying questions were asked and answered, Mrs Hepworth looked at her daughter and patted her hand. 'I can see that they need you, my darling. They may have little chance of success without your skills to help them.'

George nearly choked on the biscuit he was eating. Aubrey's eyes widened. 'You don't mind her going with us?' he asked.

Mrs Hepworth smiled. 'I find modern society to be a limiting force, diminishing the scope of human endeavour. I utterly reject the moderate, the safe, the comfortable. To venture is to gain. Both Lionel and I agreed on this, which, paradoxically, led to many arguments.' Her gaze softened. 'But we knew we wished to raise a daughter who would live a free life. We wanted her to reach for the stars, for that is the most certain way to attain them.'

'Trust your children,' Lady Fitzwilliam murmured.

'Of course. Trust them. They will fall, occasionally, but they will fly.'

Lady Fitzwilliam applauded. 'You, naturally, are a Suffragette?'

'What intelligent person isn't?'

Lady Fitzwilliam looked at Caroline. 'Do you understand what you're becoming involved with?'

'No. But I doubt that anyone here really understands what we're facing.'

'Holmland. Plotters and conspirators. And the Magisterium – which may be against us or for us,' Aubrey said. 'We cannot count on anyone.'

'Aubrey,' said Lady Fitzwilliam, 'what do you propose as our first course of action?'

'George and I have uncovered a secret message, similar to one that summoned the Holmlanders to the Society for Non-magical Fitness in Greythorn, where they were met by the Magisterium. It indicates a meeting in the Mire, tonight.' He frowned. 'George and I planned to attend. Disguised, of course.'

'Where did you see this message?' Mrs Hepworth asked.

Aubrey explained about the agony columns and how they'd been used to relay secret instructions.

'So who placed the message?' Mrs Hepworth asked. 'The one that lured the Holmlanders to that Fitness Society?'

'Ah.' Aubrey paused, finger in the air. The Holmlanders could have put the code in the newspaper, unaware that a trap was waiting for them. The Magisterium? No, their set-up at the Society for Non-magical Fitness indicated that they were simply prepared to wait for their prey, staffing the reception area just in case innocent visitors dropped in – as they had.

Aubrey had a disturbing thought. He'd cracked the cipher message. Had someone else? Someone who wanted to orchestrate a confrontation between the Holmlanders and the Magisterium?

'I'm not sure who placed that message,' he admitted. 'But I'm not sure it's important at this stage.'

Mrs Hepworth frowned. 'But why would the Holmlanders pay any attention to a second ciphered message if the first led them to a trap?'

Aubrey could see that Caroline did not inherit her intelligence solely from her father. 'Excellent point,' he said. 'I was coming to that.'

'And those vile pamphlets,' George said. 'What were they doing at that place? What had the Holmlanders to gain from trying to ruin your father's reputation?'

He mentally thanked George for bowling up an easy one, a nice long hop outside off stump. 'Father is the leading voice for resisting Holmland aggression. When he wins the election, Holmland will have a much more difficult time in achieving its aims for an empire. Ruining his reputation is a simple way to make sure that doesn't happen.'

'So,' Mrs Hepworth said, 'the Holmlanders appear well mixed up in this, and decidedly up to no good. But why would they traipse off to the Mire tonight? And why do you feel you have to be there? How does that help your father?'

Lady Fitzwilliam patted Mrs Hepworth on the arm. 'Thank you, Ophelia. You've cut to the heart of the matter.' She looked at her son. 'Aubrey?'

Aubrey stood, facing his mother, George, Caroline and Mrs Hepworth. They looked at him with expressions of interest, hope, caution and worry, but also a desire to do something instead of waiting, passively, for news. It was a desire he well understood. In all circumstances, he preferred to take matters into his own hands, to forge his own path. He was not a log, drifting downstream towards the waterfall. He was a fish, fighting the current with all his might. Even if he was dragged over the edge, he'd be struggling all the way down to the rocks.

The attempted assassination of the Crown Prince. The Black Beast of Penhurst. The murderous shade at the professor's workshop. Powerful magic was at the heart of these events, powerful magic of a new and revolutionary kind. Getting to the bottom of this puzzle could help his country and his father, but it could also help him in finding an answer to his condition.

A solution was close, but he just needed some time.

He looked at the expectant faces in front of him. 'What do you think?' he said to them, opening the floodgates.

Immediately, four people started to talk at once, with their theories of who did what to whom, where and when. Argument and counter-argument, polite but forthright, bounced from one to the other as explanations grew more and more tangled.

Aubrey began to pace, thinking.

The golem. The Black Beast. The shade. The Magisterium. Banford Park. Holmland. The stolen notebook. Professor Hepworth. The pamphlets. His father's disappearance. He needed to put them together and make the links into a chain.

The others in the room ignored him, enmeshed in elaborate constructions of their own.

He rubbed his hands together, then seized a small brass box from a vase stand. *Let that be the golem*, he thought. He dragged over a side table. On the way, he grabbed an onyx cube, a stone die, two marble pestles, a crystal hemisphere, a tiny book with a red velvet cover, a music box, a silk fez and a tobacco pouch. Humming, he arranged them on the smooth table, one on top of the other, shifting them around in an irregular lattice – first a wall, then a mound, then two columns spanned by the red velvet book. He gazed at the structure, but hardly saw it.

He cleared his throat. The discussion died down, not without some reluctance, but soon the others were looking at him.

'Father went to the Magisterium building, Darnleigh House,' he said. 'If they have him, he's still there. But if he were intercepted along the way, by Holmlanders who are eager to remove him from the political scene, as we've established, *they* have him. It is urgent, therefore, that we find these Holmlanders. The best hope – the *only* hope – we have of finding them is to go to the Mire tonight. If they think their cipher is compromised, they won't arrive. If they think it's safe, they'll come.'

'And lead us to Sir Darius,' George concluded.

'And if he's in Darnleigh House?' Caroline asked.

'Mother,' Aubrey said, 'if you don't hear from us by noon tomorrow, I want you to call Bertie. Let him know that you think the Magisterium has Father.'

Lady Fitzwilliam looked as if she wanted to argue with this, but she changed her mind. 'I will.' She pinned Aubrey with her gaze. 'Find him, Aubrey. I don't care how, but go and bring him back home.'

'I will.'

Lady Fitzwilliam took Mrs Hepworth's arm. They left, talking in low voices. Caroline followed.

'You coming, old man?' George asked.

'In a minute.'

Alone, Aubrey put his hands together, satisfied. He was going to find his father. Nothing would stop him from that. It wouldn't matter who had him, Aubrey would find him.

He turned to go and grinned wryly at the edifice he'd built on the table. It had helped him think, and it wasn't a bad construction at all, considering what he'd had to work with. It was firm and solid. Solid enough, anyway. He wouldn't want to nudge it just *there*, for instance, because it could get a little shaky. He rubbed his chin. Maybe it did need a little support on one side.

He looked around and his gaze landed on a small, dark object that was hidden behind some white plumes from a plant his mother had brought back from South Arenta. It was perfect.

He paused when he had it in his hand. It was wooden, no bigger than his thumb, made from a dense, black timber so finely grained that the whole figure seemed to be looped and whorled, as if made from a whirlwind. The figure was only vaguely human, with the merest hint of limbs and a head. The face had no features.

He slid it in between the onyx cube and the fez. It fitted perfectly and stabilised the whole construction.

Aubrey left the room, still thinking.

Twenty

*L*ADY FITZWILLIAM OFFERED MRS HEPWORTH A PLACE to stay for the night. After some discussion, she agreed. Aubrey watched as they went up the stairs. 'And so to the Mire,' he said to Caroline and George.

'The Mire, at midnight?' Caroline shook her head. 'We must be on our mettle.'

'Even on our mettle, we need some help.'

'Jack Figg?' George said.

'Yes. And it's time for Tommy Sparks, too.'

George grimaced and glanced at Caroline. 'You think that's wise?'

'We can't go looking like this. Tommy's well known. He moves easily through the Mire.'

Caroline crossed her arms and glared. 'I refuse to go any further until you two stop speaking in riddles.'

Aubrey considered this. 'Perhaps we need to show you what we're about.'

While Caroline and George waited, Aubrey went to his dressing room. His heart was beating faster. He found the box at the rear of an upper shelf.

Tommy Sparks was inside.

A bowler hat with a frayed brim and scuffed crown. A long, patched jacket which had once been brown. Flannel trousers. Boots with new soles, but holes in the uppers.

As Aubrey put on this disreputable costume, he felt the thrill of release, becoming Tommy Sparks. Being this rogue gave him the chance to escape from the responsibilities of being Aubrey Fitzwilliam, once heir to the Duchy of Brayshire.

He changed his posture. He dropped his shoulders a little and pushed his chin forward, enough to alter his profile but not enough to appear exaggerated or grotesque. Inside his boots, he shifted his weight so he was standing slightly on his toes. When he looked in the mirror he saw someone who wasn't Aubrey Fitzwilliam.

Instead, he saw a street scrounger who mixed with barge folk, pilgrims, dock workers, costermongers and beggars, someone who listened to gossip and rumours, who tried to divine the mood of the people. He grinned. 'What a 'andsome chap,' he said aloud. He slipped easily into Tommy Sparks's voice, slightly higher pitched than his usual. He tipped his hat and sidled out of the dressing room to find Caroline and George.

They were in Lady Fitzwilliam's drawing room. George rose when Aubrey entered, but Caroline remained seated. She frowned.

'Hullo, miss!' Aubrey tipped his hat, then stuck his thumbs in the rope belt around his waist. 'Tommy Sparks, at your service.'

George smiled. 'Miss Caroline Hepworth, meet Tommy

Sparks. Tommy Sparks, Miss Caroline Hepworth.'

Caroline scowled. 'This is what you need to take us to the Mire? This pantomime creature?'

Aubrey staggered back a step or two in mock horror. 'Wounded, I am, wounded to the 'eart! The lovely Miss Hepworth finks I'm nothing but a creature!'

'Settle down, Aubrey,' George said. 'Save the perform-ance for the streets.'

Aubrey coughed and shook himself. 'Sorry,' he said, with his normal voice. It took an effort, as if Tommy didn't want to leave. 'Tommy does tend to take over.'

'I see,' Caroline said.

Aubrey massaged his neck. 'And you mustn't call me Aubrey when I've put on Tommy Sparks. No-one in the Mire knows me as Aubrey.'

Caroline nodded. 'This Tommy isn't inconspicuous, is he?' She raised an eyebrow. 'And he's a little forward.'

Aubrey took off his hat and studied its brim. 'Ah, yes. He tends to be like that. Especially with the ladies. He's quite a favourite.'

'I can imagine,' Caroline said dryly.

'And what about us, Aubrey?' George said.

Aubrey grinned, but this time it was not a Tommy Sparks grin. 'Wait here.'

He came back with two costumes.

'You want me to be a beggar,' Caroline said. Her voice was flat. She held up a ragged dress that looked as if Aubrey had plucked it from the gutter.

George screwed up his face. 'Me too? A beggar?'

'It's an excellent disguise. You and George can pretend to be mutes, which isn't unusual in the Mire. Beggars can go anywhere. People see the rags, not the person. They won't remember you.'

George shook his beggar's clothes. 'No fleas?'

'No. Just lice.'

George dropped the rags and took a step back. 'Lice!'

'I was joking.'

'I hope so,' Caroline muttered.

'Trust me,' Aubrey said. 'They look dirty, but they're actually quite clean.'

Caroline looked at him. 'Why do you have women's clothes?'

Aubrey felt his cheeks flaming. 'Well, just in case, you know. I've had them for ages. It's the sort of thing I collect, for study, you know . . .'

'You're babbling again, Aubrey.'

'Ah.'

George laughed. 'You've used those clothes, haven't you, Aubrey? You've dressed as a woman beggar!'

'Not for some time, I haven't.' He stopped. 'That is to say . . .'

Caroline stood. 'No need to be embarrassed. It makes good sense. I'm pleased to hear that you're not trapped into old-fashioned thinking. Now, where can I get changed?'

Aubrey showed Caroline and George to spare rooms, then went back to his own, wondering what sort of preparations would be useful. In the end, he stuffed an assortment of bottles, powders, scraps of paper and other possibilities in the capacious pockets of his coat. For a moment, he studied the mess of papers and books on one of his tables. It was the latest stage of his research, which had been extending in many directions. He'd been making an effort to bring his findings together, to take stock of possible remedies for his condition. Some were desperate, some were most unlikely, but he did have one that looked as if it could do something for him. He'd teased it out, refining it and eventually constructing a spell, but he'd shied away from it. It was rough, crude, and not without its dangers. It needed testing, developing, work. He rubbed his forehead. *Time. I need more time.*

George entered the room. He wore trousers that were torn off just below the knee. His shirt and jacket were threadbare. Jammed on his head was a hat that looked like a pie that had been stepped on. He was not smiling. 'I feel foolish.'

'Don't worry, George. No-one will notice you.' Aubrey tucked a feather in his pocket and looked around, wondering what else he should take.

George cleared his throat. 'That Caroline . . .'

Aubrey looked up. 'Yes, George?'

'Very *capable* young woman, wouldn't you say? Resourceful, clever?'

'Hmm. I thought she daunted you? You've changed your tune.'

George shrugged. 'Presentable, too. In a stylish way.'

'What are you getting at, George? Has she piqued your interest?'

'Not my type, old man. Or rather, I doubt that I'm her type. She doesn't need a plodder like me.'

'Then what is it?'

'I just wanted to make sure you realised she was *your* type.'

Aubrey didn't have time to answer. Caroline joined them before he could extract more from George on this issue. She stood unselfconsciously in her beggar's rags. 'Well?'

Aubrey studied her. The dress dragged on the ground, billowing around her. The collar had been torn off, leaving a frayed edge. The sleeves were much too long and Caroline had pushed them up. This made her forearms look enormous and puffy. Her hat had once been a collection of colourful fabric flowers, but was now a brown mess. To Aubrey's eye, there was no possibility of mistaking her for a beggar, but he hoped that the darkness would obscure Caroline's extraordinary features.

'Your posture is too good. Slump your shoulders and stoop a little. You too, George.'

'Better?' Caroline asked. She hunched, letting her head fall forward.

'It's uncomfortable,' George complained.

'You'll get used to it. Now, George, tangle your hair and smear on some of this.'

Aubrey gave a small pot to Caroline. She unscrewed the lid. 'Makeup.'

'False dirt and grime. It's quite convincing.'

Soon, Aubrey was faced by two convincing beggars. *In the dark, at least*, he thought. *At a distance*. 'Good enough,' he declared. 'Are you ready?'

'Ready enough,' George said.

'Yes,' Caroline said.

'Let's go, then.'

AUBREY FELT THE CHILL AS SOON AS HE STEPPED OUTSIDE. Rain was on the way.

The constellations were difficult to see behind the blanket of fog and smoke that hung over the city, but occasionally a star would appear and stare down at the unlikely trio.

First, Aubrey led them towards the river. They soon left Fielding Cross behind as they worked their way deeper into the bowels of the city. Gone were the sounds of the occasional piano in a parlour. Instead they had the shifting chorus of noise: guard dogs, pub brawls, clattering machinery, running water and indistinct caterwauling in the night.

They made their way through Newpike, the Narrows, Royland Rise and Downmarsh. They skirted braziers surrounded by sooty-faced men and crossed train tracks. Drizzle began to fall when they reached Little Pickling. The tang of burning coal, hot asphalt and rotting wood dampened and changed, becoming both more diffuse and more challenging.

After about an hour, through rain that grew heavier, they came to the Crozier district. Aubrey strode along Hayholt Street, waving at the few skulking passers-by. He skipped across a gutter that ran thick with refuse and turned down Creeland Lane. Sagging brick buildings looked as if they were held up by the many posters from the Army of New Albion which, in badly spelt and very large letters, denounced the King as a foreign puppet. He stopped at the only dwelling that showed a light. Grinning, he pounded on the door.

It swung open and a tall, thin young man stood there. He wore round spectacles and fingerless gloves. He had a pencil behind each ear; they stuck through a thatch of brown hair. Two cats were at his feet and they stared evenly at the visitors.

'Jack Figg!' Aubrey crowed. 'Aren't you going to ask us in? It's wet enough to drown a duck out here!'

Jack Figg didn't say anything. He nodded, stood back and allowed them to enter the tiny room.

A large, battered desk took up one entire wall. Papers and pamphlets were piled up high on it. They also stood in shaky piles to either side, next to four wooden crates and the only chair in the room. When the door was closed, Jack Figg stood and crossed his arms. 'I'm honoured,' he said mildly. He glanced at Caroline and George. 'Have you brought some poor souls who need help?'

Aubrey ran a hand over his face and sighed. He put Tommy Sparks away for a while. 'Hello, Jack. Things are moving apace.' He waved at his beggar friends. 'This is Miss Caroline Hepworth and George Doyle, whom you've met before, when he was a little better dressed.'

Jack shook hands with George. 'Good to see you again, Doyle.' He bowed to Caroline. 'Miss Hepworth. You wouldn't, by any chance, be related to Ophelia Hepworth?'

Caroline smiled. 'She's my mother.'

'Ah! One of my favourite artists. I think her *Adonis at Bay* is the lushest painting I've seen.' He frowned. 'She's much undervalued.'

'Yes,' Caroline said. 'You saw her work at the Academy?'

'Charlie, the nightwatchman, is a friend of mine. I see most of the Academy's exhibitions after dark. It's not ideal, I grant you. I'd prefer to see them with natural light. But the Academy has a habit of turning away riff-raff like me.'

Aubrey watched this with interest. 'I hate to interrupt,' he broke in, 'but we have more important matters to discuss.'

'Take a seat,' Jack waved a hand, 'or a crate. I hope you can tell me what's going on around here.'

'What do you mean?' Aubrey asked.

'Strange times, at the moment. Lots of unrest.'

'Such as?' George asked.

Jack frowned. 'I haven't seen so many agitators at work for a long time. They're haranguing, hanging posters, encouraging people to disobey authorities, calling for war, warning against war . . . And so many pamphlets!' He gestured at his own. 'Mine are getting lost in the avalanche at the moment.'

'Ah,' Aubrey said.

'And hotheads are getting organised, too, recruiting members, looking out for mischief to do. The Army of New Albion, the Patriot League, the Reformists.' He shook his head. 'It's making the struggle even harder.'

Aubrey wondered how much of this was the doing of the Holmlanders. Stirring up the masses was a useful tactic before a war.

'Jack,' he said, 'we need to go to the Mire. The burnt church.'

Jack lifted an eyebrow. 'The burnt church? Well, that's interesting. You're the second person today who's talked of the burnt church.'

'Who's the other?'

Jack looked at his hands in his lap. 'You know how I work. I don't give the name of my informants or my comrades in the struggle.'

'This is important, Jack,' Aubrey said. His face was serious. 'The fate of the country is at stake.'

Jack snorted. 'Well now, you can understand how that makes me bleed inside, seeing as how this country has been responsible for the plight of the working class.' He stood. 'Do you know how many babies die in this neighbourhood before they're six months old? D'you know how many children leave school before they're ten, just so they can earn some money to help feed the family?'

Aubrey reached out and put a hand on Jack's arm. 'I do know,' he murmured. 'Remember?'

Jack blinked, then laughed a little, embarrassed. 'You caught me making a speech.'

'You don't need much encouragement.'

'No, I don't suppose I do.' Jack sighed. 'Aubrey actually does understand the way things are,' he said to Caroline and George. 'If it weren't for him and his family, there'd be no medical care in this whole part of the city.'

Aubrey groaned. 'Jack.'

'It's true. The Broad Street Clinic is funded by your family, thanks to you.'

Caroline looked at Aubrey. He shrugged. 'Jack showed me the sights when I first came down here. I realised something had to be done. If we waited for the authorities to act, we'd still be waiting at the end of time.'

'That's the truth,' Jack said. 'Well, I've been reminded of my obligation. What was it you wanted to know?'

'Not through obligation, Jack,' Aubrey insisted. 'But because it's the right thing to do. My father's disappeared and we're trying to find him.'

Jack lifted his head. 'Why didn't you say so? Sir Darius gone? How can I help?'

'You said someone today mentioned the burnt church,' Caroline said.

'A friend of mine. A Holmlander.'

At the three-way intake of breath, Jack crossed his arms and looked defiant. 'Yes, a Holmlander. I'm not afraid to admit I have Holmland friends. Workers across the world are united in their struggle. We don't see nationality as important.'

'It's not that, Jack,' Aubrey said. 'It's just that Holmlanders could be involved in this matter.'

'Sir Darius's disappearance?'

'And other associated intrigues. How long have you known your Holmlander friend?'

'A few years. He travels a lot, he tells me. He goes back to Holmland and then returns here. He's an organiser.'

'I'm sure he is,' George said. 'And what else does he tell you?'

Jack frowned. 'He told me that he's on the run from the authorities. They want to stop his activities. Another example of the state trying to crush the workers.'

'You'd be hiding him, then?' Aubrey said. He kept his tone neutral.

'In a manner of speaking. He's safe.'

Aubrey grinned and a little of Tommy Sparks crept into his voice. 'Come now, Jack. You'll have to do better than that. We're very interested in talking to this fellow.'

'You can't. When he found out where the burnt church was, he left.'

Aubrey studied Jack. His friend was a committed man, dedicated to improving the lot of people around him. He'd educated himself through books he'd managed to put his hands on and it was his fierce, untutored intellect that led him to write and print pamphlets aimed at rousing the masses.

His greatest flaw was, however, that he was too trusting. Aubrey remembered the last time he'd seen von Stralick. The Holmlander had been wounded in the confrontation at the Society for Non-magical Fitness.

'And did you get medical help for him? Head wounds can be messy,' Aubrey asked.

'He didn't need it. Most of his ear was missing, good and clean. A plaster stopped the bleeding.'

'So it *was* von Stralick you were sheltering,' George blurted.

Jack looked defiant. 'He's a good man.'

'It doesn't matter,' Aubrey said.

'We need to get to the burnt church,' Caroline said, echoing his thoughts. 'Quickly.'

Jack looked at Aubrey, who nodded. 'It's very important.'

Jack did not move for some time, then he lifted his head. 'You're sure this is for a good cause?'

'On my honour,' Aubrey said.

'I'll take you, then. But I think it may be wise to get someone to come along with us.' Jack fetched a coat and a long scarf, which he wound around his neck. 'Follow me.'

The rain had grown heavier and was hammering on roofs, making a noise like hissing drumbeats, all out of rhythm. As they walked through the flooded streets, Aubrey began to feel the night pressing in around him. The thoroughfares grew narrower, buildings crowding on either side. Shadowy figures, solitary or in small groups, flitted through the wet, never talking, never acknowledging each other.

The rain lessened and turned into fog, then back again to rain. They trod along an old towpath beside a canal that had become a communal dumping ground. It was choked with ash, chunks of concrete and stone, household refuse and dead animals, and was heavy with the stink of decay.

Jack Figg led them under a road bridge, then through an abandoned factory that now seemed to be the home for a thousand people. By the light of a few guttering fires, they wound their way through the piles of rags that were sleeping men and women. Moans, the cries of babies and the deep, phlegmy cough of the terminally tubercular were the accompaniment to their night journey.

Aubrey clutched his coat shut as they stepped through this nightmare. When he emerged once more into the drizzle, he tilted his head and let the rain run over his face. He glanced at George and Caroline and saw their dazed expressions. 'Many people live like that,' he murmured.

'It's inhuman,' Caroline said.

Jack shook his head. 'They're as human as you, Miss Hepworth. They're just struggling to live, that's all.' He jabbed a finger at the factory. 'They say there's a war coming, but I've been fighting a war for years. A war against that.'

They walked on in silence. Jack brought them to the remains of a small quarry where brickworkers had long ago given up on scraping out more clay. It formed a bank, along the top of which ran a railway. The bottom of the quarry was a heap of scrap iron and timber.

Jack took a length of iron from the heap and banged on a rusty oil drum.

A slab of timber lifted and fell aside to reveal a hole. Faint music rose from it and Aubrey smelt an odd mixture of soap and cloves

A huge, bald head poked up. A huge neck followed, then a mighty pair of shoulders. 'Jack?' said a voice like thunder.

'Hullo, Oscar,' Jack said. 'I've got some friends who need to go to the burnt church.'

'The Mire?' Like a whale sounding, a vast white shape emerged from the debris. 'Righto, then.'

When Oscar dragged himself from the rubble and stood, Aubrey realised that he was the biggest man he'd ever seen.

He was at least seven feet tall, but his bulk made him look

even taller. He rolled as he walked, settling each foot on the ground as if unsure it would support him. Aubrey could only see his legs from the knees downwards, so immense was his belly. His bald head was round and enormous, but smooth and unmarked like a baby's. The rain rolled off his naked scalp. He wore a robe-like garment, made of old hessian bags, and he carried a large, empty sack slung over his shoulder. His feet were bare, and Aubrey guessed it was because he'd couldn't find shoes to fit.

Oscar smiled and took a step forward. 'Who are you, then?' His voice was a basso profundo, a voice that could have come from deep in the earth.

Aubrey couldn't help myself. He took a step back.

Jack interposed himself. 'Oscar, these are my friends. I want you to take care of them.'

Oscar stopped, smiled once more and stared. Again, Aubrey was reminded of a baby and he wondered how old Oscar was. 'Righto, then. Friends.'

Without another word, the giant heaved his bulk around and waddled off. Aubrey and the others stared at his mighty back.

Jack chuckled. 'You're not the only one with interesting friends, Aubrey. No-one will bother us with Oscar along for the ride.'

'I can believe that,' Caroline said. 'Who is he?'

They set off. 'I don't know, and neither does he,' Jack said. 'I found him a few years ago. He was in a cellar, naked and afraid. He was about half his current size, but had no idea how he got there or who he was. I cared for him until he was capable of managing for himself. He's still growing, you know.'

George steadied a plank and they crossed a noxious pool. 'Still growing? But he's a monster!'

'I fear that may be right,' Aubrey said. He leapt off the plank. 'There's magic involved, isn't there, Jack?'

Jack sighed and patted Oscar, who towered above him. 'Things happen in this part of the city that you wouldn't believe,' he said. 'It's a desperate place. People do things to survive.'

Caroline looked at Oscar, pity in her eyes. 'What happened to him?'

'If a magician needs a human subject, they always come to this part of the city. I can't say for certain, but Oscar could have been someone's idea of an experiment. Perhaps it went wrong. Perhaps it had the desired effect. I can't say.'

'Sometimes people volunteer,' Aubrey said. 'For a pound or two, it doesn't matter how ghastly the proposed experiment is, someone will step forward.'

Caroline touched Oscar on the arm. 'Is that what happened to you?'

'I don't know.' He smiled.

'He has a music box,' Jack said. 'He makes enough money as a bodyguard and labourer to feed himself. He's happy enough.'

'Are you?' Caroline asked the giant.

Oscar smiled again. 'I don't know.' He lifted his arms and dropped them to his sides. 'Righto, then.'

Oscar turned and climbed up a muddy slope, littered with broken bottles. He waited beside a tumbledown fence and called to them. 'Righto, then. Nearly there.'

Jack puffed up the slope, reached his gigantic friend and patted him on the hand.

Aubrey slipped as he clambered up the slope. George grabbed his arm, digging his boots into the mud and steadying them both. He dragged Aubrey up, then reached out and helped Caroline. With George's solid strength, they were able to reach the deserted road where Jack and Oscar stood. The uneven cobblestones were slick where the rain had melted whatever ordure and filth had gathered there. A single street light hissed, shedding a sickly yellow glow that made urinous streaks along the surface of the road.

Jack pointed towards it. 'The Mire.'

The Mire had the narrow streets and uneven cobbles of the other districts they'd passed through. The two- or three-storey houses leaned against each other, as if they'd had a very fine night out. Slate roofs were slick with rain, but few boasted functional gutters, so water cascaded in waterfall-sized torrents to the stones below.

Aubrey paused. Even at this distance the Mire sounded distinctive. It was noisy, with the sounds of music, shouting and general carousing, a good-natured happiness that had been absent from the tired and despondent districts they'd been through. As they turned corners, they began to run into more people. Hurrying, staggering, crawling, running, chasing, darting people.

The Mire. Aubrey grinned. *It might be grubby, but it has energy.*

When they plunged into the Mire, passing through a narrow lane that was flanked by two competing taverns, it became obvious that not all the passers-by were poor. Three well-dressed men walked past, flanked by two scowling bodyguards. Two of the men seemed to be enjoying themselves, but the third had an expression of barely controlled terror on his face.

Despite his Tommy Sparks persona, Aubrey was glad for Oscar's presence. They kept close by the massive giant like pilot fish around a great whale. He rolled along the cracked and uneven pavement, his head turning from side to side, constantly smiling.

'Don't look about too much,' Aubrey urged his friends as they passed an oyster shop where a brawl was sending bleary-eyed patrons into the streets amid a hail of shells, cheering and abuse. 'Act as if you know your business, that you belong here.' He grinned as he walked, letting everyone know that this was the most natural place in the world for him to be.

A woman leaned out of a second-storey window. Her hair was fiery red and her dress was made of purple velvet. 'Tommy!' she sang out. 'Tommy!'

Aubrey waved and threw her a kiss. Then he saw both Caroline and George staring at him. 'Ah, yes. Irene Dubois. Ballet dancer. Loves it here.' He turned and waved again, but the woman had vanished.

Humanity swirled around them and Aubrey revelled in the way that the strange mingled with the ordinary. He saw a casual assault as a pedestrian had a bag dragged over his head before being whisked away. A few moments later, he saw a woman with snakes for arms wrap them around the neck of a sailor and haul him in through an open window. The sailor was laughing.

The crowd thickened and Oscar surged ahead. Light spilled out onto the pavement from an upper-storey window and the sound of a badly tuned but enthusiastically played piano accompanied singing that Aubrey was sure was inspired by alcohol, not talent.

He had a feeling that they were walking in a gigantic spiral, always bearing left at intersections, making their way through the riot that was the Mire. He glanced up, looking for landmarks. They were passing a pair of narrow whitewashed buildings, three storeys high.

Aubrey shepherded his friends back just in time to miss being hit by a deluge of foul-smelling liquid.

George shook a fist at the wild-haired, cackling figures leaning out over the edge of the roof. 'I say!' he began, but Aubrey tugged his sleeve.

'Walk on, George.'

'What?'

'Look around. No-one else has even noticed. If you get angry, our friends up there will feel they've scored a victory. And don't even think of charging up there to berate them. They'll have clubs, sticks and hard fists and will be happy to relieve you of any valuables.'

George snorted, but Aubrey was pleased to see that his friend kept an eye on the rooflines as they pushed through the chattering throng.

They passed a gap in a row of houses where one dwelling had sagged even more than its neighbours and had collapsed. Opportunities like this were never missed in the Mire, and a wrestling tent had been erected on the ruins. Oil lamps blazed outside and a line of excited customers snaked into the entrance, while an organ-grinder entertained them with sounds that were somewhat like music, just not as tuneful. The tout at the front of the tent took one look at Oscar and shook his head. He was a small, bald-headed man with narrow eyes and a voice that could saw through glass. 'Sorry, friend. I know the sign says "£10 If You Stay In The Ring For One Round With Our Champion" but you're not what we were expecting.'

Oscar just smiled. 'Righto,' he said and sailed onwards, the others with him.

The Mire invigorated Aubrey. He loved its diversity, its life and the sheer unexpectedness that lay around every corner. It let him see another aspect of life in Albion. Rogues and saints rubbed shoulders in the Mire, as did honour and disgrace, charity and theft, hope and despair, all in a single square mile.

They went on until the crowds dwindled and the lights began to grow fewer. Aubrey noticed more and more deserted buildings, more actual ruins, not as many places of music and light. The rain began to fall heavily again and he held his coat closed as best he could. Water dripped from the frayed brim of his bowler hat.

The street ended with two mounds of rubble, one on either side. It then gave out onto a large open space, a hundred yards or more across, sloping upwards. In the darkness Aubrey could see the familiar maze of stone, stunted trees, and mounds of shattered masonry, the wilderness that surrounded the ruins that had once been St Agnes' Cathedral.

Once upon a time, the cathedral must have been a proud sight, crowning the top of the hill, looking over the city towards the other high points – Stoweside, Royal Park, Calmia. It would have been majestic.

Now, all he could see was the shell of the cathedral dark against the night, standing alone on the top of the hill like an abandoned sentinel. One wall was almost intact, reaching skywards, arched gaps that were once stained-glass windows. The other walls had fallen in the fire. Two pillars had miraculously survived, while the rest were mere stubs in what had been the nave.

Aubrey knew the cathedral graveyard was still there. It was a jumble of fallen headstones and the remains of tombs on the far side of the hill. He was glad they didn't have to go through it. Despite the rain and the years, the smell of ash and burnt wood was heavy in the air. He frowned as his magical awareness came across traces of magic everywhere he looked. It was blurred and indistinct and he couldn't tell if the magic was recent or the remnants from years of foul experiments.

'Righto, then,' Oscar announced. 'Burnt church.'

Rain sluiced down the gutters and poured off the rooftops around them. Aubrey was wet through. Caroline and George were both sodden. George looked irritated, but Caroline was calm, gazing towards their destination. 'Lights,' she said.

Aubrey turned and saw glimmers of light in the wilderness, small pinpricks of red, orange and yellow. 'We oughtn't run into anyone out there,' he said, thinking of the experimental outcasts, 'but we must be on our guard. We don't know how many Holmlanders will be appearing.'

Jack moved until he was standing with his back against the remains of a wall. 'What are you going to do now?'

'A meeting is going to take place here at midnight. What time is it now?'

Jack consulted a battered pocket watch. 'Half past eleven.'

'Plenty of time.' Aubrey looked at Oscar. 'Can he remain behind? He's a little conspicuous.'

Jack frowned. 'He can, but is it safe without him?'

'We'll move more quickly alone.'

'Oscar,' Caroline said. He looked down at her and smiled. 'Will you be all right if you stay here?'

'Yes.' He reached out with a meaty hand and – very gently – patted Caroline on the head.

'What about you, Jack?' Aubrey asked. 'Will you come or would you prefer to stay?'

'I should stay with Oscar. He's not used to being out alone at night.'

'Keep well hidden,' Aubrey said.

'I will.' Jack stopped, staring over Aubrey's shoulder. 'Someone's out there.'

Aubrey looked in the direction of his gaze and saw someone flitting from shadow to shadow.

'Damn him,' George said through gritted teeth. 'It looks like von Stralick. He has a rifle.'

'Are you sure?' Caroline asked. The rain was getting harder.

Aubrey reached into his pouch and pulled out a rough circle of enchanted glass. He closed one eye and held it to the other. 'It's definitely von Stralick. He has a bandage on the side of his head. He seems to be alone.'

'Why does he have a rifle?' Caroline wondered. 'What's he after?'

'Protection?' Jack suggested. 'We brought Oscar, he brought a rifle.'

'But why a rifle?' George said. 'That's a marksman's tool, not for self-defence.'

'There's one way to find out,' Aubrey said. 'Let's see what he's up to.' He gazed towards the ruins. 'George, you take point position. Stay fifteen, twenty yards in front. Caroline, you next. I shall come last, slightly off to your left.'

It was by the book. Or, at least, by the teachings of the Scholar Tan. *But I have something good old Scholar Tan didn't,* Aubrey thought. He took a pouch out of an inner pocket of his jacket.

'Before we set off,' Aubrey said to Caroline and George, 'there's something I need to do.'

After the incident at the shooting weekend, Aubrey had devoted some research time to the magic behind the clay golem assassin. He hadn't been able to determine exactly how to animate and control such an intricate creature, but he had established a spell for making a less sophisticated version.

'I thought we might need some scouts,' he said, and took a lump of clay out of a pouch in his pocket.

Caroline and George watched, fascinated, as Aubrey took the fist of clay and worked it between his hands. Muttering the spell he had rehearsed, Aubrey broke off a piece the size of a pea. With deft movements, he fashioned it into a rough human shape – two arms, two legs, a featureless head. Then, with care, he used his fingernail to inscribe a symbol on its blank forehead. He pronounced a short, sharp spell over it.

When Aubrey placed the mannikin on the wet ground, it quivered.

'Good Lord,' George whispered.

The mannikin swelled, its rough arms and legs becoming smoother, growing larger until it was the size of a thumb. It bent in the middle, sitting up. Then it popped to its feet and stood, swaying slightly.

While this was happening, Aubrey had fashioned another. He continued to work the lump of clay, breaking pieces off, making figures, inscribing symbols, repeating the spell. He was applying a number of laws – Symmetry, Contiguity, Action at a Distance, Sympathy – in a novel way. It was challenging.

In a short space of time, a dozen mannikins were standing in a line, arms outstretched like faceless gingerbread men.

Aubrey took a deep breath. 'Go. Observe. Report back to me.'

The three-inch-tall mannikins trembled, then dispersed, running stiff-legged into the darkness, splashing through puddles and wading through mud.

Caroline nodded. 'Clever.'

Aubrey was aware enough to be amused at how much he appreciated the comment. Then he simply enjoyed it, even though the magical effort had sapped him. 'It's an experiment. They're simple things, and their vocabulary is very limited. Let's see what happens. If they bring back some intelligence, it may be invaluable. If they don't . . .' He shrugged.

Caroline pointed. 'Look.' Von Stralick was darting up the slope, veering from side to side as he sprinted towards the ruined cathedral.

'He's making use of cover,' Aubrey commented, 'not running in a direct line, in case someone is watching him. He's experienced.'

'We can catch him,' Caroline said.

Aubrey glanced at her. Eyes bright, she looked eager, unafraid. *No-one could mistake her for a beggar*, Aubrey thought. *What was I thinking?*

George squinted and scanned the terrain ahead. 'I can't see him. He must have entered the cathedral.'

Caroline frowned. 'Making for a rendezvous?'

'No doubt.'

Aubrey glanced at George. 'Forward, then.'

George, as point man, went first. He disappeared into the darkness.

Caroline went next, then Aubrey. The ground under-foot was wet but hard, which made the going slippery. He angled towards a clump of bushes, edged around them, then ran from tree to tree, hunched over, until he reached a mound of broken bricks. Panting, he sat with his back to the rubble. His stomach felt hollow and he paused, gathering himself. While he consolidated his strength, he looked at the view.

From this vantage point, the city was laid out around him, glittering like a million stars, each light the result of ingenuity and application, meant for holding back the night, but without realising what a fairyland they would create. Incidental beauty, unmarred by forced design. He shook his head in wonder.

Movement in the wilderness caught his eye. At first, he assumed it was Caroline or George, but he realised that this movement was some distance away. For a moment he wondered if he'd leap-frogged von Stralick and moved ahead of him, but he discarded this idea. He could see that, whoever it was, he was making his way through the graveyard on the other side of the hill.

Aubrey took out his enchanted-glass viewer and peered through it.

The stranger flitted from tombstone to tombstone, keeping low to the ground. Aubrey found it hard to fix on him. His gaze shifted and slipped, sliding off the blurry form, after which it took him some effort to find him again. The intruder was indistinct, almost as if he were wrapped up in a cloud of shadows. It was like searching for hidden figures in one of the pictures he'd enjoyed as a child.

Interesting, Aubrey thought, and he felt the distant tang of magic. Now he was aware of the phenomenon, he scanned as much of the slope as he could. He felt chill when his gaze lighted on three other shadowed figures.

He jumped as someone emerged from the night. 'Aubrey,' Caroline whispered and she glided to his side.

A moment later, George joined them. 'I scouted ahead. The way is clear, right up to the ruins.'

Aubrey pointed, doing his best to track one of the ghostly visitors as it darted towards the remains of a tomb.

George whistled soundlessly. 'Quite a popular place, St Agnes', tonight.'

'Who are they?' Caroline whispered.

'No idea,' Aubrey said. 'But there's magic involved. See if you can follow their progress for more than a few yards.'

Caroline peered towards the church grounds. After a moment, she frowned. 'How odd. It's hard to keep my eye on them.'

'That's high-level magic, providing such stealthy masking,' Aubrey said.

'Who could it be?' George asked.

'A fine question,' Aubrey said, frowning as he considered the possibilites. 'Are these the Holmlanders? Or someone else . . .'

A rough voice cut through the night. 'All right, you three. Don't move.'

Aubrey started to get to his feet, but before he could move the ominous sound of a revolver being cocked came from the darkness.

'Don't try it.'

Two men scrambled over the broken masonry. One was tall and wearing a dark cutaway jacket and a bowler hat. Water dripped from every hem, edge and cuff and his scowl seemed as much directed at the rain as at what he'd found. The other wore a heavy overcoat and cloth cap. He was the one wielding the revolver, which he kept moving, unsure of where to aim.

'Damn! I thought they were beggars, but they're not,' the taller man said. 'It's youngsters.'

'What do we do now?' the other man said. The pistol jiggled as he sought guidance from his partner. Aubrey tried to lean away.

'Damn, damn, damn!' The taller man spat on the ground and looked around. 'We can't stay here. Bring them.'

'Get up,' the pistol-wielder snapped.

Aubrey rose. They didn't sound like Holmlanders. What were they doing here?

'Move it. That way.'

They were herded towards the burnt church and urged through a gap in the broken wall.

It was an immense space. St Agnes' had been enormous, large enough to hold a coronation. The hard stone floor was empty except for rubble and the few burnt timbers that were either too large or too ruined to be scavenged.

They were marched along the length of the nave, towards the apse where the altar would once have been. The two side wings of the transept, intersecting the nave, extended to either side. Aubrey could almost see the worshippers filling the great space, the priests leading the procession.

'Stop there,' pistol-wielder said and Aubrey's vision of the cathedral of long ago vanished. 'Turn around.'

The taller man ran the palms of his hands against his jacket. 'I wish you three hadn't come here.'

'So do we,' Aubrey said. 'Let us go and we won't come back.'

The taller man looked pained. 'I'd like to, son, but we can't operate like that. Things are too serious.'

'We won't tell anyone,' Caroline said. Aubrey saw her inching closer to the man with the pistol. She held her hands out as if pleading, but Aubrey could see the tensing of her body and the way she balanced on the balls of her feet.

'Easy, now,' the pistol-wielder said. He took a step back.

'It's not our decision,' the taller man said, appealing for understanding. 'We'll have to see what the others say.'

He knelt and picked up a fist-sized piece of stone. He banged it against the floor three times.

Aubrey's eyes widened as a floor stone creaked upwards. A lantern, a pistol and a face appeared. The face was long and thin, adorned with a drooping forked moustache. The man looked like a walrus rising through a hole in the ice. 'Ames? Briggs? You saw the message?'

'Aye, it's us, Holroyd,' the pistol-wielder said. He glanced at his partner. 'Ames, steady the trapdoor.'

Ames, the taller man, seized the stone and assisted those below in lifting it. Briggs, the pistol-wielder, gestured with his head. 'Now, you three, down you go.'

Ames leaned towards the hole. 'We've got three prisoners coming down, Holroyd.'

He stood aside and Briggs waved them towards the ladder. Aubrey looked at both of them. 'Are you sure you want to do this?'

'Get moving,' Briggs growled.

Aubrey shrugged and climbed down the ladder. Caroline, her face set in hard lines, went next. George was last.

The soft light of the lantern lit a long, narrow space. The walls and the floor were made of tightly fitting stone blocks. The walrus-moustached Holroyd stood at one end, holding a lantern. He looked dismayed. Two other men stood behind him and murmured to each other. 'This way,' Holroyd managed. 'Mind your step.'

This courtesy, more than anything, convinced Aubrey that they were in the hands of amateurs. That worried him. He'd rather they were professionals. Professionals were steady, predictable. Amateurs were usually inexperienced. They could do anything.

He leaned against the stone wall. His heart was hammering and he felt cold sweat all over his body. He needed to rest.

Behind him, Ames and Briggs clattered down the ladder. Together, they eased the trapdoor shut.

They marched down the passage for ten yards before it opened into a chamber about five yards square. Lanterns hung from brackets, lighting the space and the table and chairs that were arranged in the middle of it. The passage continued on the other side of the chamber, stairs disappearing into darkness.

Ames and Briggs put their heads together and muttered, while Holroyd and the nameless two others watched their prisoners. They appeared to reach a decision. Briggs gave the pistol to Ames, took a lantern from the wall and disappeared down the stairs.

'Where are we?' George asked Aubrey.

He looked around. 'I can't see any tombs or coffins, but it must be the crypt. Perhaps the remains were removed.'

'No talking,' Ames growled. He brandished his revolver.

Briggs reappeared with a coil of rope over his shoulder. 'Sit down,' he said and he handed the rope to Holroyd. 'Tie them back to back.'

'The girl too?'

'Yes.'

Holroyd was firm without being cruel. He bound them with the experience of someone who has worked with ropes all his life, with hard, flat knots well out of reach.

When Holroyd was done, Aubrey sagged against George. Immediately, he could feel his friend flexing his muscles, working against the bonds. Aubrey was sure that

George was strong enough to stretch the ropes and slip out, but it would take time, something he was sure was in short supply.

George nudged him and he jerked his head upright. 'Sorry.'

'You're unwell?'

'Not the best.'

Aubrey felt Caroline's slender strength next to him and she, too, was carefully working against her bonds. 'Are you sick?' she asked.

'Not exactly.'

Holroyd frowned. He crouched and held a lantern close to Aubrey's face. His eyes went wide. 'I thought I recognised him.'

'What is it?' Ames said. 'Holroyd, what're you carrying on about?'

Holroyd straightened. He pointed at Aubrey. 'The lad. I've seen him before, better dressed than that. He's Sir Darius's son.'

'No,' Ames said. Briggs looked startled and stared at Aubrey.

'What are we going to do?' Briggs said. He looked at Aubrey as if he were an unexploded bomb.

'Down the stairs,' Ames said. 'We need to discuss this.'

Briggs, Holroyd and the two others followed Ames into a deeper part of the crypt, grumbling.

'What next?' Caroline said. She didn't sound frightened. She sounded calculating.

'It's not good, I'm afraid,' Aubrey said. 'They're using their names. That either means that they don't think it'll do us any good to know who they are, or that they're careless. Either way, we're in a situation.'

'Who *are* these men?'

'Well, they're not Holmlanders,' Aubrey said. 'And that makes things very complicated.'

'How so?' Caroline asked.

'Where's von Stralick? Where are the rest of the Holmlanders? And what of the magically shrouded newcomers we saw? These men are a third party.' He shook his head. 'Too many variables here.'

Footsteps and the bobbing light of the lantern in the passage announced the return of their captors. None of them looked happy but Ames had put away his pistol, for which Aubrey was grateful.

Holroyd puffed air through his moustache and frowned. He looked to his colleagues and they waved him forward. 'This is very complicated,' he said.

'We were just saying that,' Aubrey said in a weary voice.

'It's not your presence, actually, that's the worst thing. It's who you are.'

'My father's son,' Aubrey said.

'Exactly.'

Holroyd wiped his hands together. 'Great man, your father. The hope of the country.'

Aubrey blinked. 'I beg your pardon?'

'He's the only one who knows what's good for the country, he does. Not afraid to speak his mind, either.'

Aubrey had heard these sort of reverential tones before. 'You served with him, didn't you?'

Holroyd looked thoughtful. 'In the Mataboro conflict. I was a sapper attached to his regiment. I never heard him give an order for something he wasn't prepared to do himself. When I was doing earthworks, demolitions, he made me show him how to lay a charge, the burn rates for fuses, things like that. Good man, he was, for an officer.'

Caroline had had enough. 'Exactly who are you? What are you doing here?'

Holroyd's eyes darted from side to side, to his co-conspirators.

Briggs stepped forward. 'We are the Army of New Albion, the true patriots of this benighted nation.'

Aubrey's brain was racing, trying to fit this new piece of intelligence into the puzzle. *The Army of New Albion? What were they doing here?*

'War is in the wind,' Holroyd said. 'Holmland aggression has made that clear.'

'Not to mention the growth in their military,' Briggs added. 'Their navy's doubled in size in the last three years. The sinking of the *Osprey* was a test of their new naval strength.'

'And it's obvious that Holmland sees Albion as the only real opponent to their plans for an empire,' Holroyd continued.

Aubrey nodded, hoping to encourage them to talk, even though they weren't saying anything new. The more they talked, the more likely it was that they would say something useful – and the more time George would have to work free.

'But this country has grown soft,' Ames said, his eyes narrow. 'Too many appeasers, too many who are prepared to give in, to turn a blind eye to those onion-eating scum.'

'The Prime Minister,' Briggs said.

'The King,' Holroyd added. He crouched in front of Aubrey. 'They're not like your father, lad. He's the man we need in charge of this country. He won't put up with the antics of the Holmlanders. He'd show them that Albion isn't a nation of weaklings and cowards. He'd stand up to them.'

'I see,' Aubrey said, when it seemed as if an answer was expected. He wondered if he should tell them of the disappearance of his father, but decided to keep that one to himself for the moment.

Briggs shook his head. 'He should still be Prime Minister, he should.'

Ames snarled again. 'That Armitage, I never trusted him.'

Holroyd looked worried, plucked at his moustache and glanced at his colleagues. As he did, Aubrey realised that these men were desperate. They might not be hardened criminals, but they had the air of people who had committed themselves to drastic action, even at great personal cost. They had the look of the fanatic about them.

His growing sense of optimism was doused by this thought. Fanatics had a habit of not being worried about their welfare, or of those around them, as long as it advanced their cause. It could explain why they were so forthcoming with their explanations.

Holroyd glanced at his colleague. 'Steady, Ames, steady.'

Ames whirled and thrust his face in Holroyd's. 'I've had enough of steady! Steady isn't going to save this country! It's action that's needed!'

Holroyd held up his hands palms outwards and spoke softly, as if to an angry dog. 'Of course, of course. That's why we're here tonight, remember? Planning, final details, timing.'

Briggs glanced at Aubrey. 'Lad, how'd you like to see your father leading this country again?'

'He will. After the election.'

Ames laughed savagely. 'Not a chance. The King's all but given the Prime Minister his blessing. The Holmlanders are telling everyone how impressed they are with our PM. Your father's reputation is being torn down. It's all cosy and wrapped up for the Royalists.'

Holroyd seemed uncertain where this conversation was going, but he didn't interrupt.

'What if,' Briggs said, 'the King and the PM weren't around any more? That'd put Prince Albert on the throne – and he and your dad get along like a house on fire. No more cosy Holmland-loving statements coming from the palace. We'd have strength instead of weakness.'

'The King's not a proper Albionite anyway,' Ames spat. 'He's Holmlander through and through. He deserves to die.'

The chamber was silent after Ames's venom. Finally, Aubrey spoke up. 'How many relatives did you lose when the *Osprey* was sunk?'

Ames stiffened. Briggs took him by the arm. 'We all lost people to those treacherous Holmlanders,' he said. 'I lost a cousin, same as Holroyd. Ames lost two brothers. Stokers, they were. Never had a chance when the ship sank.'

Ames's face contorted with anger. 'And Rollo Armitage and his cronies just caved in. Accepted the apologies and pretended all was well. Traitors. They deserve some of their own medicine and we're going to give it to them!'

Holroyd nodded. 'It's time to act. Things are getting dangerous for us. We were lucky to avoid the authorities up in Greythorn last week.' He sighed. 'You called this meeting to check our preparations, Ames?'

Ames looked startled. 'I thought the message was from you.'

They both looked at Briggs. He shook his head. 'Wasn't me. You told me about the meeting, Ames.'

Caroline had been silent for some time, but Aubrey had

felt her tensing. She coughed a little and leaned close to him. 'Get ready,' she breathed.

Aubrey didn't have time to wonder what she meant. She rose to her feet in one sinuous action, casting the rope aside.

Holroyd, Briggs and Ames stared, Ames fumbling for his revolver. The other two had their backs to her. 'Now, lass,' Holroyd said, 'you don't want to get hurt.'

'No,' Caroline said and then she sprang. Ames didn't have a chance to move. Caroline kicked the revolver out of his hand and struck him in the mid-section with the flat of her hand. He collapsed, gasping for air.

George threw off the last of the ropes and launched himself at Holroyd, who back-pedalled frantically, arms whirling, only to run into a roundhouse kick from Caroline. He staggered against the wall, knocked his head against the stone, and slid to the floor.

Caroline twisted and dropped into a crouch. One leg shot out and she spun around, sweeping the nameless two off their feet. They fell into a tangled heap. Caroline straightened up, balanced on her toes, but the men simply lay there, staring at her. Aubrey wanted to applaud, but instead he dragged himself to his feet.

'All right, love, all right,' Briggs said nervously. He eyed the revolver on the floor, but instead shuffled over to Ames and prodded him with a foot. 'Get up. Let's get out of here.'

'What about them?' Ames snarled. He was still holding his midriff. Aubrey wondered if Caroline had broken a rib for him.

'Leave them,' Holroyd said, tottering over. 'You won't say anything, will you, lad? We're just trying to do the right thing for the country. And your old dad.'

Aubrey decided to throw in his ace while they were off balance. It might turn up something useful. 'He's missing,' he said. 'Someone's kidnapped him.'

Holroyd's face fell. 'That's not good.'

'Holmlanders have taken him,' Ames snarled. 'We have to move, fast!'

'We'll do what we can to help him,' Holroyd said. 'All right, lad?'

Aubrey was silent. Holroyd seemed satisfied with this. Briggs picked up a chair and jabbed it at Caroline, then he held it in front of him as they backed out of the chamber. There was a boom as the stone trapdoor opened, and the Army of New Albion were on their way.

The noise echoed in Aubrey's skull and he felt as if were about to vomit. His knees were weak and a vast, rushing noise was in his ears. The effort of the spell-casting and the tense situation were combining to fray at his physical condition. He was deteriorating, and the call of the true death was growing stronger. 'Dangerous men,' he whispered to George, who had put an arm under his shoulders to support him.

'What?'

'Grief, fanaticism, stupidity and a cause. Explosive mixture.'

'Is he all right?' Caroline asked George.

'No. We have to get him home. He needs rest.'

An unmistakable sound rang out and Aubrey's head jerked up.

'Rifle shot,' George said.

Caroline raced for the ladder and Aubrey was left with George.

Another shot sounded.

'That will be von Stralick, I'd expect,' Aubrey whispered. He closed his eyes and sought for strength.

'I'd say so. How do you feel?'

'Barely holding myself together. It's got worse.'

'Be strong. It'll be all right.'

Aubrey opened one eye and looked at his friend. 'You always say that.'

'Well, I'm a very positive person.'

'Wait a moment,' Aubrey said. He bent his head. He was trembling, drained. The tugging at his soul was sharp and painful. It felt as if it would be dragged out of his body at any time. He doubted he had the strength to resist it.

Two more shots cracked.

Trapped, with a gunfight going on over our heads, he thought. *Father missing, the King about to be killed. I suppose I have no time to waste.*

He attempted a grin, but it wouldn't work properly. He motioned to George.

'Yes, old man?'

'George.' Aubrey sought for words, but they all seemed cheap and theatrical. 'Go and see what's going on.'

Aubrey watched his friend go to the foot of the ladder where Caroline was crouching. Dim light was coming from the open trapdoor.

He was left with no choice. He had to use an untested spell. Of course, an untested spell had placed him in this parlous situation . . .

He would not allow himself to make the same mistakes he had then. This spell might be untested, but it would be rigorous. It was raw and unrefined, but he had hopes that it might derive power from this crudity.

The aim of the spell was to bind his soul to his body again, to bring them back to their natural state of unification. If successful, it should shield him from death's untimely call. He could not afford, however, to sever the golden cord that led through the portal to the other side. To restore himself fully, he needed to learn how to recall the cord and close death's door. This was beyond him at the present.

The spell used elements he'd rephrased into a modern terminology of his own invention. Some were derived from the spell he had used for the fly that spied on his father. Others came from his death magic research. The whole expression was unique, and the final signature element indicated this. Aubrey hoped he'd be proud of it. If it worked, it would do more than stabilise his condition, it would give him some important results towards establishing a new language for magic.

He dropped his head and closed his eyes. He relaxed as much as he could. He began.

He spoke barely above a whisper, hardly moving his lips. This made crisp pronunciation even more difficult, but he felt the syllables rolling out with precision and clarity, with no slurring. Each element fell into place as if it was meant to be there. The transitions between each element were perfect, neither stretched nor condensed.

In a surprisingly short time, it was done. When he uttered the final syllable, it was like dropping a stone into a bucket of water. Ripples spread outwards through his body, reaching a boundary where they rebounded and rolled inwards again. In an instant, he felt as if his entire being was humming, vibrating faster and faster. He opened his eyes and everything was blurred. Inwardly, he continued to shake more and more until he felt as if he were going to fly apart.

Suddenly, stillness. Aubrey took a long, deep breath. He was still there. The spell had worked. He felt strong, stronger than he had for some time. His head was clear. He got to his feet and joined Caroline and George at the ladder. 'What's out there?'

'It's hard to see,' Caroline said, coming back down. 'Too many shadows. I couldn't see the sniper. Holroyd and the others are scattered around the church, hugging the walls, trying to guess where the shots are coming from.'

'What can we do?' George asked.

Aubrey considered. 'The right moment will present itself if we are ready for it.' He grinned. It was the sort of thing the Scholar Tan would say.

He glanced at the trapdoor at the exact moment a bolt of violent purple light burst through it. He threw up an arm and closed his eyes, but purple and green flashes danced underneath his eyelids. His skin prickled unbearably as a boom and a high-pitched hiss rolled down from overhead, followed by shouts and screams.

He opened his eyes gingerly, to see Caroline and George doing the same. George was slapping dust off his beggar's rags.

'We have our distraction,' Aubrey said.

He bolted up the ladder and out through the trapdoor, not giving himself time to think. He threw himself onto his belly and tried to take in his surroundings.

Dozens of globes of light were hovering in the body of the church – purple, red and gold. They varied in size from marbles to footballs and were darting at the members of the Army of New Albion. Another cluster was swooping upwards like a flock of birds.

Magic, Aubrey thought as his skin itched.

Ames was standing in the middle of the nave. He was flailing his arms and screaming. 'Rats! Get them off me! Rats!'

Holroyd was hunched against the wall, as if trying to make himself as small as possible. His shrieks made the hair stand up on the back of Aubrey's neck.

Nearby, another man lay. Blood was streaming from a shoulder wound, but his curses and demands for assistance indicated that he was another member of the Army of New Albion, and still among the living.

Briggs was trapped in the middle of a flock of globes, running for his life along the length of the nave. He turned his head to see if he was being followed and ran into one of the pillars. He toppled like a tree and didn't move.

Aubrey winced as three rifle shots cracked flat and hard. Ames danced on his toes. 'Rats!' he screamed. 'The rats are everywhere!'

Caroline surged up the ladder. She threw herself next to Aubrey and George was at their side an instant later. Together, they scrambled into a tangle of rubbish and rubble. It offered concealment and a wide view of the extraordinary events unfolding in the ruins.

'Rifle?' George asked, panting.

'I saw a flash. Coming from there, I think.' Aubrey pointed at the pile of broken masonry in the remaining corner of the ruin, where the flock of globes was congregating. They flew past, darting in and out like hungry seagulls.

'Von Stralick?' Caroline said.

'I'd say so. He's after Holroyd and his friends.' Aubrey pointed. 'But he looks trapped up there now. Not by Holroyd's crew, though. There's no magic about them.' He gnawed his lip. They really should withdraw while they could. Their position was safe, but for how long?

'Then who's controlling those globes?' Caroline asked.

'I'm not sure. George, do you have the pistol Ames dropped?'

'No, old man. I couldn't find it.' George looked pale, but calm. 'Might've been useful.'

At that moment, a giant voice rolled into the burnt church. 'THROW AWAY YOUR WEAPONS AND COME OUT. YOU ARE OUTNUMBERED AND OUTPOSITIONED. THROW AWAY YOUR WEAPONS AND COME OUT.'

Aubrey recognised the voice. 'Craddock,' he said. 'The shrouded figures we saw must have been the Magisterium. Those magical globes would be their work.' Aubrey shook his head. How did the Magisterium fit into this?

The coloured globes clustered together and began to quiver. Slowly, they faded and vanished. A score or more black-garbed figures entered the ruined cathedral, vaulting over the crumbled wall, stepping through the gaps, and scrambling over falls of stone.

Holroyd's wails grew louder and even less coherent. Ames stared wildly around, no doubt wondering where the rats had gone. Then he gaped at the black figures.

'SURRENDER!' came Craddock's magically inflated voice.

Aubrey tensed. He could feel something, deep in his bones. It grated, made his teeth ache. His neck prickled, then began to burn. Someone was preparing to cast potent magic, with a distinctive nature he'd felt before. 'Someone else is here,' he muttered.

George stared around the burnt church. 'Who?'

'I'm not sure,' Aubrey said, but the magic in the air reminded him of that which had animated the assassin golem, which had begun the chain of events that had brought them here.

The floor started to vibrate.

Caroline looked at Aubrey, but he frowned and shook his head. 'I have no idea.' He rubbed the bridge of his nose. Common sense suggested that it was a good time to slip away, while the Magisterium was busy with rounding up the would-be regicides. But this new magical presence was intriguing.

'This way,' he said, and crept towards what could once have been a balcony supporting a choir stall but was now a pile of rubble. He heard Caroline's exasperated sigh, but when he glanced over his shoulder both she and George were following.

The stones were solidly lodged against each other, having been too large to cart away easily. They proved to be easy to scale and provided good cover. Aubrey hauled himself up until he was able to lie flat in the shadow of a cracked slab of marble.

Holroyd and the others had been cornered by the thirty or forty black-clad Magisterium operatives and a few others, whom Aubrey recognised as Special Services agents. The fight seemed to have gone out of the Army of New Albion and they stood with heads down, shoulders sagging. Aubrey saw Craddock standing on the side, allowing the Special Services agents to conduct the arrest. Craddock was scanning the burnt church, one long finger lying along his cheek, his entire posture suggesting he was ill at ease.

Then the night was torn apart.

At first it was a single note, then a collection of deep, sonorous sounds, as if the largest organ in creation had all stops pulled out and all keys depressed at once. Aubrey clapped his hands to his ears. *Perhaps we should have left, after all*, he thought.

Somewhere nearby, stone crashed to the ground. George stifled an oath and stared about, wildly. Caroline's eyes narrowed. She looked poised, taut, ready to move in any direction.

Holroyd shrieked. He shot out his arm and pointed. 'They've come!' he screamed over the blast of noise that swelled, peaked and then started to subside.

Aubrey stared. Ghostly forms were rising through the stones.

Skeletal, mortified, gruesome, with remnants of ragged clothes, they drifted upwards until free of the stone. Aubrey could see through them as they floated, bony fingers by their sides. Their eyes were black and empty. Dozens, then hundreds of the spectres emerged from the stone until the ruined cathedral was filled with a ghastly congregation.

At the sight of the apparitions, the Magisterium operatives stumbled back, before grouping together under Craddock's barked instructions and presenting a united front. Chanting rose from their formation and the coloured globes reappeared, hurtling at the apparitions.

This seemed to spur the spectres into action. A wild, wordless chorus went up from them, then they raised their bony hands and surged towards the Magisterium operatives.

'Look,' whispered Caroline. 'Holroyd and the others have gone.'

'Where's von Stralick?' Aubrey wondered.

'If he has any sense, he'll leave while he can. And I think we should take the opportunity too,' Caroline said.

Aubrey grinned. 'After you.'

The apparitions closed with the Magisterium operatives, who seemed dismayed that the coloured globes had no effect on them. They fell back and began to resort to other measures – conjurations of half-visible creatures, ear-splitting lightning bolts, gusts of cold and heat, spatters of light that made Aubrey's eyes hurt.

One of the operatives was gripped by a spectre, but the ghost was slashed away by something that swooped in a blur of motion, a small, black, deadly shape.

George gripped Aubrey's arm. 'Did you see that?'

'No.'

'I did,' Caroline said. She stared at Aubrey. 'It was the same as in Father's workshop.'

George's face was grim. 'The Magisterium is using shades? Then could they be the ones responsible for your father's death, for the golem, everything that's happened?'

Aubrey chewed his lip. Craddock's motives had never been easy to discern. Could he be weaving a subtle web with the aim of achieving power unparalleled in Albion?

He shook his head. Craddock did not seem ambitious for power and status, not like so many others Aubrey had seen. Not like the Prime Minister. Not like the Foreign Secretary. It had to be someone else.

'We mustn't jump to conclusions,' he finally said. 'For a start, we can't assume that the Magisterium was behind the shade in Professor Hepworth's workshop.'

George looked frustrated, but there was no time to argue as their attention was drawn back to the nave of the church. The apparitions were slowly being annihilated by the Magisterium operatives. Bolts of magic were shredding the spectres, but they had managed to injure three or four operatives, who were slumped with their backs to the cracked base of the pillar.

But Aubrey's attention was caught by movement at the top of the pillar. Watching from this precarious vantage point was a man, but a man shrouded in magic so as to hide his identity. It was like looking through poorly made glass for, while the figure was tantalisingly apparent, Aubrey could make out nothing distinctive at all, except that the mysterious watcher seemed to be holding a stick in one hand. Aubrey frowned. Or was it a wand? Could someone have found a genuine magic wand?

This watcher was surrounded by a dozen or more shades, but he paid little attention to them even though they were attacking, slicing towards him before veering off. Aubrey saw one skim too close. The watcher slapped at it almost absently, backhanding it into oblivion. The shade folded in on itself and vanished.

The watcher leaned forward, studying the Magisterium operatives clustered at the base of the pillar. Aubrey could feel the power emanating from him. He had used potent spells to raise the spectral horde, combinations of approaches that Aubrey had never thought possible. The spells were audacious, full of bravado, and Aubrey realised the watcher was using them again. More apparitions rose from the floor of the burnt church and shambled to reinforce the dwindling ranks of their fellows, but the watcher was not content with this show of power. Aubrey gasped as, with almost scornful ease, the watcher called a rain of fire down on the hapless Magisterium operatives.

Aubrey knew, in theory at least, how difficult such a spell was. Uniting water and fire required such a strong application of the Law of Opposites that few seriously considered attempting it. Even experimenting with such a spell required an ego far beyond that of commonplace magicians.

With a hissing, crackling roar, the liquid fire cascaded down on the Magisterium operatives but, just before they were enveloped in the blazing torrent, a protective dome sprang up, neatly shielding them from fiery death. Aubrey was impressed by the training and teamwork that had allowed the operatives to respond so quickly.

He felt a tug on his sleeve. 'We should go,' George whispered.

Aubrey sighed, nodded, and allowed Caroline to lead them away from the magical battle. She made good use of cover, moving from shadow to niche, always avoiding open ground. Aubrey struggled to keep up with her decisive progress. The ruins were lit up by the rain of fire and the magical bolts that pierced it as the Magisterium fought back, sending shadows dancing across the crumbling stonework. Aubrey took a last look at the watcher. He was standing on top of the pillar, hands on hips, and Aubrey had the distinct impression he was laughing.

Who *was* he?

It took them some time, but they managed to leave the ruins and stagger back to where they'd left Jack and Oscar. Behind them, the burnt church was a riot of hurtful light, strange smells and cries that did not belong in this world.

From out of the darkness and the rain, Jack Figg's voice greeted them. 'Glad you're back. We've got a surprise for you.'

When they drew closer, Aubrey saw that Jack was standing next to a horse and cart. The driver was a small, dark man, who tipped his cloth cap to Caroline and gave a lopsided grin as water poured from the brim.

'Charlie will take us back to my place,' Jack said, 'and then he'll forget he ever saw us. Right, Charlie?'

The driver waved a hand and mumbled. It sounded as if he had a doormat stuck in his throat. He jerked his thumb at the rear of the cart and Aubrey didn't need a second invitation. He dragged himself aboard, watching as Caroline vaulted in with the grace of a dancer.

'Where's Oscar?' George asked when he'd settled on the rough, wet timber and the cart set off with a jerk. The horse glumly splashed its way through an enormous puddle.

Jack was sitting next to the driver. 'That's the other part of the surprise,' he said over his shoulder. 'Some speed please, Charlie. It's best to be well away from here.'

The driver growled at the horse. Immediately, it lurched forward over the uneven cobblestones, picking up pace until the cart was bouncing along, every jolt making Aubrey's head ache. He screwed up his face and peered through the wind-whipped rain.

Charlie obviously knew the best routes. The cart slid wildly around corners, clattered down narrow laneways and along noisome drains, but never had to stop for traffic. Aubrey clutched the side of the cart with a strength that surprised him and he wondered what would happen if a pedestrian staggered out of one of the many doors they passed.

Charlie had some difficulty getting his horse to stop. It appeared as if the nag had enjoyed the exercise. It looked almost disappointed when the cart rolled to a halt outside Jack's hovel. The light from the single window showed that someone was inside.

Jack climbed down from the cart. George helped Aubrey, while Caroline alighted and patted the horse on the flank. It turned its head and stared at her quizzically.

'Thanks, Charlie,' Jack said, but the enigmatic driver was already moving off through the rain without a word or a backward glance.

'A good man,' Jack said. 'His wife was very ill until your clinic helped her, Aubrey.'

Aubrey wished he'd thanked the driver. The cart ride had given him a chance to gain some strength after his exertions at the burnt church.

Caroline stepped up and rapped on the door of Jack's hovel.

Oscar opened it, his bulk filling the doorway almost completely.

Inside, sitting on a bench, was a man with a large bandage covering the side of his head and another wrapped around his hand. He looked pale and strained.

'Say hello to Hugo von Stralick,' Jack said.

Twenty-One

THE RAIN DRUMMED ON THE ROOF OF THE HOVEL WHILE Jack explained how they'd come upon the fleeing von Stralick and insisted he join them. The Holmlander sat on the bench with Oscar's massive hands on his shoulders, restraining him. The bandage on his hand had begun to redden as blood seeped through and he cradled it with his good hand.

Aubrey was perched on the desk. Jack had given Caroline the only chair, while George and he sat on boxes. One of Jack's cats jumped into his lap and looked unhappily at the bedraggled intruders.

'Well, Hugo,' Jack said to von Stralick. 'I know now that I shouldn't have told you the way to the burnt church. Why didn't you tell me you were a spy?'

Von Stralick attempted to shrug, but winced under Oscar's firm grip. 'Greetings, Miss Hepworth, Mr Fitzwilliam, Mr Doyle. I trust you have recovered from the wretched shooting party we shared?'

'Quite,' Aubrey said. 'What happened to your hand?'

'I've lost a finger.' Von Stralick managed to make it sound as if it was merely forgetfulness rather than a throbbing wound. 'One of those ghouls at the burnt church ripped my rifle from me and happened to take my finger with it.'

Aubrey was impressed by von Stralick's calm. And despite the bandages on his wounded ear and maimed hand, he looked clean and presentable. He'd smoothed back his black hair and had somehow kept his moustache trimmed. He spoke without any noticeable Holmlander accent.

Jack sighed. 'Hugo? Why didn't you tell me what you are?'

'I thought you knew I was a spy.'

'I thought you were a troublemaker, that was all.'

Von Stralick smiled a little. 'I'm very good at what I do.'

'Then why did you miss at the burnt church?' Aubrey cut in. 'You fired a number of shots and didn't hit anyone.'

'I'm a good spy, but a mediocre assassin.'

'Then why were you shooting at all?' Caroline asked.

Von Stralick gazed at the ceiling. 'My, that rain is heavy, isn't it?'

Aubrey fumed. 'You're not going to say anything?'

Von Stralick smiled and spread his hands. 'I have a duty, you understand.' He wrinkled his brow. 'I . . .' He coughed, covering his mouth with his good hand and wincing as he jolted the other. 'Excuse me,' he said. 'It must be the weather.'

Suddenly, his eyes opened wide in surprise. He touched his chest with his good hand and uttered a pained grunt.

'Quickly,' Caroline said. 'It's his heart. Lay him on the floor!'

Oscar looked puzzled and stood back as Jack seized the

sagging von Stralick. George helped and they stretched him out on the only uncluttered part of the floor. His eyes were closed and his face had turned a flat grey colour. He was breathing shallowly.

Caroline knelt beside the stricken Holmlander and began to loosen his tie. 'Undo his jacket,' she ordered George, who hurried to do her bidding. 'Jack,' she snapped, 'where's the nearest doctor?'

Aubrey was frowning, thinking hard. At the instant that von Stralick had reached for his chest, Aubrey had felt the insidious tang of magic reach into the room. Something malevolent was afoot.

He stumbled off the desk and joined Caroline, kneeling by the inert Holmlander. 'He's stopped breathing,' Caroline said.

Aubrey placed his hand on von Stralick's chest. 'What are you doing?' Caroline demanded. He ignored her and used his magical awareness to feel what was happening.

He hissed and nearly pulled his hand away. Magical tendrils were wrapped around von Stralick's heart like a strangler fig. They were squeezing the life out of him.

Concentrating, Aubrey could discern that it was a vicious application of Action at a Distance. He grimaced. The spell was distinctive; it had all the hallmarks of the mysterious watcher at the burnt church. Aubrey could sense that he was using von Stralick's missing finger as the basis of this deadly enchantment, the body part allowing access to the Holmlander's physical being.

Action at a Distance. Aubrey knew that a primary function of this law was to establish a linkage. Much as a marionette master pulls strings to make his puppets work, so Action at a Distance could set up a connection between the spell-caster and the subject. He blinked, frowned, then he saw it: an insubstantial filament snaking off through the solid wall of the hovel, only visible to someone with magical awareness. Aubrey reached out and uttered a simple severance spell. Without a sound, the filament parted and faded.

Von Stralick's chest heaved. With a tortured rasp, he sucked in a huge breath, then another, as his hands clutched the air. In a moment, he was sitting up, shaking his head.

Jack Figg fetched water in an earthenware mug. Von Stralick sipped it and nodded his thanks.

Shaken, Aubrey stood. He went and leaned against the desk. 'Someone wants to kill you, von Stralick.'

Von Stralick tried to smile, but it faded before it reached his lips. He touched his chest with his fingertips. 'Magic?'

'Indeed. Very unusual magic, too. Perpetrated by the unknown party at the burnt church.'

'I saw him,' von Stralick said, 'but I could not make him out. He set his ghouls on me.'

'He hasn't given up on you, it seems.'

Von Stralick looked troubled. 'I see. This changes matters, somewhat. I feel as if I am not in possession of all the facts.' He winced. 'May I resume my seat on the bench? It must be more comfortable than this floor.'

Jack and George helped the Holmlander to his feet and then eased him to his seat. Oscar shuffled to one side.

Von Stralick rubbed his neck with both hands. 'I feel that it is most important to identify this mysterious party. For all our sakes.'

Aubrey studied the Holmland spy. The man was wary, disconcerted, but he might have useful information. Aubrey told himself to step carefully here.

He thought of the grand structure of supposition and assumption he'd built up and realised he'd already begun shifting the pieces around in his mind. He thought back to the whorled timber trinket he'd added at the last moment to stabilise the structure he'd made back at Maidstone. *It looks as if I needed that piece after all*, he thought.

'Perhaps this mysterious foe has been manoeuvring this whole situation from behind the scenes, since the shooting party.' He frowned and tried to concentrate. 'He is powerful – strong enough to confound Craddock and the Magisterium, cunning enough to help the Army of New Albion escape from the Society for Non-magical Fitness. And the magic he used in the burnt church wasn't the work of an ordinary magician.'

'If it's the same person who stole my father's notebook, he'll have its assistance,' Caroline pointed out.

'Who do you think it is, Hugo?' Jack asked. 'Who is this mastermind?'

Von Stralick frowned. 'One of my first tasks when I am able to contact my superiors will be to see if they know. Someone in a position of influence? A member of the government? One of the great industrial leaders your country is so proud of? Whoever it is, their motives are not clear. It makes them all the more shadowy.'

George shook his head. 'I'm baffled.' He stood, stretched, then blinked. 'D'you have rats here, Jack?'

From somewhere near came a determined scratching.

'No,' Jack said, puzzled. 'The cats keep them away.'

'Ah, that'll be one at the door, then. Poor, wet moggy. I'll let it in.'

Jack shook his head. 'They're both inside, George. Revolutionary is under the desk and Comrade is by Oscar's feet.'

Caroline raised an eyebrow. 'Your cats' names are Revolutionary and Comrade?'

'Good, productive names, I would have thought. "Puss" and suchlike are the products of an outmoded system where domestic creatures are exploited.'

The scratching came again. Aubrey held up a hand, motioning for silence. Oscar stirred and craned his neck as George reached out for the latch. He jerked the door open. Lying on the doorstep was the mangled shape of one of Aubrey's clay mannikins. Rain tumbled on it. The mannikin lifted its head, sought for the door and found George's boot instead.

'Bring it here,' Aubrey said. 'It's come to report.'

George scooped it up. Caroline closed the door behind him and he took the mannikin to Aubrey. Aubrey held it in both hands and looked at the mess his handiwork had become. It was mostly a torso. Both legs were missing, and its arms were crossed and fused to its chest. Its clay surface looked as if it had been held over a fire, and one side of its faceless head had slumped and sagged. It twitched in his hands. 'We might have an answer here,' he said.

Von Stralick stared at the clay creature. 'What is this?'

'Aubrey's work,' Caroline said. Von Stralick sat back thoughtfully.

'Do you think it saw anything?' George asked.

'I don't know. It's too damaged to speak. It must have been caught in the magical cross-fire in the burnt church. I'm amazed it managed to drag itself all the way back here.'

At that moment, the mannikin shuddered. Aubrey went to still it, to return it to the clay from which it came, but the creature half-raised itself. As Aubrey watched, fascinated, the mannikin shook, swaying from side to side. Its poor, melted shape jerked and Aubrey had trouble holding it. Finally, with a supreme effort, it wrenched its fused arms apart. The exertion was too much for it, and the clay shape broke into two fragments.

Caroline gasped, while George and Jack let out oaths. Aubrey sat with the clay fragments in his lap. Between them was a small, silver-white object that the mannikin had been clasping.

'What is it?' Von Stralick asked, peering.

Aubrey picked it up and held it in his palm. It was cool, the size of the tip of his thumb. Roughly egg-shaped, it was gnarled in a way that was unmistakable. Aubrey recognised it immediately.

'It belongs to Dr Tremaine, the Sorcerer Royal. It was embedded in the top of his favourite cane.' As he said it, he remembered the blurred figure he had seen atop the pillar in the burnt church. He hadn't been wielding a wand or a stick, but holding his cane.

Aubrey sighed and wiped his face with a hand. He felt as if he'd been staring at a painting, trying to make sense of it, and then realised it had been hung upside down and had only needed righting. 'Dr Tremaine is our mysterious foe.'

'What?' Jack said. 'Impossible. He's dead.'

'I have to agree,' said von Stralick. 'He died in an accident at Banford Park.'

'It was Tremaine,' Aubrey repeated. It was like dropping a seed crystal into a supersaturated solution. Suddenly a lattice of consequences was forming and Aubrey found he could see much that had previously been unclear. Dr Tremaine's cane must have been lost in the magical battle in the burnt church. The mannikin had risked itself to bring back this evidence. 'This pearl is his. His death must have been a ruse.'

'But why?' Jack said. He took off his glasses and polished them. 'What is Tremaine doing mixed up in all this?'

'Playing his own game, I suspect,' Aubrey said. 'It seems as if he has moved the Magisterium, the Special Services, the Army of New Albion and your people, von Stralick, much as pieces on a chessboard.' He looked at the Holmland spy. 'But what was he doing at the burnt church?'

Von Stralick shrugged. 'I'd say I was his target. I was going to eliminate the Army of New Albion.'

'What?' George burst out. 'Why would you do a thing like that?'

'Because they're planning to kill the King,' Aubrey said slowly. He looked closely at von Stralick. 'That would mean Prince Albert would assume the throne, and he has a much stronger view about resisting Holmland aggression on the continent than his father. Isn't that correct?'

Von Stralick smiled. 'Our Elektor corresponds regularly with your King about gardening. They are good friends.'

'But Holmland wants war,' George said. 'Your generals are always talking about it.'

'No, Holmland doesn't want war at all,' von Stralick said. 'Not right now.'

Caroline narrowed her eyes. 'Later, then. At a time of your choosing.'

Aubrey pushed on with his chain of thought. 'Tremaine wanted to stop you. For some reason, he didn't want the Army of New Albion to fail. If they did, the plot to kill the King would be no more. Albion and Holmland would be friends.' He scowled. 'Tremaine wants to bring us to the brink of war.'

'Holmland would be blamed if your King was killed,'

von Stralick said. 'It wouldn't matter who was responsible. We are always blamed.'

Aubrey put his hands together and squeezed, hard. 'My father is missing, Hugo.'

Von Stralick looked surprised for an instant, before he gathered himself. 'Sir Darius? I didn't know.' He scowled. 'I don't like not knowing such things. I'm sorry, Fitzwilliam.'

'I'm sure you are,' Caroline said.

'You must believe me,' von Stralick continued. 'We would never move against Sir Darius. Not only would we be the natural suspects –'

'Which you are,' George pointed out.

'But it would harden the Albion people against us, which we do not want at the moment. Sir Darius is a very popular man.'

'I'm inclined to believe you. Which means Dr Tremaine must have my father,' Aubrey said. 'Tremaine wants war. Somehow, abducting my father is going to help advance his plot. It makes sense. From what we know of Tremaine, he likes to have more than one iron in the fire.'

'But why?' von Stralick said.

Why indeed? Aubrey thought. It came to him then, perfectly, the last piece in the puzzle. Without all his research into his own condition, Aubrey would never have seen it. Tremaine, Banford Park, magic, the Black Beast . . . Looking for a solution to his own condition, of teetering on the edge of true death, Aubrey had come across references – oblique and guarded – to a vast, inconceivable horror, something that could be satisfied under certain conditions. It was a way to power beyond belief, but it was at a cost that would be inhuman to contemplate. It was one reason why death magic was a forbidden area.

'War,' he repeated. 'Tremaine wants a war.'

'But how does he stand to benefit from conflict like that?' George asked. 'Is he working for Holmland?'

Jack jumped in. 'Or is it money? Does Tremaine own armaments factories? Is he going to get rich from the blood of the workers?'

They all looked to Aubrey for an answer. 'No,' he said eventually, 'Tremaine's game is more subtle and more terrifying than that.' He took a deep breath, then let it out. 'War as sacrifice. With Holmland and Albion at war, the whole Continent will be drawn into it.' Aubrey went on, hoping that speaking his thoughts aloud would expose holes in his reasoning, but knowing it was the only answer that made sense. 'Millions will die. With modern weapons, the Continent will be a slaughter-house. If Tremaine can harness this blood sacrifice in the correct way, he will have enough death, enough souls, to conduct the Ritual of the Way.'

'Immortality,' von Stralick breathed.

Aubrey looked sharply at him. 'How do you know about the Ritual of the Way? Are you a magician as well as a spy?'

'No magician, just a good reader. I study history. I know that the Ritual of the Way is a theoretical method of gaining immortality, but no-one has ever worked out how to arrange enough deaths.'

'The ritual is meant to grant immortality and power,' Aubrey said. 'Enough for an eternal reign.'

Von Stralick appeared to come to a decision. 'Fitz-william, look to Banford Park. Tremaine was head of that facility and we have reliable intelligence to suggest that it is not totally shut down, as was announced.' He pounded the wall with his good hand. 'Tremaine must be stopped!'

Aubrey agreed. An immortal ruler who was prepared to sacrifice millions for his own good? One who thought he was beyond petty considerations such as human life? He shuddered. A nightmare was unfolding in front of them.

At that moment, many things happened in quick succession. One of Jack's cats went out through a hole in the wall, then hissed and hurried back, confronted by the rain. The sodden animal wore an expression of utter distaste. Just as it reappeared, Oscar shifted his weight, easing his massive feet off the ground for relief then placing them back down again. Unfortunately, his left foot settled on the cat's tail.

The cat gave an ear-splitting screech and Aubrey thought, at first, that someone had launched a demon into the hovel. Oscar was startled and tottered backwards. He put out a hand to steady himself, but the flimsy wall offered no support. With the crunch of breaking timber, he toppled right through the wall and into the only other room of the tiny dwelling. He lay there, blinking.

Jack sprang to Oscar's side, then was torn between helping his friend and his spitting, hissing cat. When he saw the cat was sitting in a corner washing its tail, he left it alone. 'Oscar, are you hurt?'

Oscar sat up, smiling and wiping dust from his chest with both plate-sized hands. 'Righto, Jack. Righto.'

Aubrey smiled, but Caroline seized his arm. 'Von Stralick, he's gone.'

Aubrey turned to see the open door. George peered up and down the street. 'No sign of him.'

'Right,' Aubrey said. 'No help from that quarter, then.'

'What's the best course of action, old man?' George asked.

'I still have to get my father back.'

'And how are we going to do that?' Caroline asked.

'By finding Tremaine. Von Stralick's suspicions about Banford Park make very good sense to me. Tremaine has had plenty of time to set up equipment there since it was shut down, readying it to act as a base for his plotting.' He hummed a little, then grinned. 'Can anyone fly an ornithopter?'

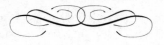

Twenty-Two

'YOU'RE *SURE* YOU KNOW HOW TO FLY AN ORNI-
thopter?' Aubrey asked.

'Of course.' Caroline reached up and tested one
of the wing struts. 'I learned years ago.'

'One of your father's friends taught you?' George
guessed.

'My mother taught me,' Caroline said. She'd abandoned her beggar's rags, revealing that underneath she'd
been wearing the loose black outfit she'd had on when
confronting the Black Beast at Penhurst. Aubrey admired
the cut of the garments as she opened the door into the
cabin, mounted the three steps and disappeared inside.

'An interesting family, the Hepworths, wouldn't you
say, George?'

'Extraordinary.'

With Jack Figg as a guide, they had gone from the Mire
to Ashfields Station in under twenty minutes. Along the

way an excited urchin joined them – one of Jack's friends – and reported that the Magisterium had left the burnt church at speed, desperately pursuing a tall man who was wrapped in shadows.

At four o'clock in the morning, the ornithopter port was deserted and quiet, as was the dirigible landing field. The only sound came from the neighbouring railway yards, where the noise of the wheel-checkers and bogie-riders rang out.

Jack left them, fading back into the night, and then it was up to Aubrey. He used a sleep spell he'd honed over years at Stonelea School, utilising the contagious nature of yawning and drawing on the Law of Sympathy, to send the two nightwatchmen to sleep.

The wrought-iron gates that led to the flight platforms were bolted, but not locked. They slipped through and found an ornithopter waiting for them.

For a moment, Aubrey stood and admired the intricate machine. Its hinged wings were beaten brass and made of a thousand separate, jointed pieces. The fuselage looked fragile, a network of metal mesh and glass, long and tapering. The whole, marvellous construction looked like a dragonfly eager to soar.

'Well?' came Caroline's voice. 'What are you waiting for? Climb aboard.'

Aubrey leaned against one of the four great metal legs. They were bent, bringing the body of the ornithopter close to the ground. 'After you, George.'

Inside the ornithopter were six seats. Aubrey took the one next to the pilot and gave Caroline the thumbs-up.

'Seatbelts,' she ordered.

Aubrey had flown in an ornithopter before, an experience that was a mixture of exhilaration and terror. He knew that it was magic that allowed ornithopters to work, for the flapping, twisting action of the wings would cause any material not magically enhanced to fall apart. Applications of the Laws of Sympathy and Correspondence allowed the metal wings to beat in the same way as the wings of birds. Other spells enhanced the power of the legs of the ornithopter, which provided the initial impetus to hurl the craft into the air.

No magical ability was required to pilot such a craft, simply skill, daring and good reflexes.

'Hold on!' Caroline said.

Even though he was ready for it, Aubrey's stomach was left behind as the four powerful legs flexed and kicked the ornithopter upwards.

George let out a whoop, but it was lost in the deafening *whoosh* of the wings as they began beating. The ornithopter lurched left, stalled, then levelled, before mounting upwards in a series of stomach-bouncing steps, wings thrashing the air.

'Higher!' Aubrey cried, grinning. Metallic clamour filled the small craft, making it sound like the inside of a foundry.

Caroline glanced at him and grinned back. Her hands and feet moved quickly over the controls and Aubrey could see no indecision, just joy. Her eyes were bright, reflecting the lights on the instrument panel. She'd tied her hair back with a piece of string and Aubrey could see her long, slender neck and the wisps there. She glanced at him again and pointed to a small box on a rack in front of him.

Inside were sound-deadeners, small yellow pieces of magically enhanced wool. He poked one into each ear, sighing with relief when the sound of the wings faded to a dull whirring, then handed the box to George.

Caroline pushed forward on the controls, sending the ornithopter swooping. Then she banked right in a sweeping arc which had Aubrey straining against his seatbelt. He found himself looking down on Ashfields Station, then Sandway, then the river.

Aubrey promised himself that he would learn to fly an ornithopter.

A FIFTEEN-MINUTE FLIGHT LATER, THEY REACHED BANFORD Park. Caroline set the ornithopter in a long, gliding circle while Aubrey looked down.

The research facility was surrounded by a forest that extended for miles. Penhurst was to the south-west, a hike through the woods. A single road led into Banford Park, where a collection of prefabricated huts stood well separated from each other, no doubt to prevent magical interference patterns from ruining experiments. A single, squat, stone building – Banford – faced a pond in the middle of the facility. All was dark and silent. The place looked as if it had been deserted for years.

'I'm going to glide in,' Caroline said. Air whistled over the rigid wings. 'Quieter.'

But more dangerous, Aubrey thought. Nothing he'd seen made him doubt Caroline's skill, but he knew that ornithopters were more responsive when the wings were beating. He tightened his seatbelt.

Caroline brought the craft around, killed some speed by raising its nose, then feathered the wings slightly. It swooped over the pond, around the stone immensity of Banford, past the research huts, then she deliberately stalled and the machine dropped onto its legs. They flexed, then steadied, and they were down.

Aubrey looked at Caroline. Even in the darkness and the dim light thrown by the instruments, he could see her cheeks were flushed and she was breathing heavily. 'Well done,' he said.

'Let's find your father,' she said briskly, after she'd composed herself.

Aubrey stumbled out of the ornithopter and crouched in the shadow of a rose bush the size of a house.

George joined him. 'What's the penalty for stealing an ornithopter?'

'Less than the penalty for failing to save one's country. Or one's father.'

Caroline slipped out of the flying machine. Aubrey noticed that her bare feet were tiny. 'Where now?' she asked.

Aubrey chewed his lip. 'I was sure there'd be lights.'

'Maybe there's no-one here,' George said. He looked to the east. 'Dawn can't be too far away. We could make for the station. We'd be well away from here in a few hours.'

'Wait,' Aubrey said. 'Let me see what I can feel.'

Aubrey spread his hand and placed it flat on the chill, damp grass. He pressed, trying to get as close to the earth as he could.

He could feel stirrings of magic close by, but the traces were stale, most likely the residue left behind by the researchers when the facility was disbanded. He sensed tiny remnants of old earth magic, forgotten charms from people long ago.

Then he felt a strange magical vibration tingling in his hand. It was muffled, shielded by subtle spells. Aubrey only sensed it because it was familiar. It had the flavour of the magical residue the golem assassin had left, and was very close in texture to some of the spells cast at the burnt church. 'It's underground. Under there.' He stood and pointed at Banford. 'A bunker, I'd say.'

'How are we going to get in?' Caroline asked.

'You don't have any other skills you haven't told us about?' Aubrey replied. 'Picking locks? Breaking and entering?'

'We could go and see if the place is open,' George suggested.

Aubrey shrugged. 'As long as we do it quietly.'

The double wooden doors of the main entrance to the stately Banford were locked. Both side doors were locked. The rear door was locked. None of the windows was open.

Frustrated, Aubrey stood before the front doors again. 'Dr Tremaine is under here. That's where the magic is.'

'How do you know?' Caroline asked.

'The magical traces lead right through every entrance. And they're fresh, a few hours at most.' Aubrey put his hand on the smooth wood of the doors. He grasped the brass handle. 'The doors have been enchanted, too. I can feel it.'

'So we need magic to get inside,' George said. 'Do you know any good unlocking spells?'

'Tremaine wouldn't want to use a spell every time he went in and out. Too tedious.'

What would he use? Aubrey asked himself. *He'd want something efficient, elegant, automatic . . .*

He'd want the doors to recognise him.

Aubrey knew that good preparation was the key to successful spell-casting. *But in this case*, he thought, *I'll have to make it up as I go along. Again.*

He hummed a little and slapped his pockets, eyebrows raising when he felt a hard, round shape in his inner jacket pocket. He reached into it and pulled out Dr Tremaine's pearl. He stared at it. 'Remember the illusion spell I cast back in Professor Hepworth's workshop?' he said softly.

'The Law of Something or Other, no doubt,' George whispered hoarsely. 'Whatever it is, old man, I'd get on with it if I were you.'

Aubrey moved to one side of the door and cleared his mind, readying himself. He took a deep breath and began.

Having cast it so recently, the spell came to Aubrey easily. He used the pearl as a focus, as it had been so close to the Sorcerer Royal for so long. Each syllable he chanted set the parameters of the illusion, while the specific sequence of terms circumscribed the effects, limiting them to Dr Tremaine's physical appearance. He shuddered at the thought of taking on any of Dr Tremaine's personality. That wouldn't do at all.

He had time to adjust the spell a little, to make it even more convincing. Aubrey's inversion of two syllables at the end of the spell, and the elimination of the falling terminal utterance, added what he thought was some *flavour* of Dr Tremaine's being. He hoped it might help deceive the guardian spells waiting for them.

He let out a deep breath and turned to his friends. Caroline stared and hissed, her hands curling into fists.

'Well done, old man,' George said in a strained voice. 'Dr Tremaine has a twin.'

Aubrey didn't feel any different, but when he looked at his hands they weren't his own. They were long, powerful and bore several wicked scars. 'Let's hope the door thinks so.'

'That's better,' Caroline said. She stood more easily. 'You can't possibly be Dr Tremaine with that voice.'

'Good,' Aubrey said, but he felt vaguely insulted. 'Stand behind me.'

Aubrey spread his arms wide and presented himself to the entrance. He grinned when the door opened with no hesitation. 'Quickly, let's find the stairs down to the bunker.'

It was easier than he expected. Behind the grand stair-case which led to the upper floors was a narrower flight of stairs leading down. Soft buttery lights began to glow as they descended, triggered by their presence. At the bottom of the stairs was an iron door and it, too, opened as they approached. A short corridor led to another iron door which swung back as they neared.

Inside was a drawing room. Aubrey blinked. Except for its having no windows, the room would not have been out of place in Penhurst or Maidstone. The carpet was richly patterned Olchester, the furniture was solid, darkly polished wood and leather. Glass-fronted bookshelves were crammed with expensive-looking volumes. A harp stood in one corner. The paintings were landscapes full of riders, peasants and haywains.

Across the room, sitting motionless on one of the large, wing-backed chairs was Sir Darius. Next to the chair stood a tall, dark figure in an extravagant fur coat.

'Father,' Aubrey breathed. 'Dr Tremaine.'

'Ah, good to see you all here!' the Sorcerer Royal said, beaming. 'I was just explaining to Sir Darius how I'd change the lbw law if it were up to me, but that can wait. Take a seat. And cancel that illusion, young Fitzwilliam. Devilishly handsome though I am, it's a mite disconcert-ing seeing myself across the room.'

A three-syllable utterance was all it took to cancel the illusion. Aubrey stared at his father. 'What have you done to him?'

Sir Darius was sitting stiff-backed, both feet on the floor, arms on the armrests of the chair. His face was impassive, drained of life. The only part of him that moved was his eyes, which met Aubrey's gaze.

Dr Tremaine chuckled. 'A simple spell. An inverse application of the Law of Animation, as I expect you've already guessed. Much safer than tying him up.'

'Let him go.'

'After taking so much trouble to bring him here? That wouldn't make much sense, would it?' Dr Tremaine clapped his hands together. 'And now you're here. Which is a capital thing, as I have a feeling that it may be useful to keep a close eye on you, young Fitzwilliam.'

Aubrey sensed Caroline slipping to his right, putting a table between the Sorcerer Royal and herself. George stood to Aubrey's left, fists clenched, glowering.

'You killed my father, didn't you?' Caroline said.

Dr Tremaine turned and studied her for a moment. 'Ah, Miss Hepworth. I haven't seen you since you were a baby.'

'You killed him,' Caroline repeated, her voice steady.

'I'm sorry,' Dr Tremaine replied, lowering his large, dark eyes. 'I loved Lionel. A great friend. A great man. A great mind. I'm glad I have his notebook to remember him by.'

His face had gone from joviality to sorrow to compassion in an instant. Aubrey blinked. It was as if Dr Tremaine had run through a series of masks, trying each one until he found one that fitted the occasion.

'But *why* did you kill him?' Aubrey asked, as he digested

the fact that the professor's notebook was in the possession of Dr Tremaine.

Dr Tremaine shrugged. 'The magic that drove the
Black Beast needed a final test. It happened to be Lionel.
Rather bad luck on his part, really. It could have been
anyone.'

It was the offhand nature of this declaration that chilled
Aubrey. Someone whom Tremaine called a friend was
killed just because he happened to be in the wrong place?

'You really are trying for the Ritual of the Way, aren't
you?' he asked.

Dr Tremaine rolled his eyes. 'I'm sorry that it's so
obvious.'

'You're planning a war,' George said through clenched
teeth.

'Just helping it along a little. To tell the truth, I think
the idiots in charge are doing a good job by themselves,
but I'm not one to leave things to chance.' He stroked his
chin and chuckled. 'My role over the last few months has
been like an invisible stage manager, really. Rewarding, if
a little frustrating.'

'You were at the Society for Non-magical Fitness,'
Aubrey said flatly.

'I made sure my Army of New Albion tools were able
to escape from that mess. Von Stralick nearly managed to
ruin everything right then by luring them there.'

'And the burnt church? You saved them there as well?'

A flash of annoyance crossed Dr Tremaine's face.
'Von Stralick's childish coded message was an obvious
trap for the Army of New Albion poltroons. I knew I had
to get there and help them escape. Alas, the Magisterium
was there in force and so my plans have collapsed. For
now.' He broke off and looked at the wood-panelled

ceiling. 'Speaking of which, it seems as if Craddock's forces have arrived.' He chuckled. 'Doesn't he ever give up?'

Aubrey heard a muffled explosion overhead. It seemed as if Dr Tremaine was right.

The Sorcerer Royal sighed. 'It looks as if I must be off. You'll forgive me for leaving so abruptly?'

'No,' Caroline said.

Aubrey turned to see that Caroline was holding Ames's revolver in both hands and had adopted a perfect shooting stance. *Where was she hiding that pistol?* he thought wildly. He had time to marvel at the tears in her eyes, then she fired all six shots without hesitating.

Dr Tremaine looked irritated and, backhanded, swatted the bullets out of the air. They bounced off a bookshelf and fell to the floor. 'Don't do that,' he said. 'I hate the smell of cordite.' He barked a few guttural words and the revolver disappeared. Caroline stared at her empty hands. She wiped her tears away with the back of her hand and started towards him.

Dr Tremaine's expression hardened. Gone was his cavalier attitude, his banter and his amusement. Instead, he was a cold and malignant creature. Aubrey could see that this was a man who was indifferent to the suffering of others. He would snuff out lives without a thought. 'Enough,' Tremaine snarled, in a voice that was deeper, rougher. 'This part of the game is at an end.'

He pointed at her and uttered two short words and Caroline was flung backwards, tumbling like a feather in a gale.

Aubrey moved to help but stopped when he saw that she'd somehow managed to land on her feet. She growled, deep in her throat, and looked as if she were ready to advance on Dr Tremaine again.

Aubrey was taken off guard by Caroline's fierceness, a contrast to her usual cool demeanour, but he could see that the pain at the loss of her father was boiling out of her unchecked – and it was leading her into mortal danger.

'Wait,' Aubrey said, and – as he'd hoped – he drew the Sorcerer Royal's ferocious attention.

'No,' Tremaine said, 'do not try to stop me.'

Even though Aubrey felt weakened by his recent spell-casting, he could not allow Tremaine to harm Caroline – or escape so easily. If he could slow down the Sorcerer Royal, distract him, perhaps he could give Craddock's operatives time to appear.

He reached into his pocket. 'I have your sister's pearl,' he said, holding it up.

For the first time, Aubrey saw uncertainty in the face of the Sorcerer Royal.

Tremaine let out a long breath. 'I thought I'd lost it. A shade attacked from behind. For a moment I thought it was one of mine, like the one I used to monitor Professor Hepworth's workshop. It wasn't. It slashed my cane from me. I didn't have time to retrieve it.'

'It's important to you.'

Dr Tremaine bared his teeth and his eyes blazed like furnaces. Aubrey felt the immense power of the man. 'Give it to me.'

'I think not.' Aubrey had no strength for anything substantial, but gambled that he would be able to repeat the spell he'd used when he took on Tremaine's appearance, but with a special addition. *Like to like*, he thought, and quickly muttered a short spell. Instantly, Aubrey was again Tremaine's twin – except this time he was shackled to the original by a magical chain, left wrist to left wrist, bound fast. The chain was massive and it radiated intense magic. He gritted his teeth. Tremaine was not leaving.

Tremaine staggered and Aubrey felt a wild, fierce joy at landing a blow against such a foe. Then something unexpected happened. Aubrey gasped, catching the breath in his throat, and he realised the bond between them was doing more than simply preventing Tremaine from leaving. He was connected to the Sorcerer Royal's being.

For a splinter of time, Aubrey was overwhelmed. A cascade of impressions rampaged through him. He was assaulted by the towering arrogance of the man, the utter and complete surrender to ambition and pride. Tremaine, at heart, was brutal, selfish, full of swagger and self-righteousness, with the passion and limitlessness of a force of nature.

The riot of sensations was suddenly cut off. Aubrey stared at Tremaine, who glared back at him before sneering, then laughing. 'You fool, Fitzwilliam! I've made my soul impervious to such dangers, but obviously you don't know how. The first lesson when you deal with life or death: take care of your own soul first!'

And Aubrey knew that while he'd been glimpsing Tremaine's being, the Sorcerer Royal had done the same to him. The magical chain was a conduit that ran both ways. Tremaine had been given an insight into Aubrey's parlous condition – and it wasn't unfamiliar to him.

Dr Tremaine jeered at Aubrey's anguish. He reached into a pocket of his fur coat and plucked out a familiar notebook. He brandished it at Aubrey. 'Even Lionel Hepworth managed to work out a handful of ways to prevent an accidental true death. You are out of your depth, boy, and you are paying for it.'

Dimly, Aubrey heard Caroline's cry of dismay at the appearance of her father's missing notebook.

'I can't let you go,' Aubrey gasped. *For more reasons than one, now. Either you or that book might just have some answers for me.*

Contemptuously, Tremaine barked a torrent of harsh, spiky phrases. With a jolt that made Aubrey gasp, the magical chain disappeared and Aubrey was himself again, his Tremaine link vanishing like smoke in the wind.

'I must,' the Sorcerer Royal said, his eyes blazing. He lifted a hand, but paused. 'Keep my pearl safe for me, Fitzwilliam.'

Tremaine spoke one word, a word of many syllables. Aubrey had never heard anything like it before. The sound hung in the air shimmering and skating on the edge of perception, but it left a bitter taste in Aubrey's mouth, a harsh, metallic tang that made him feel unclean.

Then the Sorcerer Royal disappeared.

Aubrey realised his knees were trembling. He steadied himself against a bookshelf. George started towards him, but he waved him away. He needed a moment to compose himself.

'Aubrey?' Sir Darius turned his head and worked his jaw. 'Where are we? Why are you dressed like that? And George, a beggar?'

Aubrey had forgotten he was still dressed like Tommy Sparks and that his clothes were sodden.

'I'll tell you later, Father. Are you all right?'

Aubrey went to him, only to hear feet pounding down the stairs. He turned to see Magisterium operatives crashing into the room. 'Don't!' he cried to Caroline, as the operatives surrounded her. The warning was too late for George, who swung a punch and was wrestled to the ground by three businesslike women in black uniforms, the Magisterium having no qualms about including females in its ranks. When George realised who had tackled him and thrown him to the carpet, his expression was a combination of embarrassment and delight.

Aubrey managed to get to his father's side by the time all the operatives had entered – a score or more packing into the room.

Craddock entered. 'Sir Darius,' he said. 'Glad to see you're all right.'

Sir Darius, still groggy, merely nodded.

Unsmiling, Craddock surveyed the room. 'Where's Tremaine?'

Aubrey waved a tired hand. 'You're too late. He's gone. How did you know he wasn't dead?'

'I had my suspicions. Some of my operatives were investigating, and their findings led us to the burnt church. When we arrived, we were confronted with a major magical assault.' He smiled his wintry smile. 'Soon after this, we had a visit from Tallis, of the Special Services. Apparently von Stralick, the Holmland spy, is on good terms with him. Von Stralick telephoned him to let him know what was going on – the plot against the King, your father's kidnapping – and Tallis informed us. Von Stralick also told him that you'd be heading here to look for Tremaine.'

'Craddock,' Aubrey said, 'Dr Tremaine wants to undertake the Ritual of the Way.'

Craddock's eyes widened fractionally. 'I see. That would explain much.'

'He has Professor Hepworth's notebook, too.'

'It's worse than I'd thought, then. The professor's work will help Tremaine if he's mad enough to try for the

Ritual of the Way.' He studied Aubrey. 'It seems as if we have much to talk about.'

AUBREY CLOSELY WATCHED THE ORGANISATION OF THE Magisterium and made mental notes. As dawn broke, hordes of black-uniformed operatives swarmed all over Banford Park, sifting, noting, photographing, analysing and collecting. Craddock commanded with a minimum of direction; all the operatives seemed to know what they were doing. Two of them flew the ornithopter away, returning it to the Ashfields ornithopter port.

Sir Darius, Caroline, George and Aubrey were whisked away to Darnleigh House in one of the Magisterium's anonymous black motorcars. It was a quiet, strained trip, with little conversation. Sir Darius seemed to be still affected by the spell Dr Tremaine had used, sleeping all the way. The two operatives who sat with them were polite, but not forthcoming. Their repeated answer to any question was, 'I'm sorry, but you'll have to ask Commander Craddock.'

Darnleigh House and Lattimer Hall, the headquarters of the Magisterium and the Special Services, faced each other across Grainger Square in Eastride. It wasn't a huge distance from the Mire, which amused Aubrey. He imagined a steady stream of informers flowing from the Mire to Darnleigh House, across to Lattimer Hall and then home again in a vast, continuous loop.

Darnleigh House was actually a pair of three-storey townhouses. A hundred years ago they had been bought, walls knocked out, offices installed, basements converted and one entrance bricked up. From the outside, it remained the sort of anonymous architecture that told passers-by to move along as nothing extraordinary was inside. If Aubrey hadn't known better, he would have thought the place belonged to a surgeon, or a reasonably well-to-do stockbroker, perhaps one who had come into his money early and had rather let things drift a little. Modest, discreet, slightly shabby.

On the other side of Grainger Square, the Special Services' Lattimer Hall was altogether fiercer. A fire in a row of houses had provided the opportunity for a purpose-built building to take up the entire block. A squat concrete establishment, only two storeys, it looked as if it could laugh off a cannon shot. Lattimer Hall imposed itself on the surroundings the way Darnleigh House didn't, which may have said something about the way the two agencies thought of themselves.

By the time they were ushered through the well-guarded entrance of Darnleigh House, Aubrey was beginning to flag. He was pleased that this appeared to be a healthy fatigue, not the soul-sapping exhaustion that his condition usually brought about. But he couldn't help feeling nervous as he passed into headquarters of the Magisterium.

He glanced at George, who yawned, and Caroline, who looked alert, taking in the surroundings. His father had been dazed enough for Craddock to order a wheelchair be brought for him. He nodded, eyes closed, face pale.

'Craddock,' Aubrey said, and he yawned as well, 'we've been up all night. Can the interrogation wait a while?'

Craddock raised an eyebrow. 'Interrogation?' He studied Aubrey for a moment, then he gestured at the nearest operative. 'Find recovery quarters for these people. Take Sir Darius to the infirmary.'

Aubrey was feeling woolly-headed with tiredness by the time he lay down in the small room he'd been shown to. Sleep fell on him like an avalanche. It was hours before he woke up.

When he did, he found that someone had taken off his shoes and removed his Tommy Sparks clothes. He lay in a very comfortable bed in a darkened room. Enough light came through the gaps in the curtains to show him that the room was well furnished, if a little old-fashioned for his liking. He reached out and pulled back the drapes to see Lattimer Hall frowning at him from across the square. The thought of all the Special Services people inside made him close the curtains again.

A serious young woman in the black uniform of the Magisterium was sitting on a chair watching him. 'Would you like something to eat?' she asked.

'Where's my father? Where's Caroline? George?'

She stood. 'Miss Hepworth is in the mess hall. I don't know about the others.'

'What time is it?'

'Just after noon. I'll be outside when you're ready.'

She slipped out of the door. Aubrey used the small washroom to bathe hastily. When he brushed his hair, the reflection in the mirror looked tired, but not unnaturally so. A pair of black trousers, a black shirt, tie and jacket lay on the end of the bed. They were his size and he dressed quickly.

The mess was a brightly lit room, long and narrow, with no windows. Tables were lined up in rows, ten or twelve chairs to a table. The surfaces – walls, linoleum floor, tables – were utterly clean. It reminded Aubrey of the dining hall at Stonelea School, without the smell of boiled cabbage. Instead, this place had the upright and cheery aromas of coffee, toast and boot polish.

Caroline was there. She was sipping a cup of tea, holding it in both hands as if she were cold. She was wearing the same uniform as Aubrey's escort. He thought she made the jacket and trousers look remarkably striking. Aubrey's escort took up position near the swinging double doors and watched them with the ease of someone who has watched many people and in much less comfortable settings.

Caroline glanced at him without putting down her cup. 'Where's George?'

'Probably sleeping, if I know him.'

She sipped her tea, a frown creasing her forehead, then she looked up. 'What's *wrong* with you?'

Aubrey blinked. *Now that's a big question*, he thought. 'What do you mean?'

'You're looking healthy enough now, but over the last few weeks I've seen you looking like a corpse, getting better quickly, then deteriorating again.'

Aubrey shuddered. 'Not quite a corpse.'

'Well?' She put down her cup. 'What's going on? Why was Dr Tremaine taunting you about your soul?'

A shutter rolled up and a round-faced woman leaned out. 'You want something to eat, luv? We've got egg and bacon pies, sandwiches, or a mixed grill.'

'Just tea, please.' He turned his attention back to Caroline. How much could he tell her? How much did he *want* to tell her? 'I have a condition,' he said, finally.

She rolled her eyes. 'Well, that doesn't tell me much. What sort of condition?'

He shrugged. 'It's unusual.'

'You're evading now, not babbling, and I'm still not getting an answer.'

Aubrey chewed his lip and studied her. Her eyes were green and probably the most arresting he'd seen.

He wavered. Perhaps he should tell her. It would be good to have another confidante, someone he could share his plight with. He was sure he'd benefit from her wit and intelligence. But another part of him was reluctant to show her how stupid he'd been. At least, to show her any *more* stupidity than she'd already seen.

He wanted her to be impressed by him, not to pity him.

Aubrey was relieved when, at that moment, the round-faced woman marched up to the table with a tray. 'Tea. Some bread and butter, too. You didn't ask for it but I guessed you'd be wanting it. There's milk and sugar, just in case you need it.'

Caroline opened her mouth, but Aubrey was blessed with another timely interruption.

Craddock opened the swinging doors. He wore a travelling cape and broad-brimmed black hat. Aubrey's escort, still by the doorway, stiffened and stood at attention, but Craddock didn't acknowledge her. 'Fitzwilliam. Miss Hepworth.' He didn't raise his voice, but it came clearly across the mess hall. A neat trick, Aubrey decided. 'I'd like you to come with me.'

George appeared in the doorway, yawning, in fresh, clean clothes. 'Not without me.' He waved to Aubrey and Caroline. 'No chance of food, is there?'

CRADDOCK LED THEM THROUGH THE WARREN OF DARNLEIGH House. After going down six flights of stairs, Aubrey began to wonder at the extent of the place. It seemed as if much more was underground than above street level.

They walked along corridor after corridor of closed doors. Aubrey decided that if he was ever taken by a foreign power and asked for the secrets of Darnleigh House, all he could tell them was that the Magisterium kept thousands of door-makers in work.

Strange noises and smells came from several rooms – mechanical chattering, organic whining, the smell of the sea. Aubrey's curiosity was jumping and his magical awareness constantly prickled, but he didn't think it wise to stop and ask.

At the end of one long corridor – ceiling, walls and floor completely tiled in green – Craddock opened a door. He stood back and motioned. 'Inside.'

Aubrey entered first and stepped into a hospital ward.

It had sunny yellow walls, and two rows of beds, with severe hospital chairs between the beds. Only one bed had an occupant. 'Father,' Aubrey said.

Sir Darius looked up, smiled and extended his hand. 'Aubrey. Can you get me out of this place? I've spoken to your mother and she insists I come home. There's much to be done.'

Aubrey smiled at his father's impatience. 'I'll try.'

'Good man.' Sir Darius saw Aubrey's companions. 'George, you've been keeping Aubrey out of trouble, I hope?'

'Impossible, sir. I'm doing my best just to make sure he doesn't bring about the end of civilisation.'

'True, George, and we thank you for it,' Sir Darius said.

'I don't think the Magisterium and the Special Services combined could keep Aubrey out of trouble.'

'Sir.'

'Miss Hepworth.' He turned and glared at his son. Aubrey didn't mind. 'I hope my son hasn't been imposing himself on you any more?'

'No, sir. He's been helpful.'

'Good, good.' Sir Darius looked unconvinced. 'I'm sure there's a story behind all this. I'd like to hear it soon, Aubrey.'

'Yes, sir.'

Craddock came to the bed. Sir Darius nodded at him. 'Craddock.'

'Sir Darius, I'm glad to see you're well.'

'I'm fully recovered.'

'I'm sure you are. We'll just have to wait for the doctor to confirm that.'

Sir Darius nodded. 'Craddock, thank you for your help in all this. You're doing a fine job.'

'It's what I aim for. Now, you should rest.'

Aubrey watched this exchange with interest. Had he detected an easing of tension between the two men? Years of distrust weren't broken down in an instant, but were there the beginnings here?

Sir Darius harrumphed. 'I have an election to win.' He eyed Craddock. 'No sign of Tremaine?'

'No. He's disappeared entirely.'

'I see,' Sir Darius said.

'You may not have been in any condition to hear last night, but the Special Services has rounded up the Army of New Albion.'

Aubrey let out a long, relieved breath.

Sir Darius glanced at his son then stroked his moustache. 'Why?'

'They were going to blow up the King and the PM during the King's birthday procession.'

'A week before the election?' Sir Darius looked thoughtful. 'That would have thrown a cat among the pigeons.'

'After the conspirators were all arrested,' Craddock continued, 'Tallis's people found the explosives they'd fitted under the Old Bridge, near Parliament House.'

'They were serious,' Sir Darius muttered. 'The King and the PM at once.'

'Yes,' Craddock said. 'Amateurs in some ways, but deadly serious. If they hadn't been unmasked, the King would have died.' He looked at Sir Darius. 'And the Prime Minister.'

Sir Darius glanced at Aubrey. 'Before Tremaine fled, his hold on me weakened somewhat. I managed to hear about his being behind the Army of New Albion. And his plans for the Ritual of the Way.'

'Indeed,' Craddock said. 'We have a formidable foe out there.'

Aubrey's curiosity got the better of him. 'But why did he kidnap you?' he asked his father. 'How did that help his plans?'

Sir Darius grimaced and looked uncomfortable. 'I may have forced his hand a little there. A New Albion hanger-on contacted me about supporting them. I made a few enquiries and what I heard made me very nervous, even though a plot to kill the King was never mentioned. I was on my way to see you, Craddock, to put all this on the table, when Tremaine abducted me.'

'He couldn't just kill you, of course,' Craddock noted, 'because he wanted you to lead the next government. The government which would oppose Holmland aggression most strongly.'

'Quite. Although if he thinks I'm as straightforward as that, he's underestimating me,' Sir Darius said. He raised an eyebrow. 'And what about the Holmlanders? I know they were mixed up with the Army of New Albion.'

'Von Stralick,' Craddock agreed. 'We're still determining his full level of involvement, but we're sure he was the one who lured the Army of New Albion into our trap at the Greythorn Society for Non-magical Fitness.'

George waved his hand, interrupting. 'That's right. Von Stralick told us he thought it was a good chance to get rid of them.'

'Indeed. Well, we thought we were about to capture von Stralick's spy ring, but he managed to out-manoeuvre us.'

'Ah. He wanted you to arrest the New Albionites. He saw them as a loose cannon, no doubt, liable to disrupt Holmland's own plans.' Sir Darius frowned.

'Von Stralick was remarkably forthcoming when he telephoned the Special Services. Said he was in need of a good rest and he was going back to Holmland. Before he hung up, he told Tallis to thank someone he called "young Fitzwilliam" for doing him a great favour.' Craddock studied Aubrey and waited for his response.

'A favour?' Aubrey said. 'Well, we did run into von Stralick, and he was injured. I suppose I patched him up –'

'He nearly died,' Caroline put in. 'Without Aubrey, he would have.'

'I see,' Craddock said, and Aubrey knew the head of the Magisterium was filing this away for later consideration. 'Sir Darius, I think it fair to tell you that the Magisterium has had its eye on your son since the failed attempt on Prince Albert's life. He has shown a penchant for becoming involved in dangerous matters.'

'I'm aware of that, Craddock,' Sir Darius said. 'He causes me no end of worry, even though he usually contrives to fall on his feet.'

Craddock nodded. 'Resourceful chap. He managed to get to you well before we did, and he held off Tremaine. Who knows what Tremaine would have done to you, given more time? It may have been another long-term plot of his.' Craddock looked at Aubrey. 'Remarkable lad you have here, Sir Darius.'

'I know.'

Craddock took off his hat and brushed some invisible lint from it. 'I wonder if he's ever thought of a career in the Magisterium?'

Aubrey's mouth dropped open. Sir Darius raised an eyebrow. 'Craddock, I do believe you've managed to surprise my son. And me.' He looked at Aubrey. 'My son's magical ability is a wonder to me. He can do things I've never dreamed of. His horizons are vaster than mine ever will be. I'm proud of him – and I envy him.'

Aubrey's knees felt weak. He sat on the chair by the bedside, humbled. He thought he'd known where he stood, but the rug of certainty had been pulled out from beneath his feet. Craddock's offer was unexpected, and his father's words had caught him utterly unawares. Perhaps he'd been guilty of making assumptions. Again.

Craddock gave a small movement of the lips that – on another person – could have been called a smile. 'You'll consider my offer, Fitzwilliam?'

Aubrey nodded. 'I have much to consider.'

Twenty-Three

ITH LESS THAN TWO WEEKS BEFORE THE ELECTION, Aubrey found that twenty-four hours was not enough time in a day.

Despite George's reluctance to become involved in politics, Aubrey dragged him in to help with the campaign. Together they organised the distribution of pamphlets and the hanging of posters, as well as helping to arrange public rallies and meetings. Aubrey's arms grew sore from cranking printing machines, and ink became ingrained under his fingernails. His hands were red and sore from clapping during his father's numerous speeches. He met with Jack Figg and gained his assistance in rallying workers behind the Progressive Party.

Aubrey also assumed a key role in scrutinising and editing Sir Darius's speeches. 'Adding a touch of theatre,' was how he explained this contribution to George.

Aubrey tried to involve Caroline, but she declined.

Then Lady Fitzwilliam invited her, telling her of the Progressive Party's commitment to giving women the vote. After that, Caroline made sure Sir Darius and his colleagues addressed Suffragette rallies, which provided a sharp distinction from the Prime Minister and his Royalist cronies, who refused invitations from Suffragette leaders and, at times, heaped scorn on Suffragette hopes.

Sir Darius campaigned vigorously on a platform of a strong Albion. With news of more Holmland aggression in the Goltans, this resonated with the public. The Prime Minister tried to distance himself from the King, who had the extraordinary lack of both wit and tact to have Count Herman, the brother of the Elektor of Holmland, visit his country estate. The newspapers reflected the general unhappiness with this. George made a point of cutting out the best headlines and pasting them on the walls of the tiny office Aubrey and he worked from so that whenever Aubrey looked up from typing, tele-phoning or duplicating, he saw 'Is Our PM A Holmland Man?' in large, black letters all over the walls. Aubrey wondered if Bertie had had anything to do with the invi-tation to Count Herman.

The King's birthday parade went ahead, as tradition demanded, but the Prime Minister was not overly pleased with the result. The King insisted that the royal coach was full of his imaginary friends and that Sir Rollo had to walk behind. The sight of the red-faced, waddling PM trying to keep up with the royal coach caused gales of laughter along the entire parade route.

For Aubrey, election night was a mixture of relief, tension and detachment. The Progressive Party had booked the ballroom of the Burton Hotel, which was directly opposite the Electoral Board offices in Porter

Street. While members of parliament, candidates, staff and families milled about, a constant stream of people crossed the street to bring the latest news on the counting.

Early in the evening, Aubrey felt as if he needed some solitude after the whirlwind of the previous fourteen days. He stood by a pillar, screened by a potted palm, and watched his father and mother greet people as they arrived. He was still there when he saw Caroline and her mother enter. Caroline was wearing a grey dress that made Aubrey feel as if he'd been struck, hard, in the stomach. Her face glowed as she smiled at Sir Darius. Her hair was arranged in a way that Aubrey guessed would have required a good structural magician. She wore a fine gold chain around her neck and small diamond earrings.

She looked beautiful. Her mother was with her and wore something or other. Aubrey had no idea what.

He leaned against the pillar, making sure Caroline and Mrs Hepworth didn't see him. He watched as they entered the room and quickly found George, who reluctantly bade farewell to a group of young women he'd spent much of the evening entertaining.

Aubrey took a deep breath and let it out slowly. Things were turning out well enough, he supposed. Caroline wasn't totally convinced that he was a dangerous lunatic, which was a good thing. The situation there was retrievable, given tenacity — of which he had an abundance.

The plot to propel Albion into war had been foiled. *For now*, he thought, and this cast a pall on his musings that was at odds with the optimism of the evening. *The threat of war is going to be with us for some time*, he thought, *Dr Tremaine or no Dr Tremaine*. He could see years of international tension while life tried to go on.

Then there was his 'condition'. He had steadied things, but it was temporary. It was as if he'd woven a cocoon around his united body and soul, but death was still waiting for him, a gaping maw that was calling, calling . . .

More research, more experimentation, that was his only answer. What he'd done so far had spurred his thinking about development of a modern language for magic and he had some inklings that his solution would be dependent on this, too. Along the way, he was bound to grapple with the fundamental question of the Nature of Magic as well. He needed time, more time! If only he could get hold of Professor Hepworth's notebook.

Which brings us back to Dr Tremaine, in more ways than one, he thought and he patted his fob pocket, where an irregular lump lay, a reminder of unfinished business.

He wondered how he could do all this while pursuing his goals. The events of the last few weeks had only confirmed his desire for a life in politics – on his own terms. It was the way to true achievement. But when? University first? The army first? Or what about Craddock's invitation to join the Magisterium? He was still swamped with choices.

He smiled. His escapades had shown him something: for better or worse, he was his own man. His abilities and his strengths had saved his father, while he had coped with weaknesses that were undeniably his own. The challenge of living in his father's shadow and up to his expectations had, perhaps, been a burden of his own making. It might be time to lay it down, especially with his father's recognition of his magical skill. Magic was a sphere Sir Darius had not conquered, but perhaps his son could. It could be a chance to step aside from measuring himself against the man he respected so much. So maybe magic was where his future lay. Perhaps he could carry the torch of rational magic that Baron Verulam had lit so long ago.

He grinned. *But I do love a challenge*, he thought and, for the moment, he left the future to take care of itself.

He looked at the smiling faces, the animated conversations in the ballroom. The Progressive Party was about to sweep the Royalists from power, no-one had any doubt about that. It was a time for change, for bettering society, for righting wrongs. Aubrey caught himself and smiled. He'd been the one making the speeches this time.

He looked around at the excited candidates, those who were about to be elected and become the law-makers of the land. As the evening drew out, Sir Darius and Lady Fitzwilliam circulated around the room, arm in arm, speaking to every candidate and every current member of parliament. Aubrey shook off his sombre mood and took on the role as Sir Darius's son without a tinge of resentment. He shook hands, congratulated workers, listened to stories. Eventually, he was able to sit at a table with Mrs Hepworth, Caroline and George.

'Nervous, Aubrey?' Caroline asked.

'Definitely,' he said. *Mostly around you*, he thought. 'Can't take this election for granted, you know.'

She smiled and he hoped she hadn't read his mind. '"What lies ahead can be seen if one knows enough of what lay before." Scholar Tan.'

'Ah.' She'd developed a knack of making him feel inadequate. He had almost grown accustomed to it.

'Excellent salmon, Aubrey,' George said. 'Try some?'

'Not just now.'

Mrs Hepworth — Ophelia, Aubrey told himself — leaned over. 'Your father looks very handsome. The years sit easily on him.'

Aubrey looked at his father, then back at her. 'You know him well?'

'I knew him well indeed.' She gazed at Sir Darius with affection. Aubrey noted this and filed it away for future consideration. *I knew he had a past*, he thought, *but it might be even more interesting than I'd thought.*

The confidence in the room grew as the evening progressed and the news coming from across the road grew steadily better. By midnight, champagne was being opened and poured.

Aubrey smiled. A dance band was summoned and the evening became a party. He waved to a campaign official, asked a few questions and then sat back with a foolish smile on his face.

'Have we won?' George asked Aubrey, raising his voice over the music.

'Yes. Oh, nothing official, but the result is in no doubt. The Prime Minister is apparently meeting his Cabinet and advisers, deciding how to put a good face on the defeat.'

'Grand.'

A man rushed into the ballroom and stood on tip-toes and looked around. Spying Sir Darius, he hurried to his side. A quick conversation and Sir Darius nodded decisively. With one athletic bound, he leapt to the stage and spoke to the bandleader. The bandleader gathered the musicians and ended the tune with a flourish.

Sir Darius raised his arms. He was about to speak, when he looked down. Lady Fitzwilliam smiled up at him. He grinned back and motioned for her to join him on the stage. Amid applause, she did, but she used the stairs instead of duplicating her husband's leap.

When the acclamation died down, Sir Darius cleared his throat and addressed the crowd. 'Loyal colleagues, friends and supporters. The Prime Minister has conceded!'

Aubrey knocked his chair over as he leapt to his feet. His cheers joined those of everyone else in the room. Triumphantly, George shook a fist in the air. Caroline smiled. Mrs Hepworth applauded, tears in her eyes.

A man's voice rose above the acclamation. 'Three cheers for Sir Darius, our new Prime Minister!'

The cheering rose again, shaking the chandeliers and the windows. Sir Darius waved, then led Lady Fitzwilliam from the stage, shaking hands and suffering claps on the back as they went.

Sir Darius took Lady Fitzwilliam onto the dance floor and bowed to her. He looked to the bandleader and nodded. A tune struck up and the Fitzwilliams moved gracefully into a dance. He led deftly, and she followed his moves as if they'd rehearsed for years. Every eye in the room was on them, but the couple was oblivious.

'They dance well,' Caroline said.

'Yes,' Aubrey said. 'Do you dance?'

'Yes.'

'Let me guess . . . a friend of your father's taught you?'

'Of course. I dance very well, thanks to the Count of Lower Gallia.'

'So do I,' Mrs Hepworth said. She put her chin on her hand.

Aubrey opened his mouth, but at that moment Sir Darius and Lady Fitzwilliam came to their table. 'Ophelia,' Sir Darius said, smiling, 'it's good to see you. It's been too long.'

She smiled. 'Yes.'

'Miss Hepworth, I'm glad you're here to help celebrate. Without your help . . .' Sir Darius left the obvious unstated. He coughed. 'It's time for us to leave.'

'Now?' Aubrey asked, dismayed.

'We'll let the people enjoy themselves,' Sir Darius said. 'They've earned some respite from my presence. Loyal as they are, I'm sure things will be more carefree once I leave.' He paused. 'Mrs Hepworth, Miss Hepworth – you'll join us for a small celebration at Maidstone?'

When his father made this unexpected offer, Aubrey had been tussling over the best way to say goodbye to Caroline so as to ensure seeing her again. He leapt to his feet. 'A capital idea. Just the thing. Rather noisy here, now, I mean, even though the band was a nice touch . . .'

'Aubrey,' Caroline said, 'you're babbling.'

Lady Fitzwilliam leaned across the table and patted Caroline on the arm. 'We're used to it, my dear,' she said sympathetically.

Aubrey was so delighted at the coming together of things that he felt no irritation whatsoever.

Stubbs was waiting for them when they came out of the hotel. He tipped his cap and opened the door of the Oakleigh-Nash. 'Wonderful night, ma'ams, miss, sirs.'

'Indeed,' Sir Darius said. 'It's a wonderful country.'

DUCHESS MARIA MET THEM WHEN THEY ENTERED Maidstone. She stood in the entrance hall, at the bottom of the great stairs, eyes bright, hands clasped. 'Darius,' she said. 'Well done, Prime Minister.'

Sir Darius made a face. 'That's not official, Mother. I haven't been sworn in.'

'Rubbish. It's just a formality now!'

He bent and kissed her on the cheek. 'Take everyone

to the drawing room, Aubrey,' he said. 'I have something special to help us celebrate.'

Aubrey held out his arm for his grandmother. She smiled at him and together they led the others to Lady Fitzwilliam's drawing room.

When Sir Darius rejoined them, he had a dusty bottle.

'Over a hundred years old, this port,' he said. 'I've kept it for a special occasion.'

Lady Fitzwilliam smiled. 'You didn't have time to go down to the cellar to fetch it. You must have brought it out earlier today.'

Sir Darius smoothed his moustache with a finger. 'I may have had it ready. Just in case.'

'You were confident,' Mrs Hepworth said.

'Of course,' Aubrey put in. 'We were always going to win.'

'Always?' Sir Darius said. He opened the bottle. After an instant, an aroma like dusty, sun-warmed leather filled the room. Sir Darius nodded happily and then poured the port into small crystal glasses.

Lady Fitzwilliam distributed the port and waited for her husband.

'To all of you,' he said, raising his glass. 'To Rose, for your fortitude and love. To Mother, for your high expectations and your understanding. To Aubrey, for your courage and intelligence. To George, for your loyalty and bravery. To Caroline, for your dauntlessness. To Ophelia, for your bravery and in recognition of your loss.'

Aubrey held his glass high. 'And to all of us, to the future!'

'To the future!'

Twenty-Four

AUBREY HUMMED A LITTLE AS HE LOOKED OUT OVER the Hummocks training course. He shifted the straps of his pack so the weight sat more evenly, and he realised he was disappointed that the weather was mild. A breeze blew across the course and the subtle smells of summer turning into autumn came to him – leaves beginning to dry and crisp, the wan scents of the last of the summer roses, acorns ripening.

'Are you ready, Fitzwilliam?' bawled the same Warrant Officer who'd witnessed Aubrey's previous, unsuccessful attempt on the course.

Aubrey straightened. 'Sir!'

Twenty yards away, George was leaning against the fence. He tipped back his hat and mock-saluted. Aubrey grinned.

'Enjoying ourselves, are we?' the Warrant Officer barked. 'Get started, then!'

Aubrey trotted off, the pack settling with each step. He felt good, better than he'd felt at any time since the failed experiment.

He slogged up the first mound and down the other side. While his body worked, his mind was abuzz.

Caroline came first in his thoughts. Aubrey's mother had offered her a position as her assistant, working at the museum on weekends. There was even the prospect of both of them going on an expedition to the polar sea, spending three months looking for new seabird species on the remote, icy islands. He readily admitted – to himself – that he'd miss her.

He was starting to breathe heavily, but he felt none of the telltale signs that meant he was in danger of dissolution. In fact, he was enjoying the strain of his muscles and the gritty discomfort of the uniform. It reminded him of how alive he was. He wondered if his condition had given him an appreciation of small things like that. He had cause to be grateful for much, but it hadn't ever occurred to him before to be grateful for simply being alive.

Halfway through his second lap of the course, Aubrey was not so happy.

The minor discomforts had intensified into throbbing feet, aching shoulders and a feeling of burning exhaustion, to a state where lifting his head to see the course in front of him was a major undertaking.

Nearly there, he told himself, repeating the phrase for the thousandth time. He didn't believe himself, but it had become a chorus, a chant, something to cling to. *Nearly there.*

Aubrey couldn't hear anything apart from the shuffle of his feet. All that mattered was the small stretch of beaten earth that was the trail he was following. His whole world had narrowed; the only important thing was putting one foot in front of the other.

It was an ordeal, but Aubrey told himself it was only a physical struggle. He could cope. He could succeed. After all he'd been through, he could tolerate mere bodily discomfort. It was torture, but it was tolerable torture.

Aubrey remembered the way he had dragged his soul-self against the pull of death. It had been an impossible task, resisting his end like that, but he'd done it by doing it little by little, stubbornly refusing to give in. It was a lesson he'd learned: sometimes the best way to slay a giant was to nibble it to death.

He could do it again.

By this stage, his movements were mechanical. He continued to plod forward, his rifle held extended, the straps of his pack cutting into his shoulders.

He adjusted his grip on the rifle. He gritted his teeth, refusing to surrender.

The path beneath his feet angled upwards. He felt crushed beneath the weight of the pack, but pushed on, lost in the effort.

Downwards, almost slipping, digging in, balancing the weight, pressing on.

Up again, knees bent, leaning forward, elbows spread, ankles aching.

Doing it little by little. Refusing to give in.

A THOUSAND YEARS LATER.

'Aubrey! You can stop now!'

'George?'

'Here, let me help you.'

The weight was lifted from his back and Aubrey almost fell over. He loosened his grip on the rifle and used it to support himself. He looked up. 'I did it?' he croaked.

Atkins, the Warrant Officer, scowled. 'Yes.'

He marched off.

George gripped the pack and thrust a water bottle at Aubrey. He drank, took off his helmet then poured the rest of the water over his head. 'Another trial, George,' he said. 'Another test.'

'Yes. But you did it.'

Aubrey grinned. 'Was there ever any doubt?'

About the Author

Michael Pryor has published more than twenty fantasy books and over forty short stories, from literary fiction to science fiction to slapstick humour. Michael has been shortlisted six times for the Aurealis Awards (including for *Blaze of Glory* and *Heart of Gold*), has been nominated for a Ditmar award and longlisted for the Gold Inky award, and five of his books have been Children's Book Council of Australia Notable Books (including *Word of Honour* and *Time of Trial*). He is currently writing the final book in the Laws of Magic series.

For more information about Michael and his books, please visit www.michaelpryor.com.au

**Read on for a sneak preview
of Aubrey and George's adventures in**

·HEART OF GOLD·

*A*UBREY FITZWILLIAM KNEW THAT CRISIS WAS another word for opportunity. He simply wished that he saw more of the latter and less of the former.

AUBREY GRIMACED, TIGHTENED THE LAST VALVE ASSEMBLY and closed the ornithopter's cowling. He stretched, wincing, just as his friend George Doyle spoke up. 'Aubrey?'

'Hm?'

'What's bright orange and floats through clouds?'

'Riddling, George? Really, you need to find something more worthwhile to do.'

'It's not a riddle, old man. It's what I'm looking at right now.'

While Aubrey had worked on the ornithopter, George had spent much of the evening lounging on a bench, propped on one elbow and reading the newspaper.

Now, he was peering out of the window of the workshop at the night sky. Aubrey wiped his greasy hands on a rag and strolled to see what had caught his friend's attention. 'Where?'

A pearly-grey blanket of cloud hung over Finley Moor Airfield and stretched to the south, where it reflected the many lights of Trinovant, the heart of the Albion Empire. Thunder growled nearby.

'There. That glow.' George pointed to the north-east, past the control tower – dark at this time of night – and the dirigible mooring masts. Four long grey cigar-shapes bobbed at rest. They were the pride of the Albion airship fleet, the 800-foot-long Imperial class, the most advanced lighter-than-air craft in the world.

The orange light was coming from something in the clouds – something large. Aubrey frowned, trying to make out what it was, then he gaped as it burst through the clouds. A flaming dirigible staggered across the sky, its nose angling downward, losing lift and sagging in the middle. Fire had enveloped the front third of the stately airship, puncturing the internal gasbags. Flames lit up the airfield and the countryside in a ghastly hell-light.

Aubrey's tiredness vanished. He sprinted out of the hangar, a thousand decisions competing for his attention. He flung open the door of the nearest ornithopter. It was a Falcon model, not his favourite, but it was a six-seater, with a largish cargo bay, and that was what he wanted.

George caught up and seized his arm. 'What are you doing, old man?'

'That's a Gallian airship, an RT-401. Twenty crew members are going to die up there unless we do something.'

'You've never done a night flight before,' George pointed out.

I know, Aubrey thought. *And I flew solo for the first time just two days ago.* 'How hard can night flying be?' Aubrey vaulted into the pilot's seat. 'It's the same sky, after all.'

'It's not the sky I'm worried about.' George squeezed his broad-shouldered frame into the co-pilot seat. 'It's the ground waiting for us if you make a mistake.' He shook his head. 'This is madness. Shouldn't we send for help?'

'No time. Those poor souls don't have long.' Aubrey ran through his pre-flight checklist, decided it would take too long in the circumstances, then pulled the ignition lever. The engine coughed into life and he seized the controls.

The great metal wings creaked and stretched. Aubrey used the foot pedals and the landing gear whirred into action. He felt the bird-like craft settle, tense, and then a stomach-dropping thrust as its legs kicked upwards. The wings twisted and beat, noisily driving upwards.

Aubrey forced the craft to climb almost vertically. He flicked his black hair as it fell in his eyes. 'Where is it?' he shouted over the crashing of the metal wings.

'Left!' George shouted back. 'Port, I mean! Over there, past the sewage works!' He pointed. Aubrey dragged the wheel around until the dirigible came into view overhead.

He pulled back on the wheel with all his strength, and sent the ornithopter into a testing climb. Then he levelled off and swept toward the crippled airship.

A huge gout of fire erupted from the nose of the dirigible. Aubrey gritted his teeth and wrenched at the controls. George shouted as a jet of flame reached for them, a wave of heat screaming like a flock of harpies. Their craft staggered and heeled, the port wing canting while the starboard wing flailed wildly. His heart hammering wildly, Aubrey held on, glad for the belt that kept him in his seat.

From behind them came the shriek of struts protesting under strain. Aubrey held his breath and eased off the controls. The rending noise slowed, but then he heard the sharp pings of rivets giving up and popping loose. Immediately, metal crashed against metal, grinding horribly. *Not a good sign*, he thought. With little choice, he ignored it and concentrated on keeping the craft steady.

The Falcon was approaching the dirigible almost directly head-on. Aubrey banked the ornithopter to port and swooped along the vast flank of the airship. The Falcon bucked a little, but Aubrey anticipated and held the line.

The entire front half of the dirigible was ablaze. The smell of burning rubber was harsh in Aubrey's nostrils and he grimaced. He eased the Falcon toward a tight turn around the stern of the airship, aiming to glide along the other side.

George shouted and grabbed his arm. The ornithopter, delicately responsive, dipped and shuddered. Aubrey had to strain the controls, adjusting wing pitch and attack, to right it again.

'Don't do that!' he shouted.

'Someone's in the back!'

Aubrey risked a glance as they rounded the tail of the aerial behemoth. A stocky man in the uniform of the Gallian Dirigible Corps was standing in the rear observation cockpit, waving desperately.

'We'll come back for him.' Aubrey steered toward the bow, where the gondola clung to the belly of the dirigible.

The gondola was the long cabin where the captain controlled the airship. If he was able to come alongside, he might be able to get the ornithopter to hover long enough to take on survivors. The Falcon could carry four passengers, but Aubrey was sure he could manage six, then shuttle back for the rest.

He licked lips that had suddenly gone dry, and began to edge closer to the dirigible. He clenched his teeth and concentrated on keeping his hands steady.

A mighty groan came from the airship, followed by the sharp, bright noise of metal reaching the end of its strength. Automatically, Aubrey sheered off and dropped away. Then he climbed, not wanting to get caught in the rain of debris falling from the crippled dirigible – struts, wire, shattered glass, burning fabric.

He glanced up and, to his horror, saw that the internal frame of the airship was collapsing. Tormented metal screamed and buckled. One of the motor units wrenched loose and fell, still whirring, to the ground far below. Then, without warning, the entire gondola tore away. It tilted and hung, attached along one side, then it plummeted.

Immediately, the remnants of the dirigible lurched upwards, much lighter now. The clouds opened around it, then swallowed the flaming leviathan of the air.

Sickened, Aubrey closed his eyes, grieving for the lost crew. Twenty brave souls, gone in an instant. He banged the instrument panel with a fist, cursing his failure to save them. Should he have gone for help as George suggested? Was he simply being too rash, too overreaching – again?

'What now?' George shouted.

Aubrey narrowed his eyes. He could still do something to help. 'The cockpit. The survivor.'

He scanned overhead and saw the remnants of the dirigible wallowing out of the clouds, shuddering like a great whale in its death spasms. The remaining motor units were whining desperately, but the dirigible had begun its final plunge.

Aubrey realised his jaw was aching from the tension. George grunted, then swore as oil sprayed across the windscreen.

That's all I need, Aubrey thought numbly. He couldn't see a thing through the streaks and smears of black muck.

Doing his best to stay calm, he ran through the commonplace spells he'd memorised since he'd begun learning magic. He seized on one he'd used for practical jokes, an application of the Law of Attraction. The elements were straightforward, the duration easy to handle. Usually the spell was used to make things hard to separate − to humorous effect − but this time Aubrey inverted the spell. The oil fell away from the windscreen as if it couldn't bear to be near the glass.

The ornithopter bucked, then dropped in the turbulent air caused by the burning dirigible. The flames had almost engulfed the entire airship and the heat beat on Aubrey's exposed skin. The ornithopter shuddered, then slipped sideways. He caught it with an upward wing beat, but the strain was causing the metal laminates to shred and peel. There was no natural way to bring the ornithopter close enough to perform a mid-air rescue.

It'll have to be magic, then.

George pointed. The tail of the airship had tipped upwards, like the stern of a sinking ship. A figure was in the cockpit, pressed up against the glass.

Aubrey flinched as violet-white light flashed through the cabin. Hard on its heels was an immense crack that made the ornithopter vibrate like a gong. Dazzled, with coloured specks dancing in front of his eyes, Aubrey groaned. As if they didn't have enough to contend with, the storm was closing in. The ornithopter quivered, as if it were a real bird caught in a storm.

Feverishly, Aubrey's mind seized on the comparison. The Law of Similarities came to him, the well-established components blazing across his mind, clear and sharp.

The ornithopter was like a bird. With an effort, and the properly constructed spell, he could make it more so.

He chanted the spell, dropping the values into the unfolding formula in the way that fitted best. He announced each element as crisply as he could while trying to hold the bucking craft steady.

'Hold on!' he barked to George. The interior of the ornithopter began to glow, but it was different from the dirigible's flaming red and the harsh glare of the lightning. Streaked with green and yellow, every surface began to shimmer, a spiky phosphorescence that reeked of magic. Aubrey's magical senses jangled in response.

Another boom and the ornithopter was again rocked by thunder. Aubrey wrestled controls that were growing increasingly sluggish and dragged the craft around the nose of the sinking dirigible.

George let out an oath as the substance of the ornithopter rippled. Wide-eyed, he clutched at the control panel, seeking something to hold onto, then jerked back as it flowed underneath his fingers. His face was rigid with terror as the substance of the machine shifted shape, threatening to dissolve and pitch them both into the ferocity of the storm.

Thunder bellowed, a burst of heat erupted from the dirigible and then they were no longer in the cabin of an ornithopter. Wind screamed and plucked at them as they lay flat on the back of a giant metal bird.

'Hold on!' Aubrey shouted – unnecessarily – and scrabbled for a handhold.

Aubrey was excited. The spell had worked. The ornithopter had been encouraged to assert its similarity to a real bird, to become more than a machine. Exposed to the elements, a long neck thrust out in front of them while a fan-like tail spread behind. Great brass wings feathered in the shifting turbulence, keeping them tracking alongside the stricken dirigible. Aubrey could see that the glass of the windscreen had become the glinting eyes of the creature, while the hydraulic pipes and electrical wiring conduits had merged into the body of the bird, making tendons and muscles.

Aubrey looked down and gulped. The ground was a long way away. He narrowed his eyes against the whipping wind, the heat of the flames and the smoke. His fingers dug into the metal feathers and he was thankful the bird's back was broad.

George stared at him and down at the metal bird, then grinned and gave a nod of approval. 'Don't worry, I'm not letting go!'

The metal bird clashed its way toward the observation cockpit. Aubrey urged it on.

The dirigible had finally given up the struggle. Huge rents ran across the metal skin, exposing the interior fabric and aluminium skeleton. A gasbag ripped free and, intact, shot up through the clouds. Deprived of this lift, the dirigible sank even more swiftly.

The metal bird slid sideways, then banked right in a turn that had both Aubrey and George scrabbling to stop themselves sliding off its back. Just when Aubrey had jammed his left foot against what he suspected had once been a fuel line, the metal bird plummeted and his stomach tried to find its way out of his ears.

As the metal bird dived, it screeched, a wild clanging cry that joined the tumult of the thunderstorm and the burning dirigible.

Aubrey hung on, desperately, fingers whitening with effort. Suddenly the metal bird lunged and struck the observation cockpit with its talons. Aubrey cried out as the glass shattered and the crewman fell, flailing, through the air.

Aubrey hammered at the bird's metal skin, shouting wordless oaths of anger and disbelief. What had he done? Created a monster and loosed it on the world?

The metal bird folded its wings and dived after the falling Gallian, and Aubrey was forced to cling with both hands. He squinted and tried to think of a spell to stop the creature's madness.

Then Aubrey's grip was tested again. With a crack like a giant's whip, the bird thrust out its wings and stopped its dreadful descent. The jolt threw him aside and, for a desperate moment, he had nothing to hold onto. He slid, his back scraping on bolts and ridges, until his head hung over the bird's flank. Far below, the dark and hard ground beckoned. Above was the blazing immensity of the dirigible. Of course, there now also existed the possibility of being pecked to death by a rampaging metal avian.

Another jolt sent him head first over the bird's flank, and he was only prevented from tumbling into the empty air when he grabbed a feathered ridge. While his heart raced, the world wheeled around below, a great, flat dish waiting to catch him.

Wind ripped at his clothes and made his eyes water.

Desperately trying to think of a way out of his predica-
ment, he saw the great talons of the metal bird a few feet
below him. They were clutching the Gallian crewman.
His uniform was scorched, his eyes were closed. Aubrey
couldn't tell if he was breathing or not.

His collar jerked and, for an awful instant, he thought
he was about to fall. He looked up to see George grimacing and holding onto his jacket. With George's help,
Aubrey managed to scramble up until he was again flat
on the back of the bird, panting with exertion and exhilaration at his rescue. His fingers ached from clinging to
his handholds, but he was alive!

He put his mouth close to George's ear. 'The Gallian!
The bird has him! He's safe!'

'Like we are?' George shouted. Aubrey grinned.

Blinding white light peeled the sky apart and the metal
bird was flung across the heavens. Its wings flapped in
wild, jerky sweeps. Aubrey, blinked, dazzled and
deafened, alarmed at the smell of hot metal and ozone.
Through black spots that wandered in his vision, he
looked over his shoulder to see that half the bird's tail
was missing – melted, with black charred streaks.

It had been struck by lightning.

The creature almost tumbled, then righted itself and
began a descent that was a combination of vertigo-
inducing drops and a controlled tight spiral. Aubrey
peered over the side. The flames of the still-descending
dirigible reflected in the ponds of the sewage treatment
works bordering the airfield.

Their descent continued to slow. Aubrey cheered on
the plucky bird, but the rasping tickle that signalled the
presence of magic made him alert. The feathers beneath
his fingers rippled and flowed, rearranging themselves,

shifting shape. The creature heaved, plunging a little, then Aubrey was in the battered cabin of the ornithopter again. The windscreen was cracked and the smell of scorched metal was thick in the enclosed space.

Aubrey had time to see that George was in the seat next to him and that the unconscious Gallian airman was in the seat behind. George was hastily strapping on his seat belt and Aubrey managed to do the same before the ornithopter splashed into the sewage works.

Aubrey was thrown forward and hit his head on the steering column. He jerked back, blinking, as water cascaded on the cabin roof. He gasped for air and was soon rewarded by the rich fragrance of the settling ponds. Through the window he saw, in the distance, the tattered remains of the dirigible settling with relative dignity into the swampy morass. A cloud of steam and smoke rose to the heavens.

A dense, ponderous feeling settled on Aubrey's shoulders, making them sag. It took him a moment to be able to identify it as relief. He spent a moment wondering about the flawed spell, and how he could have made the ornithopter's change last longer, but he gave up, pleased that such a quickly cobbled-together effort had worked at all.

George coughed and cleared his throat. 'Good landing.'

'What?'

'WingCo Jeffries said any landing you walk away from is a good landing.' George peered out of the window. 'Or in our case, swim away from.'

'Oh.'

The ornithopter wobbled, slipped, paused and then began to sink.

Aubrey shrugged. Just when things couldn't get any worse, they did. He glanced over his shoulder to see that the Gallian was still unconscious, but breathing. He was sprawled across the back seats like a rag doll.

Aubrey rubbed his forehead. He felt weary to the bone. The magical exertion had drained him and he knew he'd pay for it later. 'You know, George, I was just wondering why you jumped into the ornithopter with me. What were you going to do? You don't know the first thing about flying.'

'Just habit, old man. You go off on a hare-brained expedition, I tag along to try to stop you from killing yourself. Or, at least, to minimise the damage to innocent bystanders. It's a hobby, I suppose.'

'Couldn't you have taken up stamp collecting?'

'Allergic to glue, old man. You know that.'

Aubrey was silent for a time and watched the discoloured water rise up the windows. Then the ornithopter bumped and stopped sinking. Nearby, frogs started croaking.

'George?'

'Mm?'

'You remember that holiday I said we should take after the examinations?'

'Of course.'

'I think now could be a good time to take it.'

THE LAWS OF MAGIC

· HEART OF GOLD ·

At a loss after finishing their end-of-year exams, Aubrey and George travel to the Gallian capital, Lutetia, where it so happens that the lovely Caroline is studying natural history.

Aubrey wants to follow up a lead on curing his condition — though his family have other ideas, and he's soon burdened with a royal mystery to solve, old letters to procure, a missing ornithologist to locate and a spot of diplomatic espionage. These tasks should keep Aubrey occupied — but that would be underestimating Aubrey's sense of curiosity and uncanny knack of being in the wrong place at the wrong time.

Someone is stealing people's souls and turning them into mindless monsters, and the country's magical lifeline, the Heart of Gold, has been stolen, leaving the city in chaos. Aubrey, George, and a somewhat reluctant Caroline are on the case . . .

Out now!